Praise for Sue Ann Jaffarian's
Ghost of Granny Apples
Mystery Series

"*Ghost á la Mode* is a charming tale, as appealing as apple pie. I predict a long life (and afterlife) for Sue Ann's latest series."

—Harley Jane Kozak,
Agatha, Anthony, and Macavity
award-winning author of *Dating Dead Men*

"A fun new series. Ghostly puzzles are one of the trendy new themes in cozy mysteries, and this is a good one."

—*Booklist*

"Take colorful characters in a charming setting, mix in a dash of romance, add a pinch of the paranormal, and serve it up like one of Granny's famous pies. I guarantee you'll be back for seconds."

—Deborah Sharp,
author of *Mama Gets Hitched*

"A delectable paranormal cozy series from Sue Ann Jaffarian."

—*Publishers Weekly*

Gem
of a
Ghost

A GHOST OF GRANNY APPLES MYSTERY

Innis Casey Photography

About the Author

SUE ANN JAFFARIAN IS a critically acclaimed, award-winning author whose books have been lauded by the *New York Times*, optioned for film/TV rights, and praised by *New York Times* best-selling author Lee Child and Emmy award-winning actress Camryn Manheim. In addition to the paranormal Ghost of Granny Apples Mystery series, she is the author of the Odelia Grey and the Madison Rose Vampire Mystery series. Sue Ann is also nationally sought after as a motivational and humorous speaker. She lives and works in Los Angeles, California.

Visit Sue Ann on the Internet at

WWW.SUEANNJAFFARIAN.COM

and

WWW.SUEANNJAFFARIAN.BLOGSPOT.COM

Gem of a Ghost

Sue Ann Jaffarian

MIDNIGHT INK
WOODBURY, MINNESOTA

FIRST EDITION
First Printing, 2012

Cover design by Ellen Lawson
Cover illustration © 2011 Doug Thompson

Midnight Ink, an imprint of Llewellyn Worldwide Ltd.

This is a work of fiction. Names, characters, places, and incidents are either the product of the author's imagination or are used fictitiously, and any resemblance to actual persons (living or dead), business establishments, events, or locales is entirely coincidental.

Library of Congress Cataloging-in-Publication Data
Jaffarian, Sue Ann, 1952–
 Gem of a ghost / Sue Ann Jaffarian.—1st ed.
   p. cm.—(A ghost of Granny Apples mystery)
 ISBN 978-0-7387-1381-6
1. Jim Thorpe (Pa.)—Fiction. I. Title.
PS3610.A359G46 2012
813'.6—dc23

2011034466

Midnight Ink
Llewellyn Worldwide Ltd.
2143 Wooddale Drive
Woodbury, MN 55125-2989

www.midnightinkbooks.com

Printed in the United States of America

For my parents, Art (Arakel) and Margaret.
If I have one regret about my writing,
it's that you are not alive to read it.
But then again, maybe you are ...

acknowledgments

As with all my books, my heartfelt thanks go out to my agent, Whitney Lee, and my manager, Diana James, who stand by me through thick and thin.

I want to send a special word of thanks to all the folks at my publisher, Llewellyn/Midnight Ink, for their patience in granting me extra time to get this novel done. The messiness of life often snubs its nose at contract deadlines, and this book would not have turned out nearly as well had they not granted me a couple of extensions and worked around the unfinished manuscript for sales and marketing purposes.

A special acknowledgment goes to Betty Lou McBride for giving up several hours of her time to give me a detailed tour of the Old Jail Museum and a quick history of the town of Mauch Chunk (now Jim Thorpe, PA) and the Molly Maguires.

one

· · · · · · ·

"I'M BEING HAUNTED, EMMA." The words were blurted, cut and harsh, by Joanna Reid, the woman sitting across from Emma Whitecastle. Then, remembering where she was, Joanna discreetly cut her eyes at the neighboring tables to see if anyone had overheard her. Satisfied no one was paying them any mind, she leaned forward, narrowed her eyes, and whispered, "Do something."

It was an order, not a request, made without preamble.

They were having lunch at the Ivy on Robertson Boulevard, seated on the crowded patio under sun umbrellas clustered together like giant mushrooms. The Ivy was a Los Angeles bistro popular with celebrities. Two tables over, eyes shielded behind large designer sunglasses, one of the Olsen twins was seated with two other young women. Several tables in the opposite direction sat the always elegant Sidney Poitier. Conan O'Brien had been leaving the restaurant as Emma arrived. The patio was separated from the sidewalk by a white picket fence. On the far side of the busy street, standing in front of a clothing store, were a couple of determined paparazzi waiting to snap off photos of stars lunching. After catching O'Brien's departure, one had grabbed a shot of her. The other photographer had ignored her completely, which was fine by Emma.

She'd been surprised when a call came from Joanna's secretary asking if she'd be available to meet. She hadn't heard from Joanna in almost five years, not since shortly after Joanna's husband, Max Naiman, had been killed in a car accident. Emma didn't even recognize the name at first, not until the secretary amended her message to say Joanna Naiman Reid was extending the invitation. Then Emma remembered that Joanna had remarried a few years back.

Max Naiman had been a very popular action film star, best known for his franchise of spy thrillers. Before Max's death, Emma and her then-husband, Grant Whitecastle, had seen the Naimans socially on occasion, bonded not just by show business but by the friendship of their daughters, Kelly and Elaine, better known as Lainey. The girls had attended the same private schools for years. After Max's accident, Joanna shipped Lainey off to a European boarding school and threw herself into her work. She was now an executive at a major studio. Emma had tried to keep contact with Joanna after Max's death, but Joanna had never responded to the attempts. Now, out of the blue, Joanna had asked to meet with her.

Emma put down her fork and stared at her lunch companion. "What do you expect me to do, Joanna?"

Joanna flicked her left hand back and forth, the thick gold watch on her wrist and large diamond on her ring finger sparkling in the sunlight that peeked between the umbrellas. She was a woman used to giving orders and having them followed without question. "Whatever it is you people do with such things."

"*You people?*"

"You know what I mean, you people who talk to ghosts."
Joanna was still whispering, but her tone was imperious.

Emma picked up her water glass and leaned back in her chair
to take stock of the situation. She'd thought the meeting might
have to do with *The Whitecastle Report,* her popular cable TV show
about the paranormal. Emma had been courted recently by a few
studios for other projects and had wondered if Joanna was going
to throw her studio's hat into the ring. It seemed the lunch invitation was about Emma's paranormal talents, just not in the way she
had imagined.

Ignoring Joanna's bossy tone, Emma took a drink of her sparkling water, holding the fizzy bubbles in her mouth a few seconds
before swallowing. "Why do you think your home is haunted,
Joanna?"

"Not my house," Joanna hissed with annoyed urgency. "*Me.*"

Joanna Reid had the type of Southern California good looks
that came with having the right doctors and the money to pay
them, while Emma had the kind of beauty that came from genet-
ics and letting nature take its course. They were about the same
age—in the second half of their forties—and had one daughter
each. Both were tall, slender, fit, and blond. With a hand, Joanna
flicked her ash-blond hair over her left shoulder. When Emma had
last seen her, Joanna's hair had been dark brown and short. She'd
also had a different nose.

But her hair and a nose job weren't the only things Emma
noticed about Joanna. While her eye makeup was artfully applied,
Joanna hadn't been able to entirely mask the dark circles or the

sunken appearance to her cheeks. The woman was either ill or seriously worried about something.

"What's more," Joanna continued, again looking around to make sure no one was listening, "it's Max."

"Max?" Emma put down her water glass and studied Joanna with interest. The ghost of a dead husband could explain Joanna's appearance. "Can you see him? Or hear him?"

"Of course not. That's your job, isn't it?"

"*You people. Your job.*" Feeling feisty in the face of Joanna's rudeness, Emma threw the words back at her. "I'm not on your staff, Joanna. Please remember that."

Emma started to say something more but stopped when their waiter approached to check on things. After leaving their table, he hovered at the one next to them. She used the time to simmer down and focus on the air around them, trying to determine if there were, in fact, any ghosts in the vicinity. She saw and felt none.

As soon as the waiter left their area, Emma asked Joanna in a low voice, "Then how do you know it's a ghost, Max or otherwise?"

"I just know," she snapped. "It's a feeling. A cold, creepy feeling." Joanna got quiet and looked out past the fence toward the street. The paparazzi were busy snapping photos of the solo Olsen twin as she waited for the valet to fetch her car. "Yet a sense of familiarity, too." She turned back to Emma. "Does that make sense?"

"To me it does." Emma tested the waters to see if Joanna really could sense spirits or was just making it up. "Is Max here right now?"

"No."

Joanna started to take a bite of her half-eaten salad, then stopped and motioned for the waiter to come and take it away. Emma also indicated she was finished. Another waiter came by to refresh Joanna's iced tea.

When they were reasonably alone again, Joanna said in a sharp, low tone, "Familiar or not, make him go away. Now." It was another order.

"It's not that simple, Joanna. I can't just say *abracadabra* and he'll leave. I need to know more about why he's here."

Joanna gave her a disgusted look, the kind of look that said *then what good are you?*

Emma hadn't particularly liked Joanna before Max's death either. Max had been the one with the easygoing and fun personality. She'd even suspected Grant and Joanna of having a short fling years ago. The woman could be snide and harsh with others, especially with her own family. Lainey had spent a lot of time at the Whitecastle home, and Emma suspected it had been partially to escape her tyrannical mother.

In spite of Joanna's rudeness, Emma was intrigued by the idea that Max Naiman might have returned from the other side. "Has this been going on ever since Max's death?"

"No, that's what's so odd." Joanna took a long drink of her iced tea, then touched a napkin to the corners of her mouth. "It started a couple of months ago. Out of the blue."

"Hardly out of the blue, my dear." The comment came out of nowhere, taking Emma by surprise. She hadn't seen or felt the spirit when she'd looked around a moment before, but there was definitely one nearby now. It didn't materialize; it didn't have to.

Emma had recognized the deep and sexy Australian accent immediately. It was the voice of Max Naiman.

Emma tried hard not to let surprise reflect on her face as she gazed across the small table at Joanna. She need not have bothered; Joanna wasn't paying attention to her. Keeping her head as straight as if she were in a neck brace, Joanna's dark eyes, wide with an odd mixture of dread and annoyance, were darting around like newly released pinballs. Even in the warmth of the day, her bare arms were speckled with goose bumps and crossed in front of her as if warding off bitter cold. Emma had no doubt now about Joanna's ability to sense the presence of Max's spirit.

"He's here now," she said to Emma, still not allowing her eyes to focus on one spot.

"I know." Emma kept her voice low and soft. "He just arrived."

Finally Joanna's eyes settled back on Emma. "So it's true. You can see ghosts."

"When they want to be seen, yes. I can't see Max, but he just spoke. I recognized his voice."

"Don't let her kid you, Emma," the disembodied voice said. "Joanna knows why I'm here."

"I'll pay you anything you want," Joanna told Emma with cold intensity, "to make him leave permanently."

For a split second Emma thought she saw the shimmering outline of a spirit behind Joanna's chair. Then it was gone, dissipating in the warm air like a puff of steam, but not before offering up parting words: "Fix this."

"Wait," Emma called to it, forgetting she was in a public place. People near them glanced her way before going back to their business.

The waiter came over. "Is there something I can get for you, Mrs. Whitecastle?"

"No," Emma answered, trying to appear casual about her outburst. "But thank you." Used to catering to the rich and famous and their eccentricities, he retreated with a slight shrug.

Joanna uncrossed her arms and took a deep breath, the gesture letting Emma know she also knew the ghost was gone.

"What did he say, Emma?"

"He said he didn't come to you out of the blue—and that you know why he's here."

"And?" Joanna pressed, her eyes boring into Emma like drills searching for oil.

"That's it, I'm afraid." Emma picked up her glass and took a sip of water, trying to decide if the words *fix this* were meant for her or for Joanna.

"That's it?" Joanna sounded angry. Emma wasn't sure if the emotion was directed at her or at Max, or at her by proxy.

It was Emma's turn to lean forward. "What happened in the past several months to trigger his presence?"

Joanna dismissed the question and waved to the waiter for their check. "Nothing."

Emma knew she was lying. "Something brought him back. He could have been around all this time, but something brought him to the point of letting you know he was here. It's been my experience that spirits don't do that lightly. They don't go out of their way to let the living know they are around—especially those who cannot see or hear them—unless they have a purpose."

When the check was delivered, Joanna immediately slapped down a black American Express card. The waiter whisked it away.

"Isn't that why you asked me to lunch—to find out why he's here?"

"I invited you to lunch to ask you to get rid of him—to hire you as some sort of ghost exorcist. I don't care one bit why he's here."

The waiter returned with the credit card slip. Joanna scribbled her name on it. Without looking at Emma, she folded her copy of the receipt and slipped it into her blue crocodile Hermès Birkin, a handbag that cost more than the average family of four lived on in a year.

Emma persisted. "Max must have a reason for reaching out to you. Knowing that will help me communicate with him. Even then, he may not want to talk to me, and he may not leave until whatever brought him here is finished."

A sad smile sneaked across Joanna's face. "Max always had good reasons for doing everything he did ... even driving his car over the edge of that cliff."

The words stunned Emma. Max Naiman had been killed when his car spun out of control on a hairpin turn on Highway 1 just south of Big Sur. The news had reported he'd been drunk at the time. There had never been any indication the accident was deliberate on Max's part.

"Would you like to talk about it? Maybe someplace private?" Emma filled her voice with genuine concern in spite of her personal feelings about Joanna. Unwanted ghosts usually left people feeling helpless and anxious. If she could help Max, she could help Joanna. "I'm going out of town this afternoon, but maybe next week I can drop by your home."

Joanna cackled. "Right. Bring a famous ghost whisperer into the house and have Lin wonder what more could be going on? Not on your life."

Lin, Emma knew, was Linwood Reid, Joanna's present husband. Emma wasn't exactly sure what he did for a living, only that he was considered a big shot in finance.

"What do you mean by *more*?"

Joanna looked away.

"If something serious is going on in your life, it could be why Max is here. He may be trying to tell you something or even trying to warn you."

Joanna turned and glued her eyes to Emma's face. In spite of her drawn, tired appearance, Joanna's face was steely and determined. "Or trying to hurt us. Maybe he can't stand the thought that his family is finally happy."

"Look," Emma told her. "I have a small private office at my home in Pasadena. You're welcome there anytime." She paused before tossing out the next suggestion, pretty sure it would be shot down, but she had to try. "But the best solution would be for you and me to meet with my friend Milo Ravenscroft. He lives on the Westside, close to Santa Monica. He's out of town right now, but when he returns, I'm sure he'll be happy to help you."

"Milo Ravenscroft." Joanna said the name with a near snort, a cousin to her earlier cackle. "The famous reclusive psychic? That's rich."

"Milo isn't reclusive; he's shy. And he knows more about the paranormal than almost anyone else alive."

Joanna stood up and slipped on a pair of Louis Vuitton sunglasses. The meeting was over. Emma was dismissed.

Emma picked up her purse—also a designer bag, but only about 1 percent the cost of Joanna's—and got to her feet. While they were waiting for the valet to bring their cars around, Emma pulled out a business card and pen and scribbled something on the back of the card. She handed it to Joanna. "This is my office number, the one your secretary has. On the back is my cell phone. I'm here for you, Joanna. Just call if you want to talk."

Although she took the card, Joanna avoided looking at Emma and remained silent. Joanna's silver Jaguar was the first to arrive. She went to the driver's side and tipped the valet.

Emma called to her, "Max said to 'fix it,' Joanna. What did he mean by that?"

Joanna Reid stopped in her tracks. She didn't turn to look at Emma but hung suspended, half in and half out of her vehicle, for several seconds before disappearing into the driver's seat. With a squeal of rubber, she pulled away from the curb.

two
. . . .

"YOU REALLY SAW THE ghost of Max Naiman?" Phil Bowers sounded as excited as a kid meeting his sports hero. "Man, I loved his movies. My sons did, too. Never missed a one."

He and Emma were on horseback, riding side by side along a trail in the hills outside Julian, the historic gold-mining town in the mountains north of San Diego. Phil was astride Astro, his large chestnut stallion, while Emma rode Daisy, a paint with a friendly disposition that was a new addition to the Bowers ranch. Trotting alongside them were Baby and Sweetie Pie, two German shepherds who also lived at the ranch. As they rode, she told Phil about her lunch with Joanna Reid.

Emma had driven straight to Julian after leaving the Ivy, spending much of the three-hour drive thinking about her lunch with Joanna. Whether or not Joanna wanted to discuss the appearance of Max's ghost, Emma was now intrigued enough to want to know more, especially since Joanna had dropped the bomb that Max may have driven over the cliff on purpose. The question was how much did she want to be involved. The last time she had investigated a ghost's death, it had resulted in pain and turmoil for her own family.

"I didn't see him, Phil, I only heard him."

"But you knew him? I mean, when he was alive, you actually knew him?"

Emma nodded, still thinking about what the ghost had said.

"What was he like?"

The eagerness in Phil's voice brought Emma out of her thoughts and made her giggle. "Good grief, Phil, you sound like a star-struck groupie instead of a middle-aged tax attorney."

Emma glanced over at Phil and smiled. He didn't look like a tax attorney either. Seated comfortably on Astro, he looked like a mature rancher, which he was in addition to being a very successful lawyer. Most of the week he lived in San Diego close to his thriving law practice and his two grown sons. On weekends he drove up to Julian, where he lived on his family's ranch with his aunt and uncle, Susan and Glen Steveson. Emma had visited Phil in San Diego and was amazed at how easily he fit into both the ranching and the business worlds. He was a confident man, sure of himself and blessed with both intelligence and street smarts. He was also compassionate and kind.

"Hey, I wanted to be him—or at least the characters he played." Phil shot off a wink at Emma. "Any guy who got to kiss Angelina Jolie, Sandra Bullock, *and* Halle Berry is my hero."

"And what about me?" Emma asked playfully.

"What about you?"

"I've kissed Max Naiman."

Phil abruptly pulled up Astro and stared at Emma. "Are you kidding me?"

Emma slowed Daisy but didn't stop. She kept moving and shot over her shoulder, "Nope. Kissed him plenty of times."

Astro and Phil came alongside again. "Wow, my lips have kissed the lips that kissed the lips that kissed those hotties. It's like"—he paused to think—"it's like three degrees of kissing separation."

Emma giggled again. "It's not like I've had numerous passionate liplocks with Max, but our lips did touch on holidays and at dinner parties."

"That's good enough for me."

They rode along in comfortable silence until Phil halted Astro and dismounted. Emma took the cue and got off Daisy. They were at a lookout point on the trail with a lovely view of the valley below. Years before, someone had installed a bench facing the view to give riders and hikers a place to rest and contemplate.

As soon as Emma had arrived at the cabin she'd built across from the Bowers ranch, Phil had called and suggested a short pre-dinner ride. He gave her time to change her clothes and stretch her legs after the long drive from Los Angeles. When she walked over to the Bowers place, Phil and the horses were waiting, and Phil had a special twinkle in his eye that made Emma glow.

At the lookout, the dogs dashed about, running and chasing each other, while Phil pulled a saddlebag from Astro. From it he extracted an insulated bag holding a bottle of champagne. From a bag on the other side of the saddle, he produced two plastic cups and a couple of napkins.

"What's the occasion?" asked Emma.

Phil cocked an eyebrow in her direction. "I have to tell you? Tsk, tsk, tsk."

With great flair, he directed Emma to have a seat on one end of the bench and placed a napkin across her lap.

Holding the champagne bottle and pointing it away from them, he twisted off the wire cage and put another napkin over the stopper. "This could be tricky. After all that jostling on the horse, it might be a geyser."

Slowly Phil loosened the cork, bit by bit, until there was a pop. It wasn't a geyser, but some of the champagne did spill onto the ground. He turned back to Emma, pleased as punch with himself to have saved most of the bubbly.

"Madam?" he offered.

With a wide smile, Emma held out both glasses while Phil filled them. Done with his waiter chores, he put a napkin over the top of the bottle and returned it to the thermal bag to keep it cool, then he took a seat on the bench next to Emma.

He held out his glass to her. "Here's to our two-year anniversary, Fancy Pants."

She smiled at his nickname for her—a nickname that had started out as anything but friendly. "But we didn't start dating until October."

"Ah, but we met two years ago right here in Julian."

"But in mid-May, not the beginning of the month." She tried to keep her face straight while she teased him, but she couldn't.

"You going to toast with me or argue with me?"

In response, Emma leaned forward, snatched Phil's cowboy hat off his bald head, and planted a sloppy kiss on his mouth, letting her lips linger long enough to be tickled by his thick, graying moustache. With the kiss complete, she tapped her plastic glass against his. "To our second anniversary, Cowboy."

"I wanted to celebrate this weekend," Phil explained after taking a sip, "because it looks like my trip to Canada with my boys is on after all. We'll be gone for almost three weeks in May. With Richard getting married in the fall and Tom off to grad school about the same time, it will probably be our last opportunity to spend this much time together."

Emma fully understood. With Kelly away at Harvard, time with her daughter had become precious gifts snatched whenever Kelly came home. Soon both she and Phil would have empty nests. It was a sad yet exciting part of being a parent.

They sipped their champagne and looked out at the view, Emma cuddled against Phil's strong body, content with themselves and with each other. The dogs, done playing, settled down under a tree while the horses waited patiently.

Several minutes later, Phil reached again for the champagne bottle and topped off their glasses. "Do you think Max was talking about his own death when he said to fix it, or was it something else?"

"I don't know, Phil. Max had a great career going. I don't know what his marriage was like, but he didn't seem the type to crack and take his own life." She ran a hand through her short blond hair. "He did, however, like his booze and had been stopped for DUIs in the past. The suggestion that he drove off the road deliberately was probably Joanna's way of infusing the situation with additional drama."

Phil took a drink and rolled the information around in his head. "So, how can I help you with this Max Naiman thing? I have a friend in law enforcement who might be able to get a copy of the police report on the accident."

Emma straightened and leaned against the back of the bench. "There is no Max Naiman thing. Joanna asked to meet with me. We met, and she pushed aside any suggestions of mine to meet further." She took a large swallow of champagne. "End of story."

Amused, Phil topped off her glass again. "Look me in the eye, Fancy Pants, and tell me you aren't the least bit curious about what happened to Max and why his ghost has surfaced now."

Leaning forward, Emma latched her blue eyes onto Phil's gray ones. "I'm not the least—," she started, then stopped, annoyed with herself that she couldn't finish the statement truthfully. "I don't want to get involved," she said instead and looked away.

"That's not what I asked."

Blowing out a gust of frustrated air, Emma leaned back again and stared up at the branches of the trees high overhead. "You're right, Phil, I am curious about what happened with Max, and I do want to try to talk to him. But after what happened in Catalina, I'm a little gun-shy about uncovering other people's secrets."

Phil put down the bottle. Getting off the bench, he squatted in front of Emma and took her hands in his. "What happened in Catalina was not your fault." He could tell by the way she avoided looking at him that she wasn't convinced. "You brought Tessa justice. Didn't she deserve that?"

Emma nodded but still didn't look at Phil. She kept her eyes turned up toward the trees, hoping to ward off the tears she felt damming up behind her eyes.

"It was unfortunate how it played out," he added. "But the outcome was not your fault."

Emma lowered her chin and looked at Phil. "I still intend to mind my own business, whether or not Joanna calls and no matter what she offers."

"Offers?"

"Yes. She offered to pay me to get rid of Max's ghost. Pretty much said I could name my price."

"A paying gig, no less?" He laughed. "This is opening up a whole new career for you, Fancy Pants."

"I don't want a new career," she insisted with knitted brows. "I'm happy with the TV show, being a mom, and spending part of my time down here."

Phil held up an index finger. "Don't be so hasty. That TV show may not last forever."

"I'm financially comfortable, Phil, no matter what happens to that show, and you know it."

"I'm not saying do it full-time, just when someone needs help. Until now you've only helped ghosts. There might be some live people, like Joanna, who could use your services."

"No, thanks. I'll leave being a professional spirit go-between to Milo." Emma got up and stretched. "Speaking of ghosts, have you seen Granny lately? She's been MIA from the house for several days at a stretch for the past month—not like her at all."

Granny was Emma's great-great-great-grandmother Ish Reynolds, a hundred-plus-year-old ghost better known as Granny Apples because of the apple pies she had made when she was alive. Granny was the reason Emma had discovered Julian. She was also the reason Emma discovered she had the gift to see and speak with spirits—and the reason Emma met and fell in love with Phil Bowers.

"You know I can't see or hear Granny." Phil gave her a coy smile.

"Nice try, Cowboy. You may not be able to see or hear her, but you've become pretty perceptive about knowing when she's around."

"No flies on you, Fancy Pants."

Phil kicked back the champagne in his glass. He picked up the bottle and asked through gesture if Emma wanted more. She shook her head and finished off what she had. Phil emptied the remaining champagne onto the ground and packed the bottle back into his saddlebag. He did the same with their glasses, the napkins, and the cork, packing out everything they had packed in.

Emma climbed back on Daisy. "So, have you *sensed* Granny around lately?"

"Who do you think helped me pick out your anniversary present?"

"What anniversary present?"

"You're sitting on it."

"Daisy?"

"Happy anniversary, Fancy Pants. You are officially a horse-woman. We'll keep Daisy in our stable for you with our horses." Phil whistled to the dogs and mounted Astro. "Unless, of course, you don't like her."

Emma squealed with delight. "No, Phil, she's perfect."

She leaned over toward Phil. He cozied Astro up to Daisy and met Emma halfway for a thank-you kiss.

"But how did Granny help you pick out Daisy?"

He laughed. "Granny and I have developed our own communication system. We don't need a mediator." When he saw Emma's puzzled look, he continued. "It's simple. I ask Granny a yes or no question. If it's yes, she blows into my right ear. If it's no, she blows into my left ear."

"Ghosts don't have breath, Phil; they can't blow anything anywhere, although I've known them to create air currents or gusts."

"Well, somehow she moves the air on one side or the other to get her point across. I'd narrowed your gift down to between two horses. Granny cast the final vote for Daisy." He gave Emma a blunt nod. "So if the nag throws you, blame Granny."

Emma stared at Phil, stunned that he and Granny had figured out how to communicate between themselves without her, then reminded herself with a smile that Phil wasn't just smart, he was resourceful. "Are you sure it's Granny you're talking to? If you can't hear or see her, who knows who you might be conversing with. Might be the ghost of Pancho Villa or even Richard Nixon."

"Or maybe it's the spirit of Marilyn Monroe," he shot back at her. "I wouldn't mind that one bit."

Emma was about to say something sassy when her cell phone vibrated. She pulled it out of her pants pocket and looked at it. "It's Kelly." She hit the answer button. "Kelly?"

After a few seconds, Emma gave up and ended the call. "Darn, no decent reception up here."

"We'll be home soon. Hope it's nothing important."

"Before I left the cabin I emailed her, asking if she'd heard anything from Lainey Naiman lately. I'm pretty sure they're still in touch, though I'm not sure how often."

Phil had pointed Astro toward home but now turned his mount around to face Emma and Daisy. "What happened to not wanting to be involved?"

"I'm just curious, that's all."

"Uh-huh." He directed Astro back down the trail. "Then I'm sticking to the story that Marilyn Monroe helped pick out that horse."

three

· · · · · · · · · ·

As soon as they returned to the ranch, Phil told Emma to go call Kelly. He and Hector Mendoza, a strapping local high-school boy who worked at the ranch part-time, would take care of the horses. Working on the ranch was a Mendoza family tradition. Two brothers before Hector had held the job, each relinquishing it to the next in line when the current one went off to college or entered a full-time career. No longer a working ranch, Phil's family now leased out most of their land and kept just a few acres and a handful of horses for themselves.

Emma handed Hector the reins to Daisy and redialed Kelly while she strolled toward the house. Kelly's voicemail kicked in as Emma climbed the steps to the redwood deck at the back of the house. Baby and Sweetie Pie had run ahead of her and were now on the deck slurping at their water bowl while Killer, the family's tiny bichon frisé, danced and yipped excitedly from the other side of the closed patio door to welcome everyone home.

"Kelly, it's Mom," Emma said to the machine. "Sorry, we were out riding, and the reception was awful. Give me a call back." Kelly was Emma's twenty-year-old daughter. She lived in Boston, finishing up her sophomore year at Harvard.

The back patio slider door opened, and Killer made a beeline for Emma. Happy to see her, the little dog danced on his hind legs for attention. After a few pats, he sniffed around her like a bloodhound.

"He's looking for Archie," explained Susan Steveson, Phil's aunt, as she came through the patio door with a tray holding glasses of lemonade. "And Granny."

"Sorry, pal," Emma said to the white ball of fluff at her feet as she took a seat at the large wooden patio table, "but Archie stayed home this time." Killer sat at her feet looking up at her, his black button eyes bright with expectation, as if she might pull Archie out of her pocket at any moment.

Archie, the black Scottish terrier belonging to Emma's parents, often traveled with her to Julian. He'd made friends with the Bowers animals, especially Killer. Granny was also a hit with the dogs and played with them regularly. Like Emma, the animals could see and hear ghosts.

Emma shrugged at the determined animal. "Not sure where Granny is these days."

"She pops in and out," answered Susan, putting the tray down on the table in front of Emma. "But I don't think she's been around for a while."

Emma looked at Susan with surprise. "Don't tell me you chat with her like Phil does."

Susan laughed. "No, it still creeps me out, though not as much as it used to." She lowered her plump, sturdy body into a chair at the table and pushed her glasses higher up on the bridge of her nose with one finger. "But I know when she's here because of the way the dogs behave, especially Killer. He dances and runs around like he's playing all by himself."

She looked down at Killer, who'd finally realized Emma was alone and laid down on the deck to pout. "But we know better, don't we, boy?"

Susan took a glass from the tray. "So, you like Daisy?"

A wide smile crossed Emma's face as she helped herself to a glass of lemonade. "I love Daisy." Emma looked out across the property toward the stable. "Hard to believe it's already been two years since I first came to your door."

"Yes, a lot of water's gone under the bridge since my nephew tried to run you off the property." Susan chuckled. Phil's aunt was an optimist with a healthy dose of reality. "Glad you persisted. You both seem so much happier these days."

Emma reached out and briefly touched Susan's arm with affection. "Yes, Susan, I'd say we are. Both of us were going through ugly divorces then, and look where we are now."

"You think that nephew of mine and you will ever live under one roof?"

The question surprised Emma. Susan wasn't one to meddle in other people's business. Neither was Elizabeth Miller, Emma's mother, yet both had asked the same question in less than two weeks. Emma knew that Susan and her mother had become friends. Now she wondered if they were in cahoots in other ways.

"We practically live together now—at least we do when I'm here at the cabin."

Emma's "cabin" was a spacious three-bedroom, two-story home with two stone fireplaces, a combination office/den, and a state-of-the-art kitchen. It was directly across from the entrance to the ranch and shared the same access road. The cabin was located on the property where Granny's homestead had been built back in the late 1800s—property Phil and his family deeded over to Emma, returning it back to its original family.

From the time Emma had started building the cabin, she'd driven down to Julian at least twice a month. As soon as it was near completion, she and Phil started staying at the cabin in domestic bliss. When she wasn't in Julian, Phil looked after the place. He drove up to Julian from San Diego almost every Thursday night and often worked from Julian if there was no need for him to be physically at his law firm. Emma knew that he often stayed at the cabin without her and worked from the cabin, preferring the quiet over the hustle and bustle at the ranch. Sometimes Phil drove up to Pasadena, where Emma lived with her parents, but it wasn't the same as when they stayed at the cabin. Over time and without her really realizing it, the cabin had become their home.

"True," was all Susan replied, but she studied Emma with a frankness that announced living together wasn't what she meant.

Emma knew Phil wanted to marry her. They had talked about it several times. She loved Phil Bowers deeply, with a mature love she'd never had for the arrogant and vain Grant Whitecastle. Phil made her feel safe and secure and in a heartbeat could turn her insides to jelly like a lovesick teenager. More importantly, she trusted him as she had never trusted Grant.

"Susan," Emma began, "I love Phil; please don't ever doubt that."

Phil's aunt looked at Emma, her rosy cheeks softened with understanding. "I know that, dear. You wear it like those tight jeans you favor."

Emma laughed. "Are you saying my jeans are too tight?"

Susan leaned forward, saying in a conspiratorial whisper, "Not one bit. If I had your figure, I'd be wearing them, too."

She straightened and took a drink of lemonade, keeping her twinkling eyes on Emma. "I know you two will never have a traditional marriage with both of you in one spot night and day, like me and Glen. You have your career in Los Angeles, and Phil has his down here. You seem to have worked out the logistics of being together, and your kids get along fine, but I'm just old-fashioned enough to want to see you two wed." She lightly slapped the table with the hand not holding the glass. "There, now I've said it."

"It's about time someone did."

Emma whipped her head around at the voice only she heard— she and Killer. The little dog hopped up and started dancing on his hind legs.

"Granny must be here," Susan announced. Her voice was even, but a slight shiver ran through it. "That's how that fool dog behaves when she's around."

Emma looked over at the railing, where Killer was circling like a whirling dervish around a slim, hazy column only Emma and the dog could see. In short order, the column materialized into the outline of a diminutive pioneer woman dressed in a floor-length skirt, long-sleeved blouse, and boots. Her face was weathered and slightly pinched. A thick braid of hair circled her head. "You and Phil need to get hitched. He's a darn fine man."

"You show up now?" Emma said to the ghost. "Just in time for *this* conversation? How convenient."

"Don't get testy with me," the apparition shot back. "I'm just giving my opinion." The ornery ghost stuck out her pointed chin. "And I didn't just show up. I was listening while you told Phil about that Max ghost. Then I disappeared, seeing he was getting all mushy with you."

Emma sighed and turned back to Susan. "Seems Granny agrees with you and Mother about Phil and me." Emma put her glass down. "Susan, I've come to think of you like a second mother, so I'm going to tell you what I told my own mother." She fiddled with a stray leaf that had drifted onto the table. "I love Phil so much, I worry about hurting him."

"That's only natural, dear. No one wants to hurt those they love, but sometimes it happens."

"I've only known two men in my life, and I've loved both—Grant and Phil." Emma paused to put her thoughts in order, worried about coming off as tacky with a verbal misstep. "I worry about Phil being a rebound, since I met him while in the middle of my divorce from Grant." She paused to take a breath. "Maybe I should date more—see other men before deciding he's the one I want to be with forever. The last thing I want is another divorce."

Emma looked from Susan to Granny. "Do you both understand that?"

The ghost scowled. "What I understand is Phil is a good man, and you're a fool if you let him get away."

Emma smiled and turned back to Susan. "Granny just reminded me that good men don't grow on trees."

"And Granny would be right." Susan smiled at Emma. "Good women don't grow on trees either."

Susan stood up and went to the railing. She looked out over the trees and rolling land a moment before turning back around. "Do you want to date someone else? Have you met someone, Emma?"

"No to both of those questions. It's not so much wanting to date others as wondering if I should." Confused herself about her feelings, Emma hoped she was explaining herself clearly.

Granny looked at Susan. "Would you talk some sense into the little fool?"

Susan thought it only a two-way conversation. "Believe it or not, Emma, I understand what you're saying."

"That's not what she needs to hear." Granny stomped her left foot in frustration. Emma was glad Susan couldn't see or hear the ghost.

"The last thing I want for Phil," Susan continued, "would be another divorce. The first one near about killed him. I know you both love each other, but I also know that, in time, what you have now won't be enough for him."

"That's exactly what my mother advised me."

"You're mother is a very smart woman, and I'm sure, like me, she worried about making a mistake when she married. I don't know of a sensible bride who doesn't." Susan pushed off from the railing and stood over Emma, lightly touching her shoulder. "Follow your heart, Emma, and it will tell you what it needs, not just what it wants."

Susan turned to look back over the rail. Phil, done with tending the horses, was heading for the house. "But," Susan said, watching Phil walk toward them, "you hurt my nephew any more than is usual and customary in such matters, and I'll skin you alive myself."

Granny crossed her arms. "I don't know what all that customary gibberish meant, but I'll skin ya, too."

f o u r
· · · · · · · · ·

AFTER SPENDING A LITTLE more time with Susan, Phil suggested he and Emma clean up and go into town to have dinner.

"There goes that rocker again," Phil noted as they strolled toward Emma's cabin. He indicated one of several large wooden rockers on the porch. "Does that quite often, breeze or no breeze."

Emma smiled. "Must be Granny enjoying some down time. Could be that's why she's not in Pasadena as often—she might be spending more time here."

Phil shook his head while keeping a close eye on the rocker. "I'm not so sure that's Granny. Not too long ago, Granny and I were having one of our little chats in the kitchen, and I could see that rocker going back and forth through the window."

"Really?" Emma studied the rocker, which continued to move in a steady, rhythmic back-and-forth sweep, but she couldn't make out any spirit.

"It's my man, Jacob," a disembodied voice said. It moved along with Phil and Emma but didn't materialize.

Emma halted and signaled for Phil to stop. "Granny just told me that's Jacob on the porch—her husband and my great-great-great-grandfather."

"Have you ever seen him before?" Phil asked with interest, his eyes glued to the gently moving chair.

"Never. Granny always said he had no interest in coming back from the other side."

"Shortly after you put those rockers out," Granny explained, materializing into a faint outline, "he started coming back here. He used to love sitting on the porch of our cabin. Our porch wasn't as big and our rockers not as fine, but they did the job. After chores, we'd sit in quiet. I'd knit, and he'd whittle or clean and fix tools until it was too dark to see. On Sundays our son would sit on the stoop and read to us."

"You can't read, Granny?" It had never occurred to Emma that the ghost couldn't.

"I can read as long as it ain't fancy words, but Jacob never learned. He loved hearing Winston read from the storybooks he got from school."

As Emma watched, Granny's hazy image made its way to the porch. Granny disappeared as the second rocker synchronized its movements with the first.

Phil took Emma's hand. "I take it Granny and Jacob are both on the porch now."

Touched by the scene, Emma nodded in silence.

Still holding Emma's hand, Phil started down the path to the porch. "It's nice to see that love can even survive death." When they climbed the steps to the porch, Phil tipped his cowboy hat toward the rockers.

. . . .

"How about dinner at the Julian Grill?" Phil asked.

"Not the Rong Branch, where we met?"

"I considered it." Picking up his watch from the large pine dining table, Phil slipped it onto his wrist. "But the Grill is more romantic than beer and burgers. Besides, I didn't have enough time to choreograph a brawl to make it authentic."

Both had showered and dressed. Finished first, Emma had placed another call to Kelly but again only reached her voicemail. Now she watched Phil from an overstuffed chair in the living room while weighing Susan's words. She was crazy about Phil, and their relationship was so satisfying; she couldn't imagine her life without him. Her feelings didn't seem like a rebound reaction at all, but while her heart said to let go, her head told her to be cautious when it came to men in general. Susan had told her to follow her heart, but for the time being her head was running a blockade.

Getting up, she stepped behind Phil and encircled his waist with her arms, resting her chin on his brawny shoulder. He smelled of shaving cream, a special blend he ordered online and applied with a badger hair brush. She took a deep breath, imprinting it into her memory forever.

"Do you mind it very much that we're not married?" she asked.

He didn't turn around or break her embrace, but he hesitated before answering. "Did my aunt say something to you?"

"Your aunt, my mother, Granny—even my father has made a lightly veiled comment or two."

"I'll talk to Susan."

"No, Phil, don't. Susan—all of them—just want what they think is best for us." She squeezed her arms tighter around him. "I love you, Phil Bowers."

"And I you, Emma Whitecastle. But I don't want you feeling pressured to marry me. It's not like you need to make an honest man out of me—long past time for that."

She giggled, kissing and nuzzling his left ear.

"Better watch yourself, Fancy Pants, or we'll never make it to dinner."

"Hmm, I could always scramble us up some eggs ... later."

Phil removed his watch, placed it back on the table, and turned around to face her. Enfolding her in his arms, it was his turn to whisper into her ear. "Later sounds right up my alley."

. . . .

A HOUR AND A half later, while Emma was cracking eggs and separating the whites and yolks for an egg white vegetable omelet, Kelly called. Phil worked nearby, chopping onions and slicing mushrooms. Emma rinsed her hands and wiped them on a kitchen towel before answering.

"Hi, sweetie," Emma said into the phone.

"Hey, Mom. Whatcha doing?"

"Just whipping up a little dinner."

"Should I call back?"

"No, not at all. We're just making omelets and haven't started cooking yet."

When Phil signaled he could handle it without her, she walked into the living room and hunkered down on the large, comfy sofa, curling her legs up under her. A few minutes later, she returned to the kitchen, her face distraught. She put the phone down on the breakfast bar and hit the speaker feature, then hopped up on one of the high stools to listen.

"Kelly, I'm putting you on speaker. I want Phil to hear this. Start from the beginning."

"Hi, Phil."

"Hi, beautiful," he called to her. Emma smiled. Phil adored Kelly and treated her like his own. He leaned across the counter to listen better.

"Like I told you, Mom," Kelly began, her voice serious and clear, "it's just so weird that you asked about Elaine Naiman, because I was going to call you about her this weekend." Kelly paused. "Do you remember a few months ago, when I told you she got engaged?"

"Yes," responded Emma. "I congratulated Joanna about it this afternoon, and she shrugged it off. Didn't even give me a polite thank you. Is Lainey still engaged?"

"I don't know, but when she got engaged, that was all she gushed about on Facebook. She said her mother was planning this really big wedding. Then, about a month or so ago, she hardly talked about it at all. I emailed her privately about it, and she didn't respond. Now her Facebook page is gone."

Emma glanced up at Phil. They exchanged concerned looks, both knowing going silent wasn't normal behavior for a young engaged woman.

"Maybe," Emma said, "the wedding was called off, and she's either hurt or embarrassed about it. Maybe she found out something about her fiancé she doesn't want people to know. It certainly would fit with how her mother acted today."

"That's what I thought, too, Mom. Then Summer Perkins texted me that Lainey dropped out of school. They were both going to UCLA. This morning Summer sent me another text, saying she'd heard Lainey tried to kill herself."

Emma sucked in a gulp of air as if she'd been punched. It stuck in her throat like a gag.

"Mom, it gets worse. Summer heard Lainey has tried suicide more than once in the past few months and is now in some sort of facility."

Emma's hand went to her mouth. Lainey was the same age as Kelly. To think of someone so young going through something that horrible was unthinkable. "Oh, no! That poor child."

Phil reached out a hand and stroked Emma's arm. As a father, Lainey's situation was affecting him, too.

"Mom, can you do something for me?"

Emma leaned close to the phone, wanting a way to hug her daughter through the lines. "Of course, dear, anything."

"Since I can't be there, would you go visit Lainey? She always thought you were such a cool mom, and I think it might cheer her up."

"Of course I will. Don't think twice about it. What's the name of the place she's at?"

"I'm not sure, but I'll find out and text it to you."

They chatted a few minutes more before Kelly had to go. Emma reluctantly ended the call. After hearing about Elaine Naiman, she didn't want to let go of Kelly, not even electronically. More than ever, she wanted to know that her daughter was safe and stable.

"What do you make of that?" asked Phil, going back to preparing their dinner.

"It certainly explains why Joanna looked so haggard and brittle today. It probably had nothing to do with Max." She played with the phone, as if caressing Kelly through its case. "Joanna gave no indication that anything was wrong with Lainey. When I congratulated her on Lainey's engagement, she could have said something then."

"Like you said to Kelly, maybe it's embarrassment." Phil started blending the egg yolks back into the carefully separated egg whites. "Folks are always afraid that if something emotional is wrong with their kids, they'll be blamed for bad parenting. And often that's the case."

"Hey," Emma protested. "I separated those eggs for a reason. Egg white omelets are better for your cholesterol."

"Cholesterol or not, I prefer whole eggs over wimpy egg whites." He started beating the eggs, adding some milk to the mixture. "And, frankly, you look like you could use the extra calories in the yolks. You look a bit pale. Did you eat anything today?"

"Cereal and then half a seafood salad when I met Joanna."

Phil was right, she hadn't eaten enough, especially with the exercise of riding and sex thrown in. She looked after his cholesterol, and he looked after her in general. Grant never took notice of anything she ate unless it was to comment that she'd get fat if she ate too many sweets. Considering her naturally active metabolism and her enjoyment of exercise, she stayed slim as a reed and so far had managed to avoid middle-age spread.

Phil gave her a scolding look as he started sautéing the onions. They hit the hot, buttery pan with a loud sizzle.

"Let me help you," Emma told him.

"You just keep your cute keister on that stool. I can manage." After stirring the onions around until they were near done, he threw in the sliced mushrooms and got some chopped spinach ready to add just before the eggs.

"I have to do something, Phil. That phone call made me jumpy as a Chihuahua."

"Then why don't you make us some toast."

She got up off the stool and came around the counter. "Okay, but no butter. You put enough in the pan." When Phil made a face, she added, "There's some nice organic marmalade in the fridge. You can think of it as a little bite of dessert."

"Quit being such a pain in my ass, Fancy Pants."

"I'm just trying to keep you around long enough to get some use out of you." She gave him a wide grin. "You know, like taking care of an old car so it will last longer."

"Vintage, darling," he corrected. "I'm not old. I'm vintage."

Emma popped slices of whole-grain, high-fiber bread into the large four-slot toaster on the counter, filling each opening. "I wonder if Joanna thinks Max's ghost has something to do with Lainey's suicide attempts. Maybe Max is haunting Lainey, too." She pulled the jar of marmalade out of the refrigerator and placed it on the breakfast bar before starting a pot of decaf coffee.

"If so, it would explain why she was willing to break the bank for you to get rid of him." Vegetables done, Phil poured the egg mixture into the pan. "You want an omelet, or should I just scramble it all up?"

"Scrambled is fine with me."

Emma hovered over the toaster, thinking about the Naiman family as she watched the red-hot coils do their job. "I find it difficult to believe Max would intimidate his own daughter into killing herself. They were quite close, as I recall. Whenever there were parent meetings or programs at school, it was always Max who showed up, not Joanna."

"Maybe her schedule was less flexible."

"Every time? Grant almost always came with me to school functions. He may be a jerk, but until he married Carolyn and started a second family, he was always a good father and there for Kelly."

The toast popped just as Phil was dividing the eggs between two plates. He placed them on the counter, in front of two stools. Emma put the toast on a small separate plate and added it to the meal before retrieving silverware and napkins. She took the opportunity to glance out the window at the porch.

"The rocking ghosts still out there?" asked Phil.

"Nope. The chairs are both still."

They ate a few minutes in silence, each savoring the simple, cozy meal, before Phil brought up the Naimans again. "My offer's still good if you want me to see if I can get the official report on Max Naiman's death."

"Who knows, that might be a help." Emma took a sip of her coffee and looked up at Phil. He was grinning.

"I'm not involved, Phil. I'm just going to go visit my daughter's friend to bring her some comfort."

"Uh-huh." Phil brushed his moustache with his fingertips and stared at Emma, his eyes twinkling. "Tell me that again after you've seen the girl."

Emma almost threw her toast at him.

five

SERENITY PLACE WAS A residential facility for the treatment of emotional issues, located in the beautiful hills above San Clemente. The morning after they spoke on the phone, Emma received the information from Kelly about Lainey's whereabouts. She'd been happy to see it was located closer to Julian than to Los Angeles. That same morning she called Serenity to inquire about its visitation policy. After giving her name and relationship to Lainey, Emma was put on hold. When the woman on the phone returned, she advised Emma that while most visitation occurred on Sundays, Ms. Naiman had an hour of free time that afternoon at three o'clock.

The facility was lovely, though not as posh as where most of Hollywood went to get their heads screwed back on. The grounds encompassed acres of rolling hills and looked like a family resort, with small, peach-colored bungalows scattered around a large main building and a few smaller buildings. There were gardens; a swimming pool, gym, and spa; and art and music rooms. Paved paths edged with clusters of flowers led to the bungalows and other buildings. The Pacific Ocean could be seen in the distance.

When she first arrived, Emma had waited in the lobby until someone went to fetch Lainey. When the young woman saw Emma, she was clearly happy.

"Kelly is still in Boston," Emma explained, "so I hope you don't mind that it's me visiting."

"Not at all, Mrs. Whitecastle." Lainey fiddled with the ends of a clump of her long hair. "I ... I just didn't realize anyone knew I was here."

When Lainey seemed unsure of what to do, Emma held out her arms, inviting a hug. After a brief hesitation, Lainey stepped into Emma's embrace. Once there, the young woman clung to her like a life preserver for nearly half a minute. Emma stroked the girl's hair, as she would have done to Kelly, until Lainey pulled away. She did not appear sedated.

"I believe Kelly found out you were here from Summer Perkins."

"Summer?" Lainey's mouth twitched. "If Summer knows, then I guess everyone knows by now." She shrugged. "People were bound to find out, no matter how hard my mother tries to hide it."

Emma changed the subject, not sure she wanted to talk about Joanna—at least not yet. "Serenity looks charming, Lainey. Why don't you show me around?"

The two women started down one of the paths, passing a group of people being led through a yoga class by a young African-American man with dreadlocks. Lainey waved. He smiled and waved back.

"That's Jamal," she explained. "He's pretty cool. I usually take one of his morning classes."

A little farther along, they saw a tiny older woman sitting in front of an easel, painting. Sitting cross-legged on the ground next to her was the spirit of an elderly man. Lainey waved to the woman, who smiled and hoisted the brush in her right hand to return the gesture. The ghost at her feet waved to Emma.

"Who is that woman?" Emma asked.

"Her name is Mrs. Tapinsky—Ruth Tapinsky. She came here three months ago, shortly after she saw her husband murdered. I was told it was during a home robbery." Lainey turned her head to look back at the woman. "Ruth hasn't spoken a word since it happened."

"She seems friendly, though."

"Very friendly, except for the talking thing."

"You like her a great deal, don't you?"

Lainey smiled. "Yes. She's eighty-seven, and her eyes aren't that great, so I read to her a few nights a week."

"But she paints, even with bad eyes?"

Lainey leaned close. "Between her eyes and her arthritis," she whispered, "she's not that good of a painter, but she loves doing it, and I think it helps her grieving process."

Emma put a hand lightly on Lainey's back. "You have a good heart, Lainey. Don't ever lose that."

Several steps later, they passed two picnic tables. At one, two men—one young, one middle aged—sat playing chess. They also smiled and greeted Lainey.

"This place seems to suit you, Lainey."

"My mother tried to ship me off to some fancy facility in Baja, but I checked myself into here. I have money of my own, money I inherited from my father's estate when I turned eighteen. I can go anywhere I want."

"But why here, Lainey? Isn't there a place like this nearer to your mother?"

"Yes—two, in fact—but she was adamant that I not go to one of those. She was so afraid one of her friends would see me, and how would she explain that? Joanna Reid's daughter in a nut house." Lainey held out her arms as if making an announcement. "News at eleven! It was either Baja or find a place on my own."

Emma looked around at the sprawling green grass lawn and manicured shrubs. "This is hardly a nut house, Lainey."

"My doctor suggested Serenity." She glanced around like a princess taking in her realm. "They've been very nice to me here. Very down-to-earth and helpful."

She pointed to a two-story building standing next to the larger main building. "That's where they keep the *really* messed-up patients. You know, those that need constant watching and monitoring. I was there about a week when I first arrived. Now I'm in a bungalow." Emma noted that Lainey didn't seem at all self-conscious about being in the facility. "The bungalows are triplexes that share small patios. Ruth is in one of the other rooms in my bungalow."

Emma stopped walking. "How long have you been here?"

The girl took a deep breath, her eyes rolling up as she did the math in her head. "It's been just over a month, I think."

A month. Emma looked at the young woman who used to drink cocoa with Kelly while doing homework. A girl who told

41

Emma about her first kiss long before she'd said anything about it to her own parents. "How much longer will you be here?"

Another shrug. "My doctor thinks I'll be ready to go home soon."

"You don't sound convinced."

"I'm not sure what I have to go home to."

They had arrived at a patio by the pool. The pool was a long rectangle with lane lines painted on the bottom. It was surrounded by a high fence—a reminder of the safety precautions needed in such a place. In the pool, a young woman was conducting a small water aerobics class. Just beyond the pool were a couple more picnic tables situated under a few shade trees.

"Why don't we sit and visit?" Emma suggested.

Lainey nodded, and they settled in at one of the tables, Emma wishing she had on shorts like Lainey and not a cotton dress. Still, she managed to swing her legs over the bench seat in a fairly ladylike motion.

"Mrs. Whitecastle," Lainey began.

"Call me Emma." She smiled. "After all, you're all grown up and, I understand, nearly a married woman."

Lainey avoided looking at Emma. "I'm not sure that's going to happen. Not now." It was the first time she showed any sign of sadness.

"I had lunch with your mother yesterday. When I said something about the engagement, she never said it was off."

Lainey shot her a look of suspicion. "Did my mother ask you to come here?"

"Lainey, I'm here because Kelly heard you tried to kill yourself. *She* asked me to visit you, not your mother." Emma smiled and touched Lainey's hand. "And I wanted to come as soon as I heard. Your mother never mentioned to me that you were here."

The look softened. "Kelly was my best friend until my mother sent me away to school."

"She's still a close friend. She's very worried about you, as am I." Emma paused. "Did you really try to take your own life?"

Lainey took a very deep breath, her chest rising as her lungs filled with the fresh air. She looked away as color washed over her cheeks.

"I'm sorry, Lainey. I'm afraid I've overstepped my bounds. I shouldn't be prying like this."

Slowly Lainey shook her head, still not looking at Emma. "No, I want to tell you ... Emma. I think it will do me good. My mother has never asked much about it. It will be like trying to explain it to her." Lainey got up and took a few steps to one of the nearby trees. She leaned against it, looking out toward the horizon, where the ocean met the sky, melding two different shades of blue into one as deftly as the brushstroke of a talented artist. "Maybe you can go back and tell her what I couldn't."

"But she must know."

"She knows I tried to kill myself, but she never wanted to hear about what actually happened."

The scenery was peaceful, but Emma was horrified that Lainey hadn't spoken to her mother in depth. If Kelly had tried to end her life, Emma would have been all over it, wanting to know the details of how and why—especially trying to get to the root of the why. She reminded herself not to judge Joanna too harshly. People responded to tragedy in different ways, but it still sickened her like a bad stench.

"The first time I tried to kill myself," Lainey began, still not looking at Emma, "the day began like any other. I got out of bed, showered, shampooed, brushed my teeth. Three hours later I was driving my car toward one of those concrete walls that border the freeway." She finally turned to Emma. "That was about two months ago."

Emma tried to listen without displaying the shock she was feeling. Her gut was like an unbalanced washing machine trying to clean a heavy pair of sneakers. She steadied herself, understanding that if Lainey picked up on her discomfort, she might not continue.

"Perhaps you fell asleep at the wheel."

"No." Lainey returned to the table and swung her long, tanned legs over the bench to face Emma. "I clearly remember turning the car and heading straight for the wall. At the last second, I pulled the steering wheel to the left. The car hit the wall, but not head-on. The car spun out of control and slammed back around and hit the wall again."

"You were fortunate you weren't killed."

"That's what I'm told." The words changed to deadpan, as if the girl didn't care one way or the other about death. "I was banged up but okay. A couple weeks later I almost did the same thing. It was late at night. I was returning home from visiting a friend and was driving along PCH just south of Point Magu. All of a sudden I got this overwhelming urge to slam my car through the barrier and into the ocean. "

The loud gasp escaped Emma's lips before she could stop it.

"I know what you're thinking," Lainey said before Emma could speak. "You're thinking like father, like daughter."

Emma wasn't about to lie. "Yes, initially, but you weren't drunk, were you? And you didn't go over the cliff."

"No, Emma." Lainey paused and studied Emma like a curious puppy. "That doesn't feel right. Can I go back to calling you Mrs. Whitecastle?"

"Of course. Whatever makes you more comfortable."

"I wasn't drunk," she insisted. "I'm not much of a drinker. I hadn't had anything alcoholic in days, maybe longer. But like with the wall, I felt compelled to do it, like I was being told or ordered to do it. At the last minute, I snapped out of my zombie daze and turned the wheel, just like the time before. The barrier scraped the entire right side of my new BMW."

Emma clutched her hands together. Could it be that Max Naiman was trying to kill his own daughter, or was Lainey suffering from a real psychosis?

"My mother about went berserk when she found out about the second car. She insisted I see a shrink, which I did. And things were better until about five or six weeks ago, shortly before I came here."

Emma was almost afraid to ask but did. "And what happened then?"

"I almost succeeded."

"Another car accident?"

Lainey shook her head slowly back and forth while lifting the right side of her knit jersey. Just below her breast was a large cotton bandage. She leaned back so Emma could get a good look.

"Fourteen stitches, though the stitches are out now." She made the announcement in a tone as dry as hot sand. "I was holding a chopping knife, cutting vegetables for dinner, when I had this urge to stab myself."

"More voices or orders?"

"Yes. At least I think so."

Again Lainey got up from the table. She crossed her arms in front of herself as if chilly. Emma's eyes scanned the area, wondering if there were spirits present, especially Max.

"I'm up here, Emma."

In a slow movement, Emma looked up toward the voice, pretending to weigh Lainey's words. At first she couldn't see him, but finally her eyes distinguished the figure of the ghost of Max Naiman. He was sitting on the low branch of the largest tree, swinging his legs back and forth like an impish five-year-old. Emma wanted to speak with him but knew she couldn't with Lainey present.

"This time, though, it was really weird," Lainey continued.

Emma returned her attention to Lainey.

"I was looking down, watching the knife get closer and closer to my chest ... to my heart ... like I was a bystander instead of the one it was happening to and doing it."

Lainey uncrossed her arms and pretended to hold a knife in a double grip, its tip aimed at her heart. Chills vibrated down Emma's spine like she was watching a horror movie, and to her, she was.

"It felt like something was holding my hand back," Lainey explained. "Like I was struggling with myself for control of the knife and losing. Just before it went in, my body jerked to the left, and the knife tore into my right side. There was a lot of blood but nothing serious." She looked up, not realizing she was staring directly at the ghost of her father. "It almost felt like someone pushed me out of the way, but I was alone."

Lainey relaxed her arms. "It was after that Mom decided I should be shipped off to a nut house."

Emma started to say something, but Lainey held up a hand to stop her. "I know, I know. This is not a nut house." She leaned forward, putting both of her hands flat on the table, determination showing on her face for the first time. "But let's face it, Mrs. Whitecastle, it really is."

Emma studied Lainey's face. It was fresh and pretty, with smooth olive skin, large brown eyes, a perky nose, and full rosy lips. An awkward girl, she'd grown into a beautiful woman. Only the girl's eyes belied the fear she was suppressing.

"Lainey, do you actually hear someone telling you to do these things?" Emma glanced up. Max was still in the tree, but his legs were motionless as he listened to his daughter.

"You think I'm nuts, don't you? Like everyone else." Lainey straightened. "And maybe I am."

"I'm not judging you, dear. I just want to know if you really hear the voices."

After crossing her arms again, Lainey turned her back on Emma and stared out at the blue horizon. "No, not audibly anyway." She turned back. "It's like I'm two people, and one of me is trying to destroy the other."

"Do you still get those urges?"

"Not since I've been here."

"And what about your fiancé? What does he think of all this?"

At the mention of her fiancé, tears started dripping down Lainey's cheeks as if on cue. Emma got up and went to her. The young woman sobbed against Emma's shoulder.

"I love Keith so much, Mrs. Whitecastle. But how can I marry him like this? How could he ever want me, knowing how unstable I am?"

Kelly had filled her mother in on Keith Goldstein, Lainey's fiancé, when she'd told her about Lainey's engagement a few months earlier. A premed student, Keith had met Lainey at a party last fall. Kelly had met him when she was home for the holidays and had found him both smart and likeable.

"What does Keith say about all this?"

Lainey pulled away. "At first he was very concerned and thought maybe I had blacked out while driving. He's premed at UCLA."

Emma nodded. "Kelly told me that."

"He nagged me into getting a complete physical, but my doctor found nothing physically wrong with me." She took a deep breath. "When it happened a second time, the doctor ran more tests, and I also went to a therapist. The therapist thought it might have something to do with my father—some sort of delayed reaction, especially since it involved running a car off the road."

Emma shot a look at the tree, but Max was gone. "Had anything like this ever happen before?"

Lainey shook her head quickly back and forth, her long dark hair swaying. "I was destroyed when my father died. It was horrible. And after my mother sent me away, I was miserable for the first year; I was so lonely. But I've never thought about killing myself."

Lainey took a seat back at the table. This time she sat facing out and leaned back against the table top. "Through all this Keith was great. He was so concerned about me. But when I stabbed myself—" She stopped and looked down, her hair covering her face. Emma could hear sniffles.

"After the stabbing," Lainey continued, "he said it was obvious to him I didn't want to get married." She looked up at Emma, her face streaked with tears. "He said whether I knew it or not, I'd rather die than marry him."

"Why would he think that?"

"Because it started right after we got engaged. The first accident happened less than two weeks after he gave me the ring. Oh, Mrs. Whitecastle," Lainey wailed. "Keith said horrible things to me after the stabbing."

Emma sat down next to Lainey, who was now sobbing into her hands, and put an arm around the girl.

"He said I was like one of those animals … you know … the ones who'd rather chew off their leg than be trapped. I got so mad I threw my engagement ring at him and told him to go to hell."

"Did you feel trapped, Lainey?"

She dropped her hands and looked up at Emma with genuine surprise. "Absolutely not. I loved Keith; I still do. I knew I wanted to marry him two weeks after we met." She wiped her face with the back of her hand and sniffed. "Ask Kelly. I told her that when I saw her in December."

"Where's Keith now?" Emma dug into her purse and pulled out a tissue and handed it to Lainey.

After cleaning herself up, Lainey continued. "We moved in together right after New Year's. I own a condo near campus. It was convenient for both of us."

"He's still in the condo?"

"He started staying with a friend, another guy at school, after we broke off our engagement, but when I decided to come here I told him to stay in the condo while I was gone. It would be better for his studying, especially so close to the end of the school year. After school ends, he'll move out." Again the tears started.

. . . .

EMMA WAS ALMOST TO her SUV when she heard someone call her name. She turned to see a thick, older woman wearing a white lab coat and white orthopedic shoes walking toward her with surprising energy, in spite of a slight limp.

"Mrs. Whitecastle, a moment, please," the woman called.

Walking back through the parking lot, Emma met the woman halfway.

"Mrs. Whitecastle," the woman said, "I'm so glad I caught you. I'm Dr. Garvey, Kitty Garvey, Lainey's doctor here at Serenity Place." She held out her hand to Emma, and Emma shook it.

"You're the facility's resident doctor?"

"Actually, my husband, Dr. Michael Garvey, and I own and operate it." She smiled. "Everyone calls me Dr. Kitty. He's Dr. Mike."

Dr. Kitty had a wide, friendly face, with lined cheeks and fluffy silver hair. Rectangle-shaped glasses with red plastic frames perched on her nose, secured by a multicolored beaded chain that hung around her neck.

"Do you have a moment?" the doctor asked Emma. "It's about Lainey."

Emma became alarmed. "She said she's doing much better. Is that not the case?"

"Oh, no, she is doing much better." The doctor smiled. "She's such a charming young woman, isn't she? The residents and staff both love her to bits." The doctor paused and adjusted her glasses. "I understand you've known her a long time—that you're the mother of one of her childhood friends."

"That's right. I've known Lainey since she was a little girl."

"Do you intend to come back and visit her?"

"Should I not?" Before Dr. Kitty could answer, Emma added, "I know she got upset during my visit today, but I think it did her good."

"It did her a great deal of good, I'm sure." The doctor paused. "Mrs. Whitecastle, let me be blunt. You're the first person who's visited Lainey since she's been here. When you called today and inquired about visitation, I was standing in the reception area. I told the desk clerk to give you special permission to visit today during our afternoon free time instead of waiting until Sunday, our usual visiting day."

"Joanna Reid, Lainey's mother, hasn't been here?" Emma's anger toward Joanna threatened to boil like a teakettle.

"No, I'm afraid not. She hasn't even called. Lainey's young man called a couple of times when she first got here, but not lately." The doctor pursed her lips. "Lainey has mentioned you and your family in our talks. I think it would be good for her if you visited again."

"Of course, Doctor." Emma considered an idea she had while speaking with Lainey. "In fact, I was thinking of inviting her to my cabin in Julian for a visit. It's about ninety minutes from here. It's peaceful, and I have access to horses. As I recall, Lainey used to ride when she was a girl."

The doctor beamed. "I know Julian well. Dr. Mike and I go there every year for their apple festival."

"Can Lainey leave the facility?"

"She can leave anytime she wants, although I think she still needs a bit more time with us, at least until we're sure she's going home to a stable environment. But for a short weekend, I think it would do her a world of good to visit you in Julian."

"How about next weekend?" Emma suggested. "I can pick her up on Friday afternoon and bring her back on Sunday evening."

"Before we tell Lainey, how about you and I talk by phone later in the week. Let's see how she's doing before we get her too excited."

In agreement, Emma pulled a business card out of her purse and wrote her cell number on the back, as she had with Joanna. She handed it to the doctor. "Call me anytime, Doctor, about anything having to do with Lainey."

Dr. Kitty studied the card. "You're *that* Whitecastle? The one who does those shows on the paranormal?"

Emma nodded, pleased the doctor hadn't asked if she was related to Grant Whitecastle or the burger company. "Yes, that's me. Do you watch the show?"

"Goodness, no. I've just heard about it from several friends who enjoy it. They'll be tickled to find out I've met you in person."

The doctor leaned in and whispered. "Please don't be offended, but personally I think it's a lot of hooey."

Hooey nor not, Max Naiman chose that moment to show himself again. He didn't materialize completely, but Emma definitely discerned a slight outline of haze standing next to the doctor.

"Fix this, Emma," Max said, his face narrowed with concern. "Please."

six

· · · · · ·

"SIMMER DOWN, YOU'RE GOING to bust a button." Granny studied Emma with her signature scowl.

"But Granny, Lainey's own mother hasn't called or visited her in a month. Doesn't that get your goat?"

"Of course it does. That poor child needs a mother at a time like this. Good thing you visited."

"But I'm *not* her mother," Emma stressed. "She should have her own mother, not some stand-in."

"From what you've told us so far about Joanna Reid," said Phil, only hearing Emma's side of the conversation, "in this case, the understudy is much better than the original. At least I know you're a wonderful mother."

They were seated on the porch of the cabin. Phil and Emma were dressed to go into town for the dinner at the Julian Grill they'd skipped the night before. Emma was perched on the porch railing. Granny was fully materialized and seated in a rocker next to Phil. She rocked gently back and forth, the chair barely moving under her spirited power. The empty rocker to Granny's left was not moving at all.

"Where's Jacob tonight?" Phil asked, noting the still rocker.

Granny glanced at the chair. "He'll come around after you folks leave for your supper." Emma relayed the answer to Phil.

Phil feigned hurt. "What? He doesn't like our company?"

"What he likes is peace and quiet," the ghost answered. "He's not gonna have that with the three of us yammering like magpies about this poor girl." Again, Emma acted as interpreter.

Granny gripped the arms of her rocker and looked at Emma dead-on. "So, chief, what's our assignment?"

Emma nearly fell off the railing with surprised laughter.

Phil sprang from his chair to steady her. "You going to fill me in, or do I have to play twenty questions with Granny?"

Once Emma stopped laughing enough to catch her breath, she repeated what Granny had said. Laughing himself, Phil turned to the chair he assumed held the ghost. "Granny, you do say the damndest things. Where do you come up with this stuff?"

Emma ran a hand over her face. "From TV, where do you think? Now that it's not football season, my mother says Granny has become addicted to crime dramas."

Granny stopped rocking and twisted her face into an even deeper scowl. "Now just a cotton-picking minute. Who do you think turns on the TV and watches them shows with me? It ain't Dr. Miller, that's for sure."

After being fed Granny's comment, Phil buried his face in the side of Emma's neck, just below her ear. His laughter tickled her skin. "She has a good point, *chief*," he said, his breath warm on her neck. "Your mother is her enabler."

Playfully Emma pushed Phil away. "Enabler or not, there is no assignment." Emma looked directly at the ghost when she spoke. "You got that, Granny? We're simply going to help Lainey through these tough times if we can."

Granny was not happy. "But what about that ghost haunting her mother? He could be haunting Lainey, too."

"That ghost is Max, Lainey's father. And while I'd hate to think he's causing his daughter's suicide attempts, it does seem Lainey is having some paranormal experiences and doesn't realize that's what they are."

Seeing that both Phil and Granny were giving Emma their undivided attention, Emma continued. "I questioned Lainey about what she remembers right before each attempt on her life. Each time she remembers feeling very cold."

"So if it is Max making her do this stuff," Phil said, "it means she can hear him."

"Not necessarily," Emma explained. "When I asked her about the voices, she said it wasn't something she heard as much as something she felt. Like she *felt* driven to kill herself—almost as if she were obeying some unseen master."

"Evil master," added Granny.

"I agree, Granny. Whatever is causing her to do these things is evil."

Phil shook his head. "It's unconscionable that a parent, even the ghost of a parent, would do such a thing to his own daughter."

Emma's face turned sober. "Parents have been known to do horrible things to their children, Phil. Or don't you read the news?"

"But I thought you said Max was a good dad when he was alive."

"He was, at least that I could see. But who knows what happened right before his accident or after he died."

Granny shook her head at Emma's comments. "I've never known any spirit changing from being a decent sort while alive to being evil after death. Death might take them by surprise and they may be upset for a bit, but in time they get over it. But if a person was nasty in life or angry about something at the time of their death, there's a good chance they'll be a nasty spirit. Remember that Mrs. Manning? Her ghost was spiteful. Lainey's mother sounds like she might be a humdinger in the afterlife, too, if she don't change her spots."

After Emma's translation, Phil looked at Granny. "So whatever you were in life is how you spend eternity?"

"Not always, but for the most part," answered Granny. "Though I've seen some not-so-nice spirits become quite pleasant after a while. If a person does change after they die, it's more likely they were unhappy while alive and find peace in death. *Rest in peace* ain't just some saying you carve into a headstone."

Emma repeated Granny's words to Phil.

"So," Phil began after digesting Granny's explanation, "if Max Naiman was a good and loving dad while alive, it's unlikely he'd harm his daughter now."

Granny got up and went to Phil's side. Standing on tiptoe, the tiny ghost blew into his right ear.

Phil winked at Emma. "There's my answer."

Open mouthed, Emma stared at the two of them. "Unbelievable."

When Granny took her seat in the rocker again, Emma told them about seeing Max. "Max showed up today when I was visiting Lainey. He didn't say a word, just watched her, almost like a guardian angel. When I was leaving he showed up, but I couldn't say anything to him in front of Dr. Garvey without looking like a wingnut."

"Did Max say anything?" asked Granny.

Emma nodded, still lost in thoughts of Max Naiman. "His parting words to me were *fix this*."

Phil looked surprised. "Weren't those the same words he said at the restaurant?"

"Yes. Guess they were meant for me after all, except this time he said 'please.'"

After a few beats of silence, during which Emma thought about Max and Lainey, she turned her full attention to her present company. "I hate to cut our weekend short, Phil, but I need to head back to LA tomorrow morning. There are two people I want to talk to before Monday, if I can—Joanna Reid and Keith Goldstein."

"I thought Joanna didn't give you her contact information."

"She didn't, but Lainey did, as well as Keith's."

"You going to run this by Milo, too?"

Emma shook her head. "Milo left yesterday for a series of paranormal retreats in England. He's one of the presenters. Tracy went with him."

Tracy Bass was Emma's closest friend and a college professor. While Tracy couldn't see or hear ghosts, she was very interested in the paranormal. She and Milo Ravenscroft had met when Emma first started discovering her special talents, and the two had, in time, become lovers.

"I thought Milo hated stuff like that."

"Normally, yes, but this is more of an educational thing. They do two week-long retreats back-to-back with very small groups at some old castle. Tracy encouraged him to do it." Emma smiled. "Personally, I think Tracy just wanted a free vacation in England. After the retreat, they're going to do some traveling around the countryside."

Phil nudged a stray rock on the floor of the porch with his boot. "How about I come with you, then?"

"Why?"

"I'd feel better if you'd let me come along, Emma. These things tend to get you into hot water. I'd worry less by your side."

"But what about your work? You must be swamped getting ready to leave for your trip with the boys."

"I hadn't planned on doing much this weekend, and I'll bring along my laptop just in case I do need to address something. We can take separate cars, and I'll drive back to San Diego on Monday morning."

Emma smiled at him. "Are you sure?"

"I wouldn't have offered if I wasn't."

Emma put an arm around Phil's waist and snuggled. "It would be nice to spend the rest of the weekend together, and my parents would love to see you."

"Not to mention," Granny added, "they'd feel better knowing Phil had your back while you go snooping around."

Emma frowned at Granny. "I don't need Phil to watch my back, Granny."

"Yes, you do, you little fool. And tell him to bring his gun."

Emma stomped her right foot once on the ground. "And he's *not* bringing his gun."

Phil chuckled, easily filling in the gaps in the conversation without a translator. Emma slipped her arm away and turned to him, her hands on her hips. "You're not bringing it, are you?"

"I hadn't thought of it, but maybe it's not such a bad idea." One look at Emma and Phil amended his comment. "No, Fancy Pants," he assured her with a laugh and a soft stroke of her arm. "I'll leave my gun at home."

Emma gave him a quick, solid kiss. "Thank you."

"Humph." Granny got up again from her chair and started for the far end of the porch, her image beginning to fade. "You're both a couple of fools."

"Granny," Emma called to her. "There is something I'd like you to do for me, if you want."

The ghost spun around, her lined face wreathed with eagerness. "I knew there'd be an assignment." She floated back, coming to a halt in front of Emma and Phil. She looked up at Emma, her mouth pursed with purpose. "Shoot, chief."

seven

· · · · · · · · · ·

Linwood and Joanna Reid lived in a Beverly Hills mansion located north of Sunset Boulevard near Greystone Mansion. It was an imposing estate with a tall, thick white wall around the perimeter and a large iron gate guarding the entry.

Emma drove up to the gate, aligning her Lexus SUV with the security intercom. After hitting the buzzer, she announced her name, and the gates magically opened.

Phil, sitting in the passenger's seat, looked astounded. "Just like that, *open sesame*? I thought this woman didn't want to see you again."

Emma shot him a sly look as they drove through the gate and proceeded down the circular drive to the front of the magnificent house. "When I called Joanna this morning on the way back from Julian, she still didn't. So I applied a little pressure."

Catching a cocked eyebrow from Phil, she explained sheepishly, "I sort of blackmailed her—or threatened to. I told her I'd seen

Lainey and that I'd tweet her whereabouts and circumstances on Twitter if Joanna didn't see me."

Phil was aghast. "But you'd never do that. Not in a million years."

"Of course I wouldn't, but Joanna doesn't know me well enough to know that." They pulled up just beyond the wide marble front steps, and Emma killed the engine. "Desperate times call for desperate measures. An hour later, she called back with a time to come by."

Unbuckling his seat belt, Phil asked, "Do you even have a Twitter account?"

Emma flashed Phil a coy smile and looked up at the huge house. "This is nothing like the home she had with Max in Malibu. It was large but charming and less ..." She stalled for words.

"Stuffy and pretentious?" Phil suggested. "I've been in museums smaller than this."

A middle-aged Latina in a maid's uniform answered the door and showed them in. The inside of the home was as elegant as the outside, with a double staircase and opulent furnishings. In the foyer, another maid was busy dusting. Fresh flowers and expensive sculptures adorned most of the tables. Impressive and important art covered the walls. Phil stopped at one painting, studied it, and gave off a low whistle.

The maid showed them through the house and out the back. Following a stone path through a carefully planned flower garden, they crossed the large, sloping lawn to a patio overlooking the pool, where they found Joanna seated at a table under a shade umbrella. She was wearing immaculately pressed walking shorts and a crisp cotton sleeveless blouse, both in white. A pair of designer sunglasses, different from those she wore Thursday, were in place. In front of her was a carafe of coffee and a single delicate cup and saucer.

When the maid asked if there was anything else Joanna required, Joanna waived her off. "Nothing, Bonita. They won't be staying long."

"Nice little place you have here," Phil observed. When Joanna didn't invite them to sit down, he pulled out a chair for Emma and took one for himself.

Joanna pulled down her sunglasses and scanned Phil top to bottom as if he were an item at a grocery store checkout. "And who might you be?"

Emma made the introductions. "This is Phil Bowers, a close friend. Phil, Joanna Reid."

Phil held out his right hand to Joanna. "I'm Emma's man-toy," he said in a deadpan voice.

Joanna offered up a tight-lipped smile but didn't take his hand. Instead, she readjusted her sunglasses and turned to Emma. "I see you traded up."

"That's the general consensus," Emma replied, remembering her suspicion that Joanna had once had an affair with Grant.

"Speaking of trading up," continued Emma, "this is certainly a lot more house than you had in Malibu."

Joanna looked around the flawless grounds. Her mouth remained a slit, not giving away her feelings. "Yes, Lin has lived here for years." She turned to look at Phil and Emma again. "I never did like that house in Malibu. It felt cramped, and there was no room for a proper garden."

Emma took her own look around the grounds, noting that the Malibu house would have fit into a corner of Joanna's present digs like a second garage.

Joanna took a sip of her coffee. "I heard you had to move back in with your parents, you poor dear."

"Not had to, Joanna, chose to. I own a home in Julian and split my time between there and Pasadena."

"Julian? Never heard of it."

Emma was glad Granny wasn't present. She took folks' not knowing about Julian very personally. "Julian is a lovely little town in the mountains north of San Diego." She turned and smiled at Phil. "Phil and his family are from there."

Joanna sneered. "How quaint."

"In fact," added Emma, getting ready to stir the pot, "Serenity Place is about halfway between Julian and Los Angeles." She turned again to Phil. "Isn't that right, Phil?"

"Almost to the mile if you take the 5 Freeway."

Joanna removed her sunglasses and glared at Emma. "All right, Emma Whitecastle," she hissed through perfect white teeth. "What the hell kind of game are you playing?"

"I'm not playing a game, Joanna. I don't play games when a young woman's life is involved."

Emma cleared her throat, giving herself time to control her emotions. "You're the one who called me up and ordered me to get Max's ghost out of your life. You're the one who implied his death wasn't an accident—that he killed himself. Yet you never told me poor Lainey has had three suicide attempts in the past few months. More importantly," Emma pointed an accusatory finger at Joanna, not caring one bit how rude the gesture was, "I understand you have not once visited your daughter or even called her. Are you punishing Lainey because she refused go to the facility you chose, the out-of-sight, out-of-mind place in Mexico?"

"You don't know what you're talking about."

"Next to you, Joan Collins is mother of the year."

"Bravo, Emma."

Emma's head snapped up in time to see the ghost of Max Naiman materializing. He slowly and silently clapped his hands as he walked toward them.

"Never knew you had that kind of spunk, luv."

As he had the day before, Max was wearing jeans and an open chambray shirt over a plain tee shirt, making Emma remember how often he wore that combination while alive. He'd been of average height, lean and muscular, with wavy black hair and naturally high cheekbones fashion models would drool over. At that instant it struck Emma how much Lainey looked like her father, except that Max had rugged good looks and his daughter's face was as smooth as a fresh peach. He ambled over to the table, as relaxed and laid-back in death as he had been in life. When he approached Joanna, she started to shiver. She reached for the white sweater on the back of her chair, but it slipped to the ground.

Phil got up. Retrieving the fallen sweater, he placed it gently across Joanna's shoulders, noting at the same time how chilly it was at her end of the table. Before returning to his seat, he caught Emma's eye over the top of Joanna's head. After cutting his eyes side to side, he shot her an inquiring look and mouthed, "Max?" She returned a slow, deliberate blink, hoping he took it as a yes; he did. Returning to his seat, he kept his senses sharp.

"It's over eighty degrees out, and I'm cold," Joanna complained in a shaky voice. "I must be coming down with something."

"The same bug you had at the Ivy?" Emma asked.

Clutching the sweater tight, Joanna stood up. "It's time for you to leave. Lainey is none of your business."

Max bent forward and placed his hands on Joanna's shoulders. Instantly she began to weep and sat back down, her imperious behavior dissolved into a puddle. He said something to his widow, but Emma couldn't hear it, though it was enough to cause Joanna to shake anew. Max laughed at her distress.

Looking directly at the ghost, Emma asked, "Why are you tormenting her?"

The ghost gave Emma a slow, lazy smile and started to fade. "I always liked you, Emma. You were good to my daughter. Be good to her now. She needs you."

Emma shot to her feet. "Wait, Max. I need to speak with you." But the ghost had disappeared.

"He's gone?" asked Phil.

"Yes."

Emma looked at Joanna, whose thin shoulders still vibrated from her soft crying. "What did Max say to you, Joanna, to get you so upset?"

Joanna raised her head. Taking off her sunglasses, she looked at Emma. Her tears were ruining her eye makeup. "He said something to me?"

Emma moved around to Joanna's side of the table. Perching on the edge, she studied the distressed woman. "You knew Max was here just now, didn't you?"

Joanna closed her eyes and moved her head up and down slowly.

"But you didn't hear him speak?"

"No." Joanna raised frightened eyes to Emma's. "What did he say?"

"I don't know, Joanna. I could see him whisper something into your ear, but I couldn't hear it."

Phil leaned forward, ready to put his attorney interrogation skills to work. "If you couldn't hear him, then why did you get so upset?"

Joanna's eyes shifted from Emma to Phil and back to Emma. "It was the way I felt. It's the way I feel every time."

"Tell us," encouraged Emma.

No longer cold, Joanna shrugged off her sweater. It fell between her back and the back of the chair. "Whenever I think Max's ghost is around, I get so cold—bone-chilling cold—and a weight presses on me until I think I cannot bear it; it's like I'm being smothered with something damp and cold like a heavy, wet blanket."

With shaking hands, Joanna picked up her coffee cup. It was almost empty. She reached for the carafe, but her hands were still shaking and her grip undependable.

Emma noticed and picked up the carafe, refilling Joanna's cup. "Could you feel a weight just now?"

Joanna picked up the cup with two trembling hands. "More than ever."

"He put his hands on your shoulders when you stood up and pressed down until you sat back down."

"Can ghosts do that? Touch you, I mean?" The fear in Joanna's eyes doubled.

"Look, Joanna," Emma began, keeping her voice calm. "I'm still learning about this stuff, but one thing I do know for sure is that ghosts cannot harm the living physically."

Joanna cast Emma a disbelieving look before taking a sip of her coffee.

"It's true," Emma assured her. "They can intimidate and frighten us." She thought of Granny. "They can even annoy or bring comfort. But they cannot physically harm us. Remember that."

Emma pushed off the table. Pulling a chair close to Joanna, she asked, "When exactly did Max start coming around? Was it before or after Lainey's first suicide attempt?"

Joanna nearly dropped her coffee cup. Emma reached out and placed her hand over Joanna's to steady it and guide it back to its saucer.

"You don't think he's behind Lainey's …," she swallowed, "her problems, do you?" Joanna sounded genuinely shocked. She picked up a linen napkin from the table and started patting it around her smudged eyes. "I can't believe that. He adored Lainey."

"He's frightening you, why not her?" asked Phil.

"Because it wouldn't make sense," Joanna responded. "Max and I, well, we had our ups and downs, and for the couple of years before his death, it was mostly down. Affairs by both of us. His drinking. My nagging. A few months before he died, we decided to start over and recommit ourselves." She looked at Emma. "Don't you remember, Emma? We even restated our vows."

"That's right," Emma confirmed. "I remember now. You had a ceremony under a gazebo on the beach."

"Yes. We even had new wedding rings." Joanna started tearing up again. "Mine was a platinum band encrusted with diamonds, with a large solitaire in the center. His was this impressive band with a single large square-cut diamond, a vintage piece from an estate sale." She sighed deeply, lost in thought. "We were just beginning to be happy again when Max started falling apart."

"You mean his drinking?" asked Emma.

"Not at first. It started with erratic behavior. He was snappish and impatient with both me and Lainey, and he always seemed distracted. Then the drinking started up again." She cast her eyes down toward the peaceful swimming pool glistening in the sunlight like a large crystal sculpture. "The night he went over the cliff near Big Sur wasn't his first incident."

Emma was taken aback by the announcement. "He tried something like it before?" She glanced over at Phil and saw that his eyes were glued to Joanna, watching and weighing her words and facial expressions, checking for any flaws in her commentary.

"Not a car accident, but just a few weeks prior to that he went on a real bender. He used a bottle of thirty-year-old Scotch to wash down a bottle of sleeping pills."

Emma weighed the truth of Joanna's story. "I don't recall hearing about that."

Joanna gave up a sad chuckle. "Of course you didn't. The studio, his agent—everyone—managed to squelch it. He did it at the house in Malibu while I was at my office and Lainey was at school. His agent found him in our bedroom when he dropped by for a meeting. He called a private doctor. One used to dealing with celebrity screw-ups." Another sour laugh. "Had it happened today, with all the social media and bloodthirsty gossip mongers, it probably would have been all over the news." Joanna glanced at Emma. "Just like your ugly divorce."

Inside, Emma flinched, remembering how her personal life and the divorce battle with Grant had been featured on every celebrity news program, entertainment Internet blog, and supermarket checkout rag.

Joanna straightened in her chair. "We also caught a break because it happened on the same day Jan Banks decided to kill his pregnant wife."

Jan Banks—another Hollywood horror. Banks had been the star of a long-running TV prime-time game show. On the day the network announced it was canceling the show, Banks returned to his home in Bel Air, shot and killed his young wife, then turned the gun on himself. When it happened, it had dominated the news for days.

In his chair, Phil shifted uncomfortably and cleared his throat. "I remember that day."

Emma gave a slight nod. "Yes, me too. Jan and Grant were friends." She reached over and patted Joanna's arm. "I'm sorry, Joanna. I had no idea."

"A couple of weeks later, Max seemed almost his old self. He'd even stopped drinking. Driving over that cliff was the last thing any of us expected."

Joanna started to take a drink of her coffee but decided against it. "Lainey doesn't know about the pills, Emma. I'd like to keep it that way. We told her Max had an allergic reaction to something he ate and went into anaphylactic shock. He was horribly allergic to shellfish, so it was an easy sell. Max's death was difficult enough for her without adding an earlier cover-up."

Emma got up and went to the edge of the patio to think. It was a large area with several cozy arrangements of outdoor furniture, like a living room without roof or walls. She stood looking down the steps that led to the lower level and its large deck, cabana, and pool house. A few moments later, she returned to the table.

"Close to his daughter or not, you still don't think Max had anything to do with Lainey's suicide attempts? It seems too coincidental to me that he doesn't, especially if he showed up about the same time they started occurring."

"But you said ghosts can't hurt us."

"Not physically," Emma repeated, "but who knows what other influences they might be capable of. While I don't want to believe that Max is behind this, Lainey is being tormented by something. She told me each time she tried to kill herself, it felt like someone was telling her to do it."

Joanna looked aghast. "I didn't know that."

Emma fixed the other mother with an accusatory eye. "You would have if you'd taken the time to listen to the poor girl. Haven't you even checked with her doctors about her progress?"

With shaking hands, Joanna returned her sunglasses to her face. "I didn't want to know," she said in a clipped but quiet tone. "I couldn't bear it, and I had other very serious matters to consider."

"More serious than your own child?" Emma wanted to slap her.

"Halloooo," a man called from the house.

Phil and Emma turned toward the sound. Joanna didn't.

eight

· · · · · · · · · ·

Linwood Reid took the path from the house down to the patio at a confident clip. He was tall and lanky, dressed in conservatively colored golf apparel. On his head was a white cap from Hilton Head. He came toward them with a tall drink in his hand and a wide smile on his face.

"Hello, dear." Lin bent down and kissed his wife on her cheek. "I didn't realize you had company."

Emma could have sworn she saw Joanna recoil at her husband's touch. It wasn't a sharp jerk but a slight turn of her face and shoulders away from his affectionate gesture, an almost imperceptible tic.

"How was your game, Lin?" Joanna asked dutifully.

"Great. Won a whole three dollars from Gains and the boys." He laughed and winked at Emma and Phil. "High stakes, huh, folks? We each put a dollar in the pot. Winner gets the pot, a free drink, and bragging rights."

"Lin," Joanna said, "this is Emma Whitecastle and her friend Phil Bowers."

Phil stood and reached out a hand to the man. They shook. "I enjoyed that article about you in *Forbes* last month."

"You in finance, Phil?"

"Tax attorney down in San Diego."

Lin nodded agreeably and turned to Emma, appraising her physical appearance, fresh and inviting in a pale blue summer sheath. Clearly he liked what he saw. "Whitecastle? You related to that ass on TV?"

Considering both she and Grant had their own TV shows, Emma suppressed the urge to ask which Whitecastle ass Lin meant. Instead she said, "Grant Whitecastle and I divorced almost two years ago."

"Good for you. Never liked that tacky show of his."

Lin looked down at the table and noted the coffee for one. "We need to get you folks some refreshments." He pulled a cell phone from his pocket. "I'll call Bonita, and she'll be down here in a jiff. What'll you have?" He raised his crystal highball glass. "I'm having G & T. Sound good?"

"No, thank you, Lin," Emma said quickly. "We were just leaving."

"You sure? Won't take but a minute."

"No, thank you," confirmed Phil. "We need to shove off soon. We have another appointment."

With a look of disappointment, Lin put away his phone and folded his long body into the empty chair next to his wife, opposite Emma. He put down his drink and took off his cap to wipe his forehead with a white handkerchief pulled from a pocket. "Quite a scorcher on the links today."

Under his hat, Lin's hair was a damp mass of short gray waves. His face was tanned and lined with shallow ruts, like bicycle tire grooves in soft earth. Both his lips and nose were thin and irregular. He appeared to be quite a bit older than Joanna.

Lin's dark eyes were not nearly as congenial as his outward demeanor. Small and alert, like that of a rodent, they measured Emma and Phil as carefully as a fine tailor cutting expensive fabric. "I've never met you folks before. You old friends of Joanna's?"

"From a long time ago," Emma offered. "When Max was alive and I was married to Grant, we saw each other often. Our girls went to school together and are still great friends."

"Emma went to visit Lainey at that place." Joanna stared into her coffee cup when she spoke.

Lin laughed. "You mean that hippy-dippy place in San Clemente?"

"Serenity Place seemed quite lovely to me," challenged Emma. "And Lainey appeared content. Her doctor told me she's greatly improved."

Lin replaced his cap. "We tried to get her into a place that would provide real help, not some touchy-feely summer camp for spoiled brats."

"Lin, please." Joanna glanced at her husband. "Lainey wanted to go there, and she did. She's getting help, and that's all that matters."

"Help. Bah! All she's receiving is reinforcement of her bad behavior."

Lin turned his gaze from Emma to Phil, looking for confirmation of his opinion. He received none. "My stepdaughter is a drama queen, plain and simple."

Emma felt her eyes narrow in anger in spite of her attempt to keep her face a blank tablet. "You don't believe Lainey tried to kill herself?"

He weighed his thoughts like whole coffee beans before letting them spill. "I believe she tried to make it *appear* as if she were killing herself."

Lin leaned back in his chair and crossed one long leg casually over the opposite knee. "But, come on, we all seem to be reasonably intelligent people here. If someone really wanted to kill themselves, they would eat the barrel of a pistol or something irreversible like that." He raised his glass to make the point. "The first two attempts were clearly daddy rage, and the last was a joke." He took a long sip of his cool drink. "Who in the hell tries to stab themselves?"

Phil asked dryly, "You've never heard of hara-kiri?"

Lin ignored the comment. "Just spoiled, unbalanced baby divas looking for attention, that's who does things like that."

Emma wasn't watching Lin. Her eyes were on Joanna's hands. While she appeared calm, her fingers were fidgeting with the china coffee cup as if it had a paper label that could be peeled off.

· · · · · · · · · · · · ·

"Did you find that man as insufferable as I did?" While Emma talked, her fingers were flying, typing out a text message to Kelly on her phone.

At the wheel of Emma's SUV, Phil chuckled. "He was pretty full of himself, that's for sure." He glanced over at Emma. "What are you writing over there, a novel?"

"I'm asking Kelly if she's ever met Linwood Reid or if Lainey mentioned him to her."

"Remind me to find that *Forbes* article for you."

"I'd love to read it." Emma finished the text off with *xoxox, Mom* and put her phone away. "You didn't tell me you knew who he was."

"And you didn't tell me Joanna was married to Linwood Reid. You only said her last name was now Reid. Being married to him explains that palace of a house, though."

"Yes, that was pretty amazing. Both you and I live in lovely, large homes, but next to that, we might as well be living under an overpass of the 405 Freeway. Even that monstrosity I shared with Grant is a shack next to the Reid home."

The GPS in Emma's car directed Phil to turn left off of Sunset at the edge of the UCLA campus. "So who exactly is Linwood Reid?" she asked.

"He's some big global money guy. Built a fortune financing a variety of successful high-risk, high-return ventures, anything from treasure hunting to oil expeditions. He's also a major player in international construction and energy companies."

"Like Halliburton?"

"Not Halliburton, but companies like it. Although here's a trivia tidbit for ya." Phil flashed her a grin. "He's supposedly a close pal of Dick Cheney."

"A pal close enough to shoot?"

Phil laughed and turned left at another intersection, following the next instruction called out by the automated voice of the GPS. They were on their way to Lainey's condominium to see Keith Goldstein.

"Where did he make his seed money? You have to have money to start to turn it into money of his present magnitude."

"There's a lot of speculation on that. It's well known he was one of the pirates in the Enron mess."

"One of the executives?"

"No, one of the initial investors. One who bailed with a boat-load of cash just before it all turned to shit."

"Just savvy or an inside tip?"

Phil shrugged. "Who knows. It was never proved he knew anything about the internal finances of the company." He made another turn onto Wilshire Boulevard. "There were also rumors of him being involved in selling guns overseas."

"What?" Emma nearly snapped her neck as she whipped around to stare at Phil.

"Again, nothing was proved, but the rumors claim he pro-vided financial backing for international gunrunners and made an obscene amount of money."

"Wow. I may have traded up, but it seems Joanna didn't, at least not in character."

Phil blew her a loud, sloppy kiss.

"Speaking of wow." Phil pulled into a circular drive of a high-rise building on Wilshire Boulevard. "Are you sure this is where Lainey lives?"

"This is the address she gave me."

After the doorman directed them to visitor parking, they made their way into the marble-encased lobby to face the concierge.

"Yowza!" said the disembodied voice of Granny. "Is this a hotel?"

Emma turned to Phil and pretended to whisper something to him. "Nice time for you to show up, Granny. Max popped in at Joanna's, then popped out just as quickly."

"Hey," the ghost said with annoyance as heavy as her boots. "I've been trying to get him for ya, but it's not like he's standing around on the other side waiting for me to pick him out of a lineup."

Knowing this wasn't the time and place to argue with the cranky ghost, Emma plastered a smile on her face and turned to approach the dark-skinned young man at the desk. He gave her a gracious nod and closed-lipped smile. He was movie-star beautiful, with black slicked hair and intelligent eyes the color of dark roast coffee. His name tag said Shaheen.

"Shaheen, I'm Emma Whitecastle. I believe Elaine Naiman in 1202 called about giving me access to her apartment." Emma dug out her wallet and presented her ID to the man. He glanced at it, then checked something on the computer recessed into his desktop.

"Yes, Ms. Whitecastle," Shaheen said in a softly accented voice, "Ms. Naiman called yesterday with instructions. If Mr. Goldstein isn't at home, we're to give you a key."

He picked up a phone and punched in a number. After a few moments, he put the phone down. "It seems Mr. Goldstein is not in." Shaheen unlocked a cabinet in the desk console and from it plucked out a key and handed it to Emma. "You can take one of the two elevators to your left to the twelfth floor. Unit 1202 is all the way down the hall, an end unit."

Emma and Phil took the elevator. Granny had taken off again.

"When I was in college," Phil said during the ride in the mirror-walled elevator, "I shared a run-down two-bedroom house with three other guys. Our furniture was hand-me-downs from family, and our tables and bookcases were made from planks of wood and bricks."

"I know what you mean. My digs weren't that ... um ... rustic, but I did share a modest apartment with my cousin Marlene. It wasn't too far from here, but it was a world apart in amenities."

"That's right, you went to UCLA, didn't you, Fancy Pants?"

"Both Grant and I went there. We met during our junior year."

When the elevator doors opened, Emma immediately saw Granny. The ghost was in the midst of materializing. She stood just beyond the elevator, patting her foot on the hallway carpet with impatience.

"What's the matter, Granny?" Emma asked the ghost. "You didn't want to keep us company?"

"Don't like those darn contraptions, not one bit. They're like coffins that move."

Emma repeated the comment to Phil, who shivered and shook his head. "That's something to remember for our trip back down."

"I'm a bit confused," Phil said as they started walking down the quiet hallway with Granny floating alongside. "Did you tell Lainey you were coming here to interrogate her fiancé?"

"Not exactly."

Both Phil and Granny stopped and stared after Emma. "What exactly *did* you tell her?" Phil asked.

Emma stopped halfway down the hall. Just as she was about to say something, a door to her right opened and a slight, middle-aged man with thick black glasses with circular frames came out carrying a tiny orange Pomeranian. He smiled at Emma, then noticed Phil and nodded to him. The dog noticed Granny and started yipping with excitement.

"Baxter," the man clucked at the dog. "Shush." He turned his attention back to Emma and Phil. "Can I help you folks?"

"We're looking for number 1202," Emma told him.

He pointed in the direction they had been heading. "All the way down to the end, on your left."

Phil took Emma's elbow. "Thanks." They started back down the hall.

The man put Baxter down on the carpet, and the little dog went nuts, wagging his tail and pulling on his leash to follow Emma and Phil ... and Granny.

The man laughed. "Are you folks carrying raw filet in your pockets?"

Granny, sensing she was the problem, disappeared.

Phil chuckled. "The little guy must smell our animals. Between our horses and dogs, we have quite a zoo at home."

Picking up the excited dog, the man gave them a final smile and headed for the elevator.

Phil tugged gently on Emma's elbow. "So, what did you tell Lainey?"

"You're not going to drop this, are you?"

"Nope."

"I simply asked Lainey if there was anything she wanted from her apartment while I was up in Los Angeles. She was very grateful and gave me a short list of items, mostly makeup and a couple articles of clothing."

"Uh-huh. But you really wanted to get inside her place and see if you could get a sense of Max's presence, right?"

"Yes, and this seemed a good way to do it without alarming her." When they reached the door to 1202, Emma inserted the key. "I couldn't exactly ask her about her father's ghost, could I?"

"Lying, threatening folks with blackmail—doesn't quite sound like you, Fancy Pants."

She opened the door several inches, then stopped. "I'm sorry, Phil, if you're disappointed in me, but I did what I felt I had to do to help the girl."

"Don't get so defensive, Emma. I'm not disappointed—intrigued, yes. This is a side of you I haven't seen before. I find it rather fascinating." He paused long enough to plant a short kiss on her lips. "As long as you don't use those new talents on me."

"It's a deal, Cowboy."

"Are you two going to moon after each other all day or do some work?"

Emma turned to the ghost. "There you are, Granny. I thought you'd left."

"I did, but just until that fool dog got out of the way."

Phil pushed the door open.

"Wow!" exclaimed Phil, stepping inside Lainey's condominium just behind Emma. "Exactly how rich *is* this girl?"

nine

· · · · · · · ·

"WHO KNOWS? MAX WAS no Johnny Depp, but at the time of his death he was bringing in between twenty-five and fifty million a year."

Phil stopped in his tracks. "How do you know?"

"I thought you read *Forbes*. Each year they publicize the top-earning actors in Hollywood."

"I must have missed that issue. Or else I blocked it out of my mind so as not to cause brain damage."

"Lainey said she received an inheritance on her eighteenth birthday. I'm sure that was substantial enough to fund this place."

They walked deeper into the apartment. The great room was huge and was partitioned off into a sitting area and formal dining area by the use of expensive area rugs over a glistening hardwood floor and clusters of sofas and chairs in bold colors and designs. A large table with enough textured fabric chairs to seat eight dominated the dining area.

"This doesn't seems like the home of a college student at all," noted Phil. "It looks straight out of a design magazine."

"This is hardly a crash pad, and I'll bet it was professionally decorated."

"Fancy-schmancy," added Granny. "I prefer Kelly's digs."

Emma turned on her heel to face Granny. "Kelly's? How do you know what Kelly's apartment looks like, Granny?"

"I meant her room at the Millers' house. Much more appropriate for a young woman in school."

Two walls of the great room were composed of floor-to-ceiling windows, providing a panoramic view of most of Los Angeles. The largest wall of glass was divided by a large natural-stone fireplace. Sliding doors led out to a wrap-around patio containing several lounge chairs, small tables, and charming potted plants.

The solid walls of the condo were painted a dark but muted yellow, almost a deep, soft gold, that played nicely with the furniture. A long mirror, framed in black, hung on the wall over a sofa. In the dining area, a matching mirror hung over a modern built-in buffet. Artwork on the walls was also framed in black.

In front of the largest sofa sat a square coffee table made of a huge slab of glass resting on a stone pedestal. In the middle was a tall, graceful orchid arrangement. On the table, scattered around the orchid, were glasses and beer bottles and a dish that had been used as an ashtray. It was then Emma noticed bits of clothing tossed about.

Identifying jeans, a tee shirt, and a skimpy top in the mess, Emma next picked up a hot pink lace bra from the arm of one sofa. "I guarantee Lainey did not leave this place like this a month ago."

Phil eyed the bra, one brow cocked in suspicion. "And even if she did, I'm sure this place comes with an experienced housekeeper who'd make sure stuff like this wasn't lying about."

Next to the sofa were two pairs of shoes—a pair of men's athletic shoes and a pair of high-heeled sandals. A few feet away from the sofa, almost to the doorway leading to a long hall, Emma toed a pair of bikini underwear that matched the bra.

She entered the hallway and peeked into the first room. It was a kitchen with state-of-the-art appliances, granite counters, and a nice-sized eating area. It was also a cluttered mess of dirty dishes, empty beer bottles, and glasses. On the counter were open bags of chips and half-eaten deli sandwiches, along with two empty pizza boxes.

"The food on the counter and dishes stacked in the kitchen aren't more than a day old," she reported when she returned to Phil. "Looks like a party went on here last night."

"Humph," scowled Phil. "While the cat's away, the fiancé will play."

"Ex-fiancé," Emma corrected. "But it still seems very thoughtless considering he's living in her luxurious apartment."

Granny came floating in from the hallway. "That bathroom is a wonder. Makes the ones at the Miller house seem like outhouses."

"I'll tell my mother that, Granny. She'll appreciate it, I'm sure."

"No need to get sassy about it. I was just saying." The ghost sniffed. "Guess you also don't want to know nothing about the man passed out in the back room."

Emma threw the bra down on one of the sofas and turned to Phil, lowering her voice to a whisper. "Granny says there's someone passed out in the back."

When Emma started for the hallway, Phil grabbed her arm. "Stay here," he ordered. "I'll check it out."

Picking up a sculpture from a nearby table, Phil held it like a police baton and started down the hallway past the kitchen doorway. Emma held back, then followed close on his heels. He glanced back. "I told you to stay."

"I'm not Archie," Emma hissed back at him. "I go where I please."

Shaking his head, Phil returned his attention to his mission.

"See," Granny said to Emma. "I told you he should've brought his gun."

The hallway was long and wide, with the solid areas painted the same color as the walls in the great room. Frosted glass doors took up most of one side. Emma quietly scooted one glass door back. It glided open soundlessly on a track to reveal a large and neatly organized closet. On the painted wall, framed photos and mementos hung in an artful arrangement like a pictorial display of Lainey's life. Emma's eye caught on several photographs of Max with Lainey and Joanna, and even a couple that included Kelly when the girls were young. There were also some taken recently of Lainey with a young man.

Phil slowly opened a door on the frosted glass wall side. It revealed a den with a built-in desk and bookcase unit. On the desk was a laptop and a printer with school books stacked around it. The room was cozier than the great room and appeared more lived in. There were glasses and bottles and empty plates with dirty napkins on the table in front of the sofa. Across from the sofa, a massive flat-screen TV hung on the wall.

The next door on the other side revealed a good-sized bedroom with a large window, through which the afternoon sun beamed brightly. It was nicely decorated like the rest of the condo, but obviously not the master bedroom. In this room, several boxes were stacked against one wall, along with ski equipment. Two high-end bicycles were parked against another wall.

The next room was a large bathroom almost the size of the bedroom, with a sunken soaking tub, dual sinks, and a shower that could fit four comfortably.

"Jesus," Phil said to Emma in a barely audible volume, "that bathroom is nearly a religious experience."

"So Granny told me," she whispered back.

On the other side of the bathroom was a bedroom much like the first, though not used as much for storage. Both bedrooms had doors connecting them to the bathroom.

"Psst," Granny whispered, even though only Emma could hear her. "Quit lollygagging. It's the last room at the end."

At the end, facing the hallway, were a set of double doors. Keeping the sculpture aloft, Phil gently turned the knob and peeked in. Sensing no danger, he pushed the door open more to show Emma what Granny had found.

On the huge California King four-poster bed was sprawled a young man with dark locks of hair from whom gentle grunts and snores emitted. He was on his stomach and naked, only partially covered by the tangled sheets.

"Hey," called Phil in an authoritative tone. "Buddy, get up." He took a step forward. "Come on, rise and shine."

The man in the bed moaned and turned slightly, revealing he was not alone. Next to him was an equally naked young woman with messy long blond hair.

Emma went to the large bank of windows. As in the great room, they were floor to ceiling and opened out to a balcony. She opened the blinds quickly, flooding the room with warm sunshine. The bodies on the bed starting moving like snakes disturbed in their nest. Not too fast, but there was life, evidenced by moans and the shifting of limbs.

"What the hell," the man said.

Shielding his eyes with an arm, he turned away from the window as he flipped onto his back. The woman remained on her stomach and moaned.

Phil approached the bed and poked the guy in the shoulder. "Come on, pal, get up. We have some questions for you."

The man raised up on his forearms and shook the sleep out of his brain like a dog shaking off water. His head of short black curls danced with the movement. As soon as he focused on Phil, he went on alert.

"Hey, man!"

With youthful speed and reflexes, he got to his feet and stood ready to defend himself, fists clenched and ready. Though much lighter than Phil, he was about a half foot taller and thirty years younger. Using caution, Phil stepped back but didn't step down. The kid hadn't noticed Emma yet.

Off to the side, Granny danced around from foot to foot like a prize fighter. "You can take him, Phil." Once again, Emma was glad Phil couldn't hear Granny. He didn't need any distractions at the moment.

"Who are you, and what do you want?" The young man's voice vibrated with a lick of fear, but he kept his fists up and ready.

"We're friends of Lainey's," Emma told him from her spot by the window. "You Keith Goldstein?" He looked like the young man in the photos in the hallway, but Emma wanted to make sure.

He snapped his head around at the sound of Emma's voice, then whipped it back to keep an eye on Phil. He didn't seem to notice or care that he was naked. Emma moved from the window so that the kid could keep both of them in his sights, hoping it would make him less wary. The girl on the bed stirred, slowly wakening, oblivious to the drama unfolding a foot away.

Granny shimmied up to Emma. "Will someone please tell the lad to put his knickers on."

"The lady," Phil prodded, "asked if you're Keith Goldstein. Answer her."

He glanced between the two of them. "Yeah, that's me." He lowered his fists but didn't unclench them. "Is Lainey okay? Did something happen to her?" He sounded genuinely concerned.

"Keith," Emma began, taking a step toward the door. "We need to talk to you about Lainey. Why don't you put some clothes on and meet us in the living room."

"Maybe I should call the police instead."

"Still playing the tough guy, huh?" Phil pointed to the phone next to the bed. "Why don't you call down to the front desk. They'll tell you Ms. Naiman gave them permission to let us in today."

"The concierge called first," Emma added, "but I guess you were too passed out to hear the phone."

"Will someone please get some clothes on the boy?" Granny paced, trying to keep her eyes averted. "It's indecent."

"We'll see you out in the other room." Emma started to leave, then stopped. "And while you're putting on your pants, you might want to wake up Sleeping Beauty. It's after three in the afternoon."

. . . .

WHEN KEITH GOLDSTEIN JOINED them in the living room ten minutes later, he was alone. Phil and Emma were seated on the large sofa talking quietly between themselves. Keith was wearing jeans and a souvenir tee shirt from a rock concert. His feet were bare and his dark hair combed back away from his face, his curls semi-contained. He wore glasses with thick, black rectangle rims. He was an average-looking man in his early twenties, with nerdy overtones and a narrow face speckled lightly with acne scars. In one hand he carried a freshly opened can of Coke.

Emma crossed her arms and gave him a disgusted once-over. "This is how you treat Lainey after everything she's been through?"

He plopped down on the sofa across from them and took a drink of his soda. "Who are you again?"

Smoothing the skirt of her dress, Emma used the gesture to gather her patience like an errant chick. "I'm a longtime friend of Lainey's family, and Kelly's mother."

He digested the information as he took a long pull from the soda. "Kelly? That's Lainey's girlfriend at Harvard, right?"

"Yes."

"Yeah, Kelly White. I met her last December. Pretty cool chick."

Emma almost corrected him on the name but didn't. "I saw Lainey yesterday, Keith. She wanted me to stop by and pick up a few things for her."

Keith shot to attention. "How is she? Is she getting better?" His voice overflowed with hope.

"Yes, her doctor is pleased with her progress."

"Awesome."

Before Emma's motherly instincts could rise up and scold Keith, the girl from the bed emerged from the hallway wearing an oversized tee shirt. From the drape of her garment, it appeared it was all she was wearing. Unlike Keith, she hadn't even made an attempt to brush her hair or wash her face. Her honey-highlighted hair was wavy and well past her shoulders. Emma thought she recognized her.

"Just need to get my clothes." The young woman didn't seem at all embarrassed by the situation.

"It's about Lainey," Keith told her as she gathered her underwear, shoes, and other clothing as casually as picking flowers in a field. "They said she's doing better."

"That's great." Her words were upbeat; her tone—not so much. Clothing bundled in her arms, she sat on the arm of the sofa next to Keith and crossed her legs, leaving nothing to the imagination.

"You're Summer Perkins, aren't you?" asked Emma as she studied the girl's makeup-smudged face.

"Yeah," the girl answered as she studied Emma back. "And you're Kelly's mom—Mrs. Whitecastle, right? The ghost lady from TV." She sneered when she threw out the ghost part.

"That's right. It's been a long time since I've seen you, Summer—not since you girls were in high school. It's nice that you all still keep in touch."

Summer shrugged. "Lainey and I used to hang out a lot."

"Used to?"

"I mean, we're still good friends and all, but with her in the nut house, it's kind of hard."

Emma leaned forward, her face pinched in anger. Phil put a hand gently on her arm as a warning to take it slow. Emma ignored his gesture and fixed her eyes on Summer. "You're such good friends, you're keeping her fiancé company? In Lainey's own bed, no less?"

"411, Mrs. Whitecastle, they're not engaged anymore."

"It's true," Keith confirmed, though he had the good grace to look guilty. "Lainey and I broke up just before she left for Serenity. She gave me the ring back and everything."

"Hey, gramps," Summer suddenly called out. She uncrossed her legs and spread them, aiming her crotch at Phil. "Take a picture, it'll last longer."

Phil was flustered. "I can assure you, young lady, I was not looking at you."

"Yeah, right. All you old pervs do it. You know you do." She flashed Phil a sly grin. "Just so long as you don't touch."

"Summer, chill," Keith ordered as if he were giving a sharp command to a bad dog.

Granny moved in close to Emma. "Phil was not looking at that tramp's hoochie. He was looking at something else."

"I know," Emma said under her breath.

"What?" Summer snapped at Emma. "What did you call me?"

"I didn't call you anything, Summer. I was just saying I think you should go."

"You're not the boss of me."

The girl was stretching Emma's patience to the limit. Kelly wasn't perfect, but she was polite and sensible and seldom insolent. "We have things to discuss with Keith that don't concern you."

"Do as she says, Summer," Keith told her, not sounding too pleased with her behavior either.

Phil held up a hand halfway as if waiting to be called upon. "I was looking, Summer, not at you but at that gorgeous ring on your left hand. Does your fiancé know you spent the night here?"

The girl looked down at her left hand, which sported a very large square-cut solitaire. "This isn't mine, it was Lainey's. I was trying it on last night and forgot it was there. So relax, you don't have to tattle on me to anyone." She gave Phil another catlike smile. "Or were you thinking more along the lines of blackmail?"

"Just go, Summer," ordered Keith.

With her clothes in her arms, Summer stalked down the hall to the master bedroom, treating everyone to the loud slam of the door behind her.

"Don't mind Summer," Keith told them. "She's messed up, but she's cool."

Emma looked at Keith as if he'd lost his young mind. "She's definitely messed up, Keith, but she's far from cool. She's in more need of Serenity Place than Lainey is."

ten
· · · · · ·

AFTER AN AWKWARD MOMENT during which Keith took time to
absorb Emma's blatant warning about Summer, he explained,
"There's nothing going on with me and Summer. I've been really
down lately—the thing with Lainey, studying for exams—it all
kind of piled up on me. Some of our friends came by last night to
cheer me up. Summer was with them. They brought food and
beer. We played video games. That's it."

The parent in Emma wasn't mollified. "You played video games
from bed?"

Keith nosed the pedestal of the coffee table with a foot. "I guess
I got drunk, and Summer and I hooked up after. That's all."

Looking for some manly backup, he turned his eyes to Phil.
"Man, you know how it is."

Under different circumstances, Phil would have given him a
small smile of support, but he had sons, and while boys would be
boys, he wouldn't want either of them to hook up with the likes of

Summer Perkins, not even for an evening. Instead, he asked Keith, "Do you still have feelings for Lainey Naiman?"

Keith put his Coke down on the glass table. He leaned forward, resting his forearms on his knobby knees. "Yeah, I still do. I'm crazy about her."

"Lainey believes you think she tried to kill herself because she didn't want to marry you," Emma told him. "How'd she get that idea?"

Looking anywhere but at Emma, Keith took a deep breath. He placed the palm of his right hand on his chest and rubbed slowly, as if soothing a suspected heart attack. "I guess I sort of told her that."

Emma pushed. "You likened her to an animal who'd rather chew off her foot than marry you, didn't you?"

Phil hung his head like a broken hinge. "Oh, son, you didn't!"

Keith looked up, his brown eyes drooping behind his glasses. "I know, I was a complete dumbass. I just didn't know what else to think. We were having a fight. After I said that to her, she took the ring off and threw it at me. I'm only in the condo until she returns from Serenity. My stuff's all packed and ready to go."

"Lainey believes something was driving her to do what she did," Emma said. "She must have told you that."

"Yeah." Keith ran a bony hand over the stubble on his chin. "She told me she felt like she had no control over her actions—like she'd space out and then snap out of it just as she was about to die." He eyed Emma, his face still as stone. "Do you believe that?"

"Yes, Keith, I do. I don't think Lainey was responsible for her actions, and I want to get to the bottom of it."

Keith sat perfectly still as he mashed what Emma said together with his feelings. Picking up his soda, he took a long drink, tipping back the can until it was empty. He put it back on the table, the sound tinny and hollow as it connected with the glass table.

"If it's not me causing Lainey's problems, do you think I have a chance to win her back?"

Emma was quiet, but Phil gave it to him straight. "Hard to say with Summer in the mix. If she's the one who's told everyone where Lainey is, I'm sure she's going to happily tell Lainey or Lainey's true friends, like Kelly, about this little indiscretion."

"Oh, god!" Keith hung his head, cradling it in his hands.

"You might want to be the one to tell her," Phil suggested. "Man up, and let her know how you feel and how sorry you are."

Emma got up to stretch her legs. She walked to the patio door and looked out at the gorgeous view, studying the cluster of Century City high-rise office buildings that popped up in the distance like dandelions. She turned back to Keith. "Was everything else okay between you and Lainey? No other issues that might have upset her, or dreams or feelings she was having right before these incidents?"

When he shrugged, she asked, "What about your parents? Did both sides approve of your upcoming marriage? After all, you are both quite young and still in school." She took a step back toward the men and leaned her hands on the back of the sofa where Phil sat. "I know I'd be concerned if Kelly wanted to get married at this time in her life."

Keith gave the question some thought before answering. "At first my folks were concerned about Lainey. They knew she was the daughter of someone famous and cautioned me about life in the fast lane. But when I took her to Seattle to meet them, she melted their hearts, especially after she told them she doesn't want to stay in LA after we've finished with school. They saw for themselves she isn't at all like those rich bimbos they hear about in the news. She's smart and down-to-earth." A small smile crept across his face. "As far as my folks are concerned, there are only two things I've done 100 percent right in my life—set my sights on becoming a doctor and fall in love with a nice Jewish girl."

"And Lainey's parents?"

After a deep sigh, Keith shook his head in disgust. "My parents are definitely not going to like them."

It was Phil's turn to make a guess. "I take it they didn't take to you as your parents did to Lainey?"

"They're psycho. Her old man called me a gold digger right to my face."

The ghost of Max Naiman popped into view just behind Keith. "Don't look at me. I like the boy."

Emma caught Phil's eye as she asked Keith, "You mean Linwood Reid, her stepfather?"

"Yeah. He actually had the balls to offer me fifty thousand dollars to drop Lainey like a lead weight."

"Is that the Max character?" asked Granny.

Emma nodded but kept up her conversation with Keith. "What did Lainey say about that?"

"I didn't tell her." Keith got up and disappeared into the kitchen.

"Max is here," Emma whispered to Phil. "He likes Keith."

"So do I," returned Phil, "in spite of Summer."

Granny eyed Max up and down. He winked at her, causing Granny to giggle like a schoolgirl. "I gotta watch me some of his movies."

Keith returned clutching another Coke. "That booze made me dry as a sand dune." He looked down at the can as he popped the top. "I'm sorry. Would you guys like something? We've got tons of Coke, even some beer still left."

"No, thanks," Phil answered for both of them.

Emma wasn't through with the Lin Reid topic. "Why didn't you tell Lainey about Lin's offer?"

Keith took a drink before answering and squelched a burp. "Excuse me." Sitting back down, he said, "Lainey doesn't get along with her stepfather at all. Not sure why, but she can't stand him. She once told me he had her husband all picked out for her—some clown nephew of his or someone like that. Maybe that's why."

"So Lainey being engaged to you gummed up his plans." Phil leaned forward and moved the orchid out of the way to see Keith better.

"I guess."

Max moved in front of Emma. "This boy isn't the gold digger. Reid is."

Emma's attention clicked onto the ghost. Without thinking, she asked Max, "Why do you say that?"

Not realizing Emma was speaking to a spirit, Keith answered, "Well, as long as she's with me, she can't date his nephew. Although she's met him and doesn't like him, so I'm not sure how Lin thought he was going to change her mind."

Max looked at the boy, letting him finish before he answered Emma's question. "Lainey doesn't have all her inheritance. She gets the bulk of it when she turns twenty-one in five months. I think Reid wants to get his hands on it. He's already wormed his way into Joanna's money by convincing her they didn't need prenups."

Emma clutched the back of the sofa. "Keith, did you know about Lainey's inheritance?"

"Sure, that's how she could afford this place."

"No, not the money she received at eighteen. Did you know she was to inherit a larger sum upon her twenty-first birthday?"

From the surprise on his face, both Emma and Phil knew he didn't.

Emma wasn't sure how or if Lainey's suicide attempts tied in to her inheritance or Lin Reid. While Lin did seem to exercise some control over Joanna, she couldn't imagine how he could manage to push Lainey to the brink of killing herself, if he did have a hand in it at all. It just seemed improbable.

"You know what the weirdest part of all this is?" asked Keith. "When we were with Lainey's parents, her mother seemed to be totally in agreement with Lin. But her mother offered me money to make sure I married her."

"What?" everyone, even the two ghosts, asked almost in unison.

"Yeah." He ran a hand through his hair, loosening it into a riot of short tendrils. "Joanna came here one day shortly after Lainey went to Serenity and handed me twenty grand in cash. *In cash!* She said there was another eighty waiting for me the day I married Lainey."

Phil stared at Emma. "What in the hell is wrong with those people?"

Without waiting for an answer, he turned to Keith. "Whatever made Lainey do what she did, I don't think it had anything to do with you. Not a damn thing."

"I'd like to believe that."

Without a word, Max started floating down the hallway toward the master suite, Granny following him like a lovesick puppy. It reminded Emma of Summer. The girl hadn't come out yet. "Summer's taking a long time."

Keith turned and glanced down the hall. "She's probably showering first."

"Or," Phil added, "stalling to make a point."

Emma made a sour face, then stopped when Phil caught her in the act. He merely grinned at the childish behavior and patted her arm. "Patience."

After taking a deep breath, Emma said, "Keith, I'm inviting Lainey to my home in Julian next weekend. Would you like to drive down and see her? It's not here and it's not Serenity. Think of it as someplace neutral where you two can talk out your problems."

"She might not want to see me."

Phil considered the invitation. "I think that's a great idea, Emma. And if it's uncomfortable for them, Keith can stay at the ranch instead of under the same roof."

He turned to Keith. "My ranch is just across the way from Emma's cabin. It will give you two space when you need it."

Before Keith could answer, Granny popped into view. "Come quick!" she told Emma. "It's the girl."

Without explanation, Emma dashed around the sofa and sprinted down the hallway toward the master bedroom. Phil, realizing something was wrong, was right behind her. Bringing up the rear was a surprised Keith.

When she got to the double doors, Emma grabbed the knob and started twisting and turning while shoving on the door.

"Something's wrong with Summer," she told the men.

"Out of the way, Emma." Phil slammed his sturdy shoulder against the door. It shook but didn't give. Keith, still stunned, watched. "Come on, son," Phil shouted. "Give me a hand here."

Keith lined himself up with Phil, and the two of them hit the door with their shoulders like side-by-side battering rams. The thick, expensive door buckled but didn't give.

"What's going on?" asked Keith between grunts and slams.

Emma shook with impatience to get inside the room. "I think Summer's in trouble."

"One more time," said Phil. "One, two, *three*." On three, the two men hit the door, breaking it open. They spilled into the room like floodwaters, with Emma wading through them.

eleven
. . . .

"Summer, no." Emma wanted to shout the words, but she didn't dare in case the sound startled the girl any more than breaking down the door had. Instead, they squeaked out of her in a soft plea as she stepped past the men and cautiously made her way to the open door to the balcony.

Summer was partially dressed, wearing only skinny leggings and her lacy pink bra. On her feet were her high heels. Her hair was a tangle of golden vines spilling down her shoulders and across her face and neck. She looked like an exotic wild animal. Teetering precariously, one foot on a patio table, the other on the railing of the balcony, she peered over the edge to the ground twelve floors below. Standing next to her, his eyes glued to her face, his arms outspread as if to catch her, was the ghost of Max Naiman.

"Summer!" Keith called and started for her.

Grabbing his arm, Phil held him back. "Careful. You don't want to spook her."

At her name, Summer turned around and pushed hair from her face. She saw them, but it was clear the image wasn't registering. Her eyes were glazed and unfixed.

"What's she on?" Emma whispered to Keith.

"Nothing that I know of," he whispered back. "I've never even seen her smoke dope."

"Help her, Emma," pleaded Max, not taking his eyes off of Summer.

"There's something not natural about that girl," Granny said to Emma.

"Granny's right," added Max. "It was the same with Lainey."

Motioning for the men to stay behind, Emma took another step toward the balcony. "Summer, come here, dear. I have something for you." She kept her voice light and inviting, forcing the fright out of it for the sake of the girl.

Summer looked at Emma, and for a brief moment happy recognition sparked her eyes. "You're Kelly's mom." Her tone was totally devoid of the earlier insolence.

"That's right, Summer, I am." Another careful step. "Remember when you girls used to stay at our house?"

The girl on the balcony nodded slowly.

"You and Lainey and Kelly. Paula and Charlotte, too. You'd go to the dances at school, then to our house for a sleepover."

"Mr. Whitecastle would make us blueberry pancakes."

"That's right." Emma had forgotten that. Before he was super famous and became so self-centered, Grant had been a gem of a father. "Why don't you come down from there? We can make blueberry pancakes together. Wouldn't you like that?"

Again Summer nodded, this time accompanied by a small smile.

"Good job, Emma," Max encouraged. "I think you've got her."

Granny wasn't so sure. "Hold on, there's something wrong here."

Granny was right. Just as Summer started to take her foot off of the railing, a shimmering haze outlined her body, and Summer retreated back into a stupor, the earlier smile gone.

"What's going on?" Phil asked in a low voice. Behind him Keith watched, dumbstruck.

"I'm not sure," Emma responded. "But I think there's another spirit here. And not a very friendly one." She glanced back at Phil. "Do you see anything odd about Summer?"

"She just retreated into a trance again."

"Exactly, and there's a haze surrounding her."

"That I can't see."

"Granny, Max, do you know who that is with Summer?"

Both ghosts responded in the negative, but Max added, "That's exactly how Lainey looked each time she tried to kill herself."

"Whoever you are," Emma said, speaking at Summer but not to her, "leave the girl alone. She's innocent."

Keith moved closer to Phil. "What in the hell is going on?" His voice shook with fear as goose bumps sprouted on his arms like air bubbles on a baking cake.

"I think Summer is being haunted," Phil told him as quietly as possible.

Keith's mouth fell open. "What the—"

"Shhh," Phil cautioned. "Let Emma handle it."

"Summer, look at me," ordered Emma, her voice low but stern. "Look at me," she repeated in a stronger voice.

Summer shook her head slightly and tried to focus, fighting for control of her own body. "What's happening to me?" She started weeping.

"Stay focused, Summer," Emma encouraged. "Take your foot off the ledge and stay focused on me."

The girl latched her eyes onto Emma's again. "I'm so cold." She wrapped her arms around herself.

"I know, dear, but you'll be warm in a minute. Just take your foot off the ledge."

From far below came the blast of multiple sirens.

"Sounds like the police are here," Phil said. "Someone must have seen her on the ledge."

Max glanced over the railing. "Fire and police."

After relaying the information to Phil and Keith, Emma told Keith, "Go to the front door and wait. They'll be up here in a minute."

Keith hesitated, not wanting to leave Summer, but in the end he did as he was told.

Emma returned her attention to the girl. "Help is coming, Summer, but you have to be brave and do as I say. Take your foot off the railing."

Summer removed her foot from the balcony railing and placed it next to the one on the table. Granny and Max watched, frozen in their tracks.

"Good," said Emma. "Now come down off the table. Slowly, one foot at a time."

The frightened girl didn't move. The haze around her thickened, enveloping her like a cocoon. She put her foot back on the railing. Emma felt sick to her stomach.

"Whoever you are," Granny said to the hidden ghost, "show yourself. This child's done nothing to you."

While they watched, Summer battled for her life, struggling against the spirit wanting to control her mind and her actions.

Emma moved closer. "Please leave her alone," she begged of the unknown spirit. "Whatever you want, I can help. This girl cannot."

"You cannot help," a feathery female voice answered. "No one can. It is not my destiny in life, or in death, to be happy."

Summer's other foot started to move toward the railing. Phil saw it, too, and circled around, trying to edge toward Summer without attracting notice.

It was then Emma noticed the ring on Summer's hand. It seemed illuminated, but from the inside out, not from catching the sunshine that spilled onto the balcony. "Max," she said to Lainey's father, "were you wearing that ring when you died?"

He glanced at the ring. "No, that's a woman's engagement ring."

"The stone. Isn't that the stone from your ring, the one Joanna gave you?"

He drifted as close to Summer as he dared and tried to get a good look at the ring. "Yes, I believe it is." He turned to Emma, his ghostly face shocked by understanding. "Lainey was wearing that ring when she tried to kill herself. I'm sure of it."

"Summer, look at me," Emma ordered. When the girl didn't, Emma snapped her fingers. "Look at me!"

This time Summer turned her eyes to Emma and tried to focus.

"Take the ring off, Summer."

Summer looked confused. The haze around her grew as heavy as a fog bank. Her second foot finished its journey from table to rail. She bobbled. Emma and Phil gasped.

"The ring," Emma said again. She took another step forward. "Lainey's ring, Summer. Take it off."

Summer raised her left hand and looked at the stunning, light-filled rock. "But it's so pretty."

"Take it off," Emma coaxed. "It belongs to Lainey."

With her right hand, Summer clutched the ring and started to slip it off slowly, all the while keeping her eyes transfixed on it.

Excited voices drifted in from the other room, and they could hear fast footsteps in the hallway.

"Do it, Summer. Now!"

Mustering the last of her self-control, in one sweeping motion Summer slid the ring off her finger, letting it fly toward Emma. The haze around her remained but was fading rapidly.

As the emergency people entered the room, Summer's eyes cleared and she became aware of her situation. She screamed.

"You'll not deny me!" cackled the disembodied voice.

The ghost swirled around the frightened and confused young woman like a swarm of bees. Another bobble, and Summer lost her footing.

Emma's screams echoed those of the falling girl.

twelve

· · · · · · · · · · · ·

EMMA ROCKED BACK AND forth on the large leather sofa in the den of her parents' home. Although it was warm, she couldn't stop shivering. Her mother placed a heavy afghan across her shoulders and rubbed them, trying to both soothe and warm her daughter.

"There was nothing you could have done, Emma," said Phil, who sat on her other side. "As soon as she came out of her trance and realized where she was, Summer panicked and fell. And who knows what influence that evil spirit had over her, even after the ring came off."

Inconsolable, Emma continued to shiver. "I should have worked faster or noticed the ring earlier."

"The police coming in like they did probably didn't help either." He put his strong arms around her and drew her into his warmth. "You did everything you could, Emma. And if we hadn't been there, Keith might have become a suspect in a murder. Imagine if she'd jumped while the two of them were at the condo alone."

It was true, and Emma knew it. If the angry ghost did inhabit the ring, it might have enticed Summer to jump, leaving Keith on his own to explain what had happened. As it was, the police weren't too keen on the explanation that Summer might have been hearing voices. Each of them had been questioned separately. Although they didn't know what Keith told the authorities, Phil and Emma later compared their own accounts and found them almost exactly the same: Summer had been acting a bit bizarre when they first saw her. When asked to leave, she'd gotten in a snit and locked herself in the bedroom. Emma had a feeling something was wrong, and when they broke down the bedroom door, they had found Summer in a trancelike state, about to jump. Both of them had left out the part about Granny telling Emma about Summer being in danger and about the ring.

. . . .

THE RING.

In the aftermath of Summer's death, Emma had noticed the ring on the floor and picked it up, hoping the police didn't see her do it. She slipped it into a pocket of her dress.

When all the questioning was done, Keith packed up some clothes. Emma grabbed the items Lainey had requested, and they all left the condo together, leaving the police to complete their investigation. In the elevator, Emma held the ring out to Keith. He didn't make a move to touch it, even though he had not been in the room when Summer pulled it off and didn't know about the ring's deadly consequences.

"That really belongs to Lainey. The stone was her father's. Joanna gave it to us to use for the engagement ring." Keith hesitated but still didn't take the ring. "Can you give it to her when you see her?"

As much as Emma was afraid of what the ring might hold, she knew that having it in her possession might give her an opportunity to contact the ghost inhabiting the gem. She needed to find out for sure if it was the angry spirit who had made Lainey try to destroy herself and caused both Max's and Summer's deaths. She also wanted to know more about the ghost. She knew it was female, but that was it. Hopefully Granny or Max would be able to tell her more. Both of them had disappeared shortly after Summer's swan dive onto Wilshire Boulevard.

Acting as if the ring might burn her, Emma cautiously put it back into her pocket. "I'll make sure it gets returned to Lainey."

"What are you going to do now?" Phil asked Keith.

The still-shaken young man shrugged and looked away. "I'll crash with friends until school's over, then head back up to Seattle for the summer. No sense staying in LA if Lainey doesn't want me."

"You are still welcome to come to Julian next weekend," Emma told him. "At the very least, you need to see Lainey and explain what happened. Even if you go to Serenity to do it."

Keith took a deep breath and blew out two lungs' worth of frustrated air. "You're right. I'm sure she's going to see this on the news and wonder what was going on."

"I don't know how much news they allow in places like that," Phil told him. "Sometimes facilities like to monitor things that might disturb their patients."

"Phil's right, although Lainey will need to be told. Her mother might tell her, or even the police. They did ask me about Lainey."

"Yeah," Keith said, running a nervous hand through his hair. "Me too."

Phil put an encouraging hand on Keith's shoulder as he handed him more bad news. "And the media is going to have a field day with this. It's not every day a young woman falls to her death from the twelfth-floor home of Max Naiman's daughter."

More deep groans from Keith. "What a nightmare. All because I couldn't keep my pants on."

"It wasn't your fault Summer fell," Phil told Keith.

. . . .

Now, in the comfort and security of the Miller home, Phil was saying the same thing to Emma, and like Keith, she wasn't so sure. Keith wasn't at fault. He may not have understood what Emma said when she told him Summer was being haunted, but he didn't put the ring on her finger or set her on the ledge. And Phil was right: neither did she. If Granny hadn't told her about Summer being in danger, she might never have discovered the dangers of the ring.

Emma started to rise. "What is it, honey?" her father, Paul Miller, asked from his chair across from the sofa. "What do you need?"

"My purse, Dad. It's on the table in the foyer."

Dr. Miller rose and left the room, returning in a minute with Emma's handbag. He handed it to her. "You know I don't always understand all this stuff about ghosts and spirits like you and your mother do, but it does seem, from what you've told us, that there is something unnatural going on here."

"I agree, Dad."

"And it seems to me that unless you get to the bottom of it, more people might be in danger."

"But why me?" Emma looked up at her father, a retired heart surgeon. She'd gotten her looks from her mother and her tall, slim body from her father.

She looked around the room at each of them—her father and mother and Phil. "Why can't someone else do this?" She started to cry softly. "Sometimes it's too much to bear."

"Because you have the gift, Emma." The simple response came from Granny, who only Emma and her mother could hear. "You were chosen to be special. We need you."

Emma looked around the room until her eyes settled on Granny. She was seated on the floor by the fireplace. Next to her, Archie was stretched out, half on his back, as the ghost stroked his belly. When the ghost spoke, the dog thumped his tail.

"Granny's right," Elizabeth Miller told her daughter. "You do have a special gift, but I don't like you getting mixed up in these things." Elizabeth told the men what the ghost had said. "It worries me to death."

"I'm with your mother on this, honey." Dr. Miller sat on the edge of the coffee table and took his daughter's hands into his own. Emma loved the feeling of her small hands being cradled by her father's capable ones. "If that ring is a problem, why not have Lainey or her family lock it up in a safe-deposit box or sell it or even have it destroyed?"

Emma dug into her purse and located the ring. She'd stuck it into a small zippered side pocket once she and Phil were on the road back to Pasadena. She pulled it out, careful not to put it on her finger. Her mother let out a slight gasp. Even her father was impressed.

"That's some stone." Dr. Miller held out his hand for it. "May I?"

With a bit of hesitation, Emma handed it to him. "Just don't put it on," she cautioned. "We don't know for sure it's the ring that's haunted, but I don't want to take any chances."

Dr. Miller put on his reading glasses and examined the ring closely. Keeping ahold of it, he showed it to his wife, who was equally impressed. "I'm no expert, but to the naked eye that looks nearly flawless."

"And large," added Elizabeth. "Didn't you say this stone was once set in a man's ring? Seems rather large for that."

"I vaguely recall Max's wedding ring, the one Joanna gave him after they restated their vows. The stone was huge, but it was recessed in the band, so it didn't sit up like in this setting."

"I'll bet that ring is worth a mint." Dr. Miller gave it back to Emma. "Haunted or not, it shouldn't be sitting around." He got up and resettled in the club chair he'd vacated earlier.

"Why don't you put it in the safe until you can give it to Lainey?" Elizabeth suggested.

Emma's father shook his head. "They won't let Lainey have anything that valuable while she's at Serenity. She'd just have to turn around and give it to someone there to hold it for her."

"Dad's right." Emma studied the ring, both wishing and dreading further communication with the spirit within it. "I'll tell Lainey I have it and ask if she wants me to give it to her mother to hold."

"Hey," Phil piped up as a thought occurred to him. "If that stone originally belonged to Max, and Joanna only recently handed it over to Lainey and Keith, do you think that maybe she knows about the spirit?" While the other three contemplated his question, he added, "She does seem to be sensitive to spirits."

Elizabeth looked at Emma with surprise. "Is Lainey's mother like us?"

Emma smiled inwardly at the "like us" comment. Her mother could hear Granny but couldn't see her, and so far had not demonstrated an ability to hear other ghosts beyond the one time Emma had helped her see Paulie, Emma's deceased brother. Nor did Elizabeth seem to want to expand her abilities beyond that one time. Emma wished she'd set such boundaries for herself.

"I don't think so, Mother. Joanna displayed a sensitivity to Max's presence but claimed she could not see or hear him. I think it's totally possible for non-mediums to sense spirits even if they cannot see or hear them, especially those they were close to in life. I've seen it at sessions with some of Milo's clients."

She gestured with her hand to Phil. "Phil has learned to communicate with Granny and can tell when she's around."

"Really?" asked Dr. Miller with interest.

"Absolutely," answered Phil, "and not just when Emma's present. Granny and I have become quite the pals."

Phil unwrapped his arm from around Emma's shoulders and leaned forward. "Right now," Phil told them, "Granny is over by the fireplace. Just to the left of it." He looked to Emma for confirmation. After she rewarded him with a nod, he continued his demonstration. "And I'll bet she's right behind Archie, possibly low to the floor or sitting on it."

"You sure he can't see me?" Granny asked Emma.

Emma's mother sat back against the sofa cushion, her face filled with astonishment. "I'm beginning to wonder the same thing myself, Granny. I only know where you are by the sound of your voice."

Emma laughed, her first in many hours. She was also warm again and shrugged off the afghan. "They think you're holding out—that you really *can* see Granny."

Phil shook his head. He lifted the coffee mug from the end table next to him and took a gulp, stretching out his explanation and enjoying it far too much.

"All it takes is a bit of observation," he continued. Still holding the coffee cup, he pointed it toward where he rightly assumed Granny was sitting. "Archie has been glued to that spot ever since we came in here, and we all know he's devoted to Granny. What's more, right now he's all stretched out, with his tail thumping away. I'm guessing not only is Granny over there on the floor with him, but she's rubbing his belly."

Emma turned toward Granny, who was still rubbing the soft fur on Archie's black underbelly, putting the animal into doggie nirvana.

Suddenly aware of what she was doing, Granny stopped. "Well, I'll be." Archie, not at all pleased, whined.

"They also chat back and forth," Emma informed her parents.

Dr. Miller, a man of science, sat back in his chair. "This I have to see to believe."

"You mind, Granny?" Emma asked the ghost.

In response, Granny stood up.

"Granny," Phil asked her. "Do you think Joanna Reid is lying? Do you think she can see or hear Max?"

"No," Granny answered. "She can't."

"Tell Phil, Granny," Emma told her. "Mother and I can hear you, but tell Phil."

Phil stood up and moved to the middle of the room. The ghost drifted over to him. Archie got to his feet and followed, planting his butt on the carpet where Granny stopped. The Millers watched, fascinated.

When Phil repeated his question, Granny got on tiptoe and blew into his left ear.

"Granny said no, she doesn't think Joanna can see or hear Max."

"Granny," Phil said to the spirit. "Do you think Emma should help Lainey and this new ghost?"

The ghost gave it some thought before blowing into Phil's left ear.

"No? You don't think she should?"

Granny moved her head and blew into Phil's right ear.

"Oh, so you *do* think she should help them?"

"No." Granny stomped her foot soundlessly on the carpet. Archie started in surprise. She blew into Phil's left ear again, then quickly blew into his right.

"Are you confused?" Phil asked the ghost.

"Nothing confusing about it, you old fool. I think she shouldn't help the ghost, but she should help Lainey. You gotta ask the right questions, not jumble them all together."

Emma and her mother broke into laughter. So did the men when Emma's mother conveyed Granny's words.

"You gotta teach me that trick, Phil," Dr. Miller said. "Might liven up the football games she watches with us."

Phil sat down in a club chair that matched Dr. Miller's. "Nothing tricky about it. Like I said, you just have to be observant. You already know it gets a bit cool when she's here. Just watch the dog and pay attention. Left ear is no, and the right is yes."

"I ain't no parlor trick," huffed Granny in a barely audible voice. Turning on her heel, she stomped back over to the fireplace. Archie followed. Emma watched Granny retreat, noting the ghost's image was fast dissipating.

Phil watched the dog trot across the carpet, stopping short in his tracks as if he'd come across a wall. "Did Granny leave? Was it something I said?"

"She's gone," Emma confirmed. "You have to remember that being with us takes a lot of Granny's energy. The more she speaks or is visible, the sooner she has to leave us to recharge." Emma walked over and sat on the arm of Phil's chair. "Remember how I said it's not possible for Granny to blow into your ear?"

"But she did blow into my ear," Phil stated with emphasis. "Just now and before."

Emma shook her head. "She can't blow. Not really. But she can cause the air around her to move. It takes a lot out of her though." She put an arm around Phil's shoulders while she explained. "Today, when Joanna thought she was being forced back down into her chair, Max was doing it. He was causing the atmosphere around Joanna to weigh her down. But right after that, he disappeared again. He'd used up his energy. Even petting Archie is like that. Granny isn't really petting him but moving the air around his belly so it feels like a caress. It's exhausting for her, but she loves doing it." She gave Phil a squeeze. "But not to worry, Granny will be back and her old self soon—at least I hope so. I wanted to ask her why she didn't want me to help that other ghost."

"Whoever that is," Granny answered, her whispery voice coming out of nowhere, "she's up to no good. She's killing people, Emma. I don't want you messing with her."

"Granny's back," Elizabeth told the men before reporting Granny's words to them.

"Yes, but only her voice," said Emma as she stood up.

Emma walked toward the fireplace, hoping to hear Granny better. "But I have to help that ghost if I want to help Lainey. It seems to go hand in hand."

Elizabeth continued to report the conversation to the men.

"Granny and I are on the same page here, Emma," Phil announced. "I saw what that vengeful ghost did to that poor girl today."

Emma thought about Summer's fall and what she'd just explained to Phil and her parents. "And now I'm pretty sure Summer didn't slip. I believe that ghost pushed her over the railing using the same technique Granny uses to blow into your ear."

She looked down at the ring still clutched in her hand. "She murdered Summer Perkins the same as if she'd shot her through the heart, and she'll keep on murdering unless we find out why and stop it. It's likely the spirit in the diamond was the reason Max Naiman died in that car accident."

"You think it might be a curse or grudge against the Naimans specifically?" asked Emma's father.

"I doubt it, Paul," answered Phil. "The girl who died today didn't seem to be related to them."

"But she was wearing the ring that belonged in the Naiman family," Paul pointed out.

Emma paced in front of the fireplace as she tried to remember what Joanna had told them about the ring. She spun back around to Phil. "Didn't Joanna say the ring was a vintage piece she'd found?"

"I believe she did say that."

Going to where she'd dropped her bag, Emma retrieved her cell phone and placed a call to Joanna Reid. She only reached voice-mail. "Joanna," she recorded. "Emma Whitecastle. I think I know what might have killed Max and Summer Perkins, and tried to kill poor Lainey. I need to talk to you as soon as possible." After giving Joanna her cell phone number, Emma ended the call.

"You think the police have contacted her yet?" asked Elizabeth. "She might not know about Summer unless she saw it on the news."

"Hard to say, Mother, but even if she doesn't know, mentioning Summer's death might compel her to return my call, if only out of curiosity."

Going down her list of recent calls, Emma hit the number for Serenity Place. When someone answered, Emma gave her name and asked to speak to Dr. Kitty Garvey, saying it was important and had to do with Lainey Naiman.

She was told Dr. Kitty was out but she could leave a message. "Please ask her to call me." Again, Emma left her number.

"Is that the Dr. Kitty Garvey who is married to Dr. Michael Garvey?" Dr. Miller asked.

"Yes, Dad. Do you know them?"

"I met them many years ago at a medical conference." He turned to his wife. "Remember, dear, they sat at our table during dinner one night, and later we all played bridge."

Elizabeth Miller rooted around in her memory as if looking for a pair of lost gloves. "Was that the winter conference on Kauai?"

"Yes."

"I do remember them. They were both psychiatrists, and as I recall, she had just had a terrible skiing accident and was in a cast. Was mad as can be that she was in Hawaii and couldn't snorkel."

"Dr. Kitty does have a noticeable limp," Emma reported.

Dr. Miller leaned back in his chair and rubbed his hands together. "If it's the same pair of doctors I'm thinking of, they were quite adamant about treating depression and other mental conditions naturally."

"What do you mean, Dad?"

"Naturally—without drugs except as absolutely necessary. I remember them being quite passionate about it. Said doctors and patients both were too eager to put a bandage on problems with drugs instead of getting to the root. Can't say I disagree."

"The few people I saw at Serenity Place didn't look under the influence of drugs at all. You would have thought they were on vacation at a spa with regular exercise and art classes."

"Exercise," Dr. Miller repeated. "I recall the Garveys were very big on exercise being a major part of therapy. Wholesome food, lots of physical exercise, and digging deep to discover and face personal demons."

Emma thought about Dr. Kitty's comment about hooey. "I wonder how the Garveys would feel about facing an angry ghost?"

thirteen
. . . .

"HAVE YOU DECIDED WHAT to do with that ring?" Phil called out to Emma. He was tucked into Emma's bed, reading, while he waited for her to finish brushing her teeth.

Emma came out of the bathroom, her electric toothbrush humming inside her mouth like an industrious bee. She stopped it and pulled it out. "Still thinking about it. Might offer to keep it for Lainey until she's out of Serenity. Then again, she might want me to give it to her mother." She stuck the toothbrush back inside her mouth and ducked into the bathroom, closing the door behind her. A minute later, the humming stopped.

Phil glanced at the clock on the nightstand. Emma had been in the bathroom a long time. Putting down his book, he climbed out of bed to investigate. He put his head close to the closed door but couldn't hear anything. He softly knocked. "Emma, you okay?"

No reply.

Opening the door, Phil found Emma sitting on the closed lid of the toilet, lost in thought.

"Hey, Fancy Pants," he said in a gentle voice. "What's up?"

Emma turned her head slowly to look at him. It took her a second to return her thoughts to the present. When she did, she smiled. "You look quite fetching in those PJ bottoms and spectacles, Cowboy."

Phil sucked in his gut and patted his thick chest with its sparse blanket of gray hair. "Ya think? Or is that just some crazy ghost talk?"

Emma's smile faded into overcast clouds. Turning her head away, she stared at nothing in particular, her hands clasped together.

Phil took a seat on the wide, rounded side of the custom tub across from her and leaned forward, wrapping his large hands around hers. They felt hot to his touch. "Are you feeling okay, Emma?"

She continued staring at her closed hands. "Yes, I'm fine."

"Somehow I'm not convinced." Keeping one hand on hers, he felt her forehead and cheeks. "Your hands are burning up, but you don't have a fever."

She pulled her hands away from his and opened them. Inside was Lainey's diamond ring. "It's the ring, Phil. It's giving off heat."

"I thought you put that in your parents' safe downstairs."

"I was going to, but ...," her voice trailed off, and she returned her attention to the ring.

Phil wasn't happy knowing her answer to his next question even before he asked it. "You want her to come out of the ring, don't you?"

Emma looked up, her blue eyes returned to clarity again. "Yes, Phil, I do. Until I talk to her, I can't help anyone. I've been trying to get her to come out. She did it at the condo, so I know she can if she wants."

Phil took off his reading glasses and rubbed his eyes. "Emma, I'm worried about this ghost. She seems more dangerous than any you've encountered before."

"But I need to know more about her, Phil. I think if I put on the ring, I might be able to connect with her."

Phil dropped his glasses and jumped to his feet. "No, Emma." Remembering Emma's parents were in their bedroom on the other side of the house, he lowered his voice. "You know damn well wearing that ring has caused people to die."

She scrunched her face up at him in challenge. "Are you going to forbid me, Phil?"

He stooped down to pick up his glasses and stayed in his crouch longer than was necessary, his eyes cast down at the gleaming tile floor. When he looked up, his displeasure was clear. "No, Emma, I'm not going to forbid you. You're not a child. I simply want you to consider the consequences and the people who would be devastated if something happened to you—Kelly, your parents, even my aunt and uncle."

"And you?"

He stared into her eyes, his unhappiness replaced by fear. "I'm at the top of that list, Emma. The King of the Hill. I'd be lost without you. Next to my boys, you're my reason for getting up each day."

She leaned forward and kissed him, letting her lips linger on his. "I'll be fine, Phil."

He pulled away. "Don't make promises you might not be able to keep. Until you know more about that damn ghost, you don't know what it's capable of."

"Then help me."

"How? By keeping you away from balconies, cars, and sharp objects?"

"Yes."

Phil did a double take. "You're serious."

"Yes, Phil. I am."

Without answering, he turned on his heel and went into the bedroom. He plopped down heavily on the edge of the bed, his feet planted firmly on the floor to display his stand on the matter. Emma followed, the ring clutched tightly in her hand, as if that alone might prevent the ghost from escaping like a firefly.

"Phil, I need your help." Emma stood in front of him and placed a hand on his bare shoulder. "Please."

Not mollified, he asked, "What exactly did you have in mind?"

"I want to slip the ring on, and—"

He cut her off. "Absolutely not."

She removed her hand. "At least hear me out first."

Phil crossed his arms in front of his chest. "I'm all ears."

"Now that your ears are open, how about opening your mind a little?"

He uncrossed his arms, but his brow remained suspicious.

"That's better. What I propose is that I slip on the ring and see what happens, but only with you here. If anything bad starts, you can grab the ring and pull it off my finger. We could do it tonight."

"What if the ghost doesn't want to come out and play? Except for Summer, didn't the others wear the ring awhile before it started haunting them? It might not be as instantaneous as you want it to be."

She took a seat next to him on the bed and opened her hand. In her palm the ring looked like a harmless, large stone—beautiful but hardly deadly. "I realize that, but the stone is different tonight. It's buzzing with heat and energy. I also think since the ghost revealed herself once, she might do it again, especially to someone like me."

With a sigh, Phil put an arm around Emma. "Why don't you wait and ask Milo about this first?"

"I dropped him an email before we went to dinner, and he responded shortly after we returned home tonight. He said it's very rare for ghosts to take up residence in inanimate objects. He's only seen it twice, and it was pretty benign."

"So since he doesn't know much about it and can't advise, we're flying solo on this?" Phil's face darkened.

"Yes. Milo said he wants to see it, but I'm afraid if we wait until he returns in a few weeks, the ghost might decide to leave the ring and start hurting people more frequently. Without knowing her motive, we don't know what to expect."

"What about Granny? Wouldn't it help if she were here for this?"

"Maybe, maybe not. She hasn't been around since your little demonstration in the den. I tried calling to her while I was in the bathroom, but nothing."

Emma dropped the ring. "Ow, it's getting hot again."

"Let me get this straight," Phil said as Emma bent to pick up the ring. "You want to slip on that bit of voodoo and have me stand by to make sure you don't do anything stupid, beyond wearing the ring in the first place."

Using the folds of her nightgown, Emma held the ring between two fingers. "Pretty much."

"I have a stipulation, Fancy Pants."

Emma frowned. "I knew you would."

"I'll do it, but if nothing happens, you only try it again when someone's around. You do not," he held up an index finger in front of her face, "I repeat, *do not* put that ring on again unless someone is with you. And by 'someone' I do not mean Granny. I mean someone physically able to stop you from doing something crazy."

"I promise." Emma stood up and looked around the room. "I think maybe I should sit in that chair." She pointed to an armchair in the corner upholstered to match the drapes.

"You want to do this tonight, right this minute?"

"Yes, Phil, I do. The ring is ready. I can feel it."

Giving in, he shook his head. "There goes a good night's sleep and god knows anything else we were planning to enjoy tonight."

. . . .

EMMA HAD BEEN IN the chair for over an hour, and so far nothing had happened. Lainey's ring was on the ring finger of her left hand. Her finger was slightly smaller than the ring, which moved about easily. Phil had been comforted by that, seeing it would be easier to slip it off in the event something dangerous occurred.

Phil yawned. It was just after midnight. Emma felt her own eyelids droop with sleepiness. "Maybe we should call it a night," she suggested.

"You won't get any argument from me."

Getting up from his post on the edge of the bed where he faced Emma's chair, Phil went to her and offered her his outstretched hands. She took them and let him gently pull her to her feet and into his embrace. He kissed her.

"Not everything can be resolved in one night, Emma. That ghost had a big emotional day, just as we did. She could be recharging her battery for her next move."

"You may be right."

Both beat, they crawled into bed. "Are you going to take that thing off?" Phil asked, noting the ring on Emma's finger.

She considered the jewelry, resting now without the heat or buzz of earlier. "No, I think I'll leave it on. Maybe the wearer has to have it on a bit before the ghost does anything."

Phil looked skeptical.

"Don't worry," Emma assured him. "You're right here. If I make a move, you're sure to know it."

Emma turned to her side and Phil snuggled up behind, wrapping a protective arm tightly around her. "If you so much as belch," he told her, "I'm going on alert."

fourteen

. . . .

THE AIR WAS CHILLY, *and her bare feet were cold on the hardwood floor. Emma pulled the folds of the flowing silk dressing
gown around her and tightened the belt before scurrying to the
area rug with its exotic pattern. The runner ran the full length
of the long corridor, which was illuminated by the soft, buttery
glow of wall sconces. The hallway was empty, dotted on both
sides by closed doors painted white. She heard talking from
behind one and stopped in front of it, her hand hesitating on
the ornate glass doorknob before going in.*

*Inside, a group of people in stylish but old-fashioned cloth-
ing were gathered in a well-appointed parlor. A fire burned
merrily in the hearth. Three men stood by it with brandy
glasses and cigars. On the other side of the room, three women
were seated, two balancing teacups. One of the women, the one
without a cup, looked up as Emma came in; the others ignored
her. She was not much more than a girl—barely twenty, if even
that—with a round, pretty face and dark hair piled high on*

*top of her head. She was seated in a chair in a corner. Her large
oval eyes brimmed with sadness as they stared at Emma without concern or fear.*

*"Just a firm hand," one of the older men said to a younger
man with dark, slicked-back hair and a clipped moustache. "That's all the girl needs is a firm hand to get past this
nonsense."*

*One of the women, an older woman, agreed. "Now that
you're married, she'll calm down. You'll see." She took a delicate
sip from her cup.*

*The young man glanced over at the young woman, then
turned back to the others. "I'm sure Addy will come to her
senses. She's a smart girl."*

*They were talking about the young woman in the corner as
if she wasn't there. They couldn't see Emma, but the girl never
took her eyes off of her. Behind the sadness, Emma saw and felt
the anger in the girl's heart. It smoldered like hot coals waiting
to burst into flames at the first stirring of a poker. The young
woman watched Emma in silence until her face changed, and
Emma was staring at herself. She gasped as she felt firsthand
the festering hate fueling the anger.*

It started as a moan. Then the crying started, a barely audible
weeping at first, building into a succession of groans and sobs.
Emma twisted and turned in Phil's grasp.

"Emma," he said, coming instantly awake. "What's wrong?"

*Running out of the parlor, Emma dashed down the corridor
and opened another door, looking for a way out. It wasn't an
exit but a closet, empty except for a coarse rope hanging from*

somewhere near the top. The rope was a hangman's noose.
Emma slammed the door. Going to the next door, she jerked
it open. Another closet, another noose—this one made from a
long, silken sash. Emma backed away.

"No," moaned Emma, her eyes squeezed tight. "No."

Phil shook her again. "Darling, please, wake up." He snapped
on the bedside lamp. "Wake up, Emma," he said with more force.

The corridor had lengthened, seeming to go on forever, closed
doors lined up on either side like soldiers at attention. She went
to the opposite side of the hallway and jerked another open.
Inside was the man with the moustache and the young woman.
She was in a dressing gown like the one Emma wore, her thick,
long hair undone and cascading down to the middle of her
back. The man had his coat off and his sleeves rolled high on
his strong forearms. In one hand was a strap. He lashed at the
girl—at Addy—over and over as she cowered on the bed. One
blow after another, the strap hit her back, her shoulders, her
legs. He leered at his prey as the strap whizzed through the air
to land painful blows upon its target, tearing the fine silk of her
robe. Emma ran her hands down the folds of the dressing gown
she was wearing and found it now torn to shreds.

"No!" Emma's voice climbed to a screech. "Stop it!"

Phil hopped off the big bed and rounded it, coming to sit on
the edge on Emma's side. He grabbed her shoulders, lifting them
off the bed several inches, and shook her gently. "Emma, it's Phil.
You're having a nightmare." He shook her harder.

She screamed, her eyes still shut, and fought him. "No! Leave me alone!"

Running down the corridor, Emma came to the end and yanked open the last door. Inside were the two nooses—the rope and the silk sash—hanging side by side. At the end of the rope hung the corpse of a young man. At the end of the silk sash hung Addy, limp and lifeless. Emma stepped back in silent horror and clutched her middle, noticing that the sash from her own gown was missing. Addy's corpse lifted its head and, before Emma's frightened eyes, changed into Summer Perkins.

Emma screamed.

Outside the room, Phil heard footsteps. There was one short, hard knock on the door before it was flung open. Dr. Miller stood in the doorway in his pajamas. Behind him was Emma's mother in a long summer nightgown and robe. They looked with horror at the sight of Phil Bowers shaking Emma.

Emma's father grabbed Phil by the shoulder, but Phil shook it off. "She's having a nightmare," Phil explained. "I'm sure it has something to do with that damn ghost, but I can't seem to snap her out of it."

The padding of several small feet announced the arrival of Archie. Hearing the commotion, he'd left his bed in the utility room off the kitchen and had come up the back steps, his collar and tags jingling. As soon as the dog entered the room, he whined and took cover behind the upholstered chair.

"It is a ghost," Elizabeth announced, pointing at the dog. "And it's not Granny." She stood next to the bed, chilled to her bones by Emma's state. "Emma, dear, it's Mother. Wake up."

Emma fought her way out of Phil's grasp and shoved him with ferocity. "No!"

"Don't startle her," Dr. Miller ordered. "She's deeply asleep." Going to the other side of the bed, he sat down. "Phil, get ahold of her again, but in a tight embrace so she can't thrash."

With some difficulty, Phil managed to corral Emma's flailing arms until he held her in a tight cocoon. As Emma fought, Phil began to rock her gently.

"That's it," Dr. Miller said. "Calm her down." He turned to his wife. "Talk to her, dear, softly. And keep saying her name."

Elizabeth, her eyes wide with fear, starting cooing to her daughter. "Emma, it's Mother." She reached out and stroked Emma's hair, now damp with sweat. "You need to wake up, Emma. It's time to get up."

Between her mother's voice and Phil's rocking, Emma began to calm. Her crying lessened, and her jerky movements slowed.

"That's it, Emma," Elizabeth continued, fighting her own tears. "You need to wake up. Daddy and Phil and I are all waiting for you."

Between gulps of air, Emma softly wept but continued to keep her eyes shut tight, as if they were both sewn shut.

"The ring," Phil told them. "She had the ring on when we went to bed."

"Why in the hell would she do that?" Dr. Miller asked.

"Never mind that now, Paul," Elizabeth said.

"It's on her left hand. See if you can reach it and pull it off." Phil kept his arms wrapped tight around Emma.

Elizabeth grabbed Emma's left forearm and followed it until she found her hand. Phil shifted so she could get a better angle on it. "I have my hand on the ring," Elizabeth told them. "It feels hot."

"It did earlier, too," Phil said. "Now slip it off, but don't put your own finger through it."

While Emma continued weeping, Elizabeth twisted the ring and slipped it off. Emma went limp against Phil, and her crying ceased. He laid her back down against the pillow and wiped the sweat from his brow with the back of a hand.

Emma's eyelids fluttered before she opened them wide. Just as quickly, she shut them and moaned, turning away from the light of the lamp. "What time is it?"

Her parents and Phil looked at each other with relief. Emma was back.

"Wake up, Emma," her father told her. "I need to make sure you're all right."

Emma threw an arm across her face. "Of course I'm okay, Dad, except for this blistering headache."

Removing her arm, she fluttered her eyelids again until she got used to the light. "What are you all doing here?" She sat partially up. "What's happened? Is it Kelly?"

"Kelly's fine," Elizabeth assured her. "It's you we're worried about."

Emma ran a hand through her short curls. "My hair's wet." Her hands traveled down over her nightgown, finding it stuck to her body in places. "So's my nightie." She looked to everyone, searching for an explanation.

"You were having a nightmare," Phil explained, "and we couldn't snap you out of it—at least not until we snatched that ring off your finger."

Her right hand clasped her left. "Where is it?"

"I have it, dear." Elizabeth opened her palm to show her the ring.

Falling back against her pillow, Emma closed her eyes, trying to remember what had happened.

"Did you see the ghost?" her mother asked.

"I think so." She opened her eyes and sat up again. Her mother put the ring down and adjusted the pillows against the headboard to help her.

"It was like a montage of creepy and frightening things. At one point, I didn't know if I was seeing Addy or if I was her. Then she became Summer. It was horrible."

"Addy?" questioned Phil.

"Addy?" parroted Emma. "Who's Addy?"

Again the Millers and Phil exchanged glances. "Just now, Emma," Phil said for them all, "you said you either saw Addy or was her in the dream."

While Emma tried to remember, her mother retrieved a cotton robe from behind the bathroom door and draped it over Emma's shoulders.

Emma thanked her mother, then tapped her forehead with a hand. "Addy—of course. That's the ghost's name." She pointed at the ring, which now rested on the nightstand. "The ghost in the ring is named Addy."

"Did you learn anything else about her?" asked her father.

"I ... I don't know. There was a long hallway lined with doors, and behind each door were horrible things, until the last one, which was the worst." She closed her eyes again and swallowed back fresh tears as the memory of the nooses returned. "Could I have some water?"

"Of course, dear." Elizabeth went into the bathroom and returned with a full water glass and two tablets. "Here, take these for your headache."

Emma popped the pills and slurped down the water, emptying the glass. Her mother left and returned quickly with a refill and a damp cloth.

"I saw a hangman's noose," Emma told them as her mother fussed over her, wiping her sweaty forehead. "Actually two."

"Were they hanging from a tree or scaffold or something like that?" asked her father.

She shook her head. "No, they were floating from above. One was made of coarse rope, the other was fabric. Silk, I think."

Phil cleared his throat. "Uh, anyone hanging from them?"

Emma nodded, her chin almost reaching her chest, and started crying again. "A young man hung from the rope. Addy was hanging from the silk one." She looked up. "She was dead. Then she came alive, and her corpse turned into Summer Perkins."

"Summer?" Elizabeth's hand went to her mouth.

"Yes, but before that—behind the door just before that one—I watched a man beating Addy over and over with a leather strap."

Emma stopped short. She lifted her face and looked toward the window. "Addy?"

Everyone turned to see what she was looking at, but only Emma could see the fuzzy outline drifting by the drapes. It was too close for Archie, who scooted out from his hiding place to cower by Elizabeth's legs.

"Addy," Emma said to the ghost. "Tell me what it means. How can I help you? Who was beating you?"

The fuzzy outline started filling in, and soon Emma saw the form of a woman, a young woman, in a long, old-fashioned, torn dressing gown. It was open in front, its sash missing, revealing a floor-length nightgown with lace around the neckline. Her hair was down, like it had been when she'd been beaten and hanging dead. She stared at Emma, her large eyes edged with tragedy and despair. Then she disappeared.

Exhausted, Emma dropped back against her pillow. "She's gone."

"Any idea where the poor girl is from?" asked Elizabeth.

"None," replied Emma. "But from the way the first room looked and the clothing the people wore, the time period was a long time ago." She looked at Phil. "Behind the first door was a parlor that looked a lot like the one at the Julian Hotel. It wasn't the same—it was much fancier—but it had the same style of furnishings."

"Hmm." Phil thought about the hotel in his hometown. Today it was a well-known bed and breakfast, but it was quaint and furnished to replicate the time when Julian was a booming gold-rush town. "I believe the period of those furnishings would be the late 1800s or early 1900s."

"That's what I'm thinking."

"Maybe you're channeling another ghost from Julian," he suggested. "Maybe Granny knows this Addy."

Emma considered that option, but something about it didn't feel right. "I don't think so. Although I didn't see the house I was dreaming about, the rooms I saw looked rather grand—the type of rooms and furnishings found in a mansion. Plus, the clothing they wore seemed expensive and fashionable for that time. A bit more upscale than that worn in a small country town."

Phil laughed. "Don't let Granny hear you calling Julian a small country town. She'll box your ears, or at least try to."

Dr. Miller looked at the clock. "It's nearly two in the morning. Why don't we all get back to bed?" He checked Emma's pulse. Satisfied it was normal, his hand moved up to stroke her face. "You sure you're okay, honey?"

"I'm much better, Dad, and my headache is going away. I'm sorry I woke you and Mother."

"Nonsense," said Elizabeth. "We're just so worried about you. Talking and seeing ghosts is one thing. I don't like this whole idea of you dreaming about them, too."

Emma reached out, took her mother's hand, and squeezed it. "Don't worry, Mother. The ghosts can't hurt me."

Her father wasn't convinced. "Tell that to Summer Perkins."

Shortly after the Millers and Archie left Emma's bedroom, Emma went into the bathroom to freshen up. When she crawled back into bed, Phil drew her into his arms and held her tight.

"Where's that damn ring?" he asked. "I hope you're not wearing it again."

"No chance." She cuddled close against his warm body. "I stuck it in the drawer of the nightstand. "I don't want to feel that way again."

"Well, at least the ring didn't try to kill you."

"No, it seemed more like Addy was trying to tell me something."

Phil squeezed Emma tight and kissed the top of her head. "So what's your guess? You thinking that little gal hanged herself?"

"Maybe." She thought about how she felt when she'd been Addy in the dream and the anger of Addy's current actions. "The depth of loss and despair I felt certainly indicates that, but why would she be so angry and killing people now?"

fifteen

"THAT GHOST WAS HANGED?" Granny rubbed a hand over her own neck. She'd been hanged by crooks posing as vigilantes after being accused of shooting her husband. The ghost shuddered. "We need to help her, Emma."

Emma glanced up from the papers on her desk. "Last night you didn't want me to help her."

"Last night I didn't know the poor child was strung up."

"I think she may have killed herself."

The ghost wandered around Emma's home office, a space she'd created in the Millers' guesthouse, a very large studio apartment with a bathroom and kitchenette, which also doubled as a home gym. "Where's Archie?"

"Mother took him to be groomed this morning. Dad and Phil are playing golf."

Granny seemed unsettled. "Are you sure that Addy killed herself?"

"Pretty sure, unless my dream meant something else." Emma put down the script ideas from her show and looked out the large sliding glass doors at the Millers' well-groomed back yard and garden. "There was a heaviness about the dream, Granny."

"Well, there darn well should be. The girl was beaten and hanged."

"Not darkness as in seriousness, but the way I felt during the dream. It was as if I'd been abandoned, or thought I had been." She looked at the ghost, who now lingered by the oil painting Emma had picked up last year on Catalina Island. The portrayal of Avalon Bay hung over the loveseat across from Emma's desk.

"I felt totally lost and without hope, like the darkness at the bottom of a well, with no chance of escape." She took a deep breath. "I think that's how Addy felt."

Granny turned to Emma. "So now what are we going to do?"

"I called Serenity this morning and spoke to Dr. Garvey. The police were out there last night and questioned Lainey. Dr. Garvey said she's quite shaken over Summer's death but is holding up, although they had to sedate her last night so she could sleep. It was the first time in weeks Lainey has needed medication."

"They didn't let you talk to Lainey?"

"I did speak with her briefly after I spoke with Dr. Garvey. She did seem okay in spite of everything. I told her Keith gave me her ring, and she asked me to keep it until she was out of Serenity."

"Did you tell her about Addy and the ring?"

"No, I didn't. At least not yet. I was going to tell Dr. Garvey, but it sounds so far-fetched, I'm sure they'd try to lock *me* up." Emma shook her head. "It really is an outlandish theory—a haunted ring that tries to kill people. How is that even possible?"

"Some things simply defy explanation. How is it possible you and me can chat like this, with me being dead for over a hundred years?"

"Good point."

"Or me," said another voice out of the blue.

Both Granny and Emma turned in the direction of the voice in time to see the ghost of Max Naiman materialize.

Emma was excited to see him. Not knowing how long the elusive spirit would stay, she got straight to the point. "Max, did you know the stone in your ring was haunted?"

The spirit of the movie star drifted over to Emma. Granny perked up like an adoring groupie.

"No, not until yesterday. But right before my crash I'd started wondering if I might be possessed, like in a horror movie. I knew it was a stupid thought, but I didn't know what else to think."

"Did you tell anyone?"

The ghost shifted, moving back and forth in a nervous pattern.

"Emma's here to help you and Lainey," urged Granny.

"It's too late for me." Max turned, his hazy face twisted in anguish. "But you must help Lainey. I don't think she's out of danger yet."

"I have the ring, Max," Emma told him. "The ghost that killed you and Summer can't hurt her."

"You don't know that for sure. That ghost might decide she doesn't need the stone to go after her victims. Maybe she thought Summer was Lainey."

Emma rose from her chair and approached Max. "Are you thinking Addy—that's the name of the ghost in the ring—has a bone to pick with your family in particular?"

He shrugged, then twisted his neck several times, as Emma remembered him doing while he was alive. Max had suffered several injuries while doing his own stunts for movies, and his neck had always been tight after. It was funny how old personal tics and habits followed an individual into death.

"I don't know, Emma," he answered honestly. "Once I told Joanna about how I felt I was being possessed. She laughed—told me to get off the booze and stay off. I wasn't drinking at that time, but I started up again shortly after out of sheer desperation. I can't tell you how often thoughts of killing myself entered my mind before I finally sent that car over the cliff."

Emma stared at him. "So you did kill yourself?"

"Technically, yes, but I remember at the time feeling I had no control over my actions."

"Like Summer Perkins climbing up on the ledge. I don't think she did that on her own." Emma turned to stare out the window, then turned back to Granny and Max as a thought occurred to her. "But Lainey managed to turn the wheel at the last minute on both car accidents. And she fought to keep the knife from hitting a vital organ."

Max shook his head. "All three times I was there. I got her to yank the wheel of the car, and I deflected the knife."

Emma was intrigued. "You were able to do that physically?"

"I don't know how I was able to do it. I think it was more about concentrating on her mentally, like bringing her out of it at the last minute as I tried to physically move her."

"So it was some sort of emotional connection you made with Lainey?" In her head, Emma took notes. She was always learning from the ghosts about what they could or couldn't do. Often they themselves didn't understand the full range of their abilities.

Again, Max shrugged, but this time his neck remained stationary. "I remember putting all of my energy into it, like I was pushing a heavy car, trying to get it to move, while begging her to snap out of her trance. When it was over, I was so exhausted, I simply faded."

"Like you did when you used your energy to push Joanna back down into her chair yesterday. Or how she always feels weight on her when she thinks you're around."

"Yes. Dealing with Joanna is exhausting. It was when I was alive, too." He let out a sad little chuckle. "I've been trying to force her to pay attention to me, even though she can't see or hear me."

"She knows you're there, Max. Believe me, she knows, even if she didn't believe you when you told her about being possessed."

Emma saw Max starting to fade and rushed to her next question. "Why does Joanna avoid dealing with Lainey?"

"They were never close," he told her, his voice becoming feathery. "Joanna was always jealous of Lainey and of the time I spent with her, but it has become worse since Linwood entered the picture."

. . . .

"I need to know about that ring, Joanna."

"Charming office, Emma. You can work out while you ... ah, do whatever it is you do." With disdain, Joanna indicated the treadmill and other exercise equipment that took up half of the guesthouse. "Must be how you keep your trim figure."

"Nothing like multitasking," Emma answered with false cheerfulness.

Joanna Reid was seated on the loveseat across from Emma's large desk. She wore immaculate linen trousers and a mint-green silk top accessorized by a gold necklace and diamond stud earrings. Emma wore navy blue capri pants and a white tank top. On her feet were white Keds.

After her dream of the night before, Emma had called Joanna several times that morning, demanding answers. Once Joanna understood that Emma was going to be a pest about asking her more questions, she gave in, agreeing to meet Emma Sunday afternoon at the Miller home in Pasadena.

"Where's the ring now?" asked Joanna.

"In a safe."

"Please get it for me, and I'll be on my way."

Emma shook her head. "Can't do that. I spoke to Lainey this morning, and she asked me to hold it for her. It's hers, after all. You gave it to her."

"I can call Lainey, too," Joanna sneered. She took out her phone. "You'll just have to give it to me in the end."

In spite of her intention to remain calm and professional, sarcasm escaped Emma's lips. "You don't call your daughter the entire time she's at Serenity Place, and now you expect to call and make her do something she clearly doesn't want to do?" She narrowed her eyes at Joanna. "Do you even have the number to Serenity Place?"

"I don't need it. I'll call Lainey's cell phone."

"Cell phones aren't permitted by patients. You have to go through the main desk to reach anyone."

Ignoring Emma, Joanna punched a button on her cell phone and put the device to her ear. After several moments and no answer on the other end, she ended the call with a hard jab at the screen of her phone.

Emma leaned forward in her desk chair. "Whatever influence you may have had on Lainey in the past, or whatever intimidation you used to get her to do what you wanted, it's over, Joanna. It ended when she checked herself into Serenity instead of the Baja facility, and she's only going to become stronger after this."

"That Baja clinic would have been the best place for her."

"An overpriced luxury prison where they drug their guests day and night?"

Joanna stared at Emma, her mouth open. "It is not. It's highly regarded. Lin knows a lot of people who've been there and rave about it."

"Lin recommended it? So you didn't check into it yourself before insisting your daughter go there?" Emma was disgusted, and she let it show.

"My father and I did some checking into that place this morning," Emma continued. "He's a doctor, you know. Turns out it's nothing more than a cushy place for the rich and famous to stash the more embarrassing members of their family. Or it's a haven for those pretending to seek help, especially those under court order. Drugs are handed out like candy. Last year a patient overdosed on heroin."

"You're lying."

"I wish I were." Emma sat back in her chair. "Lainey and her doctor chose Serenity Place because of its reputation for therapy without drugs. Your daughter is flourishing there, and you'd know that if you had any maternal decency."

Joanna jumped to her feet, her face full of rage. "You know nothing about me." She slung her purse over her arm and started for the door, then turned sharply about on her designer shoes. "I came here because you wanted to ask me questions. I accommodated you, and *this* is how you treat me?"

"You haven't answered any of my questions. It's obvious you came here to get the ring. Did you know it was haunted?"

"A haunted ring? Don't be ridiculous." Joanna made a sound of disgust in her throat. "When you told me that on the phone, I thought you were having a breakdown of your own."

Emma rose and took a few steps toward her. "Where did that stone come from, Joanna?"

"I told you. I got Max a new wedding ring. That stone was set in his ring when I bought it."

"And where did you buy it?"

Joanna hesitated before answering. "A shop over on Fairfax. A small shop that specializes in vintage and estate jewelry. I wanted to get him something special."

"The name, Joanna."

"I don't remember." Seeing Emma's skeptical look, she added, "Really, I don't. A friend recommended it to me. It's a small family-owned store near the old farmers' market."

"Well, that's a start." Seeing Joanna hesitating about opening the door, Emma decided to try to reel her back in. "Would you like something to drink, Joanna?" She went to the mini fridge in the kitchenette and opened it. "I have diet soda and Snapple tea, also diet."

"Nothing stronger?"

Emma checked again. "There's a nice chardonnay in here, too. It was opened yesterday." She glanced over at Joanna. "Or I could go into the house and get the hard stuff."

Joanna Reid walked back to the loveseat and perched on the edge like a bird ready to take flight at the slightest hint of danger. "I suppose the wine will have to do." She put her purse down on the small ottoman that also served as a coffee table.

Emma pulled the bottle out of the fridge and got down two rose-colored wineglasses from the cupboard above. Uncorking the bottle, she filled each halfway, emptying the bottle. She walked over to the loveseat and handed one to Joanna before sitting on the opposite side of the loveseat.

"There's a ghost in the ring," Emma said, cutting directly to the issue at hand. "The ghost of a young woman who is very angry. She convinced Max to kill himself and did the same with Lainey."

Joanna took a sip of her wine. "Do you really expect me to believe that?"

"You believe Max's ghost has been haunting you, so why not a haunted ring?"

"I was wrong. He's not haunting me. I was just being paranoid."

"No, Joanna, you weren't. As I've told you before, Max has been visiting you, and he's worried about Lainey. Max was with me at the condo when Summer fell."

Joanna nearly dropped her wineglass but managed to hang on to it. "That's impossible."

"He was there. He tried to help Summer, but the ghost in the ring got to her first."

"Did you tell the police that?"

"No, I didn't. Do you really think they'd believe it?"

"Why would anyone believe that nonsense? Including me?"

"Why, indeed." Emma twisted the stem of her glass between two fingers. "But in spite of what you're saying, I think you *do* believe me. At least you believe that Max has been trying to reach you. He also thinks Lainey is still in danger, even though she doesn't have the ring."

Joanna took a big swallow of the wine. "Do you think she's still in danger?"

"I'm not sure. It depends on what the ghost in the diamond wants. I've made contact with her."

Tilting her glass, Joanna drained the wine like water. Emma noticed the nervous gesture and continued. "Her name is Addy. I think she died in the latter part of the 1800s or possibly around the turn of the century, perhaps by hanging herself."

Joanna appeared shaken. "Do you have any more wine?"

"No, and besides, it's a long drive back to the Westside. You need to stay sober."

Joanna hung on to the wineglass, clutching it to her chest like a favorite teddy bear. She didn't look at Emma but stared off toward the far wall.

"Do you know anyone in your family's history or Max's named Addy? It could be short for Adeline or Adelaide."

Joanna shook her head. "No." She turned and faced Emma, refocusing. "No," she repeated, "I don't." She took a deep breath. "Didn't you say ghosts can't hurt us—or was that simply your own personal theory?"

"I think this ghost influenced or enticed Max and Lainey into hurting themselves. Same with Summer." Emma put her wineglass down. "Max told me he stopped Lainey each time."

"What?" Joanna's mouth hung open.

"It's true. He was there with Lainey in the car and the time in her condo when she tried to stab herself. He was somehow able to stop it at the last minute. He's watching over her, Joanna, like a guardian angel."

"He always did love that child to distraction. Not sure why death would change that."

Emma studied her. "Are you jealous of Lainey? Of her relationship with her father?"

Joanna gasped. "Don't be ridiculous. Just because I'm not the smothering type of parent you are, don't think for a minute I don't care about my child."

"And what's going on with Linwood?" Emma hoped the quick change of topic would throw Joanna off balance.

"What do you mean? What does he have to do with this?"

"You seemed nervous around him. You're a lot different when you're on your own."

Again Joanna jumped to her feet. "My relationship with my husband is none of your business." She slammed her wineglass down, nearly breaking it. Grabbing her bag, she headed for the door again. "Whatever is threatening Lainey, get to the bottom of it. Contrary to what you might think, I *do* care for my daughter. After, you and Max can both go straight to hell ... if he's not there already."

sixteen
· · · · · · · · · · · · ·

EMMA FED THE PARKING meter next to her car and pressed the lock button on her key fob. As soon as her SUV gave off the alarm-set tone, she started walking up Fairfax. She'd cruised the few blocks in the vicinity of the farmers' market twice before spying several small jewelry stores just north of Beverly.

Phil had left early in the morning to return to San Diego and his law practice. They'd spent a good part of Sunday evening going over the facts they had so far on the ring and the ghost. Emma was going to do some research into the ring's history. She didn't know if jewelry stores kept information on estate pieces, but it wouldn't hurt to ask. Tucked inside her purse in a velvet pouch was Lainey's ring.

Her landmark was the farmers' market at Fairfax and Third. Joanna had said the jewelry store was near it. As she drove by, Emma glanced at the famous collection of souvenir shops, restaurants, and food booths that had been a tourist destination for decades. Today it was referred to as the "original" farmers' market to distinguish it from the dozens of community farmers' markets that rotated throughout Southern California on a weekly basis. The area around it had exploded over the years and included the upscale Grove, a mega shopping and entertainment complex, but the white clock tower still stood at the market as a reminder of a quaint and slower time.

When she and Grant were first married, they would often come down to the farmers' market early on a Sunday morning. They would grab a cup of coffee at one booth and a fresh pastry at another and sit at the small clusters of tables among other early morning Angelinos to pore over the *Los Angeles Times*. Before they went home, they'd pick up fresh produce and bread. Those had been good times, before Grant's career took off and changed him into an egomaniacal serial skirt chaser.

The first jewelry store she checked out had the usual basic inventory, nothing special. When she inquired at the second shop about estate pieces, she was directed farther up the block to another shop called Sachman & Sons.

The storefront of Sachman & Sons was the least imposing of the three. Its front windows, set on either side of the door, displayed the usual necklaces and rings. A small placard was posted in the right window announcing that they specialized in the purchase and sale of estate jewelry. To back up their claim, the right window had a small display of some lovely vintage pieces, including some exquisite cameos. Another small sign announced that the store bought gold.

Through the window, Emma saw a man working behind a counter. The door to the shop was locked. Another small sign posted on the glass front of the door invited customers to ring the doorbell on the right side for entry. About a foot and a half above the bell was affixed an ornate mezuzah, a case containing scripture found on many Jewish doorposts.

Emma poked the center of the doorbell and heard a buzzer sound within the store. The man looked up from his work and studied Emma. A second later, she heard another buzz, and when she tried the door, it was unlatched.

The store was small but bright and cheerful. A U-shaped glass display case filled with various items of jewelry, coins, and fine accessories lined three sides. Behind them were glass wall cases spotlighting other objects.

"Good morning," the middle-aged man greeted her as she entered. He was tall and slight and wore a dark suit with a white shirt and dark tie. His angular face, with its long, straight nose, sported glasses with thick black frames and a close-cropped beard and moustache of gunmetal gray. Perched toward the back of his thinning hair was a simple black yarmulke.

"Good morning," Emma replied back with a smile. She approached the counter. "I have some questions regarding estate jewelry. Are you Mr. Sachman?"

"I am Joseph Sachman, one of the sons. Did you have something to sell, or are you looking to purchase?"

"Neither, though you do have some lovely cameos in the window. You don't see them much anymore."

The man smiled and nodded. "They are a particular favorite of my mother's, though women don't wear them as they used to."

"My mother also loves them." Emma glanced back at the window display but could not see the items facing the street.

As if reading her mind, the proprietor said, "Mother's Day is coming up."

Emma gave a soft laugh. "That's exactly what I was thinking." She turned back to the business at hand. "But today I'm actually looking for information on a piece you may have sold several years ago, maybe five or six years back. Do you keep information on your better estate pieces?"

"For insurance purposes we keep a detailed inventory on everything. If an estate or antique piece is of particular interest, we might also keep some side notes. Are you sure it was purchased here?"

"Pretty sure. It was a very large diamond set flush in a man's band." Emma pulled a small pouch out of her purse and emptied it onto one of the velvet pads sitting on the counter. Lainey's engagement ring tumbled out. "The stone in this ring was set into a man's band that you sold to a friend of mine, Joanna Reid." She paused to correct herself. "Her name was Joanna Naiman then. She bought it as a gift for her husband Max."

"Max Naiman, the movie star?"

"Yes. He died shortly after. Recently the stone was removed from his band and reset for his daughter's engagement ring." Emma indicated the ring on the pad. "This is that ring."

Mr. Sachman pointed to the ring. "May I?"

"Yes, of course."

The jeweler put on his glasses, then picked up the ring and examined it. "Lovely stone." He took off his glasses, brought out a jeweler's loop, and brought it to his eye to check the stone further. When he was finished, he put his glasses back on. "What is your connection to this ring?"

"In speaking with Mrs. Reid and her daughter, we've come to believe this stone may have a fascinating history connected to it. They are interested in looking into it, and I'm assisting them." Emma pulled out one of her business cards and gave it to Mr. Sachman. He examined it.

"I remember when Mr. Naiman passed. Very tragic. I did not personally sell his wife the original ring, but I believe I do remember it. It's not often we have such large diamonds set in men's rings. Let me see what we have in the way of records."

He put the ring back down on the velvet pad and walked to the other side of the store to a computer. Emma picked up the ring and followed him on her side of the counter.

After a few hunt-and-pecks at the keyboard, during which Mr. Sachman offered up a few hems and haws, he turned his attention back to Emma. "We did sell Mrs. Naiman a man's ring with a stone of this size. In fact, it seems we sold that ring twice."

"Twice?"

"This shop is patronized by entire families, generation after generation. That gentlemen's ring was purchased here many years ago, then resold to us when the owner died, along with other estate items."

"Who owned it before the Naimans?"

Returning to the keyboard, he continued his search. "Interesting." The comment was made to the computer screen but still caused Emma's ears to perk up. "Would you excuse me a moment?"

Before Emma could say anything, Mr. Sachman ducked through a door marked Employees Only.

While she waited, Emma's eyes wandered over the items in the display case. Sachman & Sons really had some exquisite antique pieces. She found a few more cameos and studied them through the glass, thinking one really would make a lovely gift for her mother.

"Wow, look at all this stuff."

Without turning, Emma said to Granny in a whisper, "Do you think Mother would like one of these cameos?"

The ghost materialized and peered at the brooches Emma indicated. "Sure do. They're beautiful. I used to have one. Jacob gave it to me when our son was born. Not as fine as these, but I did love it."

"Which one do you think she'd like the most?"

"I like this one—it looks sort of like the one I had." Granny pointed to a fine carving of a woman with a crown of flowers.

"That is lovely. Maybe when we're done here, we'll have a look at it."

The ghost looked around. "If you're not buying something, why are you here?"

"I'm hoping they can tell me about the stone in Lainey's ring. This is where Joanna bought it."

Emma heard the office door open. "Now *shhh*."

The ghost crossed her arms. "Humpf. It's not like he can hear me."

Mr. Sachman remained by the office door. "Would you please follow me, Mrs. Whitecastle." When she hesitated, he added, "My father would like to speak with you, but it is difficult for him to come to the front of the store."

Going between a break in the large counter, Emma went behind the display and followed Joseph Sachman through the door. Granny followed them.

The back of the store was smaller than the front and was divided into two sections. The larger portion contained a compact kitchen with mini fridge and microwave and a small round table with two chairs. Industrial shelving held boxes of supplies such as bags and boxes, large rolls of gift wrap in plain silvery blue, and rolls of white ribbon. Straight back was the back door to the shop, and to the side another door that was slightly ajar. Through that door Emma spied the corner of a sink and guessed it to be the bathroom. Everything was neat as a pin.

The other part of the room was sectioned into a private office. Its door was open, and it was through there Mr. Sachman directed Emma.

The inner office contained a large safe and an L-shaped desk that also doubled as a work table. A black gooseneck magnifying lamp hovered over bits and pieces of a watch in mid-repair. Behind the desk sat a fragile old man with a white beard and silky white hair. Like his son, he wore a dark suit and a yarmulke, though his was ringed with embroidered images of the Star of David. In his delicate hands was Emma's business card.

"Mrs. Whitecastle, this is my father, Isaac Sachman. He may have the information you're seeking."

"Mrs. Whitecastle, please," said the old man. He indicated a seat across from him on the other side of the desk. "You'll have to forgive me for not standing, but my legs are rather withered from arthritis. Fortunately, it has spared my hands, which in my line of work is a blessing."

Emma sat in the chair.

"Would you like some tea?" he asked. "Joseph can make us some." His voice was edged with a European accent and had the wobble of age.

Emma smiled at both gentlemen. "No, but thank you."

Joseph gave her courteous nod. "I must return to the front. I leave you in the best of hands, Mrs. Whitecastle."

From across the table Isaac Sachman studied her, squinting his aged eyes to slits. "Why do you *really* want to know about that particular stone, Mrs. Whitecastle?"

Emma fidgeted like a schoolgirl who didn't know the correct answer when called upon. She tried not to look at Granny, who was standing at the edge of the table watching Sachman. "As I told your son, I'm looking into the history of the ring purchased for Max Naiman."

"Joseph tells me you have the ring."

"No, just the stone from it. It was reset into an engagement ring for Max's daughter, Elaine."

"May I see it?"

Emma opened the hand in which she clutched the ring. It had grown warm, but Emma didn't know if it was because of the heat of her body or that Addy was active. She held the ring out to the jeweler, who took it and examined it closely.

"This certainly does look like the stone from the other ring." He held it under the magnified lamp. "Yes, same distinct fire as I remember."

"Mr. Sachman, do you know the history behind this stone, such as where it came from? Your son said something about your store selling it twice."

The old gentleman gave her a small knowing smile. "One of the reasons I got into the specialty of estate and antique jewelry was my fascination with the people who owned such beautiful things. My family and I came to this country when I was very young. We were quite poor. My father was a watchmaker, and I learned that trade from him at a very early age. When I was older, I apprenticed to a jeweler in a fancy store in New York and learned all about fine gems and metals. Many rich people came into the store, spending with extravagance when they were happy and flush, then selling when their fortunes waned. All quite fascinating to a young man who was taught to be frugal and sensible whether your pockets be empty or full."

Grasping the lower end of Lainey's ring, Mr. Sachman held it up between them. The large diamond sat high and proud on its prongs.

"A fine piece of jewelry isn't discarded like worn clothing or an old, battered sofa. It endures long past the life of its original owner, most often passing from generation to generation, like a family name, but sometimes sold in a time of desperation or apathy."

"And this stone?"

"Tell me, my dear, what is *your* suspicion about this particular stone?"

Emma looked the old man dead-on. "I believe it has a very tragic past."

"Which includes your friend Mr. Naiman?"

"Yes, including him."

Still holding the ring, the old man tapped Emma's business card, which now sat on the desk to his left, with his other hand. "I know your television show, Mrs. Whitecastle. I have seen it a few times. Very interesting. Given the topic of your show, it is even more interesting that it is you who is inquiring about this stone."

"As I mentioned, the Naimans were friends of mine. Their daughter is still a close friend of my daughter's."

"And the fact that you are a known investigator into strange occurrences has nothing to do with your curiosity about this particular piece?"

Granny leaned in close. "He's playing with you, Emma. I think he knows the ring is haunted."

"I think you're right." Emma was looking at Mr. Sachman, but her words were meant for Granny.

"Are you speaking to me," he asked, "or to the spirit hovering just to your right?"

Emma's mouth dropped open before she could stop it. She collected herself just as fast. "That spirit is my great-great-great-grandmother, Ish Reynolds. She just told me she thinks you know the stone is haunted."

Isaac Sachman put Lainey's ring down on the table and rubbed his hands together lightly. "And she would be partially correct. I didn't know for sure it was haunted, but I've had my suspicions something wasn't quite right about it." Mr. Sachman gave a gracious head bow in the direction of Granny. "Welcome to my humble establishment, Mrs. Reynolds."

"You can see her?" Emma asked.

"Not clearly. All I ever see are small, sparkly clouds, like diamond dust floating on the air. And, unfortunately, I cannot hear them as you obviously can. I've had this ability since I was a child but didn't realize what it was until I was a young man working with that fancy jeweler. Maybe it's another reason I enjoy following the history of other people's finery—it's almost like knowing them. And gems are living things; they are born of the earth, just as we are."

Emma liked Isaac Sachman and his thoughts on gems and their owners. "Besides Max Naiman, how did the previous owners of this stone die? Do you know that?"

"My memory isn't always the best, so let me consult my notes."

He turned toward a computer that sat on the outstretched arm of the desk, but instead of pecking on the keyboard, Mr. Sachman opened a small lower drawer. From it he retrieved a ragged leather-bound journal. It bulged with scraps of paper and newspaper clippings and was held together with a thick rubber band. Removing the band, he placed it on the table between them and began flipping through the yellowed pages, all of which were filled with a small, tight scrawl.

"Here we go." From the spot he chose, he pulled a small photograph, an aging Polaroid, and handed it across the desk to Emma. "This is what the ring looked like when it was a man's ring."

The photo was of a man's wide band with the stone set flush in a dome at the middle. There was interesting scrollwork on either side of the stone, running halfway down both sides of the band. Seeing the photo brought memories back to Emma of Max wearing the ring.

"Yes, that is Max's wedding ring. Joanna gave it to him when they restated their vows."

While Emma studied the photo, Mr. Sachman read his notes on it. Out of the corner of his eye, he watched as Emma turned the photo toward Granny for her to see. He smiled and went back to his reading.

"Because of the unique nature of this stone, it seems I've done quite a bit of research on it." He flipped a page over and gave it a quick scan. "I have many notes, though I'm not surprised, considering its questionable nature." He pulled out a small newspaper clipping about Max's accident and showed it to Emma.

She leaned forward, eager to know what else was in the journal. "Besides Max Naiman, do you know how many of the previous owners died?"

"They all died, Mrs. Whitecastle, but I'm sure you meant died suspiciously."

"I did." It was clear to Emma that while the old man's legs were weak, his mind was as sharp and as clear as the diamonds he sold.

"Let's see." Sachman ran a bony finger down the pages. While he did so, Emma pulled a pen and small pad of paper from her handbag to take notes.

"Prior to Mrs. Naiman buying it, the man's ring was owned by a famous attorney in Beverly Hills. He shot himself while his wife was out of town. According to this, he'd purchased the ring himself less than a year before that happened. We bought it back from his widow about four years after his death. We had it here in the store another three years before it was purchased by your friend."

He turned another page and scanned it before finding the new information he sought. "According to my notes, before that it was owned by a banker. He bought it from a colleague of mine, but not as a man's ring—it was an engagement ring. He bought it for his fiancée, a young woman almost half his age."

Emma looked up from her notes. "I almost hate to ask what happened to him."

Mr. Sachman flipped a few pages forward. "It wasn't until Mr. Naiman's death that I started going back in time to track the ring. My notes on the earlier history are actually more recent."

He found the page he was looking for and spread the journal wide, smoothing the pages down. "Here we go. The banker bought the engagement ring many years ago, sometime in the late sixties. Shortly after, his fiancée died of an overdose of sleeping pills."

He tapped the book. "That poor family suffered."

"I'm sure any death is traumatic."

"More so this. The banker eventually did marry, and many years after his first fiancée's death, he came to me to extract the stone and reset it into a ring for his only son. That was the first time I ever saw it. I remember him telling me that he had kept it in a safe-deposit box all those years."

"So you reset the stone, not realizing it had a history?"

"Correct." Mr. Sachman took off his glasses and rubbed his eyes. He looked at Emma through eyes the color of faded denim. "His son shot himself six months later, and my customer died of a broken heart not too soon after. It was through his estate that the ring returned to me for resale, but, of course, I didn't know it was cursed."

Granny became agitated. "The sooner we get rid of that monster, the better."

"That's what I'm trying to do, Granny." Emma turned back to Mr. Sachman. "What about prior to the banker buying it? Do you know where the ring originated?"

"I'm afraid I'm not sure, but the setting was definitely Victorian, and it wasn't a copy of a Victorian design but the real thing.

There were also a few small diamonds used as accents. My customer didn't care about those when he asked me to put the stone into a man's ring. The setting was so lovely, I paid him for the setting and eventually put a different diamond into it."

Emma became alarmed. "Do you know what happened to the new owner of the setting? Maybe it has a problem, too."

"I am happy to say the owner is alive and well and still wearing the ring." Mr. Sachman winked at Emma. "You see, my son Joseph gave it to the girl he married almost thirty years ago."

"And no problems?"

"Not a one."

"Where did the other jeweler get the stone from? Did you ask?"

He consulted his notes again. "It says here he bought it through a private sale somewhere back east in the mid-sixties."

"Is it possible to speak with this other jeweler?"

"I'm afraid not. Jonas died three years ago. Cancer."

"I'm very sorry."

Isaac Sachman accepted her condolences for his friend and closed his journal. "Tell me, Mrs. Whitecastle, who or what do you think inhabits the ring?"

Emma picked up the ring and held it to the light. It was warmer than before. "Her name is Addy. She was an abused young wife who I believe hanged herself."

"Oh, my." Mr. Sachman leaned back in his chair. "And what do you propose to do now that you know this?"

Granny scowled. "She should destroy the ring, that's what the little fool should do."

Emma turned to Granny. "It's not my ring to destroy, Granny. And there's no way of knowing if that will get rid of or appease

Addy." Emma studied the ring again. "What I want to do is help Addy and save the ring for Lainey. It was her father's, after all. It has a lot of sentimental value. I just have to figure out what it will take to do both."

"Well, hurry up," snapped Granny, "before you become her next victim."

seventeen
. . . .

"You do, and I'm marching straight into the house and telling Elizabeth." The threat came from Granny. She was standing in the middle of Emma's home office, pointing in the direction of the Miller house. "And Phil."

Emma curled a lip at the ornery spirit. "Phil only understands yes or no."

"Trust me, I'll find a way to make him understand. And I'll do it tonight."

"Tattletale."

"It's not tattling if it's about something dangerous."

Trying a different tactic, Emma erased her annoyance and replaced it with reason. "Granny, I can't help Addy if I don't know anything about her."

"She's killed"—Granny paused to remember what Sachman had told them, ticking off the victims on her fingers—"she's killed *five* people, counting that Summer girl. Six if you include the banker who died of grief over his son."

Emma looked down at the notepad in front of her where she'd listed each one of the deaths. Granny was right. Five victims and one indirect death.

"And who knows how many there were before that?" the ghost ranted as she paced the office. "Or how many narrowly escaped, like Lainey."

"But you'll be here if something happens," cajoled Emma.

"No. And that's final."

Emma fingered Lainey's ring. After dinner, she'd retreated to her office with the plan of learning more about Addy. She'd called to Addy, entreating her to show herself so they could talk. She'd held the ring in her hand, trying to convey she wanted to help. It had gotten warm, but no ghost materialized.

"You're just angry because I wouldn't let Archie come out here tonight." She looked up at Granny. "It was for his own good. You know angry ghosts scare him."

"Then don't fetch her out of the ring. Leave her be. Lock it in a strong box, and throw away the key." The ghost came to a stop in front of Emma, her hazy face bright with an idea. "I know: why not throw it into the ocean like that old lady did to that diamond necklace in the movie we watched last week?"

"We've discussed that before, Granny. There's no reason why that should work. You know better than I do that ghosts need to be attached in some way to a person, place, or thing from their past or present. The ring is Addy's past thing, but now that she's made contact with us, she doesn't need the ring to come out. She only needs to be around a place or person she's made contact with in the present. Either Addy doesn't know that or she does and prefers the ring. Either way, locking up the ring or destroying it may unleash her in other ways. At least for now, the ring contains her."

"By calling her out, Emma, you're poking a sleeping, rabid dog."

Emma shook her head back and forth slowly. "I don't believe that. I think if we help her, she'll stop killing. She's lashing out because she's angry and frustrated."

Granny crossed her arms in defiance. "You've been watching too much Dr. Phil."

"I don't watch Dr. Phil, Granny, *you* do. Almost every day with Mother, and you think I don't know." Emma cranked down the frustration in her voice. She wanted Granny's help and knew that arguing with the old mule wouldn't secure her assistance. She also knew Granny was right; calling out Addy could be very dangerous. "You'll be here with me. If something goes wrong, you can fly into the house to get Mother and Dad in a flash." When Granny still didn't say anything, she added, "Remember how frustrated you felt after you were murdered. You wanted me to help you, didn't you?"

Crossing the floor several times, Granny kept her back turned to Emma. She did understand what Emma was saying. She had been frustrated for nearly a hundred years until Emma brought her peace. She turned to Emma. "But I never killed anyone, did I?"

The dead and the living stared at each other, sharing a family stubborn streak that ran as deep and wide as the Colorado River.

"Okay," Granny finally said, throwing her hands up in the air. "I'll stay with you while you wear the ring." She floated over to Emma and pointed a finger at her. "But the minute I feel you're in danger, I'm getting Elizabeth."

"Deal."

Before Granny could change her mind, Emma slipped Lainey's ring on her left ring finger and curled up on the loveseat to wait.

"Besides," she told the ghost watching over her. "We don't even know if she'll come out tonight."

"With any luck, she won't."

Emma didn't feel the same way.

"Could we at least watch some TV while we wait?"

"You watch entirely too much TV, Granny."

"What else have I got to do? It's not like a ghost can knit a sweater or get a job."

Emma shook her head and chuckled. "You have a point." She picked up the remote sitting on the ottoman and clicked on the TV mounted on the main wall of the guesthouse. "Anything in particular?"

"Just keep clicking." Granny moved toward the TV and stared at it. "There. Stop. That's *NCIS*. I like that show. That Mark Harmon's a hunk."

Emma toggled over to the channel schedule. "Looks like an *NCIS* marathon on the USA Network." She flipped back to the program and put the remote back on the ottoman. "That should keep you busy for a while. Just remember to pay attention if something odd starts happening with me and the ring."

"Don't worry; I've got your back."

Granny drifted back to the loveseat and perched on the end opposite Emma. She tried to pick up the remote, but her filmy hand slipped through it. "I gotta figure out how to work that darn TV thing on my own."

Emma walked down a narrow street. She was going downhill. It wasn't a steep incline, just a gradual one. On both sides of the street, old-fashioned townhomes and buildings in various degrees of restoration were set close together, and shops displayed wares. Cars were parked along the curb. Some were coming up the street, straight at her. Before she could jump out of the way, a Honda sedan sped through her as easily as if she were smoke. Surprised, she turned and watched it go up the street, paying her no mind. Turning back around, she met a pickup truck head-on. Emma screamed, but no sound came out. Like the Honda, it drove through her. Bewildered, she moved to the narrow sidewalk and kept walking down the street, passing people along the way. No one paid her any mind. She was wearing the same dressing gown from before, even though from the way folks were dressed it must have been chilly.

She passed several quaint buildings, including a red brick building with a black iron fence and gate. Lettering across the top of the building proclaimed it the Dimmick Memorial Library. More charming buildings, both residential and commercial, lined both sides of the street. A little farther down was an inn, its balcony railings made with the same ornate ironwork as the library. Emma kept walking until she came to a major intersection. Cars were stopped for the light. Other cars were moving through in the opposite direction. On the corner was an imposing stone building with a clock tower. A sign designated it as the court house.

Emma crossed the street, heading for a small town square, drawn to the red brick building on its edge. It was a train station. People were milling about and taking photos of it. Looking up, she saw a sign that read Mauch Chunk. When she looked back at the train station, it had changed. It was early morning. Nearby were horse-drawn carts and carriages instead of cars. On a bench in front of the train station sat a young woman with a travel case on her lap. She wore a long dress and coat with a snug bodice. The veil on her hat partially covered her face.

Feeling a bit dizzy, Emma closed her eyes to get her bearings. When she opened them, she wasn't at the train station but inside the cellar of a dark, dank building. Along the walls were openings, doorways into a series of closets. The only light came from yellow overheads and tiny openings in the boarded-up windows in each closet.

She stepped inside one, running a hand along the wall to guide her toward the speck of light. Her hand hit something hard and heavy. It was an old chain embedded into the crumbling plaster. She studied the chain, the room illuminating as her mind cleared. She wasn't in a closet, she was in a cell. An old, empty cell with thick walls of stained plaster. At the end of the chain were manacles. She stepped back in revulsion and turned to flee, but the heavy door closed, cutting her off.

As she pounded on the thick metal door, a man walked through it. She backed up. Another man came through the side wall, followed by another. Dressed in rough work clothes, with dirty hair and faces, they stared at her with hollow eyes. She backed up a few more steps until her legs hit something solid. Turning, she saw a filthy toilet built into the corner of the cell. She jumped away from it, coming face to face with yet another man as he came though the wall next to her. He was young, *with dirty, matted light hair and large, sad eyes. Around his neck was a thick rope—a hanging rope. It was the boy from her prior dream—the one hanging dead in the mansion's closet.*

He held out his hand to her, beckoning her to come with him. "Addy."

Hopelessness again filled Emma. It coursed through her body like dirty water pouring into an empty hole. She felt crushed by it, consumed and buckled by its weight, as she took his cold, lifeless hand.

"Emma!"

On the loveseat, Emma stirred, half in this world, half someplace dark and tragic.

"Wake up, Emma!"

The sound wasn't loud and solid but gauzy, as if fragmented by time and space. Still, it was familiar, and it pulled her back like a welcoming hand of help.

"Mmm." She shifted her weight on the loveseat. It was much shorter than she was, and she pulled up her legs to fit. She didn't want to go back to the jail, but somewhere in the rational part of her mind she knew she had to. She needed to know what it all meant. She drifted back to sleep.

"Emma, come back!"

Soft air brushed her face. It was fresh, and it tickled. Her eyelids fluttered in static movements of half consciousness.

"That's it. You come back right this minute or I'm going for your mother." Granny stamped her foot and blew against Emma's face as she had earlier against Phil's ear. "I mean it." She blew again and again, mustering all her energy for maximum wind.

"Mother?" Emma opened her eyes. Shut them. Opened them again. When she focused, the jail was gone. She was back in her home office. The TV was on, and she was dressed in jeans and a tee shirt. Staring down at her was the ghost of Granny Apples, looking very upset.

"Never again," the spirit snapped at her. "Never again will I let you do that. Take off that darn ring right this minute."

Emma sat up and ran a hand over her face and through her hair. She shook her head to clear it. "The ring?"

"Take it off, I tell ya. Right now." Granny paced the room in a mixture of relief and anger.

Emma looked down at her hand to see Lainey's beautiful engagement ring on her left ring finger. "But Addy didn't try to hurt me, Granny. She was trying to tell me something."

The ghost came to a stop directly in front of Emma. Her hands were on her hips. "I don't give a cow's bell about that. Take the ring *off.*"

Granny was right. The ring had proved itself to be dangerous and unpredictable, even if it was helpful to Emma. She slipped it off and got up. Walking to her desk, she found the ring's pouch and dropped it back in. She yawned and stretched as her eyes searched for a clock. "What time is it?"

"About two in the morning, I think." The ghost moved up to her and looked into her face. "You were asleep nearly four hours before you started getting all peculiar, moaning and stuff. I was worried."

Emma sat down at her desk and held her head in her hands. She was exhausted but wanted to piece together her dream before she forgot it. "I was walking down the narrow street of a town.

The buildings looked old-fashioned, but there were modern cars on the street. At the end of the street was a train station. The name of the town was posted."

"You think that was Addy's home?"

"Could be, but darn if I can remember what the name of the town is now. All I know is that it started with an *m*." She squeezed her eyes shut, trying to recapture the word, but it eluded her. "I was also in a jail cell. An old, dirty one." She opened her eyes and looked at Granny. "The ghosts of men were coming through the walls at me."

"Did they try to hurt you?"

"No, they just filled the cell, surrounding me." Emma swallowed. "One of them had a noose around his neck."

Granny stroked her own neck and shuddered. "Go on to bed, Emma. Maybe it will come to you in the morning. Then again, with any luck, maybe it won't."

"You're probably right, Granny. I am exhausted. Just like last time, the dream took a lot out of me. And I have a show to do tomorrow." She picked up the velvet pouch and started shutting down the office to go inside the house and to her own bed.

"Leave the ring here," the ghost told her.

"Why?"

Standing in front of Emma, the tiny ghost crossed her arms. "Because it's safer here."

"Don't you think the ring would be safer in the house?"

"Not the ring, *you*. *You'll* be safer if the ring stays out here. Less temptation to put it back on."

Emma turned off the TV. "Don't you trust me, Granny?"

"It's Addy I don't trust."

eighteen
. . . .

"GREAT SHOW TODAY, EMMA. One of your best."

"Thanks, Jackie. Congratulations to you, too."

In spite of her nocturnal escapade into Addy's world, Emma had arrived at the studio early in the morning for makeup and wardrobe and to go over her notes. They had one more episode to shoot before taking a break. *The Whitecastle Report* was an hour-long talk show, but it took much more than an hour to shoot. After makeup, she'd greeted her guests and chatted with them briefly about the show's format before they actually got in front of the camera. Today's show had been a panel discussing Stone-henge's history and possible present paranormal activity. Her guests included a British historian, an archeologist, and a modern Druid. Even though Emma had done quite a bit of reading on the subject and had visited the mysterious prehistoric structure years before, the show had been Jackie's idea, and she had been allowed to produce much of it.

Jackie Houchin, a young African-American woman with intelligence as impressive as her attitude, had been dividing her time between *The Whitecastle Report* and a popular travel show ever since Emma's show began. She was doing a bang-up job, and the studio kept giving her added responsibility, but it was her dream to break into mainstream TV.

"How did your interview go with NBC?" Emma asked.

"Okay, I guess. Though I'll bet over two hundred people applied for that position."

Emma hated the thought of losing Jackie, but she knew the young woman would have to move on in order to move up, and she was talented enough to deserve the chance. But television was a tough business, and talented or not, it might be a long time before Jackie was able to make the jump, in spite of the glowing references from Emma and others who worked with her.

"Keep your chin up. If not this job, something else will open up for you."

"Yeah, that's what my mom says."

"Well," said Emma, giving Jackie an encouraging smile, "I'm a mom, and I'm telling you the same thing."

After Jackie left her office, Emma opened her laptop and started poking around on Google. She hadn't had time to research what she'd learned from her dream the night before and was eager give it a try. Maybe if she started on the puzzle now, she might jiggle enough memory loose to finish it up later at home. She still couldn't remember the words on the sign at the train station, and it poked at her like a sharp stone in a shoe. She had more now than just an *m*. It was two words—two short, choppy-sounding words, the first of which started with an *m*.

Sitting back in her desk chair, she closed her eyes and tried to piece together the dream from the night before.

"Emma, wake up."

Emma opened her eyes to find Granny staring at her. "I am awake, Granny. I was just trying to remember my dream from last night."

"For a minute I thought you'd put that darn ring on again."

"The ring is at home, in my parents' safe."

"Good," Granny proclaimed with a downward jerk of her head.

"I still can't remember the name of the town posted on the train station. It's really bothering me."

"How about other landmarks?"

Emma gave it more thought. "The town looked more East Coast in design—and historical, like it was being preserved. There were mountains or large hills all around, covered with trees." She paused a moment to filter through her memory. "And a river, I think. Just past the train station, I'm sure I saw a river."

"That could be most anywhere."

"That's what's so frustrating." Emma set her fingers lightly on the laptop's keyboard as if it were an Ouija board that would lead her to the answer. "And a library. I know I saw a brick library with a sign giving its name. Remembering that name should give me a start." She looked again at Granny. "Argh! I have nothing to go on except that, and it's so frustrating. I can't research it if I don't have a starting point."

Emma's fingers stayed on the keys, itching to move and bring to life the memory caught in her head. Again she closed her eyes. Once more she pictured herself walking down the street of the town and passing the library. Her fingers started moving—*d-o-m-m*. Then they stopped.

"You got it?" asked Granny.

Emma opened her eyes. "It started with a *d*. Dommick, Dommenic, or something like that."

"A *d* library in an *m* town." Granny pointed to the laptop. "Try putting that into that there Google thingy."

"I still need more to go on." Emma took a deep breath and rubbed her temples, hoping it would come into her thoughts if she emptied them of stress. "A *d* with two *m*'s."

"Try going down the alphabet and sounding it out."

"That's a great idea, Granny."

Emma swiveled her head around, trying to relax even more. The movement created faint snaps and pops. "I need a massage."

Pushing thoughts of a relaxing massage out of her head for the moment, Emma got to work by closing her eyes again. "Dammick. Demmick. Dimmick. Dommick. Dummick." None of them held up a hand to get her attention. She tried again, reciting each more slowly. "Dammick. Demmick. Dimmick. Dommick. Dummick."

"Should I come back when you're not doing voice exercises?"

Startled, Emma popped her eyes open and sat up straight, snapping her head in the direction of the voice. At her office door stood Dr. Quinn Keenan, one of the guests on her show that day.

"Look," said Granny with enthusiasm, "it's Indiana Jones."

Emma was about to remind Granny that Indiana Jones was not a real person but stopped herself. She spoke so naturally to Granny that sometimes she forgot others could not see or hear her, much less believe in her existence. Instead, she smiled in the direction of Dr. Keenan, noting to herself that he did have an Indiana Jones appeal about him.

Dressed in jeans and a khaki shirt with a tweed sports jacket, Dr. Keenan positioned his tall, fit body in the doorway, one hand raised and posted against the frame. It was a confident, cocky pose. Emma had read his bio. He was forty-eight years old and from Philadelphia, with a PhD in archeology from Columbia and a master's degree in ancient civilizations. He'd worked with the Stonehenge Riverside Project for a number of years before recently returning to the States.

"Dr. Keenan," she began, instinctively pushing her bobbed hair away from her eyes. "I'm sorry I didn't see you there. I thought all the guests had left."

"I did leave—then a phone call brought me back."

Granny cleared her throat. "Ask him in, you little fool."

Resisting the urge to frown at the ghost, Emma indicated a chair across from her desk. "Please come in."

Dr. Keenan smiled and settled into the chair. "Thank you." He looked around her office, his eyes coming to rest on a photo of Kelly taken in Europe the summer she graduated high school. "That your daughter?"

"Yes, that's Kelly. She's just finishing up her sophomore year at Harvard." Emma's voice tinkled with pride.

"She looks a lot like you. Same color hair and Wedgwood-blue eyes."

"Uh-huh." Emma liked his flirtation but wasn't about to appear easily taken in. "She also has her father's sharpness of tongue, though she's better disciplined with it."

"Ah, yes. Your ex is the infamous Grant Whitecastle, is he not?" Dr. Keenan stifled a chuckle.

Grant wasn't a topic Emma enjoyed visiting with strangers, or even with friends. "Do you have children?"

"Yes, a son named Peter. He lives in New York. I'm heading there tomorrow morning for a visit."

"Sounds lovely." Emma decided to move along the small talk. "What did we forget, Dr. Keenan?"

"Forget?" His voice was slightly on the husky side and easy, like warm slippers for the ears.

"You said we called you back."

"Oh, that. No. The call wasn't from your studio. It was from a friend of mine who lives here in LA. We had dinner plans, but something came up. So now I have reservations at Craft and no dinner companion. I was hoping you might let me take you to dinner as a thank you for having me on your show."

"A date," Granny gushed. "Hot diggity! Indiana Jones is asking us out on a date."

Once again, Emma wanted to snap at Granny but held her tongue, something that was getting more difficult to do as Granny danced around like a fairy with a hot foot.

"Boy." Granny circled Dr. Keenan. "I thought that Max Naiman was a hunk, but this guy takes the cake."

Emma had to agree with the giggling spirit. Dr. Keenan's easy good looks were something she'd noticed before—the first time when reviewing the photo attached to his bio. His tanned face played host to rugged features, including a slightly askew nose and eyes the color of faded emeralds. Surrounding his eyes and quick-to-smile mouth were deep sun lines. His hair was streaked with gray and sun bleached to a dusty brick. He wore it longer on top, swept back away from his face, except for one wayward lock that flopped close to his left eye. Emma fought the urge to reach out and push it aside, as she'd done with her own a moment before.

"I'm sorry, Dr. Keenan," Emma began.

"Quinn or QC, please."

"Excuse me?"

"Please call me either Quinn or QC," he told her.

"*QC*, as in quality control?"

He flashed her a sexy smile of small, even teeth. "Exactly. It stands for Quinn Charles, but in college pals started calling me QC because I was so fussy about details. The name stuck. My son is Peter Charles, or PC."

Emma laughed. "I don't know if you're kidding or not."

"It's true. Everyone but his mother calls him that."

"And is he politically correct?"

"PC is of mixed race, gay, and works for Jon Stewart. You decide."

It brought out another laugh. "Your invitation is lovely, but I'm afraid after I do some research here, I'm heading home. Fighting traffic into Century City isn't exactly on my list of fun things to do on a Tuesday night, no matter how charming the invitation."

Granny was exasperated. "You're not turning him down, are you?"

"We don't have to go to Craft," he told Emma. "That was the request of my prior dinner partner, who works in that part of town."

From the way Quinn referred to his now-defunct dinner companion, Emma was sure it had been a woman.

"Tell me where you'd prefer to go," he offered.

"Seriously?" Emma leaned forward, her hands clasped together and resting on her desk. "Right now I'd like to go deep into my memory and retrieve a piece of forgotten information."

"Is it for a future show?"

It wasn't, but Emma wasn't about to tell a man called QC about Addy and the ring. "It might be; I'm not sure yet. It's a place."

"Places are my specialty." The archeologist leaned back and stretched out his long legs. "Come on," he challenged. "Tell me what you have so far. If I help you remember, you go to dinner with me."

Granny hopped up and down. "Oh boy, a game! I hope he wins."

Emma pursed her lips and twitched them back and forth as she surveyed Quinn. There was no way he was going to be able to find Addy's town any more than she could. She glanced over at Kelly's photo and let her eyes wander to the frame next to it. It was a photo of her with Phil. Their arms were wrapped around each other, and they were laughing. Quinn noticed her diverted attention.

"That your current husband?" The way he said *current* made it sound like there might be a succession of husbands in Emma's life down the road.

She turned her attention back to him, her face serious. "No, but he is a man I'm involved with."

"Are you thinking he wouldn't like it if you went to dinner with me?"

"You're a guest of my show, Dr. Keenan. He would understand."

"So it's a yes?"

"You are persistent, but you haven't won our bet yet." She looked at him, trying to decide how to handle the situation. "Tell you what: you help me find my missing library, and I'll go to linner with you."

Quinn leaned forward. "Linner?"

"That's what my friend Tracy calls it when you dine too late for lunch and too early for dinner."

"Doesn't exactly sound like fine-dining hours."

"There's a very good café right down the street from here that serves all day."

"Denny's?"

In spite of her resolve to remain unmoved by Quinn's charm, Emma let out a short laugh that came close to a snort. "You'll find out if you get that far."

Quinn got up and shrugged off his jacket, tossing it across the back of another chair. "Bring it on," he challenged.

For a brief moment, Emma latched her eyes onto his. They were deep and wide, warmth mixed with impish intelligence. She wondered what she was getting herself into.

"The names you heard me reciting are close to the name of a library I'm trying to remember," she told him. "I was about to start plugging them into Google to see if I could get a hit. I think the library is also made of red brick."

"Have you been there?"

"No, it's just something … something I once read about and want to research."

He studied her with curiosity as he gestured toward the keyboard. "Let's see what comes up."

Emma tapped in the first possibility—Dammick. Nothing, although it did suggest an Arden-Dimick Library in Sacramento, California. She clicked on the link for that library.

"That's a brick library," noted Quinn as he looked over her shoulder. Hovering over her other shoulder was Granny.

Emma shook her head. "It's too modern. The place I'm looking for looks Victorian."

"The building?"

"The whole town. Victorian and in a valley surrounded by hills and trees."

Quinn gave her an odd look but said nothing.

Emma tried the next one—Demmick. Nothing again, but the search gave her a couple of other suggestions. The first was a library called Booth and Dimock Library in Connecticut. The link brought them to the home page for the library and a photo of a large red brick building.

"How about that?" asked Quinn. "It's not Victorian, but it's definitely old."

The building in the photo was large and beautiful, with a white steeple and tall white pillars. "Too grand."

"Where exactly did you first learn of this library you're seeking?"

Emma ignored his question and went back to the search page to investigate the other suggestion—a Dimmick Library in Pennsylvania. The home page was green and offered up a lot of information, such as hours and services. She scrolled down until she found a photo of the building.

"That's it!" Emma squealed. "That's the building I saw in my dream."

"Are you sure?" asked Granny.

"I'm positive."

Quinn backed away and moved around the desk. He took his seat and stared at Emma, his eyes brimming with curiosity, his mouth pursed. "A dream? You saw that library in a dream? You said you'd read about it somewhere."

Emma looked down at her hands. The cat was out of the bag. Would he think her nuts? Taking a deep breath, she straightened her shoulders and met his stare. "It was a dream, Dr. Keenan. I saw this place in a dream, a rather disturbing one. Considering what my show is about, you shouldn't be surprised."

He leaned back, crossing one leg over the other in amused relaxation. "On the contrary, I'm not. I'm curious. Tell me what else you saw."

Emma didn't answer. Instead, she studied the photo on the web page. "It says here it's located in Jim Thorpe, Pennsylvania." *Pennsylvania.* Mr. Sachman had said his friend had purchased the original ring from somewhere back east. The dots were beginning to connect.

She looked across the desk at Quinn. "If memory serves me, Jim Thorpe was from Oklahoma. Why would a town in Pennsylvania be named after him?"

"After he died, his remains were sold to the town," Quinn explained. "They constructed a memorial to him and renamed the town. Probably some sort of bid to bring in tourists."

"You know this place?" Her surprise was short-lived as she remembered he was originally from Pennsylvania.

"I've been there. It's a charming historical town near the Poconos. It was called Mauch Chunk long before it became Jim Thorpe, and it has a very interesting history."

Mauch Chunk—the two words flashed before Emma's memory like a neon sign. They were the words she had seen on the sign at the train station.

Like sparrows fleeing a hawk, Emma's fingers flew over the keyboard of her computer until they located the website for the town. A menu of links was listed on the left-hand side. One link was for a photo gallery. A quick click and she was face to face with photos of the town. She scrolled through them, stopping at one in particular. It was the street she'd walked down in her dream. A few photos later, she saw the hotel with the iron grill work, then the train station and the clock tower.

She let the slide show of Jim Thorpe photos play, one after the other, while Quinn and Granny watched her in silence. Something inside Emma stirred with each photo. She'd been here before—maybe not physically, but she'd seen this town in the depths of Addy's ring.

When the slide show was done, Emma clicked back several photos until she saw the one for the Old Jail Museum. She hadn't seen the outside of the jail in her dream, only the inside. Going back to the town's website, she navigated the link to historic attractions. From there she found the website for the Old Jail Museum. As soon as she viewed the photos, she let out a gasp.

Quinn shot forward. "You okay?"

Granny put her face close to Emma's. "Emma, what is it?"

"Granny," she said, tapping the computer screen and totally forgetting about Quinn, "I must go here."

"Are you all right, Emma?" Quinn asked again as he came around to her side of the desk and stood next to her. His eyes scanned the computer screen, taking in the photos of the dank, dirty prison. "This is the old jail in Jim Thorpe. It's a museum now."

Goose bumps the size of small green peas broke out on Emma's arms as she navigated through the website, finding even more chilling photos of the prison. One showed a wooden gallows, another a hangman's noose. She started shivering.

"Are you alone, Granny?" she asked, still not caring if Quinn heard her or not.

"Yes, I am, Emma. Whatever is making you shiver is coming from those photos. Is that the jail from your dream?"

"Yes, it is." She pointed to one of the cell photos. "I was inside one of these cells."

Quinn looked around Emma's small office. He saw nothing outside of generic furniture. "Who are you speaking to, Emma?"

Dragging her attention away from the screen to Quinn, she said with the bluntness of a karate chop, "The ghost of my great-great-great-grandmother."

She waited for him to challenge her, to show disbelief or mockery, but instead Quinn studied her face again, then reached out and touched it. It was a light touch, just the tip of two fingers against her smooth left cheek, as if she'd disappear before his eyes if he dared to press harder. She didn't move away, but she didn't encourage him. Sensing he was trespassing, he removed his hand.

"But you said you've never been to Jim Thorpe."

"I haven't," she affirmed. "I saw it in a dream just last night."

Quinn squatted down in front of Emma. After a brief hesitation, he took one of her hands in one of his and held it like a fragile egg. She didn't pull away. "Tell me about it, Emma. Tell me about the dream."

When she hesitated, he gave her a smile of encouragement. "In my line of work, I've seen many strange and bizarre things. I've met many people like yourself all around the world—people who have connections to other worlds and beings."

He pointed to the computer screen with his free hand. "That prison has a very specific history. In the late 1870s, unjustly accused and convicted men were hanged there, railroaded by the wealthy owners of the mines in which they worked. They were called the Molly Maguires. Ever hear of them?"

"I sure did," Granny said. "It was in the newspapers even in Julian. It happened several years before I was hanged myself. The papers said those Irish men were traitors and conspirators— downright criminals."

"Granny said the men were convicted criminals."

"They were working men speaking out for better conditions in the mines. They wanted fair treatment and better wages to support their families. The owners of the mines squashed them like bugs and labeled them murderers and criminals. The investigations, arrests, and even the trials were all handled by people connected to the mining companies."

What did hanged miners have to do with Addy and her vengeful behavior? Emma couldn't see the connection. "There were men in my dream. The ghosts of men in dirty work clothes. I was inside a cell like this one, and they came through the walls at me."

"A cell like that one there?" He tapped one of the photos.

"Yes, there—where manacles are attached to the wall, and there's almost no light."

"That was a solitary confinement cell. It's in the dungeon of the prison."

"So you've been there? Inside the jail, I mean."

"Absolutely."

She clutched the hand that held hers with urgency. "I must go there, Quinn. As soon as possible."

"The jail is closed until Memorial Day weekend, but I know the owners. Maybe they will let us inside before then."

"Us?" Granny asked. "Is Indiana coming with us?"

Emma was wondering the same thing. She slipped her hand away from his. "I would appreciate any help you can give me, Quinn, connecting with the owners. And the thumbnail of the history of the place was very helpful, but I need to go on my own."

Pushing back her desk chair, she got up. "My show may be public, but the contact I have with spirits personally is very private. This situation doesn't just involve dead people but people still alive. I need to protect their privacy. I'm sure you understand."

Quinn stood up. Although Emma was tall, he was nearly a half-foot taller. He put his hands on her shoulders. "I want to help you, Emma. I'm professionally fascinated by this ... and personally fascinated by you."

She slipped out of his grasp and moved away, her mind working overtime to sort out her next move.

"I need to take a rain check on that dinner, Quinn."

"Okay, dinner's off, but at least you've dropped the *Dr. Keenan* again." He watched her with the cunning of a fox.

"I'm sorry, but I want to go to Pennsylvania right away, and I have some things I need to attend to before I go, including contacting the owners of that jail."

"As I said, I'd be happy to do it for you."

She picked up a business card from a stack in a holder on her desk and scribbled down her cell phone number and personal email address. "I know it's an imposition, especially with you flying to New York tomorrow, but it would be a great help." She slipped him the card. "They can reach me by phone or email. Tell them I plan on being in Jim Thorpe no later than Friday and would appreciate meeting with them and seeing the prison."

"Frankly," Quinn said, looking at Emma's card, "I think they're going to be very excited to meet you. They give ghost tours at the jail. It's supposedly haunted."

Emma glanced once more at the photos on the computer screen. "There's no *supposedly* about it. That jail is definitely haunted."

nineteen

. . . .

ONCE AGAIN EMMA WAS sitting across from Lainey Naiman at
Serenity Place, this time on a patio just outside the community
room and snack bar. Her plans to leave for Jim Thorpe as quickly
as possible were not jelling up. Quinn had done his part, and in
short order Emma had received an email from Betty Lou McBride,
one of the owners of the Old Jail. As Quinn predicted, the
McBrides were excited at the prospect of meeting Emma but
would not be available until the following week. This Sunday was
Mother's Day, Betty Lou had explained, and they would be tied up
all weekend with family. She suggested that Emma visit Jim
Thorpe after that.

In her excitement over finding Addy's home, Emma had forgotten about Mother's Day. She'd even bought the cameo from
Sachman's for Elizabeth. This was also Phil's last weekend in town
before his trip with his sons. The Millers and Emma had planned
on going to Julian for the weekend. She'd invited Keith Goldstein
and was going to invite Lainey, though she hadn't heard from

Keith since Summer's death. Frustrated by the delay and antsy to deal with Addy, Emma made plans to fly to Jim Thorpe first thing on Monday morning.

After spending much of Wednesday communicating with the McBrides and ironing out her travel plans, Emma had decided to head to Julian on Thursday morning, ahead of her parents, and see Lainey on the way. She'd called Dr. Kitty to clear a time and was told to be there by ten thirty, before Lainey had lunch and got down to her afternoon classes and activities.

Lainey played with her eco-friendly reusable water bottle, turning it around in her hands. "You said on the phone you know why I tried to kill myself. Is that true or just another psychological theory to add to everyone else's?" In spite of the sarcasm, Lainey's voice held hope in a fragile grasp. Holding up a hand, she started ticking off points. "My mother is controlling and doesn't love me. I'm not over my father's death. I hate Linwood. Abandonment issues. What do you have to add to the list? Oh, and let's not forget to add my fiancé's infidelity and a friend's death by dropping from the balcony of my home."

Before seeing Lainey, Emma had spoken with Dr. Kitty. Even though the doctor had made it clear in their last meeting that she considered ghosts hooey, Emma felt she needed to tell the doctor what was going on. Being a Hollywood wife had taught Emma a few tricks, like not being shy about dropping names if it could open doors. In this case, Emma dropped her parents' names, hoping it would give her more credibility. It had. Dr. Kitty's fond memories of Emma's parents and their time in Hawaii paved the way for her to at least listen to Emma's explanation about Lainey's ring.

"I'm not saying I believe this outlandish theory," Dr. Kitty had told Emma in her office just before Emma visited Lainey. "But neither do I believe Miss Naiman is or was a suicide risk. She's a survivor, and she'll survive even these recent events. But something made her try to kill herself, so why not give your idea a go. Just be delicate, if you can. And if Lainey doesn't believe it, don't push the idea."

Emma had agreed.

"Lainey, I'm not going to downplay any of the things you and your doctors have discussed in therapy. I'm sure you have some of those issues. We all have personal problems and tragedy in our lives. But I also know you're a sensible young woman and that you didn't consciously try to kill yourself."

"But something drove me to do it unconsciously?"

"Yes." Emma hesitated, wondering if she should simply blurt it out. It wasn't every day you had to tell someone a ghost was out to kill them. She wasn't sure of protocol.

Pulling the velvet pouch from her purse, Emma emptied Lainey's engagement ring onto the table between them. Seeing it brought tears to Lainey's eyes. She started to reach for it, then clasped her hands together and placed them in her lap.

"Keith called me, you know. Yesterday." She looked from the ring up to Emma. "He said he was sorry and that he'd never stopped loving me. He said being with Summer had been a big, stupid mistake."

"He does love you, Lainey. I have no doubt of that."

"He asked if there was some way I could forgive him."

"Can you?"

Lainey sniffed back the tears as she grabbed for a napkin from the dispenser on the table. "I don't know." After a brief silence, Lainey added, "But he also said I should listen to you." She gave Emma a weak smile. "Is it your job to convince me to go back to him?"

"No, Lainey, that's not my job. When all this is over, you two should privately work out your problems like any other couple."

With caution, Emma picked up the ring and placed it in the palm of her hand. There was no time like the present to jump into the deep end of crazy talk. "Lainey, I know this is going to sound nuts to you, but I believe it was this ring that caused you to try to kill yourself."

Lainey was in the midst of taking another sip from her water and nearly gagged at the words. She stared at Emma. "My *ring*? Are you kidding?"

"No, I'm not. You know that I'm involved with the paranormal, don't you?"

Lainey nodded. "Yes. I've seen your show, but I didn't realize you believed all that stuff personally. I thought you were just the host." She paused. "I once asked Kelly about it, but she just said it was your job."

What was Kelly supposed to say? Emma knew Kelly believed in Granny's existence, but talking about things like that with her friends was probably more distance than her daughter was willing to travel for the time being. And it was probably for the best.

"It is my job, but I'm also in contact with various ghosts and spirits."

Lainey's eyes popped open with expectation and more hope. "Have you seen my father?"

"Yes, Lainey, I have. He's with you a great deal. He's probably the reason you managed to thwart your own suicide attempts at the last minute. He was watching over you and protecting you."

The young woman closed her eyes as her tears changed from drips to heavy rain. "I always thought I could feel him near me, but I dismissed it as wishful thinking." Using the napkin, she blotted her eyes again. "Is he here now?"

Emma smiled to herself, noting how quickly people believed in spirits when it brought them what they sought emotionally, whether it be closure of a loved one's death or comfort. She looked around but couldn't see any ghosts, save Granny, who was hovering by the edge of the building, lost in her own interests.

"No, Lainey, he's not. But he was here the last time I visited, and he seems to spend quite a bit of time around you. He's asked me to help you."

Lainey studied the ring in Emma's hand. "But that ring was his. How could the ring want to kill me if it belonged to my father?"

"I believe the ring killed him the same way it tried to kill you."

"You mean my father didn't commit suicide, like my mother thinks?"

"Not any more than you did." Emma picked the ring up from her palm, holding it by the lower edge so the huge diamond faced skyward. It flickered with an internal fire enhanced by the late-morning sun. "As outrageous as it sounds, I believe the spirit of a young woman inhabits this diamond. What I've been able to determine so far is that her name is Addy, and she was an abused wife who lived in a small town in Pennsylvania in the late 1800s. I also believe she hanged herself when she was about your age."

Lainey leaned back, away from the ring.

"I don't know why she's going after people who wear this ring," Emma continued, "but I need to find out before she kills again."

Lainey looked up at Emma with saucer eyes. "Kills *again*?"

"I was able to trace some of the history of this ring. Many of the prior owners killed themselves. Summer Perkins was wearing it right before she fell."

A hand shot to Lainey's mouth to squelch her terror. "My ring killed Summer?"

"The night before, when she and Keith were drinking, she tried on your ring and forgot to take it off. The next morning I believe the ghost in the ring enticed her up onto the railing. Summer was behaving in a very antagonistic manner right before then."

"But neither Keith or the police said anything about the ring being linked to Summer's death."

"They know nothing about it. When Keith was in the other room letting the police in, I saw the ghost and realized the ring was the connection. I convinced Summer to take it off, thinking it would save her, but it was too late. Addy had too much influence over her. Summer managed to get the ring off but fell anyway."

Lainey put her water bottle down on the table. Getting up from her seat, she wandered to the edge of the patio, where she leaned against a support beam. She stared out over the peaceful grounds, her arms crossed in front of her defensively, as she tried to digest what Emma had just disclosed. She shivered slightly in the warm sun. Giving her time alone, Emma remained at the table and watched the activities of other residents and staff. In the distance she heard a lawn mower.

Granny floated over to Emma. "I gotta tell you something."

Emma whispered to Granny. "Can it wait? Lainey's in a lot of distress right now."

The ghost danced from foot to foot like a child needing to pee. "I think it's important."

"Okay, then."

"There's a man over by the edge of the building. I think he's spying on you."

That got Emma's attention. She started to turn to look, but Granny stopped her. "Don't look. He'll know we're onto him."

"What does he look like, Granny?"

"He's dark skinned. Young. His hair's all snaky."

"He has dreadlocks?" When Granny seemed confused, Emma added, "His hair is twisted into lots of skinny ponytails?"

"Yeah, like I said—all snaky."

It sounded like the yoga instructor Lainey had pointed out the last time she was at Serenity. Emma searched her memory for his name and came up with *Jamal.*

"He works here," she told Granny, keeping her face turned away from the side of the stucco building. "Dr. Kitty probably recruited him to make sure I didn't overstep my bounds." She paused to think, not sure if her conclusion was on target. "Still, let's be sure. Can you keep a close eye on him for me?"

Granny gave her a short salute. "I'm on it, Chief."

As soon as Granny headed off on her assignment, Emma pushed Jamal out of her mind and concentrated again on Lainey. She got up and went to the young woman; standing next to her, both of them focused their eyes on the rolling green lawn. Lainey had stopped shaking and was more composed.

"So, what now?" Lainey finally asked, still not looking at Emma.

"I'm going to Addy's hometown in Pennsylvania next week. I need to find out why she's killing people. Maybe I can bring her enough peace so she'll stop."

"And the ring?"

"I want to take it with me. I think it will help to return Addy to her home." Emma turned to Lainey. "I want you to sell me the ring."

Lainey jerked her head in surprise. "Sell it to you? But why?"

"I don't know what will happen to the stone once Addy is faced with her past, and it's too valuable to not compensate you in case it gets damaged."

Lainey returned her eyes to the landscape. "I won't sell it to you, Mrs. Whitecastle, but take the ring and do what you have to do. If the ring survives, it survives, and I'll deal with it then. If it doesn't," she shrugged, "I'm not out anything. Not really. My mother bought that ring for my father. It was supposed to represent a renewal of their relationship, but it was all a sham, like most things with my mother."

"Do your feelings have anything to do with Linwood Reid?"

She nodded. "Everything to do with him." She turned back to Emma. "You were friends with my parents, Mrs. Whitecastle, but did you know my mother was carrying on with Lin back then?"

The disclosure shocked Emma. "No, I didn't."

"Yep, right up until my parents decided to give their marriage a second chance. And how convenient that the great Linwood Reid was there to comfort her after my father died." Lainey's face hardened as she spoke. "And here's another piece of information for you: Lin tried to buy off Keith. Right after we announced our engagement, he offered Keith money to end our relationship and forget about me."

Emma remembered Keith telling her the same thing, but he'd also said he hadn't told Lainey about it.

"Apparently," Lainey continued, "he thought Keith was a gold digger and wanted to protect me." Lainey shook her head. "It's one of the things Keith told me when he called yesterday. He also said my mother later offered him money to stick around and marry me as soon as possible." She smiled for the first time since their meeting began. "He said he told them both to go to hell." She shook her head. "If anyone's a gold digger, it's Lin, not Keith."

It was the same thing Max had told her. "But Linwood Reid is a very wealthy man, why would he be a gold digger?"

"Who knows, but I know my mother has turned all of her assets over to his management. He tried to take control of mine after they married, but they were locked up in a trust managed by my father's lawyer. When I turned eighteen he tried to palm me off on his nephew—some pretentious ass much older than me. But I was onto him."

Emma tilled the information over in her head like fresh soil in a garden. "Lainey, I got the feeling when speaking to your mother that something's amiss between her and Lin. It's almost like she's afraid of him or something. She's very submissive around him and seems unhappy."

She shrugged in response. "I'm not sure what's going on, but I agree, my mother has changed. I've tried to tell her he's just a creepy common criminal in designer suits, but she won't listen."

Remembering what Phil had told her about Linwood Reid, Emma had to agree.

Lainey took a deep breath and uncrossed her arms. She faced Emma, her face softened. "Take the ring, Mrs. Whitecastle. Please. If Keith and I get back together, it will be without that ring. To me, now it will always be what killed my father. There's no way it's going back on my finger, not even if you manage your exorcism."

Emma thought about Isaac Sachman and his interest in the ring. "If the ring survives, I know a jeweler on Fairfax who will gladly buy it from you or trade it for another ring you might like more."

Emma reached out and lightly stroked Lainey's hair. The girl leaned into the affectionate gesture, her eyes welling up again. Realizing Lainey was starved for maternal love, Emma's heart broke. She made a mental note to herself to call Kelly as soon as she could.

"Lainey, would you like to come to my home in Julian for the weekend? My parents will be there, and I've invited Keith, though I haven't heard from him. Dr. Kitty said you would be able to go if you wanted."

"Thank you, Mrs. Whitecastle, Keith did mention it, and so did Dr. Kitty, but let me think about it. Okay?" She wiped her wet face with the shredded napkin still clutched in her hand. "You've given me quite a lot to think about, and I need to sort it all out." She walked over to the table, picked up her water bottle, and took a drink.

"I'm staying in Julian through Sunday. Just call my cell phone, and I'll come over and pick you up."

Back in her car in the Serenity parking lot, Emma placed a call to Kelly. As usual, it went to voicemail. Emma left her daughter a message letting her know she was going to be on the East Coast next week. Maybe after her business in Pennsylvania, she could pop up to Boston for a visit. Kelly was due home soon for the summer, but Emma didn't want to wait to see her.

"Boo!" shouted Granny, popping into the car and scaring Emma.

"For Pete's sake, Granny, even though your voice isn't loud, it's still unnerving when you do that."

The ghost laughed. It wasn't often she caught Emma off guard, and the ornery spirit liked the prank. "310-555-8168," Granny said.

"What?" Emma turned.

"310-555-8168," Granny repeated. "It's a phone number. Write it down before I forget. My memory ain't what it used to be."

Emma punched the numbers into her phone but didn't hit the call button. "Whose number?"

"Don't know, but that guy with the snaky hair called it after he spied on you and told someone everything he heard."

Emma immediately saved the number into her smartphone's memory before it could get lost. "Are you sure?"

"Of course I'm sure. He spied on you. I spied on him. I was looking over his shoulder, memorizing it."

That didn't make sense to Emma. If it was Dr. Kitty having Jamal keep tabs on her discussion with Lainey, he could have easily walked into her office to give her a full report, and it would have been more private. Emma poked at the screen on her phone until she shut off the caller ID feature that would display her number to those she called.

"What are you doing?" asked Granny. "Calling it?"

"Not until I block them from seeing my name and phone number." Done with the task, Emma hit the call button to dial the number Granny had given her. The phone rang several times before voicemail answered. Emma listened in disbelief before ending the call.

"Who was it? That doctor?"

"No, Granny, it wasn't. It was Linwood Reid, Lainey's stepfather."

twenty

· · · · · · · · · · · ·

EMMA HURRIED FROM HER car back to the office area of Serenity. "I forgot to tell Lainey something," she told the receptionist. The woman behind the desk waved her through the wide doors leading to the main part of the property.

Emma made her way through the large waiting area with sofas and chairs arranged in various conversational groupings and headed for the community room. Emma was relieved to see Lainey back to leaning casually against the post. She wasn't happy to see Jamal with her. Granny went on ahead and, without a word from Emma, set up shop next to them to eavesdrop.

Emma had to think fast. As much as she wanted to grab Lainey and drag her away from Jamal, she knew that tactic wouldn't work. Lainey liked Jamal, and it would make Emma seem like a hysteric—especially after the story about the ghost in the diamond. She had to tell Lainey what she knew without coming off as crazy and disruptive to the peace at Serenity.

Before Lainey could see her, Emma went inside and approached the desk. "Do you have a piece of paper?" she asked the receptionist. "I want to give Lainey my daughter's information, and it's probably best to write it down for her."

The woman handed her a half-sheet piece of notepaper and a pen. Emma quickly jotted, *Act naturally. Jamal works for Linwood Reid. Remember, Keith said to trust me.*

"You gotta get out there," Granny said, popping up next to Emma. "Snaky is convincing her to dump Keith for good, leave Serenity, and go back home to her mother."

Folding the sheet of paper, Emma thanked the receptionist and, as calmly as she could, walked back out to the patio. When she caught Lainey's attention, she waved and walked over to her.

If Jamal was bothered to see her, he didn't let on. He was in his early thirties, with the slim, strong body that goes with being a professional trainer. His workout clothing, black shorts and a tank top with neon blue racing stripes, fit him like a glove, showing off his buffed biceps and thighs to their best advantage. His dreadlocks were pulled back, fastened in place behind his head. He gave Emma a friendly nod of greeting when Lainey introduced them.

"Did you forget something, Mrs. Whitecastle?" Lainey asked her.

"Yes, I did." She held up the folded sheet of paper. "Kelly wanted me to pass along this note to you. It's important, so maybe I should wait for you to read it in case you have a response."

Emma turned to Jamal and smiled. "Kelly is my daughter. She and Lainey have been friends since they were little."

The yoga instructor smiled back, his smile wholesome and healthy-white against his mocha skin. "Lainey has mentioned Kelly."

Placing a hand gently on Lainey's arm, Emma guided her a few steps away from the post and turned her slightly, hoping to keep Lainey's face away from Jamal's sharp eyes. She handed her the note and held her breath as Lainey read it.

"This can't be true." Lainey's words were short and incredulous. She started to turn to Jamal, but Emma cleared her throat in warning, stopping her.

"It is. Kelly wanted you to be one of the first to know."

"I'll need a minute to think about this." Lainey studied the note with hard eyes, as if the words might change if she looked away.

From behind them, Jamal said, "Sounds like girl talk. I'll shove off and let you ladies chat." He reached out and touched Lainey's shoulder. She snapped the note shut.

"Will I see you for class later on?" he asked.

Lainey glanced over her shoulder. As a second thought, she tossed him a small, tight smile. "Absolutely, Jamal. Can't wait."

As Jamal took his leave, Emma looked in Granny's direction, trying to give her nonverbal instructions. The ghost understood.

"Right," Granny said. "I'll follow him and see what he's up to."

"Are you sure about this?" Lainey asked, her face twisted with concern.

"Yes. I overheard him talking on the phone as I was leaving." It was a lie, but Emma didn't think this was the right time to explain about Granny. "I could be wrong," she quickly added, "but he was standing by the edge of the building when we were talking before.

I think he was listening. And I don't think there are too many Linwoods in the world, at least not connected to you or this place."

"You actually heard him say Lin's name."

"Yes." Emma swallowed the lie in disgust. Phil was right, she was becoming adept at all kinds of unsavory behavior, but right now it was important to protect Lainey.

"Why would Linwood Reid be following your every move?"

"He always has, Mrs. Whitecastle." She dropped down into a chair at a nearby table with a weariness too old for her youth. "As soon as I returned from Europe, he started watching me like a hawk and tried to marry me off. It was just after I turned eighteen. I stayed with him and my mother for a while, but he gave me the creeps."

Emma's face darkened. "Was he inappropriate with you, Lainey?"

The girl's head snapped up. "You mean sexually?" She shook her head gently from side to side. "No, not at all. But he tried to control everything I did, everyone I saw. Like I told you before, he even tried to convince me to let him handle my money. You know, invest it for me." She snorted with disgust. "But I can read, Mrs. Whitecastle. I'm not some rich, spoiled bimbo with my head in the sand. Lin's been under all kinds of investigation for years. Why my mother didn't know that or didn't pay any attention to it, I have no idea. She's not a stupid woman, but she sure is when it comes to him."

She stood up again and stretched, trying to loosen the ugliness from her body, the note still clutched in her hand. She looked at it again, once more making sure it said what it did. "Keith didn't say to trust you, Mrs. Whitecastle. He said to listen to you."

"Pretty much the same in this instance, don't you think?"

Lainey tossed the remark off with the shrug of youth before continuing. "As soon as I received my inheritance, I moved out. I wanted to get away from Lin. I just know he's trying to get his hands on my money. He's absolutely transparent about it. That's why he tried to buy off Keith. If I don't marry and something happens to me, my mother will inherit my estate and get the remainder from my father's estate. It's a lot of money—much more than my mother has on her own."

A cold ribbon of horror ran through Emma as she remembered that it had been Lin who'd recommended the horrible facility in Baja. Had Lainey not insisted on finding her own help, she might be imprisoned in a place in Mexico, drugged into unconsciousness while Lin plundered her bank account.

"Why didn't you return to Europe or go somewhere else?"

Lainey sighed. "My mother and I aren't close. You know that. But I felt I should stay nearby in case she needed me."

Emma reached out and put a hand on her shoulder. "You always had a good head on your shoulders, Lainey, and a good heart."

"And by staying here, I met Keith. Even if we don't work things out, he's the best thing that's ever happened to me."

Emma let her eyes graze over the grounds of Serenity, looking for any sign of Jamal or anyone else who might be watching them. "Lainey, I think you should come to Julian with me right now, not tomorrow."

"You think I'm in danger here? Even with Jamal around, this place is pretty secure."

"I'd rather be safe than sorry." Emma cut her eyes to Lainey. "Wouldn't you?"

Lainey set her jaw with determination. "Absolutely. I'll go pack."

"Don't let her," said Granny, showing up next to the table. "Snaky's hanging around Lainey's bungalow. I think he's waiting for her."

"No," Emma told Lainey. "I think we should go right this minute."

Lainey studied Emma. "I get the feeling you know something else."

"It's just a gut feeling." Emma patted her midsection. "I think we need to get you out of here as soon as possible. I have clothes at the cabin that will fit you, and we can pick up anything else you need along the way."

After giving the matters three seconds of thought, Lainey started for the front lobby of Serenity. "Let's roll."

"Where are you two off to?" asked Dr. Kitty Garvey when Emma and Lainey crossed through the lobby. The doctor was emerging from a hallway that fed into the large waiting area. With her was the young man Emma had seen playing cards on her last visit. Dr. Kitty gave him some words of assurance and sent him off before walking over to Lainey and Emma with her uneven gait. She stood before them, her hands stuck into the pockets of her white physician's coat, waiting for an answer.

Lainey looked at Emma, waiting to take her cue. Emma wondered if she should tell Dr. Kitty about Jamal. If Linwood Reid had managed to connect with Jamal, he also could've tainted Dr. Kitty. Looking at the doctor, Emma took in the white coat over a flowing and colorful cotton skirt and simple knit top, accessorized with an impressive squash blossom necklace, and decided even if Lin had tried anything with Dr. Kitty, he would have gotten nowhere. Although her look was casual, almost a throwback to the sixties, Dr. Kitty's general air was one of solid competence and professionalism.

"Lainey's coming to Julian to visit me for a couple of days," Emma told the doctor. "You said it would be fine if she wanted to go."

"That I did." The doctor looked over at Lainey, taking in her usual tee shirt and shorts with eagle eyes. "I think it will do you a world of good, Lainey, but won't you need to take something besides the clothing on your back?"

"We were on our way to the front desk to check her out," Emma explained. "Then she'll go get her things."

Observing the nervous behavior of the two women, Dr. Kitty stepped closer, her eyes a warning signal to anyone thinking they were going to BS her. "What's really going on?"

Lainey glanced at Emma, then handed Dr. Kitty the note she still held in her hand. The doctor put on her reading glasses and scanned it several times before motioning for Lainey and Emma to follow her back down the hallway to her private office.

"Jamal knows your stepfather?" she asked Lainey once they were inside and the door shut.

"Apparently so, Dr. Kitty." She looked to Emma for support. "Though it's news to me."

"He was listening in on our conversation," Emma explained. "Then he was overheard speaking with Linwood Reid on the phone. There's no reason for one of your staff to be in touch with Lainey's stepfather."

The doctor gave it some thought. "I quite agree with that, but Jamal has been with us over a year and has never been a problem. On the contrary, he's been an exemplary employee."

"Check the last couple of calls made from his cell phone," Emma persisted. "One of them will be to Linwood Reid."

"People are allowed to know and speak with whomever they choose," Dr. Kitty pointed out. "It's what they say regarding patients that is my concern."

Lainey took a step closer to Dr. Kitty. "Jamal was trying to convince me to leave Serenity and return to my mother's house."

That got the doctor's attention. "Did he say that exactly?"

Lainey shrugged. "He said he doesn't think I need Serenity any longer, but that everyone needs family. He said I was lucky to have one that cared so much for me."

"I see."

The doctor motioned for them to follow her to a side door on the other side of the room. After knocking and receiving no response, she opened the door. It was another office, much like her own except messier. "This is Dr. Mike's office."

They walked through the room toward another door on the outside wall. Next to the door was a large window that looked out onto a small parking area with a tiny carport. There was only one car parked in the stalls.

"This is a private entrance," Dr. Kitty told them as she unlocked the door. "Emma, why don't you go back out the front way. Make sure you say goodbye to whoever is at the desk and that they see you're alone when you leave. Then bring your car to this side area. If Lainey is being watched, I'd rather no one else know just yet that she's left the premises."

twenty-one

. . . .

EMMA CLIMBED INTO HER rental car at the Lehigh Valley International Airport, located midway between Allentown and Bethlehem in Pennsylvania. Her heart beat fast with a mixture of excitement and worry. She'd left Los Angeles at six thirty that morning. After a layover in Atlanta, she landed at Lehigh around five in the evening. According to the GPS in the rental, the town of Jim Thorpe was about a forty-minute drive from the airport.

Lainey hadn't returned to Serenity. She'd been with Emma in Julian since Thursday. When Emma returned to Los Angeles on Sunday to get ready for her trip to Pennsylvania, her parents stayed behind in Julian to keep an eye on Lainey. Everyone, including Dr. Kitty, thought it best if Lainey stayed out of Los Angeles and Serenity for the time being.

Max Naiman was also on board with Lainey's newest, though temporary, arrangements. He had popped in at the cabin to keep an eye on Lainey and had taken up rocking on the porch with

Granny and Jacob. As Phil observed while watching the empty rockers moving back and forth, they were going to need more chairs.

In spite of everything, Lainey was thriving in Julian. She was an adept horsewoman and loved taking rides along the trails with Emma and sometimes Susan. She'd met the Millers years before when she was a girl and got along famously with them now. Through the online program Skype, Lainey communicated with Dr. Kitty and spent time catching up with Kelly.

When Summer Perkins died, Emma had called Kelly to let her know what had happened. Kelly had been nearly hysterical. Summer had been one of her friends, and her own mother had not only witnessed her death, but now was saying something about a ghost being responsible. Since then she'd been avoiding her mother's calls, responding to them through email only. Emma had considered simply letting Kelly think, like most everyone, that Summer had killed herself, but she didn't think it right to lie to Kelly, especially since Emma was getting so involved with the matter. Instead, she gave her daughter some space. She communicated with her by voicemail and read the impersonal return emails with patience.

On Saturday, Keith came down to Julian. He and Lainey spent many hours together, and it seemed like they might be able to work things out. Emma was happy for them. Keith seemed like such a nice, level-headed young man. When Lainey explained to him about the ring, he gave it a lot of thought before swallowing the theory, but he seemed relieved to think it might be a ghost trying to kill Lainey and not the idea of marrying him.

Shortly after leaving the airport and getting on the highway, Emma slipped on her phone's earpiece and checked her voicemail. The first call was from Phil. He was checking in from his trip. Contact with him was going to be sketchy over the next few weeks, as there would be days when he would not be accessible by phone. He said he loved her and would call the next chance he got. After a pause, he admonished her to be careful. The next message was from an irate Joanna Reid.

"What have you done with my daughter?" Joanna screamed in a tirade. "I was told she'd left Serenity, but no one knows where she's gone, or they aren't telling me. I know you have her. This is kidnapping, Emma Whitecastle. You have a daughter. Leave mine alone."

Lainey was free to tell her mother where she was. Even Dr. Kitty had made it clear it was up to Lainey to make that decision. Obviously she had decided not to let Joanna know. Emma didn't blame Lainey for keeping her mother in the dark, especially knowing Lin had placed a spy at Serenity. Dr. Kitty had informed them on Saturday morning in a quick call that she'd kept an eye on Jamal and when he had finally inquired about Lainey's whereabouts, she had pulled him into her office for questioning. At first he claimed he had no knowledge of Linwood Reid, but he finally caved under the fierce scrutiny of the two Doctor Garveys, admitting he'd been paid handsomely to keep an eye on Lainey, but that was all it was, watching over her and reporting to her stepfather how she was doing. He lost his job.

The next call was from Kelly—a half apology for being so distant. "I know you're just trying to help, Mom, but this is pretty bizarre, and I can't help but worry about you." She said nothing about Emma coming up to Boston when she was finished in Jim Thorpe.

Emma left a quick message on Phil's phone, letting him know she'd arrived safely in Pennsylvania and wished he was with her. Her next call was to her mother's cell phone, to let her parents know the same thing. Elizabeth reported that Lainey was doing fine and that the two of them had gone into town to have lunch. Her father and Phil's uncle were off playing golf. Her mother even reported that Dr. Kitty had called to say she and Dr. Mike were planning on visiting Julian in a few days and would stop to see Lainey. Emma smiled, knowing her mother was taking good care of her charge. She knew Elizabeth and Susan would gather around Lainey like protective headgear, spoiling and pampering her with kindness while serving up solid common sense. It was what the girl needed.

Following the instructions given by the mechanical voice of the GPS, Emma exited the main highway and continued along a scenic country road lined with thick groves of pines and other trees. Every now and then she'd pass a cluster of roadside businesses or go through the center of a small town. It was a peaceful drive, especially with the weather much cooler than back in California. She zipped up her jacket and lowered her window, taking in the fresh mountain air.

She was nearly to her destination when she entered a large settlement of houses. She'd set the GPS for the Inn at Jim Thorpe, the hotel where she'd be staying in the center of town, so was surprised when she passed a sign proclaiming she'd already reached the town. The homes were mostly ranch style, not Victorian as in her dream or in the photos she'd seen on the website. According to the GPS, she still had several miles to go before reaching her destination.

Driving along, something to the right of the road caught her eye. She found a place to turn around and went back, turning onto a circular gravel drive that surrounded a pink granite monument. Off to the side was a statue of an old-fashioned football player in action, the ball cradled tight in the crook of his arm while he ran. Surrounding the small park like protective hands was a thick grove of tall trees. They swayed gently in the early evening breeze.

Emma parked the car along the drive and got out to confirm what she suspected—the monument was the crypt of Jim Thorpe, the famous athlete. She'd seen photos of it online. It confirmed she was definitely on the right track.

Back in her vehicle, she continued to follow the directions. It led her through a thickly inhabited town and across a bridge. Emma's breath snagged in her throat as she caught sight of the train station and the clock tower. She tingled from head to foot, as if she'd rubbed a magic lamp or stepped from a time machine. She was in the Mauch Chunk of her dream.

A horn startled Emma. She had been waiting to make a left-hand turn on Broadway and could see the inn from the intersection. It was located on Broadway, just ahead on the right, looking exactly as it had in her dream and in the photos. All the buildings looked the same. She was so lost in her thoughts, she hadn't noticed that the light had turned red, and oncoming traffic was waiting for her to complete her turn.

After pulling into a parking spot in front of the inn, Emma got out of the car and stood for several minutes staring up the slight incline of Broadway. Turning slowly, as if filming a panoramic video, she absorbed the mixture of shops, quaint buildings, and homes, some rundown, others completely restored to their Victorian beauty. When she looked down Broadway, she was facing the same direction she'd taken in her dream. There was the train station and, just beyond it, the river.

Tugging on a chain around her neck, Emma pulled Lainey's ring out from beneath her sweater and fingered it. Before leaving home, she had run a sturdy gold chain through the ring and hung it around her neck. She'd been worried that if someone stole her purse during her travels, the ring would be lost, and Addy would be up to more menace. Emma didn't know if wearing the ring in this manner would have the same impact as wearing it on her finger, but she was willing to take the chance. "Behave, Addy," she'd said to the ring just before tucking it inside one of her bra cups, snug against her skin. "I'm here to help you."

Now in Jim Thorpe, Emma checked the ring. It was warm but only body temperature. She wondered if Addy knew where she was. "You're home, Addy. Now let's find out if you're happy to be here."

Squaring her shoulders, Emma tucked the ring back under her sweater. With one more look at the front of the red brick inn with its cream-colored, scrolled ironwork, she mounted the steps to the entrance.

The lobby was small and quaint and decorated with Victorian furnishings. Across from the main entrance was a wooden staircase, and to the right was the entry to the dining room. A man, his head buried in a newspaper, was seated next to the elevator on a red velvet chair. Emma walked up to the small counter and gave the woman behind the desk her name. The desk clerk registered her, gave her pamphlets on things to do while in town, and handed her a room key.

"Guest parking is behind the inn," the woman told Emma with a smile. "Your room is on the third floor. It's one of our mini suites. The restaurant will be open until nine for dinner."

"Is it okay to leave my car out front until I get settled in?"

"Absolutely, but remember to move it into our parking lot for the evening."

Emma thanked the woman and rolled her suitcase to the small elevator. As she waited, the man seated with the newspaper asked, "You need help with your bag, Miss?"

Turning, ready to thank him yet turn down the offer, she was surprised to see Dr. Quinn Keenan. "What—what are you doing here?"

Quinn calmly folded the paper and placed it on a nearby table before standing up. Dressed in jeans and a sweater the color of wheat, he looked even better than she had remembered. He was wearing glasses with tortoiseshell rectangular frames, adding an appealing bookishness to his devil-may-care adventure image.

"I thought you were in New York visiting your son."

"I was, but you know how it is. After two days, the kid wants the old man gone and his life back." He gave off an easy chuckle. "So I called Betty Lou to see how you two were hitting it off, and she told me you were arriving today. I thought it might be fun to see you in action."

"In action?" Emma shook her head. "Not sure what you mean by that."

He stepped closer. A woodsy soap smell, clean and natural, wafted from him.

"Come on, Emma, you're a ghost hunter. That's why you're here, and I know a lot about Mauch Chunk."

"You mean Jim Thorpe?"

"Except for the movie they made about him, I don't know much." He smiled at his own joke. "But seriously, I do know a lot about the history of this burg. Even did a detailed report on it and the Molly Maguire trials while in school. I'm from Pennsylvania, and I'm Irish. Knowing about this place was mandatory."

The elevator came. Emma stepped into it, rolling her bag behind her. Quinn followed without an invitation. They rode in silence to the third floor. He made her nervous, but not necessarily in a bad way. When they reached her floor, she got out. He followed.

"Your room is down this way," he told her, indicating the corridor to the left.

"How do you know that?"

"Because I asked for the room next to yours, although mine is actually across the hall, and it's not a mini suite. And it doesn't have a view."

Emma stopped short and glared at him, forgetting for the moment how sexy he looked. "Are you stalking me?"

"Yes." The word was blunt, delivered with a deadpan face and no further explanation.

"Dr. Keenan, I am *not* a ghost hunter."

"You're following up on a dream you had that is leading you to a haunted jail. Ghost groupie, maybe?" He looked around. "By the way, did your dead grandmother come with you?"

"Are you mocking me?" She fumed and added with a huff, "And Granny is my great-great-*great*-grandmother."

"I'm not mocking you at all, fair lady. Like I told you, I've witnessed some pretty amazing things in my travels and research, but none have come in such a charming package." His eyes scanned her quickly, assessing the slim-cut jeans, leather boots, and bomber jacket over a pale green cotton sweater. "Usually I find such interesting abilities in gnarled medicine men and toothless tribal matriarchs. Not to mention, again, I'm Irish."

"What does that have to do with anything?"

He looked astounded at her ignorance. "The Irish believe in all kinds of creatures, like fairies and leprechauns—even pookas. Maybe this granny of yours is really a pooka."

Speechless, she stood cemented to the hallway carpet, staring at him like he'd gone mad.

"Didn't you ever see *Harvey*, the James Stewart movie?" he asked when she showed no signs of movement.

"I know what a pooka is, Dr. Keenan," she said, finally finding her voice. "We did a show on pookas and other mythical creatures last spring. And, believe me, Granny Apples is no six-foot rabbit or any other imagined creature." Emma stepped closer and poked toward his chest with an index finger, stopping just short of hitting him with it. "She's the spirit of a woman who really lived and who died shortly after those railroaded miners of yours. And she was hanged, just like them, and for a crime she didn't commit. Sound familiar?"

"Simmer down. I wasn't implying she wasn't real, just that maybe she was something other than a ghost."

"Look," Emma said, trying to get a handle on Quinn's motives while battling her growing attraction to him. "I may not be an archeologist, but I do my research. I almost always visit sites I consider doing a show about. That's why I'm here."

"Liar." He made the accusation with a light, teasing voice, accompanied by a grin.

"I beg your pardon! I certainly do travel to sites. I've even been to Stonehenge." She conveniently left out the part that her visit to the famed ancient site had been years ago.

"I'm sure you do, Emma. You're definitely a professional when it comes to your work." He gave her a smug smile. "But I think you're fibbing about this being part of a future show. I mean, in the end it might be, but for now this is a personal quest." His smile widened. "You're not the only one who can sense things."

Without responding, she grabbed the handle of her bag and pulled it down the short hall, checking doors for her room number. Quinn followed. "It's the last one on the right," he told her. As he passed a door on the left, he rapped his knuckles on it lightly. "This one's mine, in case you're wondering."

"I'm not wondering anything of the sort, Dr. Keenan."

"Aw, come on, loosen up and drop the Dr. Keenan bit. You can't stay mad at me forever."

"Try me."

Stopping in front of the door she was seeking, Emma slipped in the key and opened it. The room was modest but comfortable-looking. Like the rest of the hotel, it was done in the Victorian style, and Emma noted that many of the furnishings looked like genuine antiques. There was a kitchenette with microwave and fridge, a small table with two chairs, a loveseat facing a large TV, and a queen-size bed. Off to the side of the bed, near the entrance to the small but cute bathroom, was a whirlpool tub. Not knowing how long she'd be in Jim Thorpe, she'd chosen the suite for its amenities.

She lifted her bag to the bed and went to one of the lace-covered widows. Pulling the curtain aside, she looked down onto Broadway.

"Good thing you took a mini suite," Quinn told her as he followed her in. "The other rooms are generally quite small. Some, like mine, are rather tiny."

That brought a smile to Emma's face as she remembered her stay at the Julian Hotel. "I've stayed in Victorian-era hotels before. They aren't exactly known for their spaciousness."

Quinn walked deeper into the room. "Yeah, and I bet those Victorians just loved their whirlpools."

In spite of her resolve to remain aloof, Emma laughed.

Encouraged, Quinn joined her at the window and looked out. "Just behind those buildings across the way is Race Street, and on Race is Moya, one of the best restaurants in town." He looked at Emma. "Freshen up and meet me downstairs in ten minutes. You still owe me a dinner."

She turned. His face was close to hers. She knew there were reasons why she shouldn't go to dinner with him, but for the moment they eluded her. "I'll need more than ten minutes."

"No, you won't. You're dressed fine. This town is pretty casual. Ten minutes."

She nodded, giving in. A nice dinner in good company sounded great, and she was as curious about him as he was about her.

He turned just as he reached the door. "Give me your car keys, and I'll move your rental into the hotel lot while you clean up."

With only a slight hesitation, she tossed him the keys to her rental car. If he turned out to be a crook and stole it, it was insured. Quinn was full of surprises, but her astute gut told her grand theft auto wasn't one of his talents.

Moya was a wonderful restaurant. Emma feasted on an apple salad followed by perfectly cooked grouper with crab meat. Quinn had the yellowfin tuna entrée preceded by a goat cheese and asparagus appetizer. They also killed off a particularly fine bottle of wine.

During dinner Quinn tried to pry out of Emma what exactly she was researching in Jim Thorpe, but she'd managed to keep him at bay.

"So, tomorrow," he said, divvying up the last of the wine between their glasses, "how about we have an early breakfast in the hotel dining room, provided you're an early riser. Then I'll show you around the town before you meet Betty Lou at eleven."

"How do you know I'm meeting Betty Lou at eleven?" She sat back in her chair with mild frustration. "Oh, never mind. I'm sure you just charmed it out of her like you did my arrival."

"My charm had nothing to do with it." He motioned the waiter over. "Would you like coffee, Emma? Or any dessert?"

"No dessert, but coffee, please. And make it decaf. I'd better not have anything else or I'll never get to sleep."

"Then how about a little brandy or something else in the coffee to help you?"

"Are you trying to get me drunk?" She said it with a slight smile, in spite of herself.

"Not at all." He winked at her. "At least not on our first date. I was raised better than that."

Emma sat up straight. "This is not a date, Quinn."

"Okay, then I would never get you drunk during our first business meal. How's that?"

"Much better." Emma looked up at the waiter, who stood patiently by. "I'd like a little Grand Marnier in my coffee."

After watching Emma a second, Quinn turned to the waiter. "Make that two decaf coffees with Grand Marnier."

When the waiter left to fetch the coffee, Emma leaned slightly forward. "But you are not coming with me tomorrow."

"Why not? I'm the perfect guide." He leaned forward. "You see, I'm related to the McBrides, on Betty Lou's side. That's why she gave me the information. When they bought this place several years back, out of curiosity I did additional research on its history. I know that jail and this town inside out. Whatever you saw in your dream, with my knowledge, I might be able to help you piece it together."

"I've spent the last few days reading everything I could get my hands on about this place."

"Frankly, Emma, I wouldn't expect anything less of you, but I know where all the bodies are buried. The stuff not in the history books."

Emma looked around the restaurant. There were two other couples left in the place, and one of them was getting up to leave. She watched them. They were a good-looking elderly couple and reminded her of her parents. Her parents would love visiting Jim Thorpe. She made a mental note to remember to tell them about it.

She turned her eyes back to Quinn and found him watching her. He always seemed to be studying her like a specimen—a curiosity he unearthed on one of his digs and wanted to know more about.

"Something's bothering me, Quinn."

"About me or Jim Thorpe?"

"You."

He gestured toward himself with his right hand. "Then let's hear it."

"When we were in my office that day and I was trying to find the library in my dream, you knew all along it was the Dimmick Library here in Jim Thorpe, didn't you?"

"Not entirely, but I had my suspicions it might be." He shrugged. "Victorian, red brick, the sound of the name—it all added up."

"But you didn't suggest it to me. You let me find it on my own, when you could have saved me time. Why?"

Their coffee came. He took a small sip. "Be careful," he told her. "It's quite hot."

He looked across the table at Emma. Her arms were crossed in front of her, her jaw set. She was settled in, waiting for his answer, letting him know she wouldn't move on until she got it. He surrendered. "Because I wanted to see how you worked. You know, how you processed things and problem-solved."

"And?"

"And I'm quite impressed—have been since first meeting you on the set of your show. When I realized it was Jim Thorpe you were looking for, especially Betty Lou's jail, wild horses couldn't keep me from finding out why."

He took another sip of his coffee. "It was fate, you know."

"Fate?"

"Fate that I be on your show at just that moment when you were searching for something I knew a lot about. So why don't you let me help and save you time?"

It did seem reasonable to Emma. "Okay, then. Tomorrow morning, breakfast, then how about a walking tour of the town before I meet Betty?"

"You'll find my rates very reasonable. Dinner tomorrow night should cover it."

Emma held her hand out across the table to shake on it. "But you must allow me to buy tomorrow night. After all, it is a business expense."

He took her hand, and they did an exaggerated shake on the deal. "Now," Quinn said, taking another drink of his coffee, "you ready to tell me about that dream?"

Emma opened her mouth just as her cell phone gave off a soft, insistent tone. She pulled it out of her purse and looked at the caller ID. "I'm sorry, Quinn, but I have to take this call." She got up from the table and stepped down the hall by the restrooms for privacy. She was only gone a few minutes.

"Sorry," she apologized again when she returned.

"Was that the guy in the photo on your desk?"

Emma felt her face flush and did her best to blame it on the booze in the coffee. "Yes, it was Phil. He's on a camping trip with his sons, so his calling time is rather hit or miss."

"How does this guy, this Phil, feel about your otherworld activities? Or can he see and hear them, too?"

Emma laughed, thinking about the first time Phil found out about her and Granny. "When we first met, he called me everything from a liar to crazy to psychotic. Now he and Granny are great pals."

"Seriously? Even though he can't see or hear her? Or has he developed that skill with time?"

"No, he can't see or hear ghosts. But he's very sensitive to when she's around, and they have worked out their own system of communication."

"What about the rest of your family?"

"My mother can hear Granny, but she cannot see her. I'm not sure if she can hear other spirits. Or if she can, she may be choosing to block them out."

"You and your mother." He took another sip of coffee. "Very interesting. Might be a genetic thing. What about your daughter?"

"I don't think she can see or hear them, and I don't think she wants to. She knows about Granny, and of course she knows about my show and other activities, but she seems a little uncomfortable with them."

"Give her time."

Emma played with her coffee cup, rotating it on its saucer. She wasn't sure she wanted to give Kelly time. She liked Kelly just the way she was. "Honestly, Quinn, I'd be very happy if this talent skipped Kelly altogether. Although it's called a gift, I often think it's more of a curse."

twenty-two

FOR THEIR SECOND CUP, Quinn and Emma skipped the coffee and ordered just the brandy.

"So you go around the world from dig to dig?" she asked once she convinced Quinn she wasn't ready yet to share her dream about the Jim Thorpe jail.

"Pretty much. I'm hired to help a year or two on a dig, and sometimes my contract is extended. It's a great way to see the world and meet fascinating people. I was on the Stonehenge project for the past three years. Sometimes, I give lectures at universities."

"And when you're not traveling the world, where do you call home?"

"That would be Philadelphia. Although, technically, my home is really a leased storage locker. Most of my things are there, but when I'm stateside I live with my mother in Philly."

Emma swirled the amber liquid in her brandy snifter and smiled at the small waves.

"What are you grinning about, you minx? The fact that I live with my mother at my age?"

"No. At least not really." She put down her brandy. "I'm laughing because I live with my parents, too. When I separated from Grant, my daughter and I moved in with them. After the divorce was final, they asked if I would stay. It made sense since they have a huge house in Pasadena and travel a good part of the year. I have a home in Julian, but Pasadena is my main residence."

"I've heard of Julian, but I've never been there. It's north of San Diego, isn't it?"

"Yes, in the mountains. It's a lot like Jim Thorpe in that it's a historic town that the residents are preserving as a tourist destination. But it's Western, with Victorian overtones. It's known for apples."

"And this great-great-great-grandmother of yours was from there?"

"Yes. She and her husband, Jacob, settled there originally to hunt for gold. Phil is also from there. We met when I went to Julian to learn more about Granny."

Quinn studied Emma. "I'd love to see it one day. Would you be my guide if I visited?"

"Of course I would. You should come in the fall, when they have their annual apple festival. Although Julian doesn't boast a haunted prison, we do have a tiny two-room historic jail."

They sat quietly for a few moments, sipping brandy and enjoying the warm comfort that had built up between them during the evening.

"Do you ever think about settling down?" Emma finally asked. "Or are you going to wander the globe forever?" She paused, rethinking her questions. "Which really sounds kind of wonderful."

"Not sure. I did try settling down for a while. My ex lives in Los Angeles—that's who I was going to meet at Craft that night. She's a talent agent in LA. When we met, she was really starting to climb in the business, and I had just received my PhD. When she became pregnant, we decided that I should settle in California since she made the most money. It made sense at the time, but I really hated living in Southern California, and I detested the whole show-biz scene. Finally, we called it quits, and I hit the road. Best thing we ever did. PC grew up with two loving parents who are good friends, instead of two unhappy people who felt trapped. I saw PC as much as possible, and when he was older, he visited me on my digs during school vacations."

"I know what you mean," Emma replied with a nod. "After Grant made it big, everything changed, and not for the best. Because of my show's topic and because it's on cable, it's not quite the Hollywood scene, and I like it that way."

Quinn looked around the restaurant, which was now empty except for them. "And I see the paparazzi don't follow you around anymore."

Emma groaned. "You saw some of that, did you?"

He tried to keep his face straight but couldn't suppress a small chuckle. "Only when I was in the States or London. Celebrity gossip is huge in London. I think the highlight was that brawl you two had in a parking lot."

"It wasn't a parking lot," Emma corrected, "it was my parents' driveway. That was last November, after the divorce was final. Since then, we've kept our distance from each other. The paparazzi scum aren't interested in me, only Grant, and I'm thrilled about that."

"I can only imagine what they'd do and print if they knew about your ghost activities and dreams."

Emma shuddered at the thought. "Some picked up on it, but when interest in me died, so did that. I'm sure the ghosts wouldn't like all the publicity."

Leaving the restaurant when it closed at nine, they strolled down Race Street, then back up Broadway to the inn. It was a chilly night with a cold breeze coming off the river on the other side of the train tracks.

"Yesterday," Emma observed as she zipped up her jacket, "I was wearing shorts and a sleeveless blouse."

"Nights will be cool here for a bit yet. You should be warm enough tomorrow during the day without a jacket if you wear a sweater."

At her door back at the inn, they made arrangements to meet for breakfast. "How about meeting me downstairs around nine or nine thirty in the morning?" Quinn suggested.

"Nine is hardly early enough, is it?"

He fingered the collar on her jacket. "Considering your body is three hours behind, it will think it's six. Not to mention you've had a snootful tonight. So sleep well, and get your rest. You don't know what those nasty ghosts have in store for you tomorrow."

"Sleeping in does sound lovely."

"Give me your phone."

"What?"

"Your phone. Hand it over."

She did as he asked, and he punched in some numbers. "There, now you have my cell number stored in your phone." He handed it back to her. "Now call it."

Emma hit the call button, and his cell phone rang. "There," he said, answering and disconnecting quickly. "And now I have yours. In the morning, when you get up, why don't you give me a call and let me know what time you'll be ready? That way you can sleep as long as you wish."

"You're just going to hang around and wait? Seems silly."

"Not at all. I'll have coffee and read the paper. I brought my laptop with me, so maybe I'll even do some work. So you call and let me know when you want breakfast, or even if you'd rather skip it." He gave her an exaggerated bow. "I'm at your service."

"Quinn?"

He'd started across the hall to his own room but turned around.

Emma fought the urge to kiss him, blaming the booze as the catalyst for her feelings. Instead, she opened the door to her room as she glanced back at him. "I had a really good time tonight. Thank you for the lovely dinner."

He shot her a boyish grin. "You're quite welcome. Most charming business meal I've had in a very long time."

Inside her room, Emma plopped down on the loveseat to consider her actions. She loved Phil. She couldn't entertain kissing Quinn while she and Phil were living together as they were, not even if the arrangement was part-time. She pulled off her boots and went to the whirlpool to start the water running. Alcohol or not, she was still on Pacific time, and her body thought it was seven o'clock. A hot bath on top of the brandy and wine might make up the time difference. While the bath filled, she slipped out of her clothes, neatly hanging them in the closet along with the clothing she'd removed from her suitcase before heading out to dinner.

The ring was still there, hanging from the chain snuggled between her breasts. A couple of times during dinner Emma thought she'd felt the ring heat up, but she could have been mistaken. The heat could have been generated from her own confusion about Quinn. Taking off the ring, Emma tucked it inside its velvet pouch and stored it in her makeup case. She still didn't know if wearing the ring around her neck would inhibit Addy's behavior, but she didn't want to find out. She wanted to sleep in peace tonight.

She was submerged in a hot tub of whirling lavender-scented water when her cell phone rang. She'd left it within reach on the wide ledge surrounding the tub in case Kelly called. The caller wasn't her daughter, but Tracy Bass calling from England.

"I have news," her best friend squealed over the air waves as soon as Emma answered. "Big news!"

Emma sat up in the tub, giving Tracy her full attention. "And that is?"

"We're getting married!"

"You and Milo?"

"No, me and Prince Harry." Tracy's sarcasm was short-lived by her excitement. "*Of course* me and Milo, silly!"

"I am so happy for you two."

"Wait a minute—you're not as surprised as I had hoped. Did you know about this, Emma Whitecastle?"

"Umm…"

"Don't lie to me, pal. You're not good at it." Before Emma could say anything further, Tracy gushed. "But of course you knew. The ring Milo gave me is gorgeous. Something tells me you had a hand in that." Now that her initial surprise had been sprung, Tracy's voice lowered to a loud whisper.

"I simply gave Milo some guidance, but he chose the ring himself." Emma turned off the whirlpool to hear better but remained in the tub. "Have you set a date yet?"

"No. We'll work on that when we get home. There are logistics to be worked out."

"You mean your family?"

"Yeah. Even though they aren't wild about Milo, they'll want the wedding in Chicago."

"What about Milo's family? He never talks about them to me, so I'm not even sure he has any."

Tracy sighed. "Until recently, he's never mentioned family to me either, so I'm sure there's a juicy story there. But not too long ago he let it slip that his mother lives in Las Vegas. I don't think he sees her very often. Whenever I mention us going to visit, he changes the subject."

"Makes you curious, doesn't it?"

"You got that right." Tracy paused to catch her breath. "I may not be proud of the nuts on my family tree, but I don't hide them."

Emma glanced at the clock on the nightstand. "Hey, isn't it the middle of the night there?"

"Almost three thirty. Milo's conked out cold. I couldn't sleep, but I waited to call in case you were at the office. Must be what, nearly seven thirty?"

"Actually," Emma said, glancing at the clock by the bed, "make that almost ten thirty. I'm not in California. I'm in Pennsylvania, soaking in an in-suite whirlpool in a town called Jim Thorpe. Got here just this evening."

"Huh?"

"Jim Thorpe, Pennsylvania. It's a small town near the Poconos that's full of ghosts."

"Ghosts aside, you're there because…?"

"Remember that ring I emailed Milo about last week? Seems it's haunted by a homicidal spirit from Jim Thorpe. I came here to see if I could find out more about her."

"Isn't Phil on that trip with his sons?"

"Yes, he left last night."

"So you're ghost wrangling alone? Not sure I like that, especially since you're in unfamiliar surroundings. Granny can only do so much if you get into trouble."

"I'll be fine. It's a charming town, and I'm not alone. An archeologist I had on my show last week is here with me. Seems he's from Pennsylvania and knows a lot about this place."

"An archeologist? So if danger comes calling, you're going to throw a nerdy dirt digger at it?" Tracy laughed.

"Um, it would be more like Indiana Jones swooping in to rescue me. Granny thinks he's Indiana Jones incarnate."

Tracy was silent a moment while the image sunk into her skull. "Is he as cute as Indiana Jones?"

"Cuter." Emma gave Tracy a rundown of Quinn's bio.

"Does Phil know you've invited this life-size action figure along?"

"I didn't invite him, Tracy." Emma heard the defensiveness in her voice and brought it down a notch. "He helped me figure out where Addy—that's the ghost—was from and followed me here. Seems he's related to the people who own this haunted prison I had a dream about, and he got me in for a private showing."

"Sounds reasonable, but watch your step. Okay?"

Instead of answering, Emma swished a hand back and forth in the water, making little waves in the scented bubbles.

"Okay, out with it, Emma. What else is going on?"

Emma continued making small splashes in the water while she tried to piece together her thoughts and feelings into something that made sense. "Do you think, Tracy, that maybe I should try dating other people?"

Now it was Tracy's turn to be silent. It lasted less time than Emma's. "Do you mean other than Phil Bowers? Or other people as in this archeologist specifically?"

Emma told Tracy about her conversation with Susan Steveson, then added, "Tracy, if not for Phil, I'm sure I would have kissed Quinn tonight. I know I love Phil, but now I'm not so sure I love him enough to make a life with him—not if I'm thinking of playing loosey-goosey with other men. I don't want to be that person."

"Being in love with Phil doesn't mean you're dead to other attractions, Emma. But I certainly understand your concern about Phil being the first and only man you've dated since your divorce." She paused to give it thought. While she did, Emma ran more hot water into the tub.

"Emma, do you really want to date this archeologist, or was it just the heat of the moment?"

"If I wasn't involved with Phil, Quinn would probably be sharing this whirlpool with me right now."

"Okaaaay. But I'm not talking about lust fueled by dinner and drinks. You know you can build a life with Phil Bowers. That relationship could go the distance for sure."

"I agree."

"What about this guy? Is he a sprinter or a marathon runner? More importantly, which do you want for your future? There's nothing wrong with the sprinter, as long as you know that's what he is going into it."

Emma thought about Quinn's vagabond lifestyle. Globetrotting and researching ancient civilizations certainly sounded adventurous and romantic, but how could a long-lasting relationship be built if one party's address is a storage locker?

"What do *you* want, Emma? Have you ever asked yourself that?"

"I've always wanted a marriage like my parents. No matter what life has thrown at them, they stand united and unbreakable."

"Your parents are the gold standard of marriage, Emma. They set the bar high. Hell, they're *my* role models."

"I thought I had that with Grant; now I wonder if it's possible to have such a marriage any longer. Maybe it's too old-fashioned for today's lifestyle."

"Love, loyalty, and commitment never go out of style. It just seems more difficult to maintain with all the diversions and romantic mythologies thrown at us by the media." Tracy yawned.

"You need to get to bed, Tracy. So do I. I have my jail tour tomorrow."

"Well, pal, I know you'll do the right thing, but make it easier on yourself and skip the booze and moonlight walks when you're with Dr. Hotsy Totsy. Just think about what you want long-term. And email us tomorrow after you do that research at the jail. I'm sure Milo will want to hear about that."

twenty-three

WHEN EMMA CAME INTO view of the Old Jail, it was as if someone had punched her in the gut.

"You okay, Emma?" asked a concerned Quinn when she nearly doubled over.

"Yes, I'm fine." She stood upright. "Just a small cramp. Maybe something about breakfast didn't agree with me."

"You had oatmeal and fruit. Sure it's not something else?"

"Seriously, I'm fine." Never taking her eyes off the building, she continued walking toward it as if taking her last steps on earth.

Even though she'd only seen a photo of it until now, she wasn't prepared for the emotional impact of seeing the Old Jail in person. It was an imposing gray stone edifice located on upper Broadway, just a short walk up from the hotel. It commanded a large piece of property like a sullen and brooding bully. To the right of the building was a high chainlink fence surrounding a small prison yard. To the left, a parking lot contained one car. Quinn led the way to a short set of steps to a small door that faced the parking lot. The door was unlatched.

"Betty Lou," he called as he stuck his head inside. "We're here."

"Come on in," called out a female voice. "I'm in the parlor."

Quinn stepped aside to let Emma enter first. Just inside the door to the left was a huge kitchen. Straight ahead was a hallway. To the right was a room that had been converted into a gift shop. Glass display counters were lined up on two sides and bookcases on another. On the walls were various prints and posters, including one for a movie called *The Molly Maguires* starring Sean Connery. The floor was scarred wood, clean but left rustic.

A petite woman in her late sixties with fluffy silver hair entered from the next room. She was dressed in jeans and a sweatshirt that sported a logo for the town. On her hands were pink rubber gloves, one of them holding a worn cloth.

"I'm just doing a little cleaning," she explained as she pulled off the gloves and set them down on one of the nearby counters. She looked at Emma. "We're getting ready to open for the season in a few weeks."

Quinn stepped forward and gave the woman a quick hug and a kiss on her cheek. "Betty Lou, thanks for seeing us. This is Emma Whitecastle."

Emma stepped forward and extended her right hand. Betty Lou took it and smiled. "You're even prettier than on TV."

"You watch my show?" Emma was always amazed at the number of people she met who had seen *The Whitecastle Report*.

"Not regularly," Betty Lou admitted, "but I've seen it a few times. Ever since we bought this old place, I've been fascinated by ghosts and the paranormal. I was delighted when Quinn here called to say you wanted to see the jail."

"Wait until you catch the segment of her show I'm on," said Quinn. He turned to Emma. "It airs next week, doesn't it?"

"Actually, it's on this coming Wednesday," Emma told them.

Betty Lou motioned toward the room she'd just left. "Come on in here and sit a bit before I give you the tour."

The room just off the gift shop was a lovely Victorian sitting room with a fireplace. "The warden and his family lived here at the jail," Betty Lou explained. "This was their parlor. The gift shop was their dining room."

Emma took a deep breath, half expecting to sense spirits right away, but she felt nothing. She took a seat and looked around.

"Would you like something to drink?" Betty Lou offered. "We have juices and sodas and bottled water."

"No, thank you, Betty Lou," Emma said, turning to the cordial woman. "We just had breakfast."

"Then let's get to it," announced Betty Lou, obviously excited about the topic. "How much do you know about the history of the Molly Maguires?"

"I admit I knew nothing until Quinn told me about them a few days ago, but since then I've done considerable reading on the topic and the town."

"So you know that one of the convicted men cursed this place?"

"You mean the handprint on the wall?"

"Yes. Before he was hanged, he placed his hand on the wall and declared his innocence. The handprint is still there. No matter what anyone does, it remains. It's been scrubbed, painted over, and even the plaster has been redone, yet it keeps coming back. You'll see it today. There is some discussion as to whether it was Alexander Campbell or Thomas Fisher who did it, but most believe it was Campbell."

Quinn stood by the doorway. "Emma had a dream about this place, Betty Lou, even before she knew it existed."

"Really?" An eager closed-mouth smile crossed Betty Lou's face and her eyes lit up. "How fascinating."

"Yes, I was in one of the cells and a group of men came through the walls at me. One of them, the youngest, was wearing a noose around his neck."

"I think in her dream," Quinn added, "Emma was in one of the cells in the basement."

"My, this is exciting," exclaimed Betty Lou. "It will be interesting to see if you pick up on any ghosts today."

"Do your visitors ever see spirits?" asked Emma.

"Oh my, yes, but none that I know of have ever seen actual people like that, just shadows. You know, like someone just flitted by before you can get a good look. I get the sensation I'm not alone or am being watched quite often. Many visitors have felt the presence of ghosts when they've visited."

It was then Emma saw her first ghost in the jail. It wasn't one of the miners she'd seen in her dream; it was Granny. She materialized next to Quinn and was looking him up and down, feasting on his rugged good looks. "I didn't know Indiana was going to be here," the spirit said with a grin.

Emma wanted to fill Granny in but couldn't in front of Quinn and Betty Lou.

"Betty Lou," Emma began, taking her eyes from Granny, "is there a restroom I could use before we start?"

"Of course. Right this way."

With a slight tilt of her head, Emma directed Granny to follow them.

Betty Lou showed Emma out of the parlor and across the hall to another large room with storage cabinets and cupboards. It looked like a roomy kitchen but without appliances. Under a small window to the right, the ghost of a small child, a young girl in an old-fashioned nightgown, sat playing on the floor. She looked up at Emma, her cherub face blooming with giggles like a flowerbed of spring daffodils. Not expecting to see children in a place like this, Emma was startled. She turned her attention to Betty Lou.

"Did a young child ever die within these walls? It would have been many years ago."

Betty Lou looked just as startled by the question. She stared at Emma, her answer slow and stammering. "Yes, I believe so." She took a deep breath. "Yes," she repeated as she searched her memory. "One of the wardens lost a daughter to influenza. I don't think she was more than four or five years old."

Betty Lou stopped and indicated a small door. Emma opened it to find a small, cheery restroom.

"Just come back to the parlor when you're done, Emma, and we'll start the tour." Instead of leaving, Betty Lou stood looking at Emma until Emma entered the bathroom and closed the door behind her.

After shutting the bathroom door, Emma waited until she heard Betty Lou's footsteps walking away before turning to Granny. "Where have you been?" she asked in a barely audible whisper.

The ghost looked around the small room, examining the framed pictures of flowers on the wall. "Oh, here and there. Nothing exciting about you taking a plane trip, so I thought I'd wait until you got here to pop in." Granny jerked a thumb in the direction of the door. "Though I would have been here sooner if I'd known he was tagging along. Why didn't you tell me?"

"I didn't know myself. He just showed up yesterday. He was waiting for me at the hotel when I arrived."

"Uh-huh." Granny looked at the door, then back at Emma. "I wish Phil were here."

"Why? I thought you liked Quinn."

"I do. He's a tall drink of water in the middle of a scorched desert. But I'd like him a might better if Phil were here."

"Don't be silly. He's just here to help me with this research. He knows a lot about the town."

"I saw the way he was watching you, Emma. If he's researching anything, it's you. He's sweet on you, I tell ya."

Emma flushed the toilet and washed her hands at the sink to make it seem like she'd used the facilities. "Just behave yourself, Granny. Let's not lose sight of why we're here."

"Where's Addy? Did you bring her?"

Emma was wearing a heather gray V-neck sweater over a white tee shirt. Reaching down into her neckline, she pulled out the chain and showed the ring to Granny. "I'm keeping it close but not wearing it. Seems to be working so far."

Emma noticed the ring was warm, and it wasn't from her body heat. Instead of tucking it back into its nest next to her skin, she left it to dangle between her tee shirt and bra.

Just before leaving the bathroom, Emma said, "Granny, I'd like for you to wander around this place and see if any of the resident ghosts know anything about Addy. I haven't seen any adult ghosts yet, but I'm sure they're here."

"Aye, plenty of them in a creepy place like this." Granny shivered.

"But first, could you see why that child's spirit is hanging about? Maybe she needs help reaching the other side."

"I already talked to her. She and I are going for a little walk right after I leave here."

After Granny left, Emma decided she did need to use the bathroom. After a second wash at the sink, she touched the ring under her sweater and took a deep breath. "Okay, Addy, let's find the connection between you and this jail."

Yanking open the bathroom door, Emma came face to face with a ghost. He was tall and slim, with dark hair and a long moustache that drooped down both sides of his mouth like two bushy caterpillars in an embrace. Dark, thick eyebrows hung like awnings over small, intense eyes. It was one of the ghosts she'd seen in her dream. She let out a short, static scream before squelching it.

The ghost stepped closer, almost nose to nose with her. She shivered but didn't move.

"Why are you here?" he asked, his voice neither menacing nor kind.

"You came to me in a dream. You and several other prisoners."

From the corner of her eye, she saw Quinn and Betty Lou watching her from the doorway. Quinn took a cautious step forward, but she held up a hand, signaling him to stay where he was.

The ghost kept his eyes latched on to hers. If Emma wanted to leave the bathroom, she would have to walk through him, and she knew ghosts didn't like that. She'd learned early on that if she wanted answers from spirits, the best way to get them was to be respectful.

She leaned her head closer to the ghost. If he were alive, they would have been touching cheek to cheek. "Who's Addy?"

The ghost disappeared.

Emma slumped back against the doorjamb. Quinn rushed to her side. "Who were you talking to, Emma?"

"Not a six-foot rabbit, that's for sure." She stood straight and shook herself slightly to get her bearings.

"Was it the child you saw earlier?" asked Betty Lou with excitement. "I know you saw her. How else would you have known about her?"

"No, it wasn't the girl, but I don't think she'll be coming back. She needed help getting to the other side. Granny is escorting her."

"Who's Granny?"

Quinn bent down to Betty Lou and whispered, "I'll fill you in later."

"I was just visited by one of the men from my dream." Emma described him.

Without a word, Betty Lou left them, her rubber-soled shoes hitting the floor with steps that sounded like a series of soft thumps and squeaks. She returned a few seconds later with a pamphlet on the Old Jail Museum and the Molly Maguires. She thumbed through it until she came to the page she was seeking. "Was it him?" She offered the booklet to Emma.

The left side of the booklet contained text; the right side, reproductions of drawings. The top drawing was of a man. Emma sucked in her breath and held it.

"It was him, wasn't it?" asked Betty Lou with excitement. "I always felt he was haunting the place."

Emma read the caption out loud: "Alexander Campbell."

Betty Lou tapped the picture. "He's the one most believe left his handprint on the wall."

Emma looked up from the booklet. "May I see the jail now?"

twenty-four

IN THE MIDDLE OF the hallway that connected the back door, kitchen, gift shop, and other downstairs rooms was a small ante-room. Betty Lou explained the double entry system to them—how the outside door, with its double sturdy bar locks, was secured after a prisoner entered the small holding room and before the iron gate to the cell block was unlocked for him and the prison guard to enter.

Emma stood at the threshold of the imposing iron gates and looked into the main cell block. The whitewashed walls were thicker than in the rest of the building. Betty Lou further explained how the jail was built in 1871 and had been in continu-ous use until as late at 1995.

As she stepped from the outer room through the metal gates into the cell block, Emma's body grew heavy, like she'd gained a hundred pounds in an instant. An odor tickled her nostrils. It was an underlying scent as fleeting as the ghosts who inhabited the jail, and not one noticeable to others—a fetid smell of accumulated hopelessness and anger, of defiance and defeat, even of guilt and innocence. Men and women had been rightfully incarcerated here for crimes they had committed, but others had been imprisoned wrongfully, just as some were in modern times.

Emma looked up, taking in the vaulted ceiling and the filigreed iron railing that surrounded the second-floor walkway. It was similar to the iron railings decorating the outside balconies of the inn and seemed too ornate and fine to be in such a place. Even the supports that held the second-floor walkway were decorated with cutout work. Along each wall, cells were lined up, some with iron gates for doors, some with both an iron gate and a thick wooden door. Running the length of the cell block above the doors on each side were large pipes painted black.

"The original cells had both wooden doors and gates," Betty Lou told Emma. "The gates allowed the men in the cells to see into the cell block and to socialize to some degree. The wooden doors were shut at night or when there was an execution, or if the prison needed stiffer security."

Emma took a few steps forward and noted a wide slit cut into the thick wall on the left side. Something sat on the ledge of the slit. Going closer, Emma saw it was a metal tray and a cup.

"That small pass-through goes into the kitchen," Betty Lou explained. "The prisoners would go there to retrieve their food trays, then sit at a table in the center to eat." She indicated the long tables with benches positioned in the middle of the cell block.

Betty Lou pointed upward. "Women prisoners were kept on the second floor."

There were definitely spirits milling about. Emma could feel them in the damp coolness of the air, but they hadn't materialized.

Nor did she see Granny. She didn't know if Granny had returned from her errand with the child or not, but felt she hadn't. The spirits in the jail were swirling around her, coming close, then backing away. She didn't sense many of them, just a handful. Emma knew they were watching her and understood she was different, that she would be able to see them if they chose to be seen. Their curiosity was as thick as the walls and mixed with hesitation. Quinn was behind her, and she knew he was watching her with the same look.

Emma took in the walls, the ceiling, the cells lined up like so many hungry mouths. She ran a hand along the rough texture of the wall. She'd never had such an intense experience with spirits like this before. It was nearly intimate, as if she were seeing into the soul of the structure that housed them. She wondered if it was because of Addy or because of the seriousness of the place. The one spot she couldn't bring herself to focus on was the far end of the cell block. She didn't want to look, afraid of what she might see, but knew she couldn't put it off.

Shutting her eyes, she turned her head toward the end of the cell block where the wooden gallows stood like a fearsome master. She opened her eyes quickly, ready to take in whatever was there, unpleasant or not.

"Are those the original gallows?" she asked, relieved to see that the side-by-side nooses of yellow rope were empty.

Betty Lou walked forward, leading them farther into the cell block and closer to the gallows. "No, but it is a replica of the original gallows. It was built using the same plans. Over here," she said, leading them to one of the cells, "is cell 17, the one with the handprint."

The iron gate on this cell was closed, and there was a sign posted saying photographs of the handprint were not permitted. Emma peered into the cell through the open squares of the gate and wasn't surprised to see the ghost of Alexander Campbell sitting on the small bed that was its only furnishing. On the wall across from the bed was indeed the image of a handprint. It wasn't sharply defined but was clear enough that the viewer knew immediately what it was. Campbell said nothing but looked at Emma with his head held high and straight. She gave him a courtesy nod and moved on.

All the cells were depressing and dark. Some had beds in them, some chairs and beds, some were empty. There was one horizontal, narrow window set high near the ceiling. Some had toilets. She stepped inside one of the cells but felt nothing except the closeness of the walls. She entered several, one after the other, but none was the cell Emma visited in her dream.

Something touched her elbow as she stood in the middle of the last cell. Emma jumped slightly and turned to see Quinn at her side.

"You okay?" he asked.

An odd bit of humor struck her as Emma realized Quinn had asked her that several times since they'd met.

"Yes, I'm fine. Just taking it all in."

"Any ghosts yet, besides Campbell?"

"No, at least not that I can see, but there are several here right now. Not sure who they are, though." Emma pointed to cell 17. "Campbell was just there, sitting on the bed. I'm pretty sure that handprint is his."

Betty Lou's eyes went wide. "I just got goose bumps." She rubbed her arms. "Would you like to see downstairs? That's where the dungeon cells are."

Emma gave her a silent nod, and the three of them headed through a door to the right of the gallows and down a narrow stairwell. As they followed Betty Lou down the stairs, Quinn put a hand on Emma's shoulder. She stopped and turned to him.

"What did you say to Campbell in the other room? You know, just outside the bathroom?"

Emma weighed what to say, then answered in a soft but direct manner, "I asked him who Addy was. He disappeared without answering. Either he doesn't know or doesn't want to say." Emma gave Quinn a faint smile and continued down the stairs. Surprised by her words, Quinn stared after her, watching her from behind, too surprised for a moment to follow.

If the main cell block was depressing, the basement of the jail, which housed the solitary confinement cells, was triple that in its sense of dark foreboding. It was much colder in the basement, but Emma couldn't tell if it was because of being downstairs with little to no natural light or from the presence of spirits.

"Horrible place, isn't it?" asked a familiar voice.

Emma gave the ghost a small smile of relief. "I'm so glad you're here, Granny." She spoke to Granny in a soft voice respectful of the gravity of their surroundings but not in a whisper. She didn't care that Quinn and Betty Lou were privy to the conversation. She was on the brink of learning something important. She could feel it in the cold weight that continued to invade her body. Once more she touched the ring hidden beneath her sweater, pressing it to her as if it were a talisman of protection.

"Anything about Addy yet?" Granny asked.

"No. Have you learned anything?"

Granny shook her hazy head. "This place is crawling with unhappy ghosts, but no one's talking. Want me to get tough with them?" She slapped her right fist into her left hand. There was no sound from the impact.

In spite of their dismal surroundings, the idea of diminutive Granny getting tough with the spirits of prisoners amused Emma. She smiled and shook her head at the spunky spirit. "That won't be necessary."

"Who's she talking—" Betty Lou started to say, but Quinn gently shushed her without taking his eyes off of Emma.

Once Granny left, Emma started inspecting the dungeon area while Betty Lou and Quinn watched wide-eyed with expectation. They kept a few feet away from her, giving her space without interruption.

Without the vaulted ceiling of the main cell block, the basement space felt tight, like the walls and ceiling were closing in on her slowly, compacting in from the top, bottom, and sides, like she was a piece of garbage being manipulated into a small, convenient package. The walls were rougher than those on the floor above, with old paint and plaster peeling away like skin from an orange. Dampness and mildew permeated the air like a stale cologne.

She approached the first cell. The door was thicker and heavier than those above. There was no iron door with crisscross bars to allow conversation or the prisoner to look out. The door was solid, with only a tiny opening through which communication with the prisoner could be conducted. Inside, the walls were rough-hewed, as if scraped out of the concrete with a large spoon. The ceiling was arched. Set high at the end of the cell was a window much tinier than the ones in the cells above. Betty Lou and her husband had brought in lamps to provide low-level yellow light so visitors could see inside them.

Emma shivered as she stepped a foot into the first one. She turned, slowly rotating to get a sense of the place and the people who had inhabited it during the history of the jail. She still could feel spirits around her but couldn't see them.

She left the first cell and entered the second, which was much the same except for one thing. In the second cell she could have sworn she could make out the face of a man on one wall. It wasn't an imprint, as with the hand in cell 17, but a three-dimensional outline, as if the man was trying to come through the wall but changed his mind, leaving a relief of his face protruding through the plaster.

"Don't be afraid," she said to the image. "I'm here to ask a few questions, not to bother you." The imaged faded, the wall returning to its rough flatness. Quickly Emma left the cell and went to the next one—the cell on the other side of the wall where she had seen the facial imprint.

As she crossed the threshold to the third cell, her heart began beating faster. The light in this cell came from a bare low-watt bulb at the end of a thin upright lamp pole. The small window was covered over except for a small opening the size of a deck of cards through which the sun shone like a laser pointer. The cell was the same size as the other two dungeon cells she'd seen, but it felt smaller and more cramped. The air inside this cell was different. It moved, in spite of no visible means to do so, and it was cold.

Again she did her slow pivot, taking in the details of the cell and letting the spirits present see that she came in peace. As she turned, she spied a dirty toilet built into the front right corner. It was nothing more than a toilet seat fastened to a box. The wall to the right of the toilet was the wall shared with the cell she'd just left. She stopped turning as her eyes confirmed what her heart already told her. Attached to the center of the wall were heavy chains with manacles at the end. This was the cell in her dream.

Through her sweater, she placed two fingers on the ring. "Who's Addy?" she asked the seemingly empty room.

Quinn stepped forward but didn't come close. His face was dark with concern. "Emma, do you mean Addy Ames?"

Without turning toward Quinn, Emma said, "I don't know her last name." The spirits around began manifesting themselves. "But they know her."

The first to show himself was Alexander Campbell. After him, two more appeared. Like Campbell, they appeared to be in their forties, and both had thick black beards. Emma remembered them from her dream. She remained still as they circled around her and came to rest. Keeping her right arm close to her side, she showed her palm to Quinn, signaling for him to remain where he was.

"Has Addy come home?" Campbell asked.

"Yes, Mr. Campbell, Addy's here."

"Edward will be pleased."

At Edward's name, the stone around Emma's neck turned warm. Emma touched it again, trying to assure Addy all was well.

Another ghost walked through the wall into the cell. It was the youngest of those she'd seen before, the fair-haired young man with the noose around his neck, but this time he didn't wear the hangman's rope.

As in her dream, he held out his hand for Emma to take. "Addy," he beckoned.

Emma extended her right hand toward him. "I'm here, Edward." As her hand touched that of the ghost, a shock of deep sadness and tragedy ran through her, nearly stopping her racing heart with the weight of its darkness.

"I'm back, Edward," Emma said to the spirit, her hand still touching his.

The other ghosts looked on, their faces not as stern as they had been. Quinn and Betty Lou watched transfixed, cemented to their places by the door.

Edward started to retreat back into the wall, taking Emma with him, but as her solid outstretched hand struck the stone, she stopped and dropped her hand. Tears ran down her cheeks. "I can't, Edward. It's not over. Not yet."

The ghost of the young miner came back through the wall and extended his hand again. Once more Emma took it, but this time she didn't try to follow. "I'll be back, Edward. I promise."

Emma dropped her hand and turned to look at Quinn. Her eyes were unfocused, nearly rolled back into her head, and her face was flushed. He jumped forward and grabbed her shoulders, gently shaking her. "Emma, come back to us."

twenty-five

"Emma, snap out of it," yelled Granny, popping in by her side. The ghost looked around the cell, taking stock of the other ghosts standing around watching. "Make Addy stop," she snapped at them. When the ghosts of the Molly Maguires did nothing but look on, Granny scowled, "Men! Worthless in life *and* in death."

Granny started blowing into Emma's face while she snarled at the ghost in the ring. "Let her go, Addy. Emma never harmed you. She's the only real friend you have on this earth."

"I'll call an ambulance," Betty Lou said in a worried voice and disappeared.

Emma started coming out of her fog. "No." She pushed away from Quinn. "Tell Betty Lou no ambulance. I'm fine." She turned to Granny, letting the worried ghost see she was back to herself.

Seeing Emma had returned to her senses, Quinn ran out. Emma could hear him calling out that she wouldn't need medical care. He asked Betty Lou to bring down some water instead.

When he returned to the cell a second later, Emma was staring at the wall where she'd seen Edward. Quinn watched in silence, never out of reach should she need him. Granny stood by the far wall, keeping an eye on Alexander Campbell and his men.

Emma stretched out her hand again toward the wall. Edward's ghost reached to take it. This time it was Emma speaking, not Addy through her. "Come on, Addy," Emma said, coaxing the ghost in the diamond. "Here's your chance to be free. Take Edward's hand."

"No!" Addy shouted in defiance. "It's not time."

Without warning, Emma cried out in pain and looked down. The front of her sweater, the spot over Lainey's ring, was scorched, the heat burning into her flesh.

She started pulling on the chain around her neck. "The ring," she yelled to Quinn. "Help me get it out."

Granny danced from foot to foot. "Help her," she shouted at Quinn, even though he couldn't hear her.

Quinn jumped to Emma's aid again. Staring down at her chest, he first thought it was blood, then watched as the burned area grew like a match had been held under the fabric. As Emma pulled on the chain, trying to free it, Quinn grabbed the hem of her sweater and yanked it over her head, getting the chain and ring caught.

"Wait a minute," Emma told Quinn as she became tangled in her garment. When he stopped pulling, Emma freed one arm. Moving the chain to the hand of the free arm, she kept it away from her skin while she cleared her other arm. The chain was also warm but not hot. Her sweater was ruined. So was the tee shirt under it and the bra. The small patch of skin between her breasts was stinging, but luckily the layers of fabric had kept it from being seriously injured.

She pulled the chain over her head and held it aloft, glaring at the ring. "There was no need to do that, Addy."

A fuzzy stream of light oozed from the ring, and soon Addy materialized in front of Emma. Her face was smooth and peaceful as she looked at Edward with a loving smile. "I will be back, Edward. I promise."

He held out his hand again, his young face eager and pleading. "Come with me now, Addy. We've waited so long."

Addy took his hand but didn't move to go with him. "I've hurt a lot of people," she confessed. She turned to look at the other ghosts. "Innocent people. But now I have the chance to help one of them."

"No one helped us, Addy," Campbell reminded her. "Not you, not Edward, not me or the others. Go with Edward now, and be free of the bonds of the living."

Quinn, still clutching Emma's sweater, sensed the drama he couldn't hear. He took a few steps back, hoping to see even a glimmer of the spirits. "What's going on, Emma?"

"The ghosts are having a discussion," Emma explained. "They want Addy to go with Edward. She wants to stay to finish something."

"Is it the ghost of Edward Kelly you're talking about?" The question came from Betty Lou. She had returned unnoticed. She stood at the doorway to the cell holding a bottle of water. Her face was twisted in concentration in the hope of seeing and hearing the spirits she knew existed. "He spent a lot of time in this cell before he was hanged."

Emma turned to the young man. "Are you the ghost of Edward Kelly?"

He nodded. "Aye, I am. And standing yon with Mr. Campbell are Tom Fisher and Yellow Jack."

Emma turned to the three ghosts standing near Granny and gave them a polite nod before advising Betty Lou and Quinn of what Edward had said.

Betty Lou bobbled a bit. Quinn stepped to her side, but she waved him off and leaned against the thick doorway for support. "I always knew some of the Molly Maguires were still here."

Quinn turned back to Emma. "Edward Kelly and Addy Ames were sweethearts."

Emma had surmised as much from the way the two young ghosts behaved with each other. "But who did you marry, Addy? Who beat you?"

"That would have been Ronald Dowd," Quinn answered for the ghost.

Addy shuddered at the name and became agitated. She dropped Edward's hand and floated to stand in front of Emma. "The girl is still in mortal danger."

"What girl?"

Addy pointed at the ring dangling at the end of the gold chain.

"You mean Lainey?" asked Emma.

Addy nodded. "Yes."

Protective anger bubbled to the top of Emma's emotions. "Leave Lainey alone."

"The danger is not from me." Addy started to fade.

"Stay, Addy," Emma pleaded. "Tell me what's going on."

Turning around, Emma saw Alexander Campbell was also starting to fade. His friends were already gone. Campbell floated over to Betty Lou. "Thank you, dear lady, for keeping our memory alive." He glanced at Emma. "Please tell Mrs. McBride what I said."

Emma shook her head to clear it. She didn't want to play interpreter just now. Addy had just announced Lainey's life was still in danger. That's all Emma wanted to deal with, but the stern look on Campbell's face made her take a deep breath and stop a moment.

"Betty Lou," she said to the museum owner in a rush of words, "Mr. Campbell wants me to thank you for the museum and for keeping the memory of him and the men who died with him alive."

The ghost of Alexander Campbell bowed slightly before Betty Lou McBride and took his leave.

"Oh my!" said Betty Lou. She opened the water and took a big drink of it.

With urgency, Emma turned her attention back to Addy. She and Edward were standing face to face. "Come back to me when you can, Addy," Edward said. "I'll be here." Then he disappeared into the wall.

Addy returned to stand before Emma, her image fading more by the second. She pointed at Quinn. "He can help you." Then she vanished into a stream of smoke that was sucked into the stone of Lainey's ring.

Granny floated over and stared at the ring. "In all my days, I've never seen anything like that. Gives me the willies." The ghost rubbed her arms against a chill she couldn't feel.

Quinn was just as amazed. "Did I just see smoke going into that ring or out of it?"

Emma looked down at the ring. "You saw that?"

He nodded, not taking his eyes off the large diamond. "I did."

"The smoke was going into the ring, Quinn. It was the ghost of Addy Ames returning to her haunting place. She won't go off with Edward until Lainey's safe. Lainey is the young woman who owns this ring. Addy tried to kill her before."

"And now she's worried about her safety?"

"Seems so."

Quinn started to touch the ring, then stopped and looked up at Emma, his eyes brimming with excitement. "May I?"

Emma handed him the ring. He rolled it in his fingers, feeling the cut of the facets as he searched for the life within it. He looked up at Emma. "Is this the Dowd diamond?"

Betty Lou shook off the excitement of having a ghost address her and stepped forward. "The Dowd diamond? You mean it's real?"

Emma took the ring back from Quinn. Putting the chain over her head, she tucked the ring back inside her burned tee shirt.

"You sure that's wise?" Quinn asked, holding up her scorched sweater as an exhibit to back his concern.

"I don't think she's going to try to hurt me again." Emma held out her hand for the sweater. "It's cold in here." Quinn handed it back to her.

"It was a lot colder a minute ago," Betty Lou observed. "When the ghosts were here it was absolutely freezing in this cell, like a deep freeze. You didn't feel that?"

Emma shook her head. "Usually I do, but not this time."

Quinn cocked his head and gave Emma a lopsided grin. "Then again, your clothes were on fire."

Emma pulled at the front of her sweater. There was a blackened hole between her breasts, but for now it would have to do. Anxious to reach Lainey, she reached into her jeans pocket for her cell phone.

"Darn it. My cell's back at the hotel, recharging. I forgot to take it with me this morning." She started for the door. "We have to go back to the hotel. I have to call Lainey to make sure she's okay."

Quinn pulled his phone from his pocket and held it out to her. "Here, use mine."

"Cell phones don't work down here," Betty Lou told them. "They don't work well anywhere inside the jail, and not at all down here."

After the three of them were back upstairs, Emma thanked Betty Lou for showing her around. "It's been a great deal of help."

"No, Emma, thank *you*. I can't tell you what today has meant to me." Betty Lou gave Emma a quick hug. "Now go help that Lainey girl so Addy can come back." She turned to Quinn and gave him an affectionate embrace. "You know the history of this place and of the Dowds better than I do. You help Emma."

Outside the jail, Emma called the phone at her cabin in Julian. Her mother answered. "Mother, it's me. Is Lainey all right?"

"Yes, dear, she's fine. Why?"

"Addy just told me that Lainey's still in danger. She didn't say how or why, but the danger isn't coming from Addy any longer. Maybe it's Lin. I'm not sure how Addy knows that unless she overheard it, but I don't want to take any chances."

"She's over at Susan's right now. I'll go right on over, and we'll not let the child out of our sight."

"Thank you. Where's Dad?"

"He and Glen went into town to get something—a tool Glen needs, I think. Did Addy go home?"

"Yes and no. She's home, but she won't leave the ring. I don't know the whole story yet, but I should soon." She looked at Quinn, who was waiting patiently by her side. As soon as she was off the phone, she was going to wring every scrap of information out of him she could, starting with how he knew Addy's name and the story behind the Dowd diamond.

As soon as she said goodbye to her mother, Emma stared expectantly at Quinn. "So, what's the story with Addy Ames, Edward Kelly, and Ronald Dowd? And don't spare any details."

Quinn started down Broadway. "Come on," he said. "I want to show you something, but first we need to go back to the hotel. We can trade information along the way."

Emma looked down at her ruined sweater. She wanted to change it but was antsy to learn more. "I'm okay wearing this for now. Let's just go."

He turned. "I'm not worried about your sweater, I'm worried about the burn under it. We need to get you some first aid before we go traipsing off. Burns can be nasty business and get infected easily."

"Oh, and my cell phone," Emma remembered. "I do need that. If anything happens, my mother will call that number, not yours."

twenty-six

. . . .

A KNOCK SOUNDED AT Emma's hotel door. She opened it to find Quinn holding a small paper bag aloft in one hand and two plastic bags in the other. "I have antiseptic ointment and bandages."

"What's that?" She pointed at the plastic bags. "Kind of big for a small burn, or are you planning surgery?"

He came in and put all the bags on the table. From one plastic bag he pulled out four bottles of Snapple. "I picked up some sandwiches for lunch and a few bottles of tea." He put the bag with the sandwiches in the mini fridge, along with two bottles of the tea. He twisted the top off one of the bottles left on the table and handed it Emma. "Hope you like green tea."

After she took the bottle of tea, he asked, "Now, how's that burn?"

"It's blistered a bit, but it's not bad. My clothing took the brunt of the heat. I cleaned the site off with soap and water and dried it with a clean towel." Emma had stripped to her waist and was wearing a short cotton robe over the top of her jeans. She took a drink from her bottle. It was refreshing and welcomed by her dry throat.

Quinn twisted the top off his own bottle of tea and took a long drink. "Let me have a look at it."

"I beg your pardon?"

"I am a doctor, Emma."

She laughed lightly. "Somehow, Quinn, I don't think a PhD qualifies you to give medical advice."

"No, but I've learned a lot about field medicine on digs, especially the simple things like cuts, burns, and sprains. I can even reset a dislocated shoulder or temporarily set a broken bone. You have to know that stuff when you're working in remote places."

She considered him a moment, then put down her tea and opened her robe, revealing the burn but keeping the breasts on either side of it covered. "It's nearly dead-center."

Putting down his tea, he washed his hands, then pulled Emma closer to a light to examine the wound. Emma flinched slightly when he touched her.

Quinn looked up. "I'm sorry. Did I hurt you?"

Emma shook her head and looked away. His touch didn't hurt her, it disturbed her. While Quinn grabbed the medical supplies and started tearing into the packaging, Emma studied the grain on the door to her room, trying to concentrate on anything except the fact that Quinn Keenan was touching her chest. It didn't matter that he was applying first aid; his close proximity in such an intimate manner sent shimmers of arousal through her. And she wasn't the only one sensing it. As Quinn applied ointment to Emma's wound, then covered it with a gauze bandage, folding it small enough to fit between her breasts comfortably and still cover the burn, his fingers took on a slight tremor of awkwardness. Next he applied strips of surgical tape. Emma was glad he was doing it. She could have done it on her own, but it would have been difficult to do it right. She was also having a love-hate relationship with the way it was making her feel.

"That's going to hurt for a few days," he told her when he was done. He fiddled with putting the cap on the ointment, studying it as if it were a difficult puzzle. Neither of them looked at each other, trying to ignore the charge in the air. "It shouldn't become infected if you keep it clean and bandaged. If you need me to help change the bandage, just let me know. I'll be happy to help."

"I just bet he would," snapped a disembodied voice.

Ignoring Granny's comment and presence, Emma closed her robe and tightened the belt. "Thank you, Dr. Keenan."

"My pleasure." He put away the supplies and washed his hands again. "You're a lot cuter than the guys I'm used to patching up."

"No women on those digs?"

"Them, too." He picked up his tea, still not looking at her. "Where's the Dowd diamond?"

"Here." Emma went to the nightstand by the bed and retrieved the ring. She handed it to him. "I didn't know it had a name until today."

"If it's the same stone."

"That's not the original setting. The jeweler I spoke with said the original setting was Victorian. His friend bought it from someone here in Pennsylvania in the early sixties. Every wearer has died of suicide since, except for my daughter's friend Lainey."

Emma took her bottle of tea to the loveseat and sat down. Quinn joined her.

Granny materialized next to the window, her arms crossed and wearing her signature scowl. "Does he have to sit so close to you?"

Emma shot Granny a scowl of her own but was thankful the ghost was chaperoning.

On the walk back to the inn from the jail, she'd given Quinn a quick rundown of how she had become involved, of Lainey's suicide attempts, and even of Summer's death. He'd stopped their progress several times to question her and listen with interest before continuing.

"Oh, I just thought of something." Emma popped off the love-seat and retrieved her cell phone from its charger. She also grabbed her purse and dug around inside until she located the business card for Sachman & Sons. She started punching in the numbers.

"Who are you calling?"

"The jeweler who gave me the history of that ring."

When someone answered, Emma asked to speak to Isaac Sachman and gave her name. After a short wait, Mr. Sachman came on the phone.

"I see you got my message," the old man said immediately.

Emma was surprised. "Your message? No, I didn't." She looked down at her cell to see she had two voicemails waiting. "I'm sorry, Mr. Sachman. I went out and left my phone behind. I was actually calling you for something else."

"If it is about the ring, then it is the same topic."

Emma put the phone on speaker. "I'm here with a friend of mine, Dr. Quinn Keenan. We're in Jim Thorpe, Pennsylvania, where Addy was from. I just found out the stone has a name—the Dowd diamond. Did you know that?"

Isaac Sachman gave off a low, gravelly chuckle. "I just found out the exact same thing, my dear. That is why I called. Seems the fates are determined we get to the bottom of this mystery."

Mr. Sachman cleared his throat. There was a short quiet period.

"Are you all right, Mr. Sachman?" Emma asked.

"I'm fine, Emma. I just needed a sip of water." There was another short pause before he continued. "After we spoke, the matter of this ring continued to bother me, so I called the widow of my friend Jonas, the jeweler who purchased the original ring in Pennsylvania. She told me all of Jonas's records were still stored in their garage, so I sent one of my sons over to look through them, specifically to locate sales and purchases made from the late fifties through the sixties. As I recall, Jonas was a meticulous record keeper. My son found the information and brought it back to me to look over."

"So you can confirm that the stone I showed you is, in fact, the Dowd diamond?"

"Absolutely. I also found something even more curious."

Quinn and Emma leaned toward the phone, eager to hear the news and thankful to have a diversion from their mutual attraction. Granny floated close by, her own ears keen for news.

"It seems I know the man who sold it to Jonas back in the early sixties," Isaac Sachman continued. "His name is Linwood Reid, the controversial financier."

"Linwood Reid?" Even saying it out loud, Emma couldn't believe it. She glanced up at Granny, who looked just as surprised. "Are you sure, Mr. Sachman?"

"According to Jonas's records, he bought the ring from Mr. Reid in the mid-sixties. Which is very odd, because I distinctly remember him being with Mrs. Naiman when she bought the ring from me for her husband. I'm sure he never mentioned a previous connection to it at that time."

"Did you know him before then?"

"Mr. Reid was an occasional customer who recommended our store to Mrs. Naiman and particularly that ring. I assisted them myself and remember him saying he'd seen it in the store and knew it would be perfect for Max. Of course it could be a different Linwood Reid, but it is such an uncommon name, is it not?"

"Yes, it is," Emma agreed. She handed Quinn the phone and began pacing the room as her mind spun like a Tilt-A-Whirl with surprise and possibilities.

Granny paced alongside her. "That's the skunk who hired Jamal."

"Linwood," Quinn said, holding the phone but staring at the wall as he dug through the knowledge stored in his brain. "Linwood," he repeated. "Linwood was a family name of the Dowd family, the family who originally owned that stone."

Emma whipped around. "Are you sure, Quinn?"

"Positive. Linwood Dowd was Ronald Dowd's father—Addy's father-in-law. According to local stories, he purchased the diamond in Europe for his bride, Ronald's mother. Ronald also had a brother named Linwood."

"But how is it," Emma asked, "that Linwood Reid knew where that ring was so many years after he sold it?"

The aged jeweler provided an explanation. "He could have contacted Jonas and inquired about it. Sometimes when people are forced to sell off family heirlooms, they keep track of them in the hope of one day buying them back. Few do, of course."

Emma ran a hand through her hair. "I wonder if he knew the ring was haunted?"

"That ring being cursed is a longtime legend around these parts," added Quinn.

Emma stared at him. "You mean people have known for years the ring was haunted?"

"Maybe not haunted, but for generations locals passed along stories about the ring being cursed, though most thought it was just a story, and today most believe the existence of the ring itself was fabricated to account for all the tragedy surrounding the Dowd family."

Emma picked up the ring and examined it. It remained cool to the touch. "Makes you wonder if Addy was a victim of that tragedy or the cause."

Sachman's voice came through the cell phone like that of an unseen spirit. "I hope my information was helpful, Emma."

Coming closer to the cell phone, she said, "Very helpful, Mr. Sachman. Thank you."

After the call with Isaac Sachman ended, Emma turned to Quinn armed with new questions. "Do you think Linwood Reid knew the ring was haunted and used it to murder Max Naiman? Lainey did tell me he was seeing her mother prior to her parents rededicating themselves."

Emma blew out a gust of air and continued before Quinn could make a comment. "Now I'm wondering if Joanna knew about the ring, but my gut is saying she didn't. She is nervous about Linwood, though; something is not right there."

Granny had her own theory. "Maybe the skunk also used the ring to try to kill off Lainey. He's after her money, isn't he?"

"That's right, Granny."

Quinn looked to the spot where Emma directed her comment, but saw nothing. "Is your rabbit back?" He flashed Emma a grin.

Granny hovered around Quinn, her hands on her hips, her face pinched with disapproval. "I ain't no darn rabbit, Indiana."

"Yes, Granny is back, and she'd prefer you not to call her a rabbit. Not even a famous one." Emma perched on the arm of the loveseat. "But she just pointed out another possibility. Maybe Linwood also used the ring to try to kill Lainey. He definitely wants her out of the way, and he's been trying to get his hands on her inheritance."

"Murder by haunted ring." Quinn rolled the concept around on his tongue. "If so, it's a brilliant crime. Think about it. How are the police supposed to make a charge like that stick? Then again, according to the stuff I've read about Linwood Reid, he's a genuine piece of work."

Emma tightened her grip on the ring, willing Addy to tell them more. "Quinn, did you know Linwood Reid was connected to the Dowd family?"

"Not exactly, though I did know he hailed from Pennsylvania." He stood up and stretched. "To be honest, my curiosity in the family didn't extend beyond the burning of the Dowd mansion. After that, I believe they left Mauch Chunk for good."

"When I read up on this town," Emma said, trying to sweep away her confusion, "I read about the two Packer mansions, but I don't recall anything about a Dowd mansion."

"It burned to the ground in the early 1900s. The fire was supposedly set by Ronald's third wife, Virginia Dowd."

"Tell me about the Dowds, Quinn. What do you know about the connection between them, Addy, and Edward Kelly?"

Quinn went to the window and looked out. He was silent a few moments.

"Is he thinking or sleeping?" Granny asked.

Emma shot her a look letting her know to be still.

"After the jail, I wanted to show you something." He turned around and leaned against the windowsill. "I still do. It's the perfect place to tell you Addy's story, or at least what I know of it." He shoved off and headed for the door. "Get dressed. I'll be back in a minute. We'll take the sandwiches and make a picnic of it."

twenty-seven

FROM THE HOTEL, THEY walked straight up Broadway, past the Old Jail Museum, and kept going. Quinn set a brisk pace, and after the day they'd had already, it felt good to Emma to do something physical. The mid-afternoon air was brisk and fresh and filled with the potential of cooler temperatures come sundown. When he'd returned to her room, Quinn had a small backpack. He filled it with the sandwiches and drinks from her mini fridge and a make-shift ice pack.

They moved along side by side without speaking, staying on Broadway, following its lazy curve and incline. There were fewer buildings and businesses up at this end. Quinn made a right turn onto a small side street, then disappeared into the brush on the left. Emma followed him, discovering a footpath just beyond the spring growth of bushes. They continued on the path, which climbed through a small wooded area until it broke in a clearing at the top of a small hill.

"It's beautiful up here." Exhilarated by the hike, Emma spun around, taking in the natural beauty. "Absolutely gorgeous."

Quinn dropped his backpack down on one of three well-worn picnic tables in the clearing. "Yeah, it's not that high, but it does give a great view of the town and the area around it." He pointed toward an old road on the other side of the clearing. "That's an old carriage road. We could have driven here, but I thought the exercise would do us good. You know, clear our minds."

"I totally agree." Emma stood at the edge of the clearing watching the small town of Jim Thorpe.

Quinn came to stand next to her. "How's Addy doing?"

Emma touched the small velvet pouch stuffed into the right pocket of her jeans. "So far, no bonfires. Why?"

"This was where the Dowd mansion stood. This is where Addy Ames Dowd died."

Emma sucked in her breath and held it. Wrapping her fingers around the pouch, she felt for irritation from the ring, but there was none.

Quinn gently took Emma's arm and guided her to the table with the backpack. "Come sit down and have a bite. It's been a long time since breakfast, and I have a story to tell."

He laid out three sandwiches and the two unopened bottles of tea. The sandwiches were stumpy oblongs wrapped in white paper and secured with tape. One was marked with an *e*, one with a *t*, and the last with a *v*. They looked like three oversized capsules of medication. "I wasn't sure, but I got the feeling you didn't eat red meat, so I picked up the only three sandwiches the place offered that didn't have it." Quinn touched the first wrapped sandwich, the one with the *e* scrawled on the wrapper. "We have egg salad."

He touched the next. "Tuna. And the last is grilled vegetables and Swiss." He smiled at her. "What's your pleasure, milady?"

"I'm fine with any of them, though I feel bad you didn't get one with meat for yourself." She untied her light jacket from around her waist and laid it on the bench next to her.

"I don't eat much red meat. For a while I went totally vegetarian, but it's difficult to do when you spend so much time in other countries." He lifted his long legs and stepped over the bench to take a seat across from Emma. "When the leader of a tribe butchers his prize goat in your honor, it's difficult to explain you don't eat anything with a face. Now I just eat it in moderation."

Emma laughed. "Tell you what, how about I take the egg and you the tuna. We'll split the third sandwich. That way we'll both get our veggies."

"Spoken like a true mom." He handed her the egg salad sandwich and half of the vegetable one, then dug around in the plastic bag they'd been wrapped in, producing two bags of chips and a handful of thin paper napkins. "Look, we even have napkins, thanks to the girl at the counter. How civilized."

Emma twisted the cap off of a bottle of tea and took a drink while soaking in the atmosphere. A mansion on top of this small hill would have been fantastic. Even a small house in the location would have been lovely.

"How come no one has rebuilt up here?"

"The Dowd family left it to the town to be used as a park, but I don't think they left money for its maintenance. There was some talk awhile back about a developer buying it from the city and building condos up here. I think the economy tanked those plans. In the summer, folks will walk up here to picnic or relax, but most don't even remember this spot's here. And some believe it's cursed." He took a bite of his tuna sandwich and chewed, following it up with a couple of chips. "Tell me, Emma. You're the expert here. Do you think it's haunted or cursed?"

Emma took a bite of her own sandwich. She chewed slowly, taking the time to get an overall sense of the place. "I don't see any ghosts, but I can feel something. Something very amiss." Emma stopped eating and closed her eyes to concentrate. After a moment, she looked at Quinn. "Might not be spirits at all, but I'm definitely picking up something. This place is very unsettling." She took another bite of her lunch. "Did anyone besides Addy die up here?"

Instead of answering right away, Quinn tipped back a bottle of tea for a quick swig. Another two bites and he was through his tuna sandwich. He wiped his hands on one of the napkins.

"Three people have died here that I know of: Addy, of course; Virginia Dowd; and Ronald himself. Virginia died in the fire after killing Ronald with an ax."

The news startled Emma. "Didn't you say earlier that Virginia was suspected of starting the fire?"

Quinn nodded while his eyes grazed on the peaceful view of the town below. "She torched it by setting fire to herself using kerosene."

Upon hearing the next installment of Dowd family history, Emma started choking on her sandwich. Grabbing her tea, she took a drink.

"You okay?" asked Quinn, already on his feet to assist her.

She gave him a thumbs-up while she took another drink to clear her throat. "The self-immolation thing caught me by surprise."

"According to the story," continued Quinn, who remained on his feet, "one of the servants—the butler, I believe—came across Ronald's body in the drawing room. Virginia was pouring kerosene over it, herself, and the room. When he tried to stop her, she scooped embers from the fireplace and threw them, setting the place ablaze. He barely had time to alert the others in the house to get out."

"Virginia was Ronald's third wife, correct? What happened to his second?" Even as she asked, Emma had the feeling the woman hadn't fared well.

"You know, we're sort of starting at the end of Addy's story and working backward."

"I'm fine with that." Emma took another bite of egg salad, only to find she'd lost her appetite. She wrapped up the rest of her sandwich and put it back in the bag.

"The second wife was another young woman like Addy, still a teenager when he married her less than a year after Addy's death." Quinn grabbed his half of the veggie sandwich from the table, took a bite, and swallowed. "Not much is known about her except that she died before their first anniversary. Witnesses claim they saw her walking down Broadway in her nightgown in the middle of the night. A few days later her body was found in the river."

Emma's ears pricked. "Wait. People saw her but didn't stop her? They weren't curious why a woman was walking alone in her nightgown at night?"

"A lot of the eyewitnesses believed it was a ghost—the ghost of Addy Ames, to be exact. Some swear it was Addy who lured the second Mrs. Dowd to her death—and who caused Virginia to go crazy."

Emma rubbed her upper arms from a chill that was starting from within. "That would be Addy's style."

Quinn rested one foot on the bench and leaned forward. "Well, here's a tidbit to support Addy's involvement. The Dowd diamond was a family heirloom. When Ronald married Addy, his mother gave it to him to give to her. Each time Ronald Dowd married, he gave the same large diamond ring to his bride."

"So if Addy was haunting it, she had access to her successors."

"Exactly. Ronald had three wives. Addy hanged herself. The second drowned, and the third went mad, killed Ronald, and burned down the mansion. Is it any wonder people think the ring and this place is cursed? Or any wonder why the family moved away?"

Quinn pointed at the velvet pouch, which Emma had put on the table while they ate. "Any action from within?"

"None." Emma opened the pouch and took out the ring. She caressed it. "It's stone-cold—has been ever since you saw the smoke going into it. I'm wondering if Addy's left it for good."

"Has your Granny seen her anywhere?"

"Granny's not here. I asked her to pop in on my parents to make sure Lainey's okay."

Quinn shook his head in amusement. "I can see how convenient it would be to have a friendly spirit at your disposal. It's like being in two places at once."

"Granny can be a real pill at times, and she's stubborn as an old mule, but she's always willing to help where she can, and she's fiercely loyal." Emma shot Quinn a slight smile. "She's my secret weapon. She also wasn't too keen on you patching me up like you did, even if you do remind her of Indiana Jones."

Quinn struck an action pose. "So she thinks I'm like Indy, does she?"

Emma couldn't help but grin at his antics, but she also couldn't help but think about Phil Bowers. The two men were so different in appearance, yet so much alike. Both were confident, intelligent, and accomplished, and both loved to joke and laugh. Already she felt as at home with Quinn as she did with Phil, and it unsettled her. Maybe that's what Granny didn't like—not Quinn's attentions but Emma's comfort with them.

Still holding the ring, Emma put her mind back onto the problem of Addy Ames. Swinging her legs to the outside of the bench, she got up. She took a seat on the table, placing her feet on the bench. "Now tell me about Addy and Edward."

Moving around to Emma's side of the table, Quinn took a seat on the table top next to her. "Addy Ames was a beauty, the daughter of a local merchant named Howard Ames."

"She is quite attractive," Emma commented. "At least what I've seen of her."

"Her family was well-to-do but not wealthy like the Dowds," Quinn continued. "As the story goes, when she turned eighteen, Ronald Dowd asked Addy's father for her hand in marriage. The Ames family was thrilled with the match, but Addy refused Ronald. She was in love with someone else."

"Edward Kelly?"

"Yes. It's your typical star-crossed lovers story, although it's unclear how the two met and became close. A match between them would have been unthinkable. He was from a poor family of Irish miners. Back then, the Irish were treated like animals. They were denied basic rights, not allowed to apply for jobs, not even permitted in some establishments."

Emma glanced at Quinn. "I remember that from history classes. It was much like African-Americans in the South before the civil rights movement."

"Yes. America, for all its freedoms, has never been kind to new arrivals, whether they came by force or of their own volition. Actually, much of the world is like that. People in general are fearful of others who are different from themselves. I've seen it time and time again all over the world."

Quinn cleared his throat before continuing and took a drink of his tea. "So Addy and Edward met and fell in love, even though it was forbidden by the times. Of course her family was outraged and insisted she marry Ronald Dowd. This was happening about the same time as the Molly Maguire arrests and trials, so anti-Irish sentiment was especially high. The Dowd family had interests in the mines and the railroads and was very influential. Charges of conspiracy were drummed up against poor young Edward, and he was thrown in jail with the others. He was eighteen years old."

Emma blinked back tears and hugged herself. Quinn bent down and picked up her jacket, placing it around her shoulders. He put an arm around her and kept it there for several heartbeats before removing it.

"They lied to me," came a hazy voice off to their left.

twenty-eight

EMMA TURNED TO SEE Addy standing on the edge of the clearing. The ghost was looking out over the town. "This was the view from the front porch. The porch went around three sides. It was a grand house, but to me it was a prison."

Emma nudged Quinn. "Addy's here," she whispered.

She turned her attention to the ghost, whose eyes were still fixed on the town. "Who lied to you, Addy?"

"Everyone. My father. Ronald. Even my mother." She turned to face Emma. "They said if I married Ronald, Edward would be set free. Ronald even offered to pay him money so he could start over somewhere else."

Emma's face fell with the weight of the young ghost's words. In a hushed tone, she relayed the story to Quinn before turning back to Addy. "But instead they hanged him?"

"Yes. Just a few months after Ronald and I wed." Addy moved around the clearing, studying the spot where the Dowd mansion once stood for any sign of the hated place. Emma turned to follow her with her eyes. Quinn noticed.

"Is she drifting about?" he asked.

Emma nodded. "She's moving around the clearing, to and fro, like pacing."

"I left Ronald," Addy continued, her voice a monotone but her jaw set in stone. "I left early one morning to catch the first train out of Mauch Chunk, but someone saw me at the train station and sent word to Ronald. He had two of his servants stop me and drag me back to the house."

"My dream," Emma told her. "I saw you waiting at the train station in one of my dreams."

The ghost nodded. "After that, Ronald took to beating me whenever I'd refuse his advances, which was every time. He wanted an heir, but I told him I would kill any child of his I conceived." Addy's words oozed long-embedded anger, letting Emma know she'd meant what she'd threatened.

"What's going on?" asked Quinn. Quickly, Emma brought him up to date with the conversation.

Quinn took a deep breath and blew it out. "That part wasn't in the local legend."

Addy came close to Emma and Quinn, standing directly in front of them. "Feel how cold it is right here in front of us?" Emma whispered to Quinn. He put out a hand and nodded. "Addy is right there. If the air temperature changes, she's moved away."

Emma turned her attention back to the young ghost. "So when you couldn't take it anymore, you hanged yourself. You used the sash from your robe, didn't you?"

The ghost swung her head side to side in a slow, exaggerated movement. "Ronald did that to me. He tied and gagged me, then used my own belt to hang me. He told me I could follow Edward into hell for all he cared. After, he made it look like I'd done it to myself."

Emma's hand shot to her mouth as she sucked in a quick shot of air.

"What?" asked Quinn, his eyes darting between Emma's face and the empty space in front of them.

"Addy didn't hang herself as we had thought; Ronald murdered her."

Quinn fixed his eyes directly in front of them. "Addy, is that why you haunted the Dowd diamond? For revenge?"

"Yes. No one who wore that ring was ever going to live a happy life. I made sure of that. And I made sure the ring survived. The cow that burned down the mansion wasn't wearing it when she died. It was in the Dowd safe, secure from the flames. It was also in the safe when the second wife drowned. The ring was only brought out when they went out in public." She turned her attention directly to Emma. "I use the ring, but I don't need it to influence weak minds." She let out a light, sinister laugh. "That stone embodies everything bad that has happened to me, so I used it to choose my victims."

After Emma translated, Quinn continued his conversation with the ghost. "But Addy, you killed a lot of innocent people with your actions. What Ronald did to you and Edward was wrong, but why did you want to hurt people who never harmed you?"

Without answering, the ghost turned her back on them. Before Emma could update Quinn, the ghost spun around, her pretty face contorted into pain and anger as hot and violent as molten lava. "Because I could!" she screamed at Quinn, her face nearly touching his. "Because, for the first time *I* was in control, and no one could stop me." She shook her fist in Quinn's face. "Just as no one stopped them from doing and taking whatever they wanted."

Quinn tilted his head toward Emma. "I don't know what she just said, but from the blast of cold air in my face, it wasn't pleasant."

Emma translated, then turned toward the ghost. "It's over, Addy. It's time for you to stop the senseless killing and join Edward in peace. I brought you here to end this."

The ghost lifted her chin and surveyed Emma with defiance before moving away. When Quinn started to speak, Emma clutched his hand, stopping him. The two of them sat on the bench overlooking the town once known as Mauch Chunk, Emma's hand on Quinn's, and waited, not knowing what Addy was thinking or feeling, but hoping she'd seen enough death.

Early evening was upon them. It would still be light for a few more hours, but as the sun started its descent, the air was turning cooler. Quinn moved his hand from Emma's and put his arm around her shoulders, this time keeping it there. "You warm enough?"

She nodded but didn't move from his embrace.

"She still here?" he asked.

Emma turned her head, first to her left, then to her right, until she spotted Addy. The troubled spirit was seated against a tree, her dressing gown wrapped around her legs. Her face was smooth with tranquility, and her eyes were shut in contemplation; the earlier rage was gone. "Yes, she's still here, but maybe we should go and leave her be for now. We've said what we could. The decision is up to her."

Quinn hopped off the picnic table and turned, holding out his hands to Emma to help her down. She did her own hop, which ended in a wobble. Her jacket slipped from her shoulders to the ground. Quinn grabbed hold of her shoulders but didn't remove them once she was upright and steady.

His eyes latched onto hers with intensity as he tightened his grip. "Emma, you're quite extraordinary."

A soft laugh reminiscent of a bubbling sigh escaped her lips as she stuffed the ring's velvet pouch into a pocket. "Why—because I talk to ghosts? More people than you realize can do that. They just keep it under wraps."

"No. Not because you can do that, but because you have such empathy for the dead. You genuinely feel what they feel and understand them as individuals."

His look turned her legs into jelly, and she was happy he had a good hold of her. She tried to answer with a steady voice but couldn't. Her voice, like her legs, was shaky. "Milo Ravenscroft, my mentor, told me to always remember that ghosts were once alive and to respect them as I would a living person."

"You have more than respect for them, Emma." He raised the hand on her left shoulder to her cheek, lightly caressing it with two fingertips. "You feel for them. You put yourself in their place. You take on and give their emotions life."

She dragged her eyes away from his face as she shrugged off the thought but stayed put. "If I really did that, I'd be killing people on behalf of poor Addy instead of trying to make her stop."

He laughed. "I hope not."

Emma turned her eyes back to him. She liked the way the fine lines around Quinn's eyes and mouth deepened when he laughed, as if punctuating his amusement.

He ran his hand from her cheek down to her chin and tilted her face slightly upward. Emma watched his eyes travel her face, memorizing every nuance and curve. Her eyes did the same, taking in his long reddish-blond lashes and slight bump in the middle of his nose. When Quinn's eyes lingered on her mouth, Emma closed her eyes and leaned forward. Their lips touched softly at first, each testing the willingness of the other. The first few kisses were light and playful, mere brushes of flesh against flesh. Quinn's hand cupped her face while his other hand slipped to the small of her back and pulled her to him, their mouths locking with mutual urgency.

After the second long kiss, Emma slipped her arms around Quinn's neck and abandoned herself to the feelings she'd been having since their meeting in her office.

The tinkling sound of bells filled their ears. Quinn broke their lip lock with a small snicker. "Did you order up accompaniment, or are the spirits serenading us?"

Emma broke away from him as the sound started up again. "That's Kelly." She bent down to quickly rifle through the pockets of her jacket until she located her cell phone.

"The ghost of Edward Kelly is calling you from the jail? How modern of him."

"No," Emma laughed. "Kelly, my daughter."

Emma hit the answer button. "Hi, sweetie." She turned away from Quinn, noticing at the same time that Addy Ames was gone.

"Mom, you okay? You sound out of breath."

"I was in the middle of a hike."

"Fibber," came Granny's snappish voice. The ghost popped into view just in front of Emma. "You were in the middle of a kiss that melted the bottoms of your boots."

Emma turned away from Granny. Now Quinn was in her sights again. He was packing the remainder of their lunch and trash into his backpack while keeping an eye on her. Emma turned in another direction, trying to stay away from both Granny's look of disapproval and Quinn's look of smoldering sexiness.

"You're still in Pennsylvania?" Kelly asked.

"Yes. I'm hoping to leave tomorrow or the day after and drive up to Boston to see you, if that's okay."

"That's why I'm calling. I really do want to see you, Mom, but I got a summer job, and it starts this coming weekend."

"A job?" Forgetting the two sets of eyes keeping watch on her, Emma dropped down onto one of the table seats. "You're not coming home for the summer?"

"I'll be home near the end of the summer for a few weeks."

Emma closed her eyes and pressed the phone close to her face. "Kelly, does this have anything to do with what happened to Summer Perkins? If so, we need to talk about that. I can't have you thinking I'm some sort of freak."

Silence filled the airwaves between mother and daughter. Finally Kelly said, "No, Mom, it's not. I was very upset about that, but I know it wasn't your fault." There was another pause on Kelly's end before she added, "Granny told me what happened."

Emma's eyes popped open as she turned her head to the place where Granny had been planted, passing judgment on Emma's kiss. She locked a stern look onto the spirit while speaking to Kelly.

"Granny told you? How long has this been going on?" Granny turned this way and that to avoid Emma's laser look. Pursing her lips, the ghost started whistling a silent tune and buried her hands in the deep pockets of her homespun skirt.

"I discovered I could hear Granny right after Grandpa George's funeral." Kelly was referring to George Whitecastle, Grant's father, who had died from cancer just days before last Christmas. "I was crying, and she talked to me. But I couldn't see her until after I returned to school."

Emma kept an eye on Granny, who now floated about the clearing pretending to keep her eye on Quinn, who quickly realized he wasn't the one who held Emma's interest at the moment. He watched Emma's eyes as they traveled the grassy area and kept half an ear on her conversation.

"And how often does Granny visit you?"

"Is Granny in trouble?" Kelly asked in a worried voice.

"It depends," Emma answered honestly. "Is she interfering with your studies? Or making you uncomfortable around your friends?"

"No, Mom, nothing like that. Sometimes she visits when I'm feeling lonely. She tells me what's going on at home and stories of Julian and Great-Grandpa Jacob."

"And she told you what's going on concerning Summer and Lainey?"

"Yes." Another self-conscious pause. "And about Addy Ames."

"Uh-huh." Emma had wanted to keep Kelly from the dark side of the spirit world as long as possible. It didn't bother her that Kelly was bonding with Granny. She'd half expected Kelly to develop such skills considering Elizabeth had them, too, but it did bother her that Kelly was learning so soon that ghosts could be killers. *Although*, Emma reasoned in a snap of clarity, *Lainey knew, so why not Kelly?* Kelly was a grown woman, and now that Emma knew she had the gift, she would have to guide and teach her about it as Milo had taught her. Casting her look from Granny to Quinn, Emma knew now wasn't the time to begin Kelly's lessons.

"So tell me about the job," she asked her daughter.

There was no mistaking the excitement in her daughter's voice as Kelly told her about the summer position one of her professors had secured for her. It was as an assistant to a brilliant and elderly historian, helping her to catalogue and sort her papers for her memoirs. Kelly would live at the woman's large beach house in the Hamptons for the summer. Emma understood it was an opportunity of a lifetime and one Kelly couldn't pass up.

Then Kelly said something that jarred Emma. "I was told you could come for a visit if you wanted. Phil, too. She said in my interview she'd really like to meet you. Doesn't that sound like fun?"

Phil. His name coming from Kelly's mouth hit Emma with cold, chilly guilt. Kelly said his name as naturally as if he were her father. Emma shot a glance at Quinn, then quickly turned away. "It does sound like fun, sweetie. And I'm sure Phil would like that."

When Emma finished with the call, she found Quinn standing by the footpath, ready to leave. His backpack was slung over one shoulder, and in his hands was Emma's jacket. He didn't look at her as she approached but studied the bark on a nearby tree as if it were an ancient manuscript.

As Emma passed Granny, she pointed a finger at the spirit. "We're going to talk about this later," she said in a steady, stern whisper, "so don't go disappearing on me for long."

Granny shrugged and popped out of sight as quickly as she'd appeared.

When she reached Quinn, Emma took her jacket from him. "Sorry, Quinn, but Kelly had to tell me about her new job. I was going to drive up to Boston to visit her, but that's off now." Emma passed along the information Kelly had given her about the job.

"Wow," he said, clearly impressed. "That summer job could open a lot of opportunities for her in the future."

"That's what I'm thinking. I'll miss her over the summer, but I have to let her go sometime, right?"

Quinn made no move to start down the path toward the town but stopped studying the local foliage to look at her. "So, are you and Phil going to visit her in the Hamptons?"

Emma put on her jacket against the growing evening chill. "I don't know. It's a lot to process on the fly—Kelly's job, Addy, Lainey's safety…" She let her words drift off on the breeze that had picked up.

"And me?"

Emma met his look. It wasn't challenging, but it wasn't meek and submissive. Quinn's eyes were brimming with the pain of decision.

"Look, Emma." He reached out and stroked her upper arm. "I haven't been so captivated by a woman in years." A small, sheepish smile crossed his face. "In the past, I've not had much integrity when it came to poaching other guy's girls, but for some reason I can't be that guy. Not this time. Not with you. What I feel for you isn't flirtatious sport."

Emma eased away from him. "I've been seeing Phil Bowers for almost two years, and I love him deeply; I'm sure of that. During that time, not once have I been attracted to another man. Not once, until now. I'm not a flighty woman."

"I know that. That solidness is part of what makes you so disarming and this so difficult. I'm not the sort to settle down, Emma, but you make me want to put down roots as deep as this tree." He rapped his knuckles on the thick tree trunk next to him.

"We haven't known each other very long, Quinn. We've been thrown together by this situation, and one thing led to another."

His face turned dark. "Is that what you think this is? A passing road-trip fancy involving ghosts, goblins, and a little slap and tickle?"

"I don't know." Emma's voice sharpened with frustration. "I just know I'm confused. I feel guilty one minute and don't give a damn the next. I need time to process it."

As Quinn reached for her again, the tinkling of a piano sounded from the cell phone still clutched in her hand. Emma didn't have to read the display to know the caller was her mother. The piano was her mother's personal ring tone. "That's my mother," she told Quinn, not taking her eyes from his. "It might be about Lainey."

"Your family has remarkable timing." He moved away to give her privacy as she answered the call.

"Hi, Mother, what's up?" Emma's eyes followed Quinn as he walked to one of the tables and dropped his backpack on it. His shoulders were tense and his jaw tight. He looked like a statue with clothes. She closed her eyes and turned away to concentrate on the call.

"It's just awful, Emma," Elizabeth gushed in tones of horror.

Forgetting her own dilemma, Emma went on alert. "Is it Lainey?"

"The story just broke on TV. We're all in shock."

"I'm nowhere near a TV. What's going on? Is Lainey all right?"

"Physically Lainey's fine, but we're on our way back to Los Angeles."

"Mother, what's happened?" The fear in Emma's voice caused Quinn to snap his head around in her direction.

"It's Linwood Reid, Emma. He's dead. Joanna's been taken into custody for his murder."

Before Emma could react to the news, Addy Ames appeared in front of her. Just behind her was the ghost of Edward Kelly. "You were right, Emma. It is time for me to move on." Addy glanced back at her ill-fated lover. "Thank you for bringing me back to Edward." She faced Emma again, her face smooth as alabaster. "And don't worry about Lainey. She's safe. I made sure of that."

The hand holding the cell phone dropped to Emma's side as she put her mother's news together with Addy's words of good-bye. From the phone came Elizabeth's voice. "Emma, are you still there?"

On autopilot, Emma raised the cell to her mouth without taking her eyes from Addy's face. "Let me call you back, Mother. Stay by the phone. It'll just be a minute." She cut off the call and stared at the spirit.

Quinn, seeing Emma's distress, stepped quickly to her side. "What's happening, Emma?"

"Linwood Reid was just murdered by his wife, Lainey's mother." The news caused Quinn to stagger back a step.

Emma asked the malicious ghost, "What have you done, Addy? Did you entice Joanna Reid to kill her husband?"

"I told you I didn't need the ring to carry out my plans." The ghost gave her a slow, smug smile. "Think of it as my final farewell to the Dowd family and an apology to Lainey."

With those words echoing in Emma's ears, Addy and Edward disappeared.

twenty-nine

EMMA SAT IN THE living room of a lovely and spacious beach house in Malibu. Across from her sat Joanna Reid. Beyond the glass wall that opened to spill onto a large deck seamlessly marrying the indoors with the outdoors, the Pacific Ocean sparkled like a field of teal taffeta. The house was set up on pilings. Looking out, one couldn't see the sandy beach below, just the blanket of shimmering water. The great room of the house had several clusters of furniture arranged in conversational groupings but was dominated by a large white sectional sofa reminiscent of an uncooked crescent roll. It was situated on an area rug of looped wool in a natural shade. Anyone sitting on the sofa was rewarded with the grand view of the ocean. The house was furnished in a modern minimalist style, yet it didn't feel sterile. Each of the furnishings was impeccable and appeared chosen specifically for the house. The home seemed more suited to Joanna than the sprawling mansion she'd shared with Linwood Reid and was even a better fit than the charming beach house she'd owned with Max Naiman.

"I love this house, Joanna. It's perfect for you."

Joanna looked around in a detached manner, almost as if seeing it for the first time. "It is nice, isn't it? Lainey leased it for us until the trial is over. What happens then depends on the outcome." The cockiness was gone from the former studio executive. She seemed smaller and softer, like an inflatable doll with a pinprick leak. She also seemed more at peace, even with a murder charge hanging over her head.

"I hope you don't mind that I wanted to come by," Emma told her, "but I wanted to see how you were doing. Lainey thought you might like the company."

"Actually, Emma, I was thinking of giving you a call and inviting you for a visit, but it's such a long drive to Malibu from Pasadena, and ... well," she hesitated and looked out at the sea. "I'm not going out in public much these days. Seems everywhere I go, people gawk at me like I'm some sort of sideshow."

"I understand, Joanna. It was no bother at all coming to you."

A maid entered with a tray of refreshments. It was Bonita, the maid Emma remembered from the Reid mansion. Emma gave her a smile of recognition. The maid returned it, seeming much more relaxed in her new environment. "Nice to see you again, Bonita." Bonita smiled and offered Emma a glass of iced tea.

It had been a month since Linwood Reid was killed by two bullets to his chest fired from a gun held by Joanna. She was currently out on bail awaiting trial. Lainey was standing by her mother. She never went back to the condominium in Westwood. She and Keith Goldstein had patched up their relationship, and the two of them were living at the beach house with Joanna. The condo was up for sale.

"I understand Lainey and Keith are engaged again."

Without looking at Emma, Joanna answered, "Yes, I am very pleased. He's a nice young man and loves her very much."

Joanna's answers seemed stilted, making Emma wonder if she was under the influence of a mild sedative. As if in answer to Emma's thoughts, Joanna turned her head and gave her a sardonic smile. Emma could see her eyes were clear and her mind unclouded.

"He loves her in spite of her crazy family," Joanna said with amusement. "Can't get much more loyal than that."

Joanna took a sip of tea and replaced her glass on the tray set on the coffee table. She folded her hands in her lap, ready to move forward with purpose. "I wanted to apologize to you and explain what was going on."

"You don't owe me any explanation or apology, Joanna." Emma was eager to hear Joanna's side of things but didn't want to push the issue. Lainey had filled her in on much of it, and some she'd learned from the media.

"Yes, I do. When I asked you to help me with Max's ghost, I think I knew he was here for Lainey, but it seemed so farfetched. A father coming back from the dead to help his daughter? That's the stuff that makes great Sunday night TV, not real life."

From her throat came the sound of a small wounded bird. She cleared it and continued. "I was hoping you'd tell me it was all bunk, but instead you only confirmed my suspicions. And when it all started tying in with Lainey and Linwood, I was afraid you'd find out everything—that Lin was broke and had taken me down with him. I had nothing of my own but the income from my job, and now that's gone."

Emma felt embarrassment on Joanna's behalf. The news media and tabloids had not been kind or subtle about the studio firing Joanna. "I saw that the studio let you go."

"Yes, doesn't matter that I've worked for them for sixteen years and championed many of their hit shows. They enforced the morals clause of my contract after I was charged." Another sound, a half choke, half laugh, escaped her lips. "Considering the behavior of over half the executives at the studio, that was a real kick in the pants. Morals clause, my ass."

Emma didn't want to wallow in Joanna's personal tragedy like the bloodthirsty general public was doing, but she wanted to know about the ring. "Joanna, did you tell your attorney about the haunted ring?"

She shook her head. "No. Lainey and I discussed that and thought we shouldn't because it would make everyone think I was insane, or at least my attorney might want to use it to get me off on insanity. Besides, I didn't have the ring when I fired the gun. The shooting falls squarely on my shoulders."

Emma thought about Addy Ames. The ghost had alluded to having a hand in the shooting of Linwood Reid, and Emma knew Addy didn't need the ring to cause mischief. Still, Emma kept quiet. Joanna was right; it would be viewed as crazy talk.

Joanna stood up and walked to where the room met the patio. "Did you know I was having an affair with Lin while I was married to Max?"

"Lainey told me when she was at Serenity."

Joanna turned back to Emma. A small look of surprise crossed her face like a passing cloud. "She always was a smart girl." She turned back around to stare at the sea. "When I decided I wanted to try and make my marriage work, Lin was very supportive and said we would remain friends, no matter what, and we did stay in touch as friends only. When I told him about our renewal of vows, he insisted on taking me to his favorite jeweler. He said he saw the perfect ring there for Max. And it was. Max loved that ring."

"Did Lainey tell you that Lin and his family owned the ring a long time ago?"

"Yes. She told me what you found out in Pennsylvania right after we moved to this house. Quite a story. I wouldn't mind producing a TV movie about it."

Joanna pulled a pack of cigarettes and a lighter from the pocket of her loose linen trousers. She held the pack toward Emma in invitation, but Emma shook her head. "Should have known," Joanna commented. "No one smokes anymore. I only do it when I'm nervous." She lit one and blew the smoke out toward the ocean, then leaned against the sliding door.

Emma got up, picked up their glasses of tea, and crossed the room to Joanna. "Why don't we make ourselves comfortable outside while you smoke?" Silently Joanna followed Emma to cushioned chairs arranged around a patio table.

"When did you realize Lin had a motive in suggesting that particular ring?" Emma asked as she placed Joanna's tea in front of her.

"The pieces started falling together the day I visited you in Pasadena, when you told me the ring was haunted. I remembered Lin insisting that was the ring I should buy Max, then later insisting we give the stone to Lainey to use in her engagement ring. When Lainey started having trouble, he suggested that awful facility in Cabo. As soon as I got home that day, I checked out what you said about that place, Emma, and it was all true." Joanna took a drag from her cigarette and blew the smoke in the direction of the breeze so it would not reach Emma. "Lin was going through a great deal of trouble to kill off my family for their money, and I never realized it until then."

With her free hand, she picked up her glass and took a long drink of her tea. "That's why I killed him, because he was going to kill Lainey." Her voice was being corralled into an even, disciplined tone by sheer will. "I overheard him talking on the phone to someone. He'd put a hit out on her as if she were a common thug. That's why I called you so frantic about her whereabouts."

Emma was horrified. "A hit? He contracted to have Lainey killed?" This was something neither Lainey nor the news had mentioned.

"That's what it sounded like to me. Of course this will all come out in the trial."

"Was it someone named Jamal?"

"Is that the yoga instructor from Serenity?"

Emma nodded.

"No, not him. Apparently he was hired just to keep tabs on Lainey. He really did think he was helping reunite Lainey with her family and had no idea what Lin had in mind. But using the information Jamal provided, the killer was going to slip into the facility and murder her." On the last several words, Joanna broke down into a series of choked, choppy sobs.

Emma was horrified. "Joanna, you don't have to tell me this if it's too difficult."

The distraught woman waved the comment off and continued. "The next day, I overheard him talking again on the phone. He thought I'd gone to the office, but I returned because I'd forgotten something. After talking to you the day before, I told him Lainey was back at Serenity. Jamal had told him she'd left a few days earlier. If Lin thought she was still gone, he'd have hunted her down. This way, I thought he could just keep thinking she'd returned, and she'd be safe wherever she was." Joanna's voice cracked through her tears. "But when I heard him again talking about killing her—telling this monster on the phone to make sure it looked like a suicide—I snapped." She dropped her cigarette butt into a small crystal ashtray before burying her head in her hands. "That was my baby girl he was talking about!"

Joanna stopped crying and looked up at Emma. "I went upstairs and got the gun Lin kept in his dressing room. Lin was coming up the main staircase as I was coming down. Before he could say a word, I drew the gun and shot him—twice. Bonita heard the shots. She came running and screamed when she saw Lin's body. I walked downstairs. When I got to the kitchen, I called 911."

"I was there, Emma. She's telling the truth." The spirit of Max Naiman materialized next to the railing. In the sunlight, with the ocean behind him, it was difficult for Emma to make him out at first, but soon his image came into view. "Lin was making arrangements to have Lainey killed." He shook his head. "Too bad ghosts can't testify."

Joanna looked at Emma with a mix of relief and fear. "Max is here with us, isn't he? I can feel him."

"Yes," Emma confirmed. "He's here, and he says he was there when you shot Lin."

"I thought he might have been. I felt that heavy weight I always get when he's around."

Joanna twisted her head from side to side, struggling to make out her dead husband.

"He's over there by the railing," Emma told her.

Joanna fixed her eyes on where Emma indicated, her face contorted with emotional pain. "I am so sorry, Max." She started to cry. "I should have protected Lainey better. I failed both of you."

Max moved to stand in front of Joanna. "I forgive you, Joanna. For us it's too late, but it's not too late for you to make it up to Lainey." He turned to Emma. "Make sure you tell her what I said."

Emma nodded to the ghost, then relayed his message. Joanna put her head in her hands and quietly sobbed.

As Max's image began to fade, he leaned down, putting his mouth close to Emma's ear. "It wasn't entirely Addy's influence that caused Joanna to shoot Lin." He spoke in a conspiratorial voice, as if someone else might hear. "I could have stopped it, as I stopped Lainey, but I chose not to."

Emma jerked her head to stare at the ghost as he made his confession, but she said nothing.

"Instead, Addy and I joined forces. Joanna didn't have a chance against us, especially with the emotional state she was in that day." Max stood up, his image almost gone. "And I have no regrets. Lin needed to pay for what he'd done, and he needed to be stopped from hurting Lainey ever again."

"Max," Joanna began, straining to see him. "I am so very sorry," she repeated, choking out the words.

"I'm sorry, Joanna, he's gone." Emma reached out and patted the distraught woman's hand. "And I don't think he'll be back."

Seeing Joanna shivering, Emma suggested they go back inside. Getting Joanna on her feet, she steered her back into the house and onto the large white sofa. Joanna looked beaten and frail after telling her story, and Emma wondered how she was ever going to make it through a full trial.

"I was going to leave Lin, you know?" Joanna said once she was settled comfortably. "Long before all this started."

Emma was surprised. "I didn't know that."

"That's probably what you picked up on when you said I was different around him. I'd even visited a lawyer on the sly. That's when I found out he was in a lot of trouble and owed a lot of money. He'd gone through his own fortune and most of my money. I'm sure it was his motivation for trying to get his hands on Lainey's inheritance."

"Is that why you tried to pay Keith to marry Lainey sooner than later?"

"Yes. If she were married, I thought Lin might quit dogging her, because her money would be lost to his manipulations. I wanted her taken care of before I filed for divorce."

Emma looked around and saw a cashmere throw laid across the back of a chair. She retrieved it and arranged it across Joanna's lap, pulling it up high on her chest. Joanna clutched at it like an invalid.

"I was a fool to give him authority over my accounts, but I thought he could expand them as he claimed he'd done with his own. After all, look at the house he owned—it screamed fabulous wealth, didn't it? Turns out it belonged to a business associate of his who lives in the Middle East. I lived there for several years and never knew that. Turns out his money problems were starting about the time we started our affair."

Her coral-stained lips were dry and cracked. "I was so enthralled by Linwood Reid when I first met him. It was at a party in Beverly Hills, some charity thing Max didn't want to attend, so I went alone. Max may have been an action hero onscreen, but in real life he was a simple, laid-back guy who wanted nothing more than to spend time with his family, drive fast cars, and catch an occasional wave. Lin, on the other hand, was a powerful man with friends who made international headline news. Being with him was heady stuff. It blinded me to what he really was, and by the time I found out, it was too late to save myself, but it wasn't too late to save Lainey."

. . . .

ON THE DRIVE BACK to Pasadena, Emma thought about Joanna's ill-fated attraction to Linwood Reid even though she already had a solid, dependable man in her life. Emma compared Phil to Quinn. She was pretty sure Quinn was not after her money and was nothing like Linwood Reid, but still he was an adventurer and his life was exciting, while Phil was a laid-back guy like Max.

After receiving the news about Lin's murder, Quinn and Emma had run back to the inn, where they turned on the TV in Emma's room looking for news reports about it. While Emma called her mother back, Quinn used his laptop to search for the next flight back to California for Emma. When he found it, he waved her over to the computer.

"Mother," she said into her cell phone while checking out the flight Quinn indicated, "there's a flight leaving here around eight o'clock tonight. It connects through Washington, DC, and gets me into LAX around twelve thirty in the morning. I'll be on it if I have to stow away in the bathroom."

"What about your research, Emma?" her mother asked. "You really need to get to the bottom of that ring or no one will be at peace. Dad and I can help Lainey."

"I did that today, Mother. I don't think Addy's going to be bothering anyone else again."

After hanging up with her mother, Emma called the airline and booked her return trip for that night. She had an open-return first-class ticket and had no problem getting on the short flight to DC. On the second leg of her journey, she snagged the last available seat.

Quinn wanted to go with her back to Los Angeles, but Emma had told him no, things were complicated enough. While he watched and Granny chaperoned, Emma threw her clothes and toiletries into her small suitcase. If she left soon, she'd make the flight in plenty of time.

"Wow," she said to Quinn as they said their goodbyes. They were in the back parking lot of the inn, standing next to Emma's rental car. "It feels like I've been here a week instead of just one day."

He reached out to touch her hair. "You've been one busy ghost hunter. You should come back when you have time to relax. There are lots of great things to do around here. Or maybe I should come visit you in California."

Without thinking, Emma blurted out, "You'd love Julian. I'm sure of it."

"Is that an invitation?"

Emma looked away. Around them, slender trees swayed in the breeze like a chorus of dancers. "I don't know what it is, Quinn." She turned back to look at him. "And frankly—"

"And frankly, my dear," Quinn said, cutting her off, "you don't give a damn?"

"No, not that at all," she insisted with a frown. "I was going to say, frankly, I don't have time to think about my personal life right now."

She started to get into the car but stopped and turned back to look again at Dr. Quinn Keenan. She started to say something else but wasn't sure what it was. Perhaps it had all been said.

Surrendering one last, small smile, she climbed into the driver's side of the rental car, buckled up, and turned over the engine. Granny was perched in the passenger's seat. Emma started backing the car out of the tight parking spot.

"You gonna make that flight?" Granny asked with concern.

"I have plenty of time as long as I don't have any car trouble between here and the airport."

"Good. I can't wait to get you home where you belong."

A sharp retort was on the tip of Emma's tongue, but she swallowed it. She wasn't in the mood to spar with Granny at the moment.

Once out of the parking spot, Emma turned the car toward the narrow exit. It spilled onto Broadway. A left onto Broadway, then a right at the corner, and she'd be on her way to the airport.

She took one last look in her rearview mirror. Quinn was standing a few feet behind her car, watching her leave. His left hand was stuffed into the pocket of his jeans. His right hand was against his heart.

Emma stopped the car and stared at him with heavy eyes.

"What's the matter?" asked Granny. "Did the car break down already?"

Without answering, Emma unbuckled her seat belt and climbed back out of the car. She stood for a moment looking at Quinn but not moving. He didn't move either. Taking a deep breath, Emma quickly covered the steps between them and threw her arms around his neck. Their kiss was deep and hard, finally interrupted by the honk of a horn.

Breaking apart, they saw another car coming through the tiny parking lot, heading for the exit. Emma's car blocked its progress.

Emma raised a hand to the other driver. "Just a minute."

She cupped Quinn's face in her palm for a second, then spun on her heel and did a swan dive back into her car. A second later she was on Broadway, waiting for the light at the corner.

"Humph," Granny huffed. "Was that a goodbye kiss or a see-ya-later kiss?"

"God help me, Granny," replied Emma, wiping tears away with the back of her left hand, "I don't know."

. . . .
the end

author's note

As with all my Granny Apples novels, I enjoy weaving the past with the present and fiction with reality. The Pennsylvanian town of Jim Thorpe (formerly known as Mauch Chunk) is a real place, and many of the spots Emma visits or talks about—such as the Old Jail Museum, the Dimmick Library, and the Inn at Jim Thorpe—are also real.

The Molly Maguires and their trials and executions are also a part of the history of the town of Jim Thorpe. The hanged men I mention in the book—Alexander Campbell, Edward Kelly, John "Yellow Jack" Donohue, and Thomas Fisher—were real, though I took quite a bit of liberty with Edward Kelly, the youngest of the bunch.

Feel free to visit the charming town of Jim Thorpe and the Old Jail Museum. Betty Lou McBride, the actual owner of the museum, will be happy to show you the gallows, the dungeon, and the hand-print on the wall of cell number 17.

Visit www.jimthorpe.org or www.theoldjailmuseum.com for more information about Jim Thorpe, PA, and the Molly Maguires.

**Read on for a sneek peek at the seventh book
in the Odelia Grey Mystery series...**

*Coming in
September 2012!*

EXCERPT

THE JOINT. THE SLAMMER. *The clink.* The words trekked through my brain like muddy feet across a clean floor.

The bright light above assaulted my tired, gritty eyes. All I wanted to do was go home and go to bed. I tried to think of synonyms for *bed* but failed. Instead, my mind kept to its single track like a wheel in a rut.

Hoosegow. Big house. Pokey.

I didn't know how long I'd been in this room. It was small and windowless, containing a sturdy metal table and a few chairs. Was it morning yet? It had to be. Resting my arms on the table, I cradled my head on them, face down, to escape the light.

"Really, Dev, that's all I can tell you." I spoke without lifting my head, the words coming slow, barely above a whisper, as if in church instead of jail.

Dev Frye, Newport Beach homicide detective and friend, parked half his butt on the edge of the long table. His close presence caused me to lift my head. Dev looked down with a mixture of disbelief and barely reined-in anger. He'd looked that way for hours. "Do you want to call an attorney, Odelia?"

It wasn't the first time he'd asked me that question, but this was the first time I'd seriously considered it as an option. "Do I need an attorney?" The question seeped out of me coated with fear.

I raised my head until I was upright again and looked from Dev to the other detective in the room. She'd been introduced to me as Detective Andrea Fehring.

"I thought I was just pulled in for questioning. I mean, I wasn't Mirandized or anything. That's what they do on TV when they arrest people, isn't it?" Detective Fehring, a trim woman with bobbed black hair and dark eyes, remained silent and studied me like a specimen under a glass slide. Even though there were several other chairs in the room, she stood leaning against the beige-painted wall.

Dev let out a uneven grumble that started deep in his gut. When he spoke, his usually deep, gravelly voice went up an octave, sounding like a Yahtzee cup shaken with too many dice. "No, Odelia, you're not under arrest. *Yet.*" He emphasized the last word with the sharpness of an awl puncture. "But you were found at the scene of a murder, alone, in the middle of the night, wearing a bloody nightgown."

"I wasn't found at the scene like a lost wallet, Dev." I was dangling over hot water, and I knew it. Mustering what strength I had left, I dropped the whisper, snapping at the detectives like a lobster about to be thrown into a hard boil. "I'm the one who discovered the body and called you. Remember? I've only told you that a hundred times."

Dev had been the first and only call I'd made upon finding the body. I'd called him at home. Soon after, Dev had arrived in his car, with several police cruisers as backup.

"But why were you there in the first place?" he asked, his face hard and crusty, like old bread.

A knock sounded on the door. A uniformed officer stepped in and motioned to Dev, who left after giving Fehring a meaningful look.

I was no longer in my nightie. As soon as I arrived at the Newport Beach Police Station, they'd taken it and the hoodie and jeans I'd also been wearing for evidence and gave me an extra-large tee shirt and some sweatpants to wear. Since I'd left the house in my nightgown, I hadn't been wearing a bra, and now I felt naked without one. I crossed my arms in front of my big boobs more out of modesty than defense.

"May I call my husband?" I asked Fehring.

"Detective Frye already did."

"Good." In spite of the word, it didn't feel good. I would have preferred to call Greg myself, after I'd had a chance to rehearse and soften the facts. I had thought about calling Greg while I waited with the body for Dev but dismissed the idea, hoping I could simply answer a few questions and be on my way. The plan had been to tell Greg about my nocturnal activities over a nice breakfast. I would make him blueberry pancakes with bacon—one of his favorites. Who knows, I might even have woken him up with a booty call before easing into my confession.

Upon receiving Dev's call, I had no doubt Greg sped out of our house in Seal Beach, tires on his van squealing on the pavement. And I'm sure he was also glued to his cell phone, calling either

Seth Washington or Mike Steele, both attorneys, and begging one of them to meet him at the station. Greg was going to be madder than hell over this, but at least he'd be on my side. The heated lecture would come once we got home.

Fehring stepped closer to the table, her face deadpan. "So you're the infamous Odelia Grey. I've heard a lot of stories about you."

"You shouldn't believe everything you hear." I squirmed in my chair, which was plastic and not made for someone with my bulky butt.

"Frye has a soft spot for you, but I don't. Remember that." Her dark eyes narrowed into two small ink pools. I noticed for the first time her dark hair was laced with silver strands.

If she was trying to scare me, it was working. I looked into her face and saw not a hint of warmth, only tired lines and a thin, hard mouth on a face wearing very little makeup. She could have been anywhere between thirty-five and forty-five years of age.

"They call you the Corpse Magnet, don't they?" she asked without a smidgen of amusement.

"Who's 'they'?" My words had the attitude of a combatant in a playground tussle. Fear was making me cheeky instead of compliant. My common sense tried to get the upper hand but failed. "It's not like it's on my birth certificate."

Corpse Magnet was an ugly nickname given to me by Seth Washington in a fit of exasperation and was only used sparingly by my closest friends whenever I stumbled across a dead body, which was more often than one would think. I didn't know the handle had become public knowledge. Dev must have told her.

"Don't get cute," Fehring warned. "And it's not cute when private citizens get mixed up in serious crimes. You put yourself and others in danger." She pitched forward, slapping both of her hands flat on the table across from me. I noticed her square-shaped nails were clean and trim and shined with a coating or two of clear polish. "You can put officers in danger nosing around, and that I take personally."

"Trust me, it's not my idea of a good time. It just seems to happen."

"Are you saying you just *happened* to be standing in someone else's house in the middle of the night when that woman was killed?"

"She was dead when I got there. I told you that."

Fehring stepped back and leaned against the wall again. She stuck her hands in her pants pockets and returned to studying me with laser eyes. "Personally, I think this time you did the killing yourself."

"No!" I cried out in urgency. "I swear I didn't. I—" but my words were cut off by Dev's return. With him was my husband, Greg Stevens, and Seth Washington. Seth isn't only an attorney but a close personal friend. His wife, Zenobia—better known as Zee—is my best friend. I was so happy to see them, I nearly cried. But my joy was cut short by the look on Greg's face. If Dev's face looked as hard as day-old bread, Greg's was the truck that ran over the bread. I almost peed my borrowed sweatpants.

Seth turned to Dev. "I'd like a word with my client."

As soon as Dev and Andrea Fehring filed out, I said to Seth, "I didn't know you were a criminal attorney."

Seth fixed me with his espresso eyes. "I didn't realize you needed a criminal attorney—at least not yet."

Yet. There was that annoying word again. It hung in the air alongside the one Dev had thrown out—a pair of verbal vultures just waiting to pounce and make accusations about my evening.

Greg rolled his wheelchair up to where I was sitting. No hug. No kiss. The pressurized steam coming from his ears could have heated milk for a latte. "What in the hell is going on, Odelia?"

"Calm down, Greg," Seth told him. "We need to get to the bottom of this—and quickly."

Greg looked raggedy with his light brown hair uncombed and the nighttime stubble sprouting around his usually groomed Van Dyke beard. "Seth, was it *your* wife who sneaked out of the house in the middle of the night to have a slumber party with a dead woman?"

"Of course not," Seth admitted. "Zee has more sense."

I snapped my head around to look at my so-called lawyer. "I beg your pardon? Are you on my side here or not?" When neither Seth nor Greg said anything, I tacked on, "Don't make me call Mike Steele. Please." It was more of a supplication than a threat.

After taking a second or two and several deep breaths, Greg asked, "So who's the stiff this time?"

"Please let me ask the questions, Greg," said Seth, using his lawyer voice. "I think it will go faster if I handle this."

It was in Greg's nature to take charge, but what Seth said made sense. He was, after all, the only law degree in the room. As soon as Greg nodded his assent, Seth turn to me. "So who's the stiff?"

Greg did a double take but remained silent.

"Her name was Connie Holt," I told the two of them. "She was Lily's mother."

Seth's mouth fell open; so much for his legal composure. "Lily? You mean the sweet little girl sleeping under my roof right now?"

"Yes. Connie is Lily's mother and the sister of my boss, Erica Mayfield. Like I've told the police, I found her—Connie, that is—already dead when I got to Erica's house. I didn't know who she was until the police told me."

Greg groaned. "Please tell me you did not go over to Erica's to beg for your job back."

Seth held a hand out toward us, indicating for us to be still. "Back the bus up, folks." He turned to me. "This woman fired you, and you went to her house in the middle of the night?" He took a deep breath. "Why do you do such dumb things?"

"I am not dumb." My nose twitched in annoyance while I fought to defend my actions. "I'm impulsive." I turned to my husband for support but could see he was clearly in Seth's camp on this issue. "And I wasn't fired," I insisted. "At least not yet."

"I didn't say you were dumb, Odelia," Seth clarified. "But your actions are often those of an insane person."

I turned to Greg, but he was nodding in agreement. I was on my own.

"Maybe I should call Steele," I suggested.

Greg let out a short, dark snort. "If you think he's going to be any easier on you, you've been away from him far too long."

My hubs was right. If Steele, my former boss, were here instead of Seth, he'd be crucifying me. I just wasn't sure if it would be because of my nocturnal actions or because I didn't invite him along. He'd grown disturbingly fond of sticking his nose into my amateur murder investigations. Come to think of it, so had Greg, making me believe his anger was more focused on my safety and possible future criminal record than on my actions specifically.

"We're wasting time," Seth told us. "According to Dev, they don't believe Odelia is the killer. The woman was shot twice in the chest and may have been dead several hours before Odelia called him."

"I can vouch for her whereabouts," Greg offered. "At least until about eleven. We went to a dinner party last night given by one of my basketball buddies and his wife. We got home around ten and went straight to bed. I'd had a few drinks and fell asleep just as the Channel Four news started. Odelia was in bed with me."

Seth knitted his brows as he wrote down the information. "That will help in the event they start looking at her as a suspect."

Suspect? My stomach did a flip. I took a sip of water from the paper cup Dev had brought me earlier.

"I think I got to Erica's just after one," I added. Seeing no napkin or tissue, I wiped my mouth with the back of my hand.

Remembering how Connie had looked when I stumbled across her, I shuddered. "When I arrived, Connie was staring up at the ceiling, pale and still, the front of her long-sleeved tee shirt drenched in blood. I tried to give her CPR, just in case she wasn't dead—that's how I got so much blood on me." I took another deep breath. "I told the police all this several times."

"I'm positive they're checking your clothing for gunshot residue to be sure." Seth stopped writing and looked at me. "Did they test your hands yet?"

"They applied some sort of adhesive strip to them, like they were waxing for hair removal. They also took a swab for DNA. I thought it would help if I was cooperative."

Seth nodded as he made more notes. When he was finished, he put his pen down, folded his hands, and leaned his large body back in his chair. "Okay, Odelia, tell me how you got to Ms. Mayfield's house in the first place."

"I drove."

Greg placed a hand on my arm. It was his first act of affection since entering the room, and it meant the world to me. "He means what caused you to go there?"

"Oh."

Of course that's what Seth meant, but the night's events and lack of sleep were taking their toll on my brain cells.

I dug through my tired mind for the root of my actions. When did all this craziness start to take shape? What exactly was its genesis? It had started small, of that I was sure. Like a palm-size snowball, over the past couple of days it had gathered in size with every discussion and situation until it had become a large, heavy orb too big to ignore.

I took a deep breath, ready to start at the beginning.

"It all started with Lily," I told Greg and Seth. This was not something I had told the police, because it really had just come to me.

"The little girl?" Seth asked with surprise.

WWW.MIDNIGHTINKBOOKS.COM

From the gritty streets of New York City to sacred tombs in the Middle East, it's always midnight somewhere. Join us online at any hour for fresh new voices in mystery fiction.

At midnightinkbooks.com you'll also find our author blog, new and upcoming books, events, book club questions, excerpts, mystery resources, and more.

MIDNIGHT INK ORDERING INFORMATION

Order Online:
• Visit our website, www.midnightinkbooks.com, select your books, and order them on our secure server.

Order by Phone:
• Call toll-free within the US and Canada at
  1-888-NITE-INK (1-888-648-3465)
• We accept VISA, MasterCard, and American Express

Order by Mail:
Send the full price of your order (MN residents add 6.875% sales tax) in US funds, plus postage & handling, to:

> Midnight Ink
> 2143 Wooddale Drive
> Woodbury, MN 55125-2989

Postage & Handling:

Standard (US, Mexico & Canada). If your order is:
> $24.99 and under, add $4.00
> $25.00 and over, FREE STANDARD SHIPPING

AK, HI, PR: $16.00 for one book plus $2.00 for each additional book.

International Orders (airmail only):
> $16.00 for one book plus $3.00 for each additional book.

Orders are processed within 2 business days.
Please allow for normal shipping time.
Postage and handling rates subject to change.

A spirited new series from award-winning,
critically acclaimed Odelia Grey mystery author
Sue Ann Jaffarian

A GHOST OF GRANNY APPLES MYSTERY

*Along with a sprinkling of history, this ghostly new
mystery series features the amateur sleuth team of
Emma Whitecastle and the spirit of her pie-baking
great-great-great-grandmother, Granny Apples.
Together, they solve mysteries of the past—starting
with Granny's own unjust murder rap
from more than a century ago.*

Ghost
à la
Mode

(BOOK ONE)

ranny was famous for her award-winning apple pies—
and notorious for murdering her husband, Jacob, at their
homestead in Julian, California. The only trouble is,
Granny was framed, then murdered. For more than one hundred years, Granny's spirit has been searching for someone to
help her see that justice is served—and she hits pay dirt when
she pops into a séance attended by her great-great-great-
granddaughter, modern-day divorced mom Emma Whitecastle. Together, Emma and Granny Apples solve mysteries of the
past—starting with Granny's own unjust murder rap in the
final days of the California Gold Rush.

Ghost in the Polka Dot Bikini

(BOOK TWO)

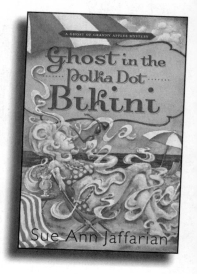

Imagine spending eternity with your backside hanging out—that's what Emma Whitecastle and Granny Apples can't help but think when they meet the ghost of Tessa North frolicking in the surf off Catalina Island. Tessa, a young starlet who died on the island in the 1960s wearing nothing but a polka dot bikini, won't cross over until "Curtis" comes for her. To help the winsome, bikini-clad spirit, Emma and Granny must find out who Curtis is and how Tessa died. Their investigation takes them from the grit and glamour of Hollywood to Kennedy-era political intrigue—before hitting dangerously close to home.

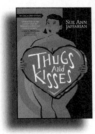

An Odelia Grey Mystery ➤

The hugely popular mystery series that features unforgettable amateur sleuth Odelia Grey

You'll love Odelia Grey, a middle-aged, plus-sized paralegal with a crazy boss, insatiable nosiness, and a knack for being in close proximity to dead people. This snappy, humorous series is the first from award-winning, critically acclaimed mystery author Sue Ann Jaffarian.

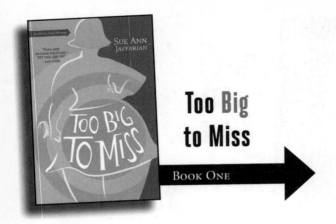

Too Big to Miss

BOOK ONE

Too big to miss—that's Odelia Grey. A never-married, middle-aged, plus-sized woman who makes no excuses for her weight, she's not Superwoman—she's just a mere mortal standing on the precipice of menopause, trying to cruise in an ill-fitting bra. She struggles with her relationships, her crazy family, and her crazier boss. And then there's her knack for being in close proximity to dead people…

When her close friend Sophie London commits suicide in front of an online web-cam by putting a gun in her mouth and pulling the trigger, Odelia's life is changed forever. Sophie, a plus-sized activist and inspiration to imperfect women, is the last person anyone would ever have expected to end her own life. Suspecting foul play, Odelia is determined to get to the bottom of her friend's death. Odelia's search for the truth takes her from Southern California strip malls to the world of live web-cam porn to the ritzy enclave of Corona del Mar.

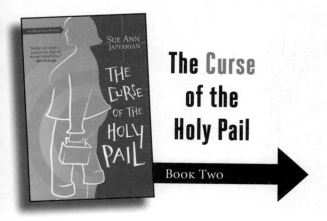

The Curse of the Holy Pail

Book Two

s the "Holy Pail" cursed? Every owner of the vintage Chappy Wheeler lunchbox—a prototype based on a 1940s TV Western—has died. And now Sterling Price, a business tycoon and client of Odelia Grey's law firm, has been fatally poisoned. Is it a coincidence that Price's one-of-a-kind lunch pail—worth over thirty grand—has disappeared at the same time?

Treading cautiously since her recent run-in with a bullet, Odelia takes small bites of this juicy, calorie-free mystery—and is soon ravenous for more! Her research reveals a sixty-year-old unsolved murder and Price's gold-digging ex-fiancée with two married men wrapped around her breasts—uh, finger. Mix in a surprise marriage proposal that sends an uncertain Odelia into chocolate sedation and you've got an unruly recipe for delicious disaster.

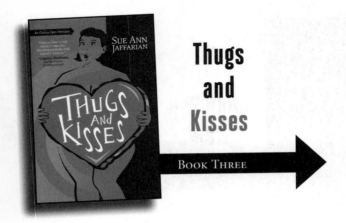

Thugs and Kisses

BOOK THREE

With the class bully murdered at her thirtieth high-school reunion and her boss, the annoying Michael Steele, missing, Odelia doesn't know which hole to poke her big nose into first. This decision is made for her as she's again swept into the action involving contract killers, tangled relationships, and fatal buyer's remorse. Throughout this adventure, Odelia deals with her on-again, off-again relationship with Greg and her attraction to detective Devin Frye.

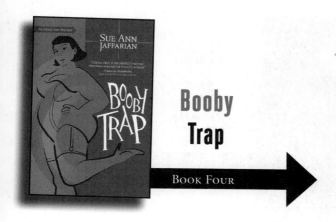

Booby Trap

BOOK FOUR

C ould the Blond Bomber serial killer possibly be Dr. Brian Eddy, plastic surgeon to the rich and famous? Odelia never would have suspected the prominent doctor of killing the bevy of buxom blonds if she hadn't heard it directly from her friend Lillian—Dr. Eddy's own mother!—over lunch one day. This mystery gets even messier than Odelia's chicken parmigiana sandwich as Odelia discovers just how difficult—and dangerous—it will be to bust this killer.

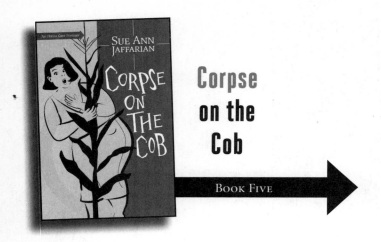

Corpse on the Cob

BOOK FIVE

What do you have to lose when you go searching for the mother who walked out of your life thirty-four years ago—besides your pride, your nerves, and your sanity? Odelia finds herself up to her ears in trouble when she reunites with her mom in a corn maze at the Autumn Fair in Holmsbury, Massachusetts. For starters, there's finding the dead body in the cornfield—and seeing her long-lost mom crouched beside the corpse, with blood on her hands…

order online 24/7 at
midnightinkbooks.com

Praise for
The Hummingbird's Cage

"A beautiful story of one woman's reinvention, with a little touch of magic that will warm your heart."
—Laura Lane McNeal, author of *Dollbaby*

"Here is a story of a woman's courage and strength, the power of friendship, and the gift of grace, which magically appears when we need it most. Truly inspired and beautifully written; you will love this novel."
—Lynne Branard, author of *The Art of Arranging Flowers*

"Brilliant and beautifully written. Unflinching. Honest. Heartbreaking."
—Menna van Praag, author of *The House at the End of Hope Street*

"So much for her veneer as an ink-stained newspaper columnist. Tamara Dietrich's *The Hummingbird's Cage* draws you in with unusual characters, unexpected twists, and a charming small town that gives us all reason to ponder: If you had the opportunity to reset your life, would you take it?"—Pulitzer Prize–winning journalist Paul Giblin

"You don't just read *The Hummingbird's Cage*; you fall into it. Dietrich's writing is descriptive in a way that fully captures each moment of a character's journey."
—Pulitzer Prize–winning journalist Mark Mahoney

The Hummingbird's Cage

TAMARA DIETRICH

NAL
ACCENT

Published by the Penguin Group
Penguin Group (USA) LLC, 375 Hudson Street,
New York, New York 10014

USA | Canada | UK | Ireland | Australia | New Zealand | India | South Africa | China
penguin.com
A Penguin Random House Company

First published by NAL Accent, an imprint of New American Library,
a division of Penguin Group (USA) LLC

First Printing, June 2015

 REGISTERED TRADEMARK—MARCA REGISTRADA

LIBRARY OF CONGRESS CATALOGING-IN-PUBLICATION DATA:

Dietrich, Tamara.
The Hummingbird's cage / Tamara Dietrich.
pages cm.
ISBN 978-0-451-47337-0
1. Mother and child—Fiction. 2. Abusive men—Fiction. 3. Domestic fiction.
4. Psychological fiction. I. Title.
PS3604.I3733H866 2015
813'.6—dc23   2014047187

Printed in the United States of America
1   3   5   7   9   10   8   6   4   2

Set in Bell MT
Designed by Spring Hoteling

To every woman with a story of brokenness.
You are stronger than you know.

Acknowledgments

Writing can be a solitary business, but getting a novel ready to pass into the hands of readers never is. Every manuscript needs gentle readers, hawkeyed nitpickers and wizards of the Big Picture.

First, to Mike Holtzclaw and Veronica Chufo for giving the first draft an early read and forgiving its countless rough edges. Novelist Leah Price, whose keen sense of plot helped add depth and drama, and whose ongoing moral support is invaluable. My fellow Pagan River Writers—Diana McFarland, Hugh Lessig, Sabine Hirschauer, Felicia Mason and Dave Macaulay. You help keep the creative torch burning every month with pizza and wine, page reviews and good humor when it's sorely needed. To jazz diva, writer and sister-from-another-mother M. J. Wilde, who has always believed in magic and miracles and, most important, in friends.

To Trudy Hale at the Porches on the James River and Cathy and Rhet Tignor at Pretty Byrd Cottage on the Eastern Shore. Their retreats were sanctuaries when I needed them—peace and quiet and blissful views from my window.

ACKNOWLEDGMENTS

My literary agent, Barbara Braun, at Barbara Braun Associates, who took on a would-be novelist and steered her toward her lifelong ambition. Editor Jenn Fisher and editorial director Claire Zion at Penguin/NAL, for seeing promise in the manuscript and shepherding it through to publication.

I can't overlook my sixth-grade teacher at Northeast Elementary. Eons ago, Betty Hinzman was the first to believe in an awkward adolescent who said she wanted to write a book one day. She'll never know how much that meant.

And last, but never least, to my mother, Betty Phillips. (See, Mom? This is what you can do with a creative writing degree.)

To all, my warmest thanks and gratitude.

The Hummingbird's Cage

Part I
Asunder

It's difficult to discern the blessing in the midst of brokenness.

—Charles F. Stanley

January 1

My husband tells me I look washed up. Ill favored, he says, like old bathwater circling the drain. If my clothes weren't there to hold me together, he says, I'd flush all away. He tells me these things and worse as often as he can, till there are times I start to believe him and I can feel my mind start to dissolve into empty air.

There's no challenging him when he gets like this. No logic will do. No defense. I tried in the past, but no more. Back when I was myself—when I was Joanna, and not the creature I've become at Jim's hands—I would have challenged him. Stood up to him. If there were any speck of that Joanna left now, she would at least tell him he had his similes all wrong. That I am not like the water, but the stone it crashes against, worried over and over by the waves till there's nothing left but

3

to yield, worn down to surrendered surfaces. That every time I cry, more of me washes away.

This is all to Jim's purpose—the unmaking of me. He's like a potter at his wheel, pounding the wet clay to a malleable lump, then building it back up to a form he thinks he might like. Except there is no form of me that could please his eye. He's tried so many, you would think that surely one would have won him by now. Soothed the beast.

In the early years, I was pliant enough. I was young and a pure fool. I thought that was love, and one of the compromises of marriage. I didn't understand then that for Jim the objective is not creation. It's not building a thing up from nothing into something pleasing. What pleases him most is the moment when he can pound it back again into something unrecognizable.

I understand what's happening—I do—but it's all abstraction at this point. I am not stupid. Or, I wasn't always. In high school I was smart, and pretty enough. I completed nearly two years of college in Albuquerque before I left to run away with Jim, a deputy sheriff from McGill County who swept me off my feet with his uniform and bad-boy grin.

In the beginning, it was a few insults or busted dinner plates if his temper kicked up after a hard day. He would always make it up to me with a box of candy or flowers from the grocery store. The first time he raised a welt, he drove to the store for a bag of ice chips, packed some in a towel and held it gently against my face. And when he looked at me, I believed I could see tenderness in his eyes. Regret. And things would be wonderful for a while, as if he were setting out to win me all over again. I told myself this was what they meant when they said marriage is hard work. I had no evidence otherwise.

A part of me knew better. Knew about the cycle of batterer

and battered. And she was right there, sitting on my shoulder, screaming in my ear. Because she knew this wasn't a cycle at all but a spiral, gyring down to a point of no return.

But I wasn't listening. Wouldn't listen. All mounting evidence to the contrary, I believed Jim truly loved me. That I loved him. Sometimes people are that foolish.

I bought books on passive aggression and wondered what I could do to make our life together better because I loved him so. The first time he backhanded me, he wept real tears and swore it would never happen again. I believed that, too, and bought books on anger management.

When I was two months' pregnant, one of his friends winked at me when we told him the news. After he left, Jim accused me of flirting. He called me a whore and punched me hard in the stomach. It doubled me over and choked the breath out of me till I threw up. Two days later, I started to bleed. By the time Jim finally took me to the clinic—the next county over, where no one knew us—I was hemorrhaging blood and tissue. The doctor glanced at the purple bruise on my abdomen and diagnosed a spontaneous abortion. He scraped what was left of the fetus from my womb and offered to run tests to see whether it had been a boy or a girl, and whether there was some medical reason for the miscarriage.

I told him no. In my heart I knew the baby had been a boy. I'd already picked a name for him. And the reason he had to be purged out of me was standing at my shoulder as I lay on the exam table, silent and watchful and coiled.

That was years ago, before the spiral constricted to a noose. I have a daughter now. Laurel—six years old and beautiful. Eyes like cool green quartz and honey blond hair. Clever and sweet and quick to love. Jim has never laid a hand on her—

I've prevented that, at least. When his temper starts to kick in, I scoop her up quickly and bundle her off to her room, pop in her earbuds and turn on babbling, happy music. I tell myself as I shut her bedroom door that the panic in her pale face isn't hers, but my own projection. That it will soon be over. That bruises heal and the scars barely show. That it will be all right. It will be all right. It will be all right.

January 7

Jim has started probation—ninety days for disorderly conduct, unsupervised. Before that, ten days in lockup that were supposed to make an impression. That was the idea, at least. But old habits—they do die hard.

He's working second shift now, which is not to his liking. Or mine. It throws us together during the day, when Laurel is at school and there's nothing to distract him. He tells me if the eggs are too runny, the bacon too dry, the coffee too bitter. He watches while I wash the breakfast dishes to make sure they're properly cleaned and towel dried. Sometimes he criticizes the pace, but if I'm slow it's because I'm deliberate. Two years ago a wet plate slipped from my hands and broke on the floor. He called me butterfingers and twisted my pinkie till it snapped. It was a clean break, he said, and would heal on its own. It did, but the knuckle is misshapen and won't bend anymore.

I clean the house exactly the same way every day. I time myself when I vacuum each rug. I clean the dishes in the same order, with glasses and utensils first and heavy pans last. I count every sweep of the sponge mop. I spray polish on the same corners of the kitchen table, in the same order, before I fold a cloth four times and buff the wood to a streakless, lemony shine. It doesn't mean he won't find some fault—the rules are fickle—but it lessens the likelihood.

Around two p.m., after he showers and pulls on his freshly laundered uniform, slings his Sam Browne belt around his shoulder and holsters his Glock 22, I brace as he kisses me good-bye on the cheek. When the door shuts behind him and his Expedition backs out of the drive, my muscles finally begin to unknot. Sometimes they twitch as they do. Sometimes I cry.

It wasn't always like this. In the beginning I was content to be a homemaker, even if I felt like a throwback. And Jim seemed pleased with my efforts, if not always my results. I learned quickly he was a traditionalist—each gender in its place. At the time I thought it was quaint, not fusty. I called him a Neanderthal once, and he laughed. I would never call him that now. Not to his face.

He had his moods, and with experience I could sense them cooking up. First came the distracted look; then he'd pull into himself. His muscles would grow rigid, like rubber bands stretched too tight, his fists clenching and unclenching like claws. I'd rub his shoulders, his neck, his back, and he'd be grateful. He'd pull through to the other side.

But over time the black moods stretched longer and longer, the respites shorter and shorter. Something was rotting him from the inside out, like an infection. The man I'd married seemed to be corroding right in front of me.

I learned not to touch him unless he initiated it. If I so much as brushed against him, even by accident, he'd hiss and pull away as if my flesh burned.

I met Jim West ten years ago on a grassy field one October morning just as the sun crested the Sandia Mountains east of Albuquerque and shot a bolt of light onto his dark mahogany hair, rimming it with silver. He was tall and powerfully built, with sweeping dark brows, a Roman nose, cheeks ruddy from the cold and the barest stubble. I thought he was beautiful. It was the first day of the annual Balloon Fiesta, and Jim was tugging hard on a half acre of multicolored nylon, laying it out flat on the frosty ground. He was volunteering on a hot-air balloon crew preparing for the Mass Ascension. All around were a hundred other crews, a hundred other bright balloons in various stages of lift, sucking in air, staggering up and up like some great amorphous herd struggling to its feet.

Jim planted himself in the throat of the balloon envelope, spread eagle, arms wide like Da Vinci's Vitruvian man, holding it open so a massive fan could blow air inside. The balloon streaming behind him was bucking as it inhaled, and Jim trembled and frowned with the cold and the effort. His dark eyes swept the crowd—many of us students from the university— and when they lit on me, they stopped. His frown lifted. He shot me the lopsided grin I hadn't yet learned to hate, and shouted something I couldn't make out over the noise of the fans and the gas burners springing to life, belching jets of fire all around us.

I shook my head. "What?"

Jim shouted something else unintelligible. I shook my head once more and pointed to my ears. I shrugged in an exaggerated *Oh, well,* and Jim nodded. Then he mouthed slowly and distinctly, *Don't . . . go . . . away.*

I turned to my friend Terri, who leaned into me with a giggle. "Oh, my God," she murmured. "He's gorgeous."

"Oh, my God," I groaned back.

A thrill shot from my curling toes to my blushing face, and suddenly I knew how the balloons felt—galvanized by oxygen and fire, bucking skyward despite themselves. It was a mystery to me why such a man would single me out—pretty enough, I guess, but hardly the type to stop a guy in his tracks. Of the two of us, it was Terri, the saucy, leggy blonde with the air of confidence, the guys would go for.

For a half hour or so, Jim toiled away, helping tie down the parachute vent, spotting the man at the propane burner as it spat flames inside the envelope, heating the air till ever so slowly the balloon swelled and ascended, pulling hard at the wicker basket still roped to the earth.

When the basket was unloosed and it lifted off at last, all eyes followed it as it climbed the atmosphere. Or so I thought. I glanced over at Jim and his eyes were fastened on me, strangely solemn. He strode over. "Let's go," he said, and held out his hand.

Gorgeous or not, he was a stranger. In an instant, the voice of my mother—jaded by divorce and decades of bad choices—flooded my head. Warnings about the wickedness of men . . . how they love you and leave you bitter and broken. But daughters seldom use their own mothers as object lessons, do they? This man who took my breath away was holding out his hand to me. Without a word, I took it.

I believed in love at first sight then.

I believed in fate.

February 15

Yesterday, Laurel asked about Tinkerbell again. Jim was there, and looked over at me curiously. I turned toward the stove to hide my face. I clenched my teeth to keep them from chattering. I pulled in a ragged breath and said as lightly as I could:

"Tinkerbell ran away, sweetie. You know that."

Tinkerbell was a little mixed-breed dog that showed up at our door last Valentine's Day—rheumy eyed, scrawny, riddled with fleas. Laurel went ahead and gave her a name before I had a chance to warn her we could never keep a sick stray. Jim would sooner shoot it, put it out of its misery, but I didn't tell her that, either. I had picked up the phone to call county animal control when I watched Laurel pull the dog onto her lap and stroke its head. "Don't worry, Tinkerbell," she said softly. "We'll love you now."

If the dog didn't understand the words, it understood the kindness behind them. It sank its head into the crook of Laurel's arm and didn't just sigh—it moaned.

I put the phone down.

We hid Tinkerbell in the woodshed and fed her till she looked less raggedy. Filled out, rested, bathed and brushed, she was a beautiful dog, with a caramel coat and a white ruff, a tail like a fox, her soft almond eyes lined with dark, trailing streaks like Cleopatra. When she was healthy enough, we presented her to Jim. I suggested she'd make a fine gift for Laurel's upcoming birthday, less than a month away.

Jim was in a good mood that day. He paused and studied Tinkerbell, who stood quietly, almost expectantly, as if she knew what was at stake. Laurel stood at my side, just as still, just as expectant, pressing her face hard against my hand.

The risk here, it occurred to me, was in appearing to want something too much. This gives denial irresistible power.

So I shrugged. "We can always give her away, if you want."

Jim's lips twitched, his eyes narrowed, and my heart sank. Manipulation didn't work with him.

"You want her, Laurel?" he asked at last, breaking out that awful grin. "Well, okay, then. Happy birthday, baby."

Laurel wriggled with pleasure and beamed up at me. She went to Jim and kissed his cheek. "Thank you, Daddy."

I was confused, but only for a moment.

Then I understood.

Jim had one more thing now—one more thing that mattered—to snatch away from me anytime he chose, quick as a heartbeat.

Two weeks before Christmas, just before Jim was jailed to serve ten days for disorderly conduct, he did.

Laurel sits on the porch sometimes, waiting for Tinkerbell to come home again. Sometimes she calls her name over and over.

"Do you think she misses us?" she asked yesterday.

Jim ruffled her hair playfully. "I bet she'd rather be here with you, baby, than where she is right now."

Every Valentine's Day, Jim gives me a heart-shaped box of fine chocolates that, if I ate them, would turn to ash on my tongue. When he touches me, my blood runs so cold I marvel it doesn't freeze to ice in my veins.

February 29

Snow fell last night, dusting the junipers in the yard, the pickets on the fence, the thorny bougainvillea bushes under the front windows, the woodshed's red tin roof. Jim was working his shift, so I bundled Laurel in her parka and mud boots and we danced in the field next to the house, twirling till we were tipsy, catching snowflakes on our tongues, our hair, our cheeks. The sky was black as a peppercorn.

This morning, Jim noticed I took longer at the dishes than I should have, from staring out the kitchen window at the red sandstone mesas still layered with unbroken snow, like icing on red velvet cake.

By noon the sun came out and melted it all away.

March 2

This evening after I put Laurel to bed, I opened the small storage space under the stairs and removed the boxes of Christmas decorations and summer clothing, the beautiful linen shade from the antique lamp that Jim had smashed against a wall, files of legal paperwork for our mortgage and vehicle loan, tax documents. Where the boxes had been stacked, I took a screwdriver and pried up a loose floor plank. In the cubby space beneath is an old tea tin where I keep my Life Before Jim.

Jim doesn't like to be reminded that I had a Life Before. Or, rather, he doesn't like me to remember a time when I had behaviors and ideas uncensored by him. A time when I wrote poetry, and even published a few poems in small regional literary magazines. When I had friends, family. A part-time job writing at the university's public information office. Ambitions. Expectations. Thoughts.

He thinks he's hacked it all away—good wood lopped off a living tree—and he has.

All but one.

My German grandmother, my Oma, who lost her father to the Nazi purge of intellectuals, used to recite a line from an old protest song:

Die Gedanken sind frei.

Thoughts are free.

No man can know them, the song goes. *No hunter can shoot them. The darkest dungeon is futile, for my thoughts tear all gates and walls asunder.*

In my tea tin I keep my first-place certificate from a high school poetry contest, the clinic receipt from the baby I lost nine years ago, a letter my mother wrote before she passed from cancer, and a note scrawled on a slip of paper: *Run, girl, run.*

It's not much of an insurrection, I know. But it's my only evidence of a Life Before, and I cling to it.

By the time Jim moved me to Wheeler, I had already banished Terri from my life. Just after I met Jim, as he began insinuating himself into every waking hour—the classes I took, the books I read, the people I hung with—Terri's enthusiasm for him waned.

"Girl, are you sure about him?" she'd ask.

I was troubled that she doubted his intentions. Or my judgment.

"Why wouldn't I be?" I asked.

"Jo, he's calling you all day. He wants to know where you are, who you're with. He's *tracking* you."

But I'd never had a serious boyfriend before Jim. My role models for romance were Byron, the Brownings, Yeats and a manic-depressive mother who cycled through the wrong men all her life. What I saw in Jim was passion and commitment. He took me on picnics in the Sandias. We rode the tram to the peak, and he proposed on the observation deck. We spent our first weekend together in a bed-and-breakfast in the Sangre de Cristo Mountains outside Santa Fe, watching the sunrise from our bedroom window. I felt caught up in a whirlwind, breathless, but happy to let it have its way with me.

Still, when he urged me to drop a study group for semester finals so we could spend even more time together, I balked. It was our first argument. There wouldn't be many more. He told me he cared for me, wanted to be with me, thought I felt the same. Disappointment infused every syllable.

I felt cornered. I blurted, "Terri thinks we spend too much time together already."

Jim's face went blank. For several seconds he didn't speak. Then, "She said that?"

I didn't answer.

"Well," Jim said quietly, "I didn't want to tell you this, but there's more to Terri than you realize. Remember when we met? Terri called me a few days later. She said she thought we should get together sometime. I told her I was interested in you, and that was the end of it."

He was studying me as he spoke.

"I chalked it up to a misunderstanding on her part. She's never called since. I didn't want you to think less of her."

My heart began to thud against my rib cage. Blood pulsed in my ears. Terri, the sleek golden girl who excelled at everything she ever tried her hand at, who could have any man she wanted—did she want mine? Was she looking out for me, or just sowing seeds of doubt to clear a path for herself?

"I thought you trusted me. Trusted *us.*" Jim shook his head sadly. "I don't want to break up with you over this."

There must be a moment when every animal caught in a leg trap runs through the minutes, the seconds, before the coil springs. Before the swing and snap of hard metal on bone. The reversible moment—the one it would take back if only it could.

Winter break was coming up, and Terri was heading home to Boston. We had been best friends since the first day of college, but suddenly she seemed like a stranger to me. By the time she returned, Jim and I were engaged and I had dropped out of school. I wouldn't take her calls anymore or return her messages. After a while, the calls stopped.

Just before the wedding, I returned home to my apartment to find a message on a slip of paper wedged in the doorjamb:

Run, girl, run.

But the reversible moment was gone.

March 6

We live just outside Wheeler, a city of twenty thousand bordering the Navajo reservation. The town is roughly equal parts Caucasian, Hispanic and Indian—not just Navajo, but Zuni and Hopi, too. It's been described as a down-and-dirty sort of place. Billboards crowd the two interstates that run into town and out again. Signs are always advertising half-off sales on Indian jewelry—mostly questionable grades of turquoise and silver crafted into belts, earrings and squash blossom necklaces, but also smatterings of other things, like tiger's eye cabochons set in thick rings and looping strands of red branch coral. The town is notorious for its saturation of bars, liquor stores and plasma donation centers. Unless you live there, or need gas or a night's sleep, or you're in the market for souvenirs of Indian Country, it's more of a drive-through than a destination.

The McGill County sheriff's office is headquartered in

Wheeler, but its jurisdiction actually lies outside the city limits—about five thousand square miles of high desert. The rugged sandstone mesas that make up the northern horizon begin about twenty miles east, and they are something to behold, rising up out of the earth in a sloping, unbroken line, bloodred and striated.

In any given year, the county might see two murders and a half dozen rapes. I know, because Jim likes to tell me, studying my face as he recounts the details, which are far more lurid than what makes it into a deputy's report. A dozen arsons, two dozen stolen cars. Four hundred people will drive drunk. Thirty will go missing, and some will never be seen again. Three hundred will be assaulted—at least, those are the ones that make their way into a report. These usually consist of brawls between men who've had a few too many, or jealous fights over a girl, or squabbles between neighbors. Less often, young men will jump a stranger for his wallet or whatever contents of his car they can easily pawn. And some are what are commonly known as domestic disputes.

If you wonder why I never became a statistic with the sheriff's office, it wasn't for lack of trying, and not just on Jim's part. If you've never been in my shoes, you likely could never understand. Ten years ago, I couldn't have. The closest metaphor I know is the one about the boiling frog: Put a frog in a pot of boiling water, and he will jump out at once. But put him in a pot of cold water and turn up the heat by degrees, and he'll cook to death before he realizes it.

After the slap comes the fist. After the black eye, the split lip. The punch that caused me to miscarry was a bad one. After that, came the fear: That I did not know this man. That I didn't know myself. That he could seriously hurt me. That he might even kill me. That there was no one to turn to, so thoroughly had he separated me from familiar people and places. He had moved me into his world where he was an authority, an officer of the law, and I was the outsider, an unknown quantity.

Then there was the shame. That somehow I had caused this. That somehow I deserved this. That this was, as he so often told me, my fault. If only I were smarter or prettier, took better care of the house, were more cheerful. If only I had salted the beans right, or hadn't left the toothpaste tube facedown instead of faceup.

In point of fact, when I finally felt the water start to boil, I did try to get help. But Jim was ready. It happened the first time he cracked one of my ribs, and I dialed 911. He didn't stop me. This was an object lesson, only I didn't know it. The deputy who knocked on the door was a longtime fishing buddy who still had one of Jim's favorite trout spinners in his own tackle box at home. By the time the deputy left the house, he and Jim had plans that Sunday for Clearwater Lake.

Jim waved the man out of the driveway, came inside and closed the door. I was leaning against the china cabinet, holding my side. Laurel was a toddler then, and wailing in her crib. It hurt so bad to bend that I couldn't pick her up. Jim came at me so fast I thought he intended to ram right through me. I shuffled back against the wall. He braced one broad hand against the doorjamb, and with the other shoved hard against the china cabinet. It toppled over and crashed to the floor, shattering our wedding set to bits, scattering eggshell porcelain shards from one end of the room to the other.

Jim was red with rage, snorting like a bull. "You stupid bitch," he said, panting hard. "Clean this up."

He stepped toward me again, this time more slowly. His

hand came up and I winced in anticipation, but he only cupped my cheek in his palm, stroking my skin. When he spoke again, the pitch of his voice was changed utterly—low and gentle, like a caress.

"And if you ever call them again, I swear to Christ I will cut your fucking fingers off before they even get here."

After that, you feel the heat, but not the burn. After that, you get on your knees and pick up the pieces, grateful you can still do that much. And after that, you lean over your daughter's crib no matter how much it hurts and pick her up and hold her so tight you think you'll smother both of you.

March 10

Laurel turned seven yesterday, and it was a good day. Jim was off and had picked up presents—a dress with ruffles and matching shoes, a DVD of *Sleeping Beauty* and a stuffed rabbit with a pink bow around its neck holding a heart-shaped pillow that read, *Daddy's Girl.* He'd suggested a coconut cake, even though Laurel's favorite is chocolate. I made chocolate, but covered it with coconut icing.

Laurel doesn't like ruffles, either, or matching sets of clothing. Left to herself, she'll pair pink stripes with purple polka dots and top it with a yellow sunhat freckled with red daisies. It will look like she's pulled on whatever has risen to the top of the laundry basket, but in fact she will spend a half hour in careful consideration of this piece with that before making her final decision. Jim jokes that she must be color-blind. He calls it "clownwear," and if he's home to see it, he makes her change. But I let her mix and match as she pleases, because she says she is a rainbow and doesn't want any color to feel left out.

March 13

Jim's probation has ended. Three months of good behavior, ten days served, an official reprimand and a misdemeanor conviction that a career man can overcome with enough time and a little effort. That was the sheriff's encouraging speech when he met with Jim and me this morning to, as he says, close the book on an unfortunate incident.

As far as he knew, we had merely argued. And I, being foolish, had taken the stairs too fast and slipped. And if it was anything more serious than this, well, he was a big believer in the healing power of time.

"I've known you two for—how long? I never met a nicer couple," he said. "You're young; you can get beyond this. You've got a daughter—Laura? Think of her. Go home. Get your family back. Forget it ever happened." He wagged his finger at Jim and laughed. "But don't ever let it happen again, Corporal."

Jim grinned. "No, sir. It won't."

As jail time goes, Jim had it easy. He was kept in a separate cell to protect him from other prisoners, some of whom he might have arrested. His buddies brought him men's magazines to pass the time, and burgers and burritos instead of jailhouse food. They shot the breeze with him and played cards to ease the boredom, the cell door open for their visits. It might as well have been an extended sleepover. Jim joked with them, lost good-naturedly at poker, winked when they delivered the magazines.

When he was finally released . . .

No, not yet. Not yet. Not yet. I can't tell it yet.

What I can say is that it wasn't my fault Jim went to jail—it was the doctor in the clinic across the Arizona state line that Jim took me to in case it was something serious. Wheeler is only a few miles from the border.

I can't remember what set him off this time—some trouble at work, most likely, that carried over. And it was mid-November, and Jim never does well during the holidays. But this time I was vomiting blood, and feverish. I was afraid I was bleeding inside, and convinced him to take me to a doctor. I swore I wouldn't say anything.

To all appearances, Jim was the concerned and loving husband, holding me up as he walked me through the doors of the clinic. He was near tears as he explained he'd come home to find me half conscious at the base of the stairs, our little daughter frantic, trying to rouse her mother. The nurses seemed as concerned for his welfare as for mine.

But the clinic doctor was young, fresh off a hospital residency in Phoenix and clearly not stupid. He could tell a bad beating from a fall. He called the local police department, which referred it back to McGill County for investigation as suspected domestic assault.

The doctor had me admitted to the small regional hospital, where I stayed for two days. During that time, he visited me to check on my progress, and to press for details.

I could tell he meant well. He asked what happened to my bent pinkie. How I came by the scar that bisects my left eyebrow. The scalding burn on my back. He said he would send someone from the local domestic violence center to speak with me, if I wished.

I didn't wish anything of the sort. He was young and earnest. To men like him, illness and injury are the enemy, and they are soldiers in some noble cause. I felt like he was flaying me alive.

"You're safe here," the doctor said.

I stared at him. He was a fool.

"Where's my daughter?" It was not a question.

Jim didn't visit me—he wasn't allowed to visit while the report was under investigation. He was put on paid leave from the sheriff's office, so he stayed in our house outside Wheeler, putting Laurel on the school bus every morning, waiting for her when she got home again every afternoon.

When I was released from the hospital, I returned home and Jim moved in with a buddy and his family. They commiserated over what was clearly a misunderstanding. A bad patch in a good marriage.

An assistant county attorney met with me once. She came to the door in heels and a tailored skirt suit that showed lots of shapely leg. Her hair was pulled back in a sleek ponytail. She wore dark-rimmed glasses, but only for effect. They made her look like a college student. I'd never met her, but knew of her—

police officers and officers of the court are members of the same team. And cops gossip like schoolgirls.

Her name was Alicia and she was full of swagger, lugging an expensive briefcase, a cell phone clipped to her belt. She couldn't have looked more out of place in Wheeler than if she'd parachuted in from the moon. If I'd had the smallest sliver of hope for rescue, which I didn't, Alicia dashed it just by showing up.

We sat at the kitchen table, the better for her to take notes. I poured her a cup of coffee that she didn't drink and set out a plate of oatmeal cookies that she didn't touch. I fed her the story Jim had made up, and she saw right through it. Just like the doctor in Arizona, Alicia pressed for "the truth," as if it were something tangible you could serve up on demand, like those cookies.

"According to the medical report, your injuries are consistent with a beating," Alicia snapped, impatient, glaring at me over her dark rims. "We can't do anything unless you help us. He'll get away with it. Is that what you want?"

I was calmer than I thought I'd be. I shook my head. "He already has."

Alicia's penetrating stare bordered on disgust. She slapped her folder closed and stood up. I was surprised—she had a reputation as a terrier, and I thought she'd put up more of a fight.

"Women like you—" she muttered under her breath, shoving her folder in her briefcase.

Something snapped inside. I stood up, too, heat rushing to my face.

"And women like *you*, Alicia," I said through clenched teeth.

She froze for a second, studying me. "What are you talking about?"

"You really should be more careful. When your boyfriend,

Bobby, knocks you around, don't call Escobar at the station house to cry on his shoulder. The man can't keep a secret. And, my God, you should know it's a recorded line."

Her pretty face turned scarlet. Later, I would regret being so blunt, so mean. But caught up in the moment, I couldn't stop myself. Laying into her felt electrifying, like busting loose from a straitjacket, and for the barest second I wondered if this was how Jim felt when he lit into me.

She slammed the front door behind her and we never spoke again. I did see her in court at the hearing for the plea agreement. Without the cooperation of the victim—that would be me—the case was weak. Jim's defense attorney and Alicia worked out a deal: if he pleaded guilty to misdemeanor disorderly conduct, the felony assault charge would be dropped and he'd serve minimal time. A felony conviction was too great a risk for Jim—it would mean the end of his police career, not to mention a lengthy jail sentence.

The judge agreed. It took all of two minutes.

To this day, if anyone should ask—and no one ever does—I would tell them the same thing I told everyone else: I got upset that day, slipped and tumbled down the stairs. I would swear it on any Bible put in front of me.

I would swear it because Jim wants it that way.

What they don't know is what happened the same afternoon that Alicia stalked out of our house.

After she left, I opened the back door to call Tinkerbell in from the yard. It was chilly, and after a run she liked to curl up on her blanket by the kitchen stove. Usually she was ready and waiting, but not that day. I called again and again, listening for her yippy bark, expecting to see her fox tail fly around the corner. But there was only uneasy silence.

I stepped outside, and that was when I saw Jim's Expedition parked to the side of the road a short way from the house. The windows were tinted, so I couldn't make out if there was anyone sitting inside. I scanned the yard again, panic rising.

That was when I saw Jim.

He was standing next to the shed, watching me. It was a bloodless stare, and it stopped me cold. I stood there transfixed, unable to speak or move. Or turn and run.

He took a slow step toward me, then another. All the while his eyes fixed on me, pinning me like an insect to a mounting board. Then he stopped. I noticed then he was carrying something in his arms. His hand moved over it, like a caress. It whimpered. It was Tinkerbell.

I opened my dry mouth, but it took several tries before I could manage words.

"Jim, you're not supposed to be here."

He smiled—but that, too, was bloodless.

"Now, that's not very nice, is it, girl?" he baby-talked playfully in the dog's ear. "Not a 'Hello,' not a 'How are you?'" He looked at me and sighed. "Just trying to get rid of me as fast as she can."

"How . . . how are you, Jim?" I stuttered, struggling to sound wifely and concerned. "Are you eating well?"

He laughed softly.

"Come here."

"We're not supposed to talk."

"Come here."

"Laurel will be home from school soon."

"We'll be done by then. Come here."

His voice was pitched so pleasant, so light, he might have been talking about the weather. I started to shake.

I moved toward him. When I was close enough, he told me to stop. He turned to the shed, opened the door and gently dropped the dog inside. Then he closed the door again.

I could have bolted then, but to what purpose? Jim was faster, stronger, cleverer. And at that moment, I didn't trust my legs to hold me up, much less handle a footrace.

Before he returned, he grabbed something that was leaning against the shed. I hadn't noticed it until then. It was a shovel—the one with the spear-headed steel blade he'd bought last summer when he needed to cut through the roots of a dead cottonwood tree. It still had the brand sticker on it: *When a regular shovel won't do the job.*

When he came back, he offered it to me. I shrank from him and shook my head.

"It's okay," he said softly. "Go on. Take it."

The shovel was heavier than I'd expected, or maybe I wasn't as strong. It weighted my arm and I had to grasp it with both hands.

"Follow me," he said.

He led me behind the shed, just short of the six-foot wooden fence that lined the rear and sides of the property. He searched the ground for a moment, considering, as if he were picking out a likely spot to plant rosebushes. Then he pointed.

"There," he said.

"Jim . . . I don't understand."

"What's to understand, idiot? You got a shovel. Use it."

His voice was mild, his mouth quirked in what might have passed for a smile. But his stare was like a knife. Like a spear-headed steel blade that would have gladly cut me in two if only it could.

I didn't dare disobey. I took a deep breath and stabbed the

shovel in the dirt. I set my foot on the shoulder of the blade and kicked. I began to dig.

The tool was built for plowing through rough ground with the least resistance. Spear it in, kick the blade deep, carve out wedge after wedge of red earth. It was easier work than I would have thought, except for one thing: I wasn't sure what I was digging.

But I had an idea.

A ragged hole was getting carved out, the pile of fresh dirt along the edge growing bigger, when Jim dragged his foot along the ground, drawing invisible lines.

"Here to here," he said.

I straightened and wiped the sweat from my face with my forearm. I leaned on the shovel handle, panting, and considered the perimeter he'd just marked off.

A rectangle. Just big enough to hold a grown woman, maybe, if her arms and legs were tucked tight.

...invillea bush

ne

scream for help. Jim wouldn't dare do anything then, would he? Not in front of witnesses?

No, of course he wouldn't.

But what he would do was take no chances. The second we heard the rumble of the bus engine, he'd do exactly what he'd come here to do, before I had a chance to run away or make a peep. Before the bus ever got close.

And after the bus had dropped Laurel off, after it had rumbled away again, Jim would still be here, with blood on his hands. And what would happen to her then?

I picked up the shovel and stabbed it back in the dirt. I had a hole to dig, and now there was a deadline.

By the time I'd finished to Jim's specifications, I was queasy from the effort. I stepped back, leaning against the fence to catch my breath, still grasping the shovel. Jim walked to the edge of the hole and peered in, cocking his head and pursing his lips. It wasn't awfully deep, but apparently deep enough.

He walked over and wrested the shovel from my grip. I cringed.

"Stay put," he said.

Then he turned and headed to the front of the shed.

I heard the shed door unlatch, heard it open, heard him mutter to Tinkerbell to stay put, just as he'd ordered me. I heard the door close.

It wasn't but a few seconds until I heard the whine again . . .

Then nothing.

I pushed myself off the fence and stood frozen in place, still trying to catch my breath. Straining hard to listen.

I heard the shed door again, this time opening. Then Jim rounded the corner, the shovel in one hand, Tinkerbell in the other, toted by the scruff of her neck.

The dog was limp, her head lolling. As I stared at her broken body, an incongruent thought raced through my mind: *When a regular shovel won't do the job.*

It wasn't my grave I'd been digging, but hers.

Jim halted in front of me, the corners of his mouth working like a tic, his eyes bright. "Take it," he said, holding the body out.

Numbly I gathered the dog in my arms; she was still warm, still soft. I could feel her firm ribs, so familiar. But there was no trace of the familiar thrum of a beating heart.

I looked at Jim, awaiting orders.

"Go on, stupid," he said. "Dump it in."

At once I turned and knelt at the hole. I leaned forward and slid her body into it. I arranged the legs, the head, to approximate something natural. I smoothed her white ruff, my hand lingering, but only for a moment. Then I stood up again.

Jim leaned the shovel back against the shed and wiped his hands on his trousers. "Don't forget to clean this. Use the hose. And oil the blade so it won't rust."

He nodded at the dog.

"Now cover that up."

There was no malice in his voice. No exultation. He sounded like any sane man might.

My legs buckled. I was on my hands and knees when he drove off.

May 18

On Jim's last day off, he took Laurel and me grocery shopping. He drove us into Wheeler to the Food Land market, and as a family we walked the aisles, Jim holding Laurel by the hand and I pushing the cart. He has lived in this town for thirteen years, since moving here from some town or other in Utah—the exact location keeps changing when he talks about it—and one way or another he knows everybody. They greet him warmly in the produce section or at the meat counter or by the bakery, and he shakes their hands and asks after the family, the kids, chatting about work, the weather, what's biting right now.

I can tell by their easy banter that they like him. They like us. They don't like me necessarily, because I am so reserved with them, and so very quiet, so deficient in small talk that I give them nothing of substance to form any real opinion. If pressed, they would probably say there's nothing about me to actively *dislike*. But they do like us as a unit.

As often as not, Jim will take us shopping like this. If he knows he'll be working, and a grocery trip is required, he will make out a list ahead of time and go over the particulars with me so I understand to buy the multigrain bread he likes, for instance, and not the whole wheat. Or the rump roast rather than the round. He will estimate the total cost, including tax, and give me enough cash to cover it. Afterward, he will check the receipt against the change, which he pockets.

Besides the Expedition, we also have a car, an old Toyota compact, which I may use with permission, for approved trips. Before and after his shifts, he writes down the mileage in a small notebook. He alone gases it up, and I know from the fuel gauge that he never puts in more than a quarter tank. He changes the oil himself. Rotates the tires. If it needs servicing, which it rarely does, he has a mechanic friend who does the work on his time off for spare cash.

From outside our fishbowl, Jim is a solicitous husband who takes care of his family. He is a hard worker with a responsible job. Good company with his friends. To women, still a striking man in his uniform.

He's invited out often for a beer after work, a weekend barbecue, but usually begs off. Family time, he'll say. For us as a couple, the invitations come less often and are nearly always refused. Some invitations aren't so easy to turn down—when a colleague retires, for instance, usually a ranking officer—and the occasion must be observed.

Two nights ago, for instance, the sheriff's wife threw a retirement party for a captain with twenty-seven years under his belt. She held it in their lovely home on a southside hill overlooking Wheeler. The weather was warm and the night was so soft, the party spilled over into their garden—it was well irrigated, green with new sod, landscaped with huge bougainvillea bushes that were heavy with scarlet bracts. I sat in a corner under a trellis of flowering vines, smelling their sweetness, listening to the Tejano music in the background, the bursts of laughter. Lanterns hung over the brick walkway; the boughs of an acacia tree glittered with strings of lights. If you closed your eyes, you could be almost anywhere.

The evening was going so well that a band of Jim's buddies didn't want it to end. After the speeches, the toasts, the cake decorated like a fishing boat, after the sheriff's wife began thanking everyone for coming, they urged Jim to join them as they moved the festivities to the Javelina Saloon, and Jim had had just enough rum and Cokes to break with habit and accept this time.

The Javelina isn't as rough as it once was. I understand that years ago it was a dive frequented by the sort of drunks who pried hubcaps from the cars parked in the business lot next door so they could bankroll their next binge—usually on a cheap, fortified wine called Garden Delight. Then it was turned into a biker bar, with loud Harleys in and out at all hours, straddled by rough-looking riders who wore dark T-shirts with slogans like *Bikers Eat Their Dead*. The bikers scared off the hard-core winos, many of whom turned in desperation to infusing Aqua Net hair spray into big gallon jugs of water. It made a cheap and wretched home brew they called "ocean."

One winter night, a brushfire ignited behind the saloon and ripped through an adjacent field where a half dozen hardcores were camped out with their wine bottles and jugs of ocean. Most managed to stagger off, but one woman couldn't get out in time. She burned alive. They never determined the exact cause of the blaze. It might have been a campfire that the wind had whipped out of control. Or it might have been a lit cigarette deliberately tossed into a patch of dry grass by someone who wasn't about to have his Harley stripped for parts.

Life is cheap in such places, but that brushfire convinced the city council to demand a crackdown on liquor establishments that cater to rough trade. The Javelina closed down. It reopened again weeks later under new management, the Harley decor still in place, because it was too costly to change out. Some bikers still drop in when they pass through town on the interstates. But now its main clientele is mostly working class—not least of all local police officers and deputies looking to kick back or decompress.

I had never been inside the Javelina before, but I'd often seen its big billboard from the east-west highway—the giant wild boar, tusked and razor-backed, charging at some unknown target in the distance.

You could hear classic country music from the parking lot and smell the Marlboro smoke and beer. I could swear I caught a whiff of gunpowder, too. Inside, the music thumped and a small disco ball revolved above couples slow dancing or boot-scooting on a dance floor thick with sawdust and stained with tobacco juice. But the color scheme was still orange and black, and a vintage Harley Davidson, stripped of its engine, hung from the ceiling above the bar.

I felt conspicuous from the start in a dress that was two sizes too big and shapeless from neck to knees. Jim's choice. The other wives seemed to glisten in their tight, pretty, shiny fabrics. In their high-heeled sandals and sling-backs. Hair curled and tucked just so, or flat-ironed till it streamed like water. Their lips were painted red, mauve and pink, and more often than not parted wide in laughter. They leaned into their men, slapping their shoulders playfully, pulling them to the dance floor. I watched them and my heart began to race, my palms to sweat. I struggled to catch my breath.

"You all right, honey?"

I looked up at a waitress with short champagne hair and gray roots, ruby lips and a look of concern in her eyes.

"Could I have some water, please?" I asked.

"You sure can," she said. "And what can I get for the rest of you?"

"Hey, Edie, when you gonna throw out that crap?" said an officer named Munoz, gesturing at the Harley suspended from the ceiling.

"Well, hell, I like that crap," Edie said. "Reminds me of the good ol' days when we had a classier clientele."

The officers hooted.

"You miss those biker freaks?" snorted an officer named Sandoval.

"I miss their *tips*." Edie rubbed her thumb and forefingers together. "You SOBs are tight as a frog's ass."

The others broke into more gales of laughter, but not Jim. He didn't like profanity in women. I thought he was choosing to ignore Edie, but after she left with the drink orders, he grinned and said:

"Well, there goes her tip."

The others thought he was joking.

The banter went on and on. I watched them as if I were outside looking in. As if I were pressing my face against a cold windowpane, marveling that people inside the bright room could be so easy with one another, so quick to laugh. I marveled the way I would if I were to parachute into some tribal village in the Amazon or Africa. It had all become something foreign to me. An alien culture. I had understood it once—once, I'd even enjoyed it—but not anymore.

I had lost all facility with people. All interest. All connection.

Worse, I began to look around the table, suspicious, searching their faces for telltale signs. For cracks in those happy, deceitful masks they presented to the world. Wondering what awful things they, too, were hiding.

The waitress returned to hand out the drinks. Sandoval's wife—CeCe, I think—called out: "Edie, when you gonna get a mechanical bull in here?"

Her husband grimaced. "Now, what in the hell would you want with a thing like that?"

"You never know—I might like to do a little bull ridin'."

He swept his arm around her and grinned. "Well, sweetheart, it's your lucky night."

In the midst of the guffaws, two big hands came down on Jim's shoulders from behind and a voice boomed, "You son of a bitch!"

Jim recognized it at once; so did I. It was the same deputy who had come knocking on our door one day to help Jim deliver an object lesson. The buddy who had turned a 911 call into a fishing date. His name was Frank.

Jim and Frank shook hands in greeting and slapped each other's shoulders and inquired after each other's wives, as if I weren't there to answer for myself. Then Frank leaned in close and muttered something in Jim's ear. Whatever the news was, it wasn't good. The grin froze on Jim's face. He stared back at

Frank and said something I couldn't hear; then they both moved away to the bar. Jim didn't return for a long time.

Close to midnight, most of the couples at our table had left. I was spent, nursing a single Dos Equis all evening, but Jim was downing Coors after Coors and growing more garrulous. When Edie came around next, he gave a *What the hell* shrug and ordered a double tequila with lime. This was not a good sign.

Munoz shook his head at him. "How in hell you expect to get home, man?"

Jim leaned back in his chair, bloodshot eyes glistening. "The way I always do when I tie one on—lights up, siren wailing."

Munoz chuckled, but his eyes were wary. He gestured at me and my Dos Equis and smiled. "Joanna here will drive you guys home. She's been a good girl."

"Fuck that," Jim snorted. "We'd just end up in a ditch somewhere."

Crack.

Munoz exchanged a surprised look with his wife, both clearly uncomfortable now.

Edie brought Jim his double shot. He slammed it and ordered another. "Easy," Munoz murmured. "Easy."

When the second one came, Jim smirked and toasted him with it.

Before Munoz could respond—if he had even planned to— he glanced past Jim to something at the other side of the saloon, and his jaw dropped a bit. "Ho-ly," he murmured. Jim turned to look. So did I.

A woman had walked into the Javelina.

That's the truest way I can describe it, except to amend it

this way: a woman didn't just walk into the Javelina—she commandeered it.

She was tall and lithe and sturdy. As tall as Jim—taller, if you counted the two-inch heels on her biker boots. Her hair was so black it shone blue, and all of it cascaded down her back like a waterfall. She looked to be in her early thirties, and wore jeans and a studded black leather jacket. She stripped off her leather riding gloves as she strode to the bar like she owned the place. The crowd parted to make room.

At her side, leaving no less of a wake, was a big man with salt-and-pepper hair and a mustache. He was also dressed in leather, and gave every impression that he could, should circumstances call for it, eat the dead.

"Is that Bernadette?" Munoz murmured.

And suddenly I understood everything—Frank's muttered message, Jim's abrupt mood shift and his hard drinking, which was so uncharacteristic for him. I had never met Bernadette, but for years Jim had made certain I knew *of* her, usually in explicit detail. She was his girlfriend from long ago, and the woman he most enjoyed comparing me to. Never, of course, in my favor.

I knew she was a mix of Navajo, Hispanic and Irish and grew up on a sheep ranch on the northern end of the reservation, near Cuba. She had left Wheeler—and Jim—before I'd ever come here. As far as I knew, this was her first time back.

Seeing the woman in the flesh, I understood why in Jim's estimation I had always come up short, and always would.

Jim was staring intently at her, glowering, working his jaw. He was breaking into a sweat, his fist squeezing the empty shot glass. Bernadette was speaking with the bartender, who nodded in our direction. She turned to look. If she was put off by

Jim's presence, she didn't show it in the least; she didn't take in my presence at all. She turned her back and resumed her conversation with the man she'd come in with.

Jim stood, and for a moment I thought he intended to leave. I stood, too, and picked up my handbag and jacket. But he took no note of me and headed for the bar. Uncertain, I trailed behind.

He stood staring at her back for some time without speaking. He stared so hard I thought he would bore tiny, smoking holes in her leather jacket. If she knew he was there, she didn't show it.

Finally he said, "I see you're still drinking tequila."

She took her time turning around. When she did, she surprised me. She barely glanced at Jim at all when she raised her shot glass and answered with a dismissive, "I still have a lot of regrets."

Mostly, she turned her attention past Jim and on me, appraising me in a puzzled way that became almost sad. Then pitying. I hugged my jacket for protection against that look, suddenly and profoundly mortified.

When she finished with me, she turned to Jim. "I hear you're still on the force. Congratulations—never thought you'd last." She smiled over her shoulder at her burly friend. "Where are my manners? Allow me to make introductions. Jim, this is my *hombre*, Sam. And, Sam, this is the reason I got my *Jim Is a Prick* tattoo."

Sam chuckled.

Bernadette leaned back against Sam and stroked his stubble lovingly. "He laughs because it's true." She turned to Jim. "Want to know where I put it?"

Now others at the bar were beginning to laugh, too. Jim's face was turning white; I could feel him vibrate with rage.

With an effort he spat out between clenched teeth: "And how does Sam here like worn-out pussy?"

Sam shifted forward menacingly, but Bernadette raised a finger that stopped him in his tracks. She was appraising Jim now with the dead calm of a stone Madonna. When she smiled, it was beatific.

"Once he gets past the worn-out part," she purred, "he likes it just fine."

The bar burst into roars of laughter. Still smiling, Bernadette leaned back against Sam, who clasped her in a bear hug and spun her on her heels back to their bottle of tequila.

When Jim became aware of me at last, he wrenched my arm so hard I thought his fingers would tear muscle. Before he pulled me toward the exit, I threw a last glance at Bernadette, who caught it as she turned toward us from the bar.

The look on my face wiped the laughter from hers.

May 20

Around two thirty in the afternoon came the growling racket of a motorcycle muffler in the drive. Then a knock on the front door. I didn't answer. I didn't intend to, but the knock came again. Then again. And, finally, a voice:

"I know you're in there."

With a jolt, I recognized the voice: it was Bernadette's.

She was the last person I expected on my doorstep, and a small part of me was intrigued. The rest of me, though, was shot through with panic. And curiosity alone couldn't tamp that down, nor stir me from my blanket on the couch. I held myself as still as I could. I didn't dare breathe.

Knock knock knock knock.

"I can keep this up all afternoon," she called out, but it sounded more like determination than threat, so I called back, my voice croaking from disuse: "Jim's not here."

"I'm not here to see that bastard," she said quietly. "I'm here to see you."

My first instinct was to batten down the hatches. To look around for something heavy to defend myself. To make up some story to shoo her off my porch and back on her bike, heading west toward Wheeler. But both would have taken more strength than I had in me.

It took a while to push myself off the couch and shuffle to the door, clutching at my bathrobe. I slipped the chain from the lock and pulled the door wide. I let her look at me.

She didn't speak for a long while. Then she muttered, "Holy shit."

I couldn't look her in the eye. I waited for her to have her fill, to assess me one more time, then leave me alone. Instead she said:

"Let's have some tea, Joanna."

She stepped inside and gently took my elbow as I shuffled painfully back to the couch. She eased me back onto the blanket. She pulled off her leather jacket and pushed up her shirt-sleeves, heading to the kitchen. She put the kettle on to boil and rummaged in the cabinets for cups and tea bags and sugar. She fixed a tray with china cups in their matching saucers, napkins, some saltine crackers, a box of tissues and a bottle of ibuprofen. She was efficient, with an eye for detail. She sat opposite me in the overstuffed chair, and we sipped Earl Grey in a weirdly companionable silence. Then she smiled.

"You ever have a tea party with a biker chick before?"

I laughed despite myself, but I felt out of practice, and it came out more of a hiccup, which hurt my sore ribs. I hiccupped again, and then again. It became a sob. My hand flew to my mouth, where the bottom lip was split and stinging.

Tears sprang to my puffy eyes, one still swelled nearly closed, spilling down my bruised cheeks. Swiftly, Bernadette was beside me on the couch, handing me tissues, letting me cry it out, in no particular hurry.

When I was done, she didn't ask what had happened. Instead, she said, "Let me show you something."

She cocked her head and pushed her long black hair to the side, holding it back so I could see the spot she was pointing to just above her left ear. I could clearly make out a gnarled white scar running five inches along her scalp.

"Bottle of Jose Cuervo," she said. "Five staples to close. Concussion."

"Did you go to the police?"

"Now, now, Jo. You're smarter than that. Even back then, he *was* the police. And he had a police buddy who said he'd swear I was whoring on Bernalillo Road, resisted arrest, assaulted an officer, got what I had coming."

I gasped. "Frank."

"I see you've met. Anyway, a split scalp—I got off easy, all things considered. I left town and never looked back."

"You were afraid he'd kill you."

She snorted. "Honey, I was afraid I'd kill *him*. I grew up on the rez. I've butchered enough game and livestock to know where the knife goes. So I guess you could say he got off easy, too. He just doesn't know it."

The prospect made my heart leap. If only she'd stayed in Wheeler, if only she hadn't left, had put her hunting knife to good use . . . "I wish you *had* killed him."

She shrugged. "That's the bruises talking."

Her indifference stung—clearly she had no idea.

Finally I asked, "Did you meet him here, or in Utah?"

"Utah? Did he tell you he was from Utah? Honey, he's from Tucumcari. The way I hear it, they ran the whole family out of town. He's never been very clear about parents, siblings, that sort of thing. I think he's pure self-invention by now." She shrugged. "Nothing wrong with that, necessarily. We're all entitled to second chances, right? But I always did wonder what he did with his first one. We were only together a few months, but that was enough. I've always been a sucker for a handsome devil—only, between us girls, I prefer them more handsome than devil. Jim was a helluva wild man then. Not so much family oriented. Did he tell you about the time he shot up a motel room?"

"Why on earth?"

"Why on earth not? That's just the way he was. Half the men in uniform back then should have been behind bars at one time or another." She gave me a sidelong glance. "I hear Jim finally made it inside a jail cell a few months ago. I only regret I wasn't here to take a picture. I would have framed it."

"A picture?" I spat the words out.

Her laughter stopped short. "Sorry. I shouldn't take pleasure in that bastard's misery, when I know damn well he takes plenty of company with him. Honey, the stories I could tell you . . ."

Her voice trailed off bitterly; her dark eyes grew darker.

I didn't know what she expected when she came knocking on my door—checking up on a batterer's wife, an hour of tea and sympathy. Penitence for poking a rattlesnake that was sleeping in someone else's lap. And I wasn't sure what I could expect of her.

But, for the first time ever, there was someone sitting right in front of me who knew Jim—the real Jim, not the affable doppelgänger he presented to everyone else. She knew him—if not to all his dark depths, then at least to his capacity for them. She had loved him, too. Once. And he'd made her bleed. Even her.

"The stories—" I stuttered. "The stories I could tell . . ."

And the next thing I knew, I was telling her—the dark things, the forbidden things, the things I'd never told anyone, could never tell anyone, especially when they pressed and prodded and tried to wring it out of me for my own good. The bruises, the bones, the burns, the scars—these are just the tangibles they can check off on any medical report. How do you quantify the words that cut as deep? The bottomless, wretched fear of more of the same?

The dam cracked; the truth gushed out. I told her about my tea tin, the groceries, the gas. The fishbowl isolation. The suffocating prison of this tin-roofed house.

The steady erosion of my own sanity. The no way out. The gut-churning horror of being forced to live every day with a monster.

I took a deep breath and braced and told her about Tinkerbell. About the grave he made me dig, the limp body, the spearheaded shovel.

About Laurel, and how hard it is to pretend to your clever child that everything's all right, that Daddy loves her, that Daddy's a good man, that Daddy would never, ever turn on her one day.

Bernadette was staring at me, expressionless. I searched her face for traces of disgust, for judgment, for compassion, for absolution. I couldn't stop myself.

I took another shuddering breath and told her what I hadn't even allowed myself to think too much about, for fear of making it real. Making it true. About the night Jim returned home from his jail stint, just after New Year's. The welcoming meal I'd prepared—pot roast, potatoes, coconut cake. Laurel had dressed pretty for her daddy in a crimson velvet dress with bows. We'd sat down as a family, and Jim seemed happy to be home, kissing Laurel good night, even tucking her in. When she was finally asleep, as I was washing the dinner dishes, Jim called for me from outside. He was in the backyard near the woodshed. He was wearing gloves, and I thought he was restacking the cordwood, but it wasn't that. As I got close, I could see his face in the lantern light, and it was twisted with the old familiar rage. My stomach heaved. He grabbed my hair and pulled me inside, yanking out hunks till I gasped. He dragged me across the shed, pulled me upright, and with his other hand grabbed an object hanging on the wall. He held it close to my face so I could make it out. It was a machete.

People disappear all the time, he'd said. He's a cop; he should know. No one would miss you, he said. Hell, no one would even notice. And if they did, he'd just tell them I'd left him and gone back to my family in another state. No one would check. No one would care.

This is my future, he told me. This is my end, if I ever, ever, ever humiliate him like that again.

Bernadette was still staring at me, her eyes still blank. I waited for her to say something. To say anything. To tell me what a pathetic wreck I was. What a terrible mother. To hop on her motorcycle and leave a trail of diesel fumes all the way to the Javelina so she could sit with Sam and tell him all about the nutcase outside town.

Instead, she said, "Show me."

She helped me up again, and slowly I led her through the

kitchen, through the back door, through the yard. When I got to the shed, I hesitated. I hadn't been inside since that night. Bernadette paused, too, for a second, then moved past to unlatch the rough plank door. She opened it and stepped in. I forced myself to follow. It was musty and close and smelled of motor oil. "This is bad," she muttered, glancing around. "Bad energy." The afternoon sun cut through the dusty window like a blade; the light was weak, but it was enough for her to scan the walls, taking in the rakes, the spades, all the garden hand tools. Then her gaze rested on one item in particular. It was a machete, hanging just where Jim had left it.

She shook her head, backing away.

She didn't speak again until we returned to the house. Then she paced the living room, her steel-toed boots clicking up and down the wood floor. I waited expectantly, not knowing for what.

"Where's your daughter?" she asked.

I told her Laurel was staying with a school friend for a few days. Bernadette nodded.

"Now, think hard. Give me a name and a number. Someone you can trust. Someone who will take you and your daughter at a moment's notice."

I shook my head, desperate. "No one. There's no one. They're all Jim's friends here. My family's gone. It's been ten years—"

"It doesn't have to be someone you know well, or even recently," Bernadette said. "You'd be surprised how many people are willing to help, if they're only asked. But make it someone as far away from here as possible."

A name sprang to mind.

"I used to know someone in Boston."

Bernadette seemed pleased. "Very good. Write it down."

There was a notepad and pen on the end table beside the telephone. She grabbed it and handed it to me.

"In two days, when Jim has left for his shift," she continued, "I'm coming back here and giving you cash and two plane tickets out of Albuquerque for Boston. Do you know where the Albuquerque airport is? Never mind—I'll give you a map anyway. You'll leave as soon as I get here, gas up your car and drive hell-bent for leather. Take nothing with you. Nothing— do you understand? By the time Jim gets home, you'll be in coach, eating peanuts somewhere over Chicago."

Suddenly the enormity of what she was plotting overwhelmed me. The insurrection was too massive, too fast. The blood was draining to my feet. I began to shake, murmuring protests.

"I can't. Wait. Please. Two days is too soon. I can barely walk. Laurel has to finish school. Laurel has to finish school. Please, she has to."

Bernadette stared at me again, but not unkindly. I was ashamed at my weakness. Oma used to tell me stories of how she and her husband and their young daughter—my mother—had fled East Germany and the communist occupation. Left their lovely home one night without warning or preparation, their dinner half eaten on the table, racing on foot toward the western border with nothing but the clothes on their backs, the barking of search dogs in the distance. I was just a child at the time, and shivered at the story, but Oma would hug me and kiss my cheek. *Mut*, she'd say. *Courage.* And here I was, frantic over pulling my seven-year-old from school early.

But of course my panic was more than that—when you're released suddenly from a dungeon, sunlight is a painful thing.

Prisoners need time to adjust. Bernadette must have understood.

She nodded. "When's the school year over?"

I did the calculation as fast as my feverish brain could manage. "Fourteen days. June fourth."

"Does Jim work that day?"

Another calculation. "Yes."

"Good. June fourth. Until then, pretend everything is okay. Nothing has changed—understand?"

"I can do that."

"No doubt. We're staying at the Palomino Motel, just up the road." She took the notepad and pen from my hand and began writing. "This is the number. Put it somewhere Jim won't find it. But don't call, understand me? Don't call unless it's life or death."

She stopped herself and chuckled. "I mean, *imminent.*"

It struck me that, whatever I was risking, this virtual stranger was willing to risk just as much. And for no good reason that I could see. I was confused, light-headed, struggling for words, trying to stammer out gratitude.

"I don't know how to repay you . . . I don't know why you're doing this."

"Don't you?" She cocked her head and smiled down at me as if I were a child who'd just said something precocious.

"Because you asked."

May 29

Something jarred me awake—not a noise or movement, but instinct. The digital clock on the dresser read 2:31 a.m., and Jim wasn't in bed beside me. The sheets where he lay were cold to the touch.

I sprang from bed, adrenaline surging, and made my way to the hallway. There, I could hear a tinny melody drifting from Laurel's room. Cautiously I followed the sound. I recognized it—a song about wishing upon a star, coming from a Cinderella music box Laurel had gotten from Santa last Christmas.

There was a night-light close enough to Laurel's little canopy bed that I could make out Jim bending over her sleeping form. My breath caught in my throat. I froze in place, staring.

Whenever Laurel had nightmares, I was the one to sit at her bedside till she fell back to sleep. She must have had a bad dream, and Jim must have heard. Watching him with her then—so gentle, so warm—was like stumbling on a stranger. At a Jim that *might* have been, but for whatever reason— because of whatever devil hunched on his shoulder, hissing in his ear—could never quite close the deal.

I watched as his fingers trailed along Laurel's cheek, the way he used to brush mine a million years ago. His expression in the obscure light so tender, it jolted me to the bone.

"Sleep, baby," he shushed.

June 3

The two weeks after Bernadette left the house passed like a forced march through a minefield. For the first time, I was glad of regimentation and rules. They ate up the hours. They helped settle my mind and keep the lies sorted into the right piles.

An odd sensation began to brew in my chest, churning it up. Night after night, I lay in bed taut as a bowstring as Jim slept next to me. I examined this new feeling, turning it over and over in my head like a found foreign object.

Finally, I identified it: *hope.*

I didn't like it. Resignation doesn't ask for anything. Pain can be numbing.

Hope has expectations. Hope can be dashed.

At times, I even found myself bitterly resenting Bernadette for laying this new burden on me—a terrible secret that seemed to press against my lips, straining to burst through as if daring to be caught. But always the resentment lifted the moment Jim left the house, the risk of discovery easing for one more shift at the station. His absences washed over me like a death house reprieve.

It helped not at all that nothing was expected of me, except to be ready when the moment came. I couldn't bear a second's idleness. Chores done, I'd rake the leafless yard, dump clean clothes out of bureau drawers just so I could relaunder them. Scrub the kitchen floor, then change the bucket water and scrub it all over again. Bite my lips till they bled.

Sometimes I'd hear the stuttering roar of a bike engine in the distance and imagine it was Bernadette or Sam. I'd wonder whether she'd ridden the two hours to Albuquerque for the plane tickets yet, or if she'd bought them over the phone and was having them mailed to her at the Palomino. Maybe the tickets were lying on her nightstand even now, just waiting for the jailbreak.

Then another thought would crush me: What if she'd changed her mind altogether? Decided to dump Jim's loser wife like deadweight? Was she even now in Durango or Flagstaff or San Antonio? At those times, it was all I could do not to pick up the phone and call the number she'd left. What stayed my hand was the realization that the only thing I could do if she answered was to pinch out a pathetic, "Are you still coming?"

The easiest thing was keeping it from Laurel. I was so well practiced in that already. And there was so much at stake.

That last night as I lay in bed, my mind could level on only one thing:

Tomorrow.

June 4

Insurrection Day

As scheduled, Laurel had early dismissal from school. The bus dropped her off around twelve thirty. She showed off her certificate for passing first grade and I suggested a fried-chicken lunch on Saturday to celebrate. Jim approved. I fought to hide my nerves, fixing my face into something neutral, waiting for him to hit the shower before work. I laid out his fresh uniform with shaking hands.

By the time he was strapping on his Sam Browne, my face was flushed. When he kissed my cheek, he paused for a second to ask if I had a fever. I don't know if it was concern in his eyes or suspicion. I blamed it on the excitement of Laurel's special day.

At 1:58 his Expedition pulled away.

Laurel changed into her play clothes of many colors and I sent her out to the backyard. I stationed myself in a chair at the front window and stared out at the road, my fingers knit together so tight my knuckles cracked, listening to every tick of the sunburst clock above the couch. I grew light-headed, and realized I was holding my breath. So I decided to time myself to the deliberate beat of the big clock—*tick, breathe in; tock, breathe out.*

At 2:33 came the distant roar of a Harley.

My heart twisted in my chest like a snared rabbit. This time, my breath caught and held till I could see motes of light. I didn't care. I sat as fixed as a tombstone, head bowed, willing with all my might for the roar to come closer.

And it did—a faraway growl from the west, growing louder and louder as it approached the house, closer to the ticking clock, closer to the harp-backed chair that was the only thing, it seemed, keeping me from sinking down to the molten core of the earth.

Closer and closer, until—

Bernadette rode up like an archangel in studded black leather on a steed of steel and chrome, a bandanna capping her head, her long hair flowing behind like a banner.

I exploded through the front door and nearly knocked her down before she had a chance to set the kickstand, hugging her hard, weeping, my eyes and nose running shamelessly.

"I wasn't sure you'd come," I choked out at last. "Thank you, thank you, thank you."

"Hell!" She gasped, laughing, staggering under the impact.

When I let her go at last, wiping at my wet face, stammering out an apology, she stripped off her gloves without a word, reached into a zippered pocket of her jacket and handed me a blank envelope. Inside were the tickets, five hundred dollars in cash, an Albuquerque street map with the airport circled in bold red marker, and a phone number and address on a sheet of lined paper.

"Your friend will be waiting for you at the airport in Boston," she said.

I swayed on my feet. "She remembers me?"

"Of course she does." Bernadette was regarding me with frank amusement. "I told her it was a family emergency and you had to leave town fast. She didn't even ask what it was—I figure you can explain when you see her. She says you and your daughter can crash with her and her husband as long as you need to."

I stared speechless at the bounty in my hands. When I looked up again, Laurel was watching us uncertainly from the side of the house. She'd heard the motorcycle rumble to the edge of the front lawn and had come to see. We'd never had such a visitor before, and she wasn't sure how to take it. Her little hands were knotting anxiously.

"Hello, *niña!*" Bernadette called out, smiling. Then she turned back to me and murmured low: "Remember—the gas station just this edge of town."

I nodded. I knew this. Of course I knew this. The game plan was ridiculously simple, straightforward. But even so, it helped to have her spell it out one more time.

"Then turn right around, and it's a straight shot to Albuquerque. Don't stop—no food, no nothing. McGill is a big county, and there's more prying eyes and gossiping tongues around than you know. Get out fast, and don't look back."

"What about you? It might mean trouble."

She grunted. "Knowing that *pendejo*, there's no 'might'

59

about it. Which is why—as much as I'd *love* to stay and watch the meltdown—Sam and I decided to pack up tonight and head out. We're thinking Reno—honey, I'm feeling lucky."

She winked and began pulling her gloves back on. "Don't linger, Jo," she murmured again, this time in earnest. "I mean it. Get your ass in gear."

I nodded, clutching the envelope to my chest. It struck me that this would likely be the last time I would ever see Bernadette—a stranger who was sticking her neck out, at no inconsiderable risk, to help a woman she'd just met. And why? Was the goodness of her heart that profound? Or was her desire for revenge against Jim that deep?

Maybe it was a mix of both, and if so, that was fine by me.

"Wait—how do I get in touch with you? How do I thank you?"

Bernadette didn't answer. She swung onto the bike and kicked it to life. She punched the throttle twice and the big engine growled back in response. Laurel covered her ears as Bernadette laughed. Then she nodded in my direction. *"Adiós, hermana!"*

She accelerated hard, her rear tire raking the edge of the lawn, spraying grass and dirt behind. The front of her bike was airborne for a second; then it squealed on the pavement as she raised a hand in salute, barreling back toward Wheeler.

"She's *loud*," Laurel said in wonder. I laughed as I dried my face on my sleeve.

"Yes, sweetie, she is that. How do you feel about going for a drive?"

For us, it was an outrageous idea. I might as well have asked if she wanted to sprout handlebars and spoked tires and go bicycling on the roof. Her eyes widened, but she didn't ask questions. I fetched the car keys from the hook inside the front door.

The air was warm; the sun was shining. The engine started right up. I felt giddy, and so weightless I could have floated up like a hot-air balloon. Laurel was studying my face so earnestly that I laughed. She smiled back, but her eyes were still so anxious I felt a pang of guilt.

No matter. I was doing this for her. For both of us.

It was four miles to that first gas station on the outskirts of town. I gave the attendant a twenty from Bernadette's envelope and began to tank up, the meter clicking away.

It was clicking for a minute or so before I noticed the choking odor of gasoline getting stronger by the second. It was then that I saw liquid running out from underneath the car, streaming toward the road.

I froze—fairly sure what it was, but not daring to believe it.

I forced myself to pull the pump handle from the filler neck of the car and set it back in its cradle. Then I dropped to my hands and knees and peered under the chassis. I saw the gas tank and understood: a hole had been punched in the side of it, near the middle. Gasoline had chugged out onto the pavement.

No wonder Jim never kept more than a few gallons in the thing. No wonder he never took it in for service, but maintained it himself or had a friend tend to what he couldn't.

A starving gas tank meant a short leash on me. And this was his insurance policy.

I pushed myself back to my feet, rocking on legs ready to buckle. I could never make it to Albuquerque on just a few gallons. There were gas stations along the way, sure, but not many. And in between were long stretches of nothing. I couldn't begin to guess if I could make it from one filling station to the next, or if I'd end up stranded on the interstate waiting for Jim to track us down—which he surely would, and most efficiently. Then there'd be nothing left but to get hauled back to the house, and what was waiting for us in the shed.

Jesus, I'd even handed him the perfect story to tell anyone who asked—his miserable, mental wife had taken their child and run off to distant parts, never to be seen around here again. He'd play the abandoned husband as skillfully as he'd played the doting one.

I groped for options. First was giving up—abandoning hope like the fickle cheat it was and driving back to the house. Chasing this last hour, these last two weeks, out of my memory. Burning the envelope and its contents, swearing Laurel to secrecy. But Jim would be checking the car's mileage after his shift, and how would I explain the extra miles? An emergency trip to the grocer's?

"Joanna?"

I turned toward a familiar voice, guts twisting. There stood Deputy Munoz in civilian clothes, tanking up an SUV with two kids inside. There was genuine concern on his face.

"You okay? You're shaking like a leaf. Is that gas coming from your car? Let me take a look."

"No!" I barked as he flinched. I caught myself, pitched my voice to something less full-on crazy. "We're all right. We're fine. We're . . . going home now."

I was backing away as I spoke, till I collided with the Toyota. Then I turned and snatched at the door handle. I fell into the driver's seat and cranked the ignition, Laurel watching, her eyes as big as hen's eggs. Munoz was heading toward the car, leaning over to peer inside. I pulled out so fast the tires squealed.

My one thought was the Palomino. Bernadette would know what to do. Maybe we could hide out there. Sleep on the floor if we had to.

It was a stupid idea, and I knew it. Selfish, too, because it would put her in more danger than she already was. But in the end it didn't matter—at the motel there was no sign of a motorcycle anywhere.

Bernadette and Sam might be back any second, or they could have checked out already and left for good. There was no time to wait and find out. And no way I'd ask at the motel office and implicate Bernadette even further.

One thing I was absolutely sure about: Munoz would be calling Jim up by now. Munoz was a good guy. He'd figure Jim would want to know his wife was having car trouble and needed help. That she looked really upset. Maybe she was sick. Maybe someone could call the motor club. Maybe Jim could swing by in his unit and help her out himself. Wives appreciate that sort of thing.

I sat idling in the motel parking lot, gripping the wheel, weighing terrible options. But the one image that crowded out every other was that of the shed behind the house and what was buried behind. The machete on the wall.

Laurel was staring at me. Willing me to do the right thing. More than ever, I felt the weight of her little life in my hands.

As I looked back into those frightened eyes, it was clear what I had to do. For her sake, if not for mine. She'd lived long enough in the shadow of a psycho.

I shoved the car in gear and pulled from the lot, beelining for the highway.

For Albuquerque, for freedom, one way or another.

The insurrection was still on.

The gas got us to the big truck stop near Continental Divide, about halfway to Grants. Grants is a good-sized town, and there'd be more stations once we got there. By now I was beginning to believe we might.

I bought three plastic gas cans, gallon size, and filled them. I loaded them in the trunk, then started to tank up.

It's a popular truck stop along Interstate 40. A family-style restaurant inside, and a bank of showers for truckers and long-distance travelers. The pumps were busy. I glanced around uneasily, trying not to stand out. Laurel's face was fixed on me through the rear window.

There was an undersized, tinny-looking car at the next pump. The driver gassing up was a young man who looked sixteen trying to pass for thirty. He wore a torn T-shirt with the sleeves rolled up and black skinny jeans. His red hair was cropped close, except where it spiked into a cowlick at the crown like a rooster, or some ironic Dennis the Menace. He was wearing earbuds, listening to music on a player that was bulging in his back pocket. His leg jiggled to a beat only he could hear. The lobes of his ears looked freakishly large, till I realized they were stretched out by plugs the size of wine corks.

Red Dennis pulled his music maker from his pocket and was glancing down at it when something on the ground caught his eye. He looked over at me and pointed under my car.

"Whoa, lady!" he said. "You're leaking!"

He said it loud enough to hear himself over his own music. Loud enough for half the people at the pumps to hear. Some of them turned to stare.

I yanked the nozzle from my car and shoved it hard back on the pump cradle. Red Dennis was heading toward me, tugging out his earbuds. His T-shirt had a Rolling Rock beer logo and a big picture of a baby in a diaper lying on its back sucking on a beer bottle. *No harm here*, the shirt read. *The kid's already shittin' green.*

Before he could get anywhere close, I was in the car slamming the door and locking it, cranking the ignition and aiming for the highway.

A quarter tank and three gallons extra would get us to Grants. Yes, yes, I was sure of it.

I checked the speedometer, determined to stick to the limit and under. I noted the mileage. I gripped the wheel with sweating palms, holding it steady, smack in the center of the right lane. I wouldn't give a patrolman any excuse to pull me over.

Two miles out, I glanced in the rearview mirror.

And there in the distance I saw it: flashing lights, red and blue. Far off, but coming up fast as a bullet train.

And I heard it: the scree and whoop of a siren.

It was eating up the distance between us with a vengeance. And I knew exactly who was behind the wheel.

Laurel heard it, too. She twisted in her seat to peer through the rear window and started to whimper.

I could barely draw a breath.

"Oh, my God," I whispered. "Help."

Part II
Borne Away

No rack can torture me,
My soul's at liberty
Behind this mortal bone
There knits a bolder one.

You cannot prick with saw,
Nor rend with scymitar.
Two bodies therefore be;
Bind one, and one will flee.

—Emily Dickinson

The First Day

There was an open window with white eyelet curtains. There was a breeze through it. There was a brass footrail with porcelain finials. A rocking chair. The smell of baking bread. Laurel's voice outside, the call of birds.

The Second Day

An old woman came with a bowl. Chicken broth. A napkin. She tucked it under my chin and fed me with a spoon. She had a severe face, thin, but her eyes were kind. Her hair was gunmetal gray, pinned back in a bun. She wiped my chin when I spilled. I tried to thank her, but my voice wouldn't come. "You sleep now," she told me, turning out the lamp, so I did.

Morning

"*Mommy?*"

Laurel's voice pulled me from a jagged sleep. A dream where I was running knee-deep in red sand and rattlesnakes. I could taste blood, like sucking on a copper penny. Someone was screaming.

I opened my eyes and Laurel was standing by the bed with a tray. It was laid with a bowl of oatmeal, a plate of apple slices, orange juice, a slice of toast.

"Let me take that, child." The old woman was there, too, lifting the tray from Laurel's hands, setting it on the night-stand. I pulled myself up, arms shaking with the effort. The woman adjusted the pillow so I could sit, then settled the tray in my lap.

"I feel better," I told her, my voice strange, croaking out of a throat nearly too parched for sound.

"Now, that's a blessing," said the woman. "You eat now."

As I did, she sat down in the rocking chair, its rails clicking against the pine floor. Laurel climbed onto the bed with me, handing me a spoon as if I were younger than she was. Then the napkin, the oatmeal bowl.

"My name's Jessie," the woman said. "Jessica Farnsworth—but you call me Jessie. This here is our farm. My husband's out sneakin' a smoke, as if I don't know. You remember how you got here?"

I shook my head.

"Simon found you out in the scrub wandering around with your little girl here. You couldn't tell us much—you were in a bad way. Laurel says you had some trouble with her daddy out there on the road."

The oatmeal caught in my throat. I took a sip of juice. When I could speak again, I said, "My name is Joanna . . . Benneman." I threw a warning glance at Laurel. "Simon's your husband?"

Her severe face broke into a delighted cackle. "Lord, no! My husband's Olin, the old fool. Simon Greenwood—he's a lo-cal man. Works in our café. Short-order cook."

I licked my lips with a tongue as dry as ashes.

I didn't remember anything about being found. Nothing about how we got here, or even where *here* was. I remembered leaving the Palomino, making for Albuquerque. Had the car run out of gas? Broken down? Did I ditch it somewhere and try to hike with Laurel through the desert? To Grants or Thoreau or some other town?

I shoved feebly at the tray with arms like bricks, the food half eaten.

"Let me take that." Jessie pushed herself up from the rock-ing chair. "You'll have a real appetite before long."

She smiled down, her gray eyes steady. Her skin was thin and clear and remarkably unlined. It seemed to radiate like rice paper backlit by a candle.

"You rest."

She bustled off with the tray.

When she was gone, Laurel nestled next to me on the pillow. "Mommy," she whispered. "Our name's not Benneman."

"I know, sweetie. But that was my Oma's name when she was a little girl like you. So I think it's okay if we use it for a little while. Can you do that?"

She nodded solemnly, her pointer finger tracing a big X across her heart. "Our secret."

Rain

$\mathcal{I}$ slept so much, I felt hungover with it. I didn't ache or hurt; I was just tired—down to my last particle. Eating wore me out. I slept through so many meals, I couldn't tell you. I'd hear kitchen noises downstairs—the rattle of pots, the clatter of dishes, the murmur of voices. Laughter. Then I'd sleep again for hours. Or years, for all I could tell.

Sometimes images of Jim flared up, but they didn't linger. He seemed to come on like a bloodhound fixed on a scent he couldn't quite make out.

I thought of Terri, too. Waiting in vain at the airport, glancing at her watch. Wondering who to call to find out why I wasn't on that plane when it landed.

But I didn't have the strength or the will to hold on to such thoughts for long.

The room kept me quilted up and safe. I drifted in and out

of sleep. When I woke, I'd watch sunbeams slant their way across the wood floor. Or listen to raindrops pinging against the roof and the windowpane in a broken staccato, like Morse code.

Laurel would visit to tell me stories of her day. Chattering on about helping Miz Jessie with the baking, the sweeping. How she went with Mr. Olin to feed the chickens and hunt for eggs. She felt bad for the hens, she said, when they discovered their eggs were gone.

Sunshine

One morning, Jessie came to help me out of bed. She laid out a white blouse with pearl buttons, a simple skirt. They fit well. She brushed my hair till it gleamed and snapped in a barrette as if I were Laurel's age.

"Now," she said. "Aren't you the prettiest thing?"

I wasn't at all sure I was ready or able to leave my little cocoon, but she led me by the hand out the bedroom door and down the stairs. My legs weren't as wobbly as I'd expected after lying in bed for so long.

Through a big kitchen, then a rear screen door to a long trestle table under a giant oak tree. Half the table was laid with embroidered white linen and floral china. Laurel was there on a wooden bench, her slim legs kicking back and forth. She jumped up and ran to me.

"Mommy!" She wrapped her arms tight around my waist. "Come sit beside me."

Someone had managed to clothe her in nearly every color found in a crayon box. A feather boa of pink and white was looped around her neck. She took my hand from Jessie and brought me to the table.

The sights and smells were overwhelming. Smoked ham, bacon, sausage. Sliced tomatoes, home fries, biscuits, pots of jam. A pitcher of orange juice and a pot of coffee. My mouth watered painfully.

"How'd you like your eggs?" Jessie asked.

Such plenty—I thought she was joking.

A man with a rough shag of white hair and a handlebar mustache was rounding the corner of the house. He was compact, dressed in a worn work shirt and a straw hat, wiping sawdust from his dungarees.

Jessie wagged her head at him. "Sneakin' another smoke, I see," she scolded. "Breakfast is on. Pour out the coffee." She headed back to the kitchen.

The man set his hat next to his plate and took a seat. He ran his hand through hair that lifted from his scalp in thick, cottony tufts that looked fit to blow off like dandelion seeds. His face was leathery and lined.

When he reached to shake my hand, his grip was firm but gentle, his calloused fingers as coarse as pumice stones. He took me in with eyes that shone a vivid blue.

"We ain't been properly introduced, ma'am. I'm Olin."

"Joanna," I said.

"Pleased to make your acquaintance. And pleased you're feelin' better."

I tried to smile. He poured out the coffee and juice while I looked around at their farm. Their house nestled in a narrow green valley that ran east to west in a long arcing curve;

it was bordered on the north by a crooked line of midrange hills.

I turned in my seat toward the south and couldn't help but gasp.

At my back was a toothy break of foothills . . . and they fed into the biggest mountain I'd ever laid eyes on. I had to crane my neck to take it all in.

Its face was deeply scored, with jagged outcroppings thrusting through thick green forests that covered all but the snowbound crest. The crest jutted into a rocky, bladelike ridge that looked sharp enough to cut steel.

The mountain dominated the valley, swallowing up a quarter of the sky. It seemed out of all time and place, like a transplanted Alp.

And it seemed almost . . . *animate.*

Aware.

And staring back at me.

I started to shiver, the ground shifting under my feet. I felt a force pulling at me. Summoning me. I gripped the edge of the bench seat to anchor myself in place.

It was as though the mountain had its own force of gravity. As if it were pivoting slowly on its axis, reaching down to collect me in its orbit. I was sure I was about to take a tumble— but just as sure I'd be rolling *up* the mountainside, not down, and plunging off—

"A sight, ain't it?"

It took what strength I had to drag my eyes away and turn back to Olin. When I did, he was cradling his coffee cup, watching me calmly. I tried to answer, but words wouldn't come, so I nodded.

"Folks give it all sorts of names," he continued. "Hereabouts, we just call it the Mountain."

I pressed my napkin to my lips. I felt flushed—a mild fever was muddling me, that was all. I'd overdone it coming down to breakfast.

"You have a pretty place," I managed finally.

Their farmhouse was stately—two stories of smooth gray stones, facing west, with wide windows and a deep porch wrapping around.

"Built it myself," Olin said. "We had ourselves a little low-slung place snug to the road at first, but I kept plowin' up field-stones every year, and the missus, she hankered for a stone house like she seen in some magazine. So I put fieldstones by till I had enough to make it for her. Sure took a while."

A red barn and a slope-roofed coop for the chickens stood behind the house. Next to the barn was an empty corral, and farther down the valley were thick groves of nut trees and fruit trees, shade trees and varieties of pine. There were many others I couldn't identify. Beyond that stood half-grown fields of wheat and corn.

I could hear water running nearby that Olin said was Willow Creek, cutting down from the Mountain. A hundred yards or so out was a little arching footbridge. And on the far side of the bridge was a boxlike building of yellow stucco with turquoise trim. It sat along a hardpan road that bisected the valley north to south, with a neon sign on the roof facing away. I couldn't make out what it said.

"Yonder's our place—the Crow's Nest Café," said Olin.

A pickup truck, mustard yellow, sat in the shade of the building. I could only guess it belonged to the short-order cook who worked there—the one Jessie said had found us and brought us to their door.

"You can't get much business out here," I said. "Remote as it is."

There looked to be miles of empty in every direction, and I was grateful for it. A moat of wilderness to keep the world out.

"We get enough," said Olin. "Not brisk—regulars, mostly. And every now and then strangers blow through."

I checked out both ends of the road. If Jim were to find us, that was how he'd come.

Olin nodded south.

"Up the road there, round the bend, is our little town— Morro. Used to be mines all through here till one day the copper played out. Most folks up and left, but some of us stayed on."

He looked about, taking in the landscape in a way that was almost loving. As if all he surveyed in every direction was as much a work in progress as his house and his fields.

Jessie was back with the eggs. "Here, honey," she said, sliding two of them onto my plate and two onto Laurel's. "Eat up."

"It's our little corner," said Olin. "Summers are hot, but they don't burn you. Winters are cold, but they don't bite. A few of us, we was born hereabouts. Others was movin' through and decided to stay on. But nobody makes it here that don't make for good company."

His blue eyes locked with mine as if he were scouting for something. I couldn't look away if I wanted to.

Finally he nodded.

"And every now and again," he said, "we get us a short-timer. I figure you for one of them."

For some reason, it stung me to hear it.

"Why do you say that?" I asked.

He smiled encouragingly.

"I figure you for a gal with a thing or two to accomplish yet," he said. He chucked Laurel under the chin. "This li'l gal, too."

Jessie turned to Laurel. "My, my! You ate every last bit on your plate," she said. "You want seconds?"

"No, ma'am. I'm full," said Laurel.

"Run along, then, and take your plate to the kitchen. Then I know for a fact there's a new swing under that tree yonder, made for a little girl just your size."

Laurel ran to the kitchen with her plate and fork, then over to a big chestnut tree near the barn. She slid into a wooden swing seat that looked freshly hewn and sanded, and kicked off. Her slim legs pumped hard. Her hair and feather boa flew.

"Mommy, watch!" she called.

"I see you, sweetie! Hold tight!"

"She'll be fine," Olin said. "She's a strong little thing."

Higher and higher she swung till she was almost parallel to the sky. She looked tiny and fragile next to the craggy old chestnut. If she lost her seat and flew off, if the rope broke, she could break a bone, or worse. But she wasn't thinking about disaster. She had a sure reservoir of courage.

"She doesn't get that from me," I murmured.

Olin and his wife traded a long look, and suddenly I could see myself through their eyes. They had to be wondering what kind of refugees had landed in their laps.

"I don't know how to thank you," I said. "I've been so confused the past few . . . days?"

Just how long had I been in that room upstairs? They weren't volunteering a timeline.

Jessie patted my arm. "You stay just as long as you need to. Laurel hasn't said much. But from what she has, well, when a woman takes it on herself to grab her child and run off from her own husband, like as not there's a reason behind it."

I stared at my coffee cup. Such people couldn't begin to understand what Laurel and I were running from. What could be hard on our heels even now.

Jessie had said Laurel told them her father had given us trouble on the road. Had he? I had no memory of it.

And just where was Jim? If only I could pinpoint him on a map . . .

"How far are we from Wheeler?" I asked.

"Head about three miles to the highway, just over the hills," said Olin, indicating the breaks to the north. "Then cut west a good thirty miles and you'll hit Wheeler right enough."

"So close," I murmured.

From the looks of this lush valley, I would've thought we were much farther from town than that. Where were the red mesas? The high desert? This place looked more like Colorado than western New Mexico.

And thirty miles out meant we were likely still in McGill County and the sheriff's jurisdiction. It would be only a matter of time before Jim tracked us here.

"Has anyone been around?" I asked. "Looking for me?"

"Not a one," Olin replied promptly, as if waiting for the question.

I hesitated, not sure what I could expect from these people.

What was it Bernadette had said? People are ready to help, if only they're asked. Even so, these two people were strangers to me. And I to them. How can you know who to trust?

I couldn't take a leap of faith like that.

But I might manage a small step.

"What Laurel said is true," I ventured. "We can't go back. We *can't*. If anyone should come asking around—even someone official—they can't know we're here. Please."

"I wouldn't fret. We ain't seen no one official in . . . how long?" Olin glanced at his wife, who shrugged. "We ain't county, you see, nor reservation. Hardly on any maps anymore."

I knew there were pockets of land leased from the federal government by homesteaders and entrepreneurs. One family east of Wheeler had leased a large tract and put up a store, a post office and an apartment compound for teachers at the nearby Indian boarding school. Decades later, they still had the land under contract.

Still, I doubted such land could be outside any sort of law enforcement.

"Morro must have police officers," I said.

"Oh, honey," said Jessie, "we haven't had need of a lawman in a long, long while."

"Ain't nothin' here we can't handle," Olin said.

Not yet, anyway. They couldn't possibly handle Jim, or see through the snake-oil charm of a sociopath when nearly everyone in Wheeler had failed for so long.

I was torn. If I tried to find out how we got here, that would lead Jim straight to us. Even reaching out to Terri was a risk—when Laurel and I didn't arrive on that plane, she would have tried to find out why. That would mean calling Bernadette, if Terri had a number for her, which was unlikely.

No, most likely it would have meant contacting Jim.

The only thing I wanted at that moment was to hide out. To lay low until I got my strength back, and my bearings. Figure out the next move for Laurel and me. Something that wouldn't land us back in that tin-roofed house, or worse.

"Listen, if anyone should come 'round . . ." I hesitated. My voice sounded thin and childlike to my own ears.

Olin leaned in again, and this time his eyes were piercing, with no hint of humor. He laid his rough hand over mine, and his touch was warm. The warmth spread up my arm like an infusion.

"Joanna." His voice was deep and soothing, the way I talk to Laurel when she wakes up in tears from a bad dream. "If such a situation should arise, I'll know how to handle it."

Olin had to be eighty, at least. Not a big man. But at that moment I understood that his frame, however slight it might seem, was forged of iron. He wasn't giving me easy assurances—he was giving me his word.

"Thank you," I choked out.

"You got any people, honey?" Jessie asked. "Family?"

I shook my head.

"Well, then." She rose briskly to gather the breakfast dishes. "About time I had some female company around here. We were never blessed with children of our own, and after a while we stopped praying for them. It's like having a family laid right in our lap, ready-made. I figure to enjoy it while it lasts."

Vantage Point

It was a struggle to settle my mind on coherent thought. It wanted to wander. It wanted to kick off like Laurel in that swing under the chestnut tree, shoot for the sky and keep going.

Staying occupied, going through familiar motions, helped to ground me. I didn't keep to my bed anymore, but helped Jessie with the chores—weeded the vegetable garden, kneaded dough, swept the heart pine floors and beat the rag rugs, hanging them over the fieldstone fence.

Jessie had to show me how to launder clothes in her big-bellied hand-crank machine—the old-fashioned kind I'd seen only in pictures. It had to be decades old, but they'd kept it in fine condition, and she insisted it still served her well. I'd hang the clothes on the line out back, fetching them in again when they were dry and smelling as sweet as buckbrush. Sometimes I'd bury my face in them and just *breathe*.

Always that terrible mountain was at my shoulder, reigning over the valley, hanging on my every move. I resisted looking at it the way you avoid looking directly at the sun, for fear it could blind you. But as with any forbidden thing, there was a strong temptation, too. To give in. To turn and steal a peek. To see what might happen if I did. But when I'd do so, the ground wanted to slide out from under me all over again, and I was reeling on the edge of a cliff.

The Mountain didn't seem to bother Laurel—she played for hours under its shadow, oblivious. I didn't dare tell the old couple how it disturbed me, or they might wonder if their houseguest was losing her mind. For all I know, they'd be right.

We landed at this place like true refugees—with just the clothes on our backs, and not so much as a toothbrush. Jessie bought clothes for Laurel at a general store in Morro—dungarees and shirts, a jacket, sneakers and socks. For me she bought yards of fabric and sewing patterns. From the styles of the dresses and skirts, some of those patterns must have been lying in store bins for years. Still, they were pretty in a vintage sort of way.

Jessie had an old Singer machine—black and gleaming, smelling faintly of machine oil—stored in a walnut housing cabinet. She'd mail-ordered it ages ago, she said, from a catalog. After supper, Olin and Laurel would play dominoes or checkers, while Jessie and I would sit in the corner, the machine whirring away.

Nearly every day, Jessie and her husband assured me they'd heard of no police search for a woman and child, but I failed to see how they'd know—they owned no television and took no newspaper. From what I could tell, their only link to the outside world was a radio—a boxy antique that picked up a single station that broadcast oldies music and radio shows.

It was as if the old couple had decided one day—decades ago—that a rustic life suited them, and they would keep just as they were for as long as they could. As if they had extricated themselves from the evolving world, and not just from its modern conveniences. Sometimes when I looked at them, I got the unsettled feeling that I was watching them through a rearview mirror, slowly receding from me.

Despite their reassurances, Jim never strayed far from my mind. I couldn't seem to shake him, however hard I threw myself into routine. I couldn't peer out a front window without expecting to see a deputy's unit speed up the dirt road or beeline for the house. In fitful dreams, police lights strobed outside, but were never there when I woke.

Back in Wheeler, whenever Jim would drive us to town, I'd stare out the car window and note all the places to hide. Every house with busted windows and an overgrown yard. Every shed with no padlocked door. Every boarded-up business. Every playhouse, doghouse, culvert.

In my mind, there was no hole so tiny that Laurel and I couldn't squeeze inside and disappear. I never imagined past that. Never imagined coming out again.

Most days, this farm felt like a good hiding place. Most days it felt safe. It was less easy to feel that way at night. After the supper dishes were washed and everyone settled in, I'd sit in a wicker chair on the porch and leave the light off. It was a good vantage point. Now and then headlights traveled up the road or down, but they never stopped.

I sat and wondered about Bernadette—by now long gone with Sam to Reno or whatever town had appeal for a woman with spirit. And about Terri, who was a true wild card. The Terri I used to know would be ballsy enough to catch a flight from Boston to Albuquerque to find out why her friend hadn't arrived. Especially if she hadn't bought whatever story Jim had fed her. *That* Terri was no fool.

But that Terri was fixed more than—what, ten years in the past? I didn't know her anymore and she didn't know me. Terri today might decide I'd flaked out on her one more time, and adios.

And that thought gave me comfort. I didn't want to be tracked down—not by anybody.

I wanted to crawl into a hole and disappear, once and for all.

A few nights ago, I asked Olin if he kept guns in the house. He told me he had a vintage carbine, two long-range Winchester rifles for hunting—one lightweight and one heavy—and a 12-gauge double-barrel shotgun. He showed me the cabinet where he kept the cartridges. He didn't ask questions.

Simon

If it seemed Jessie and her husband had removed themselves from the world, it wasn't entirely so. After some weeks, they said there'd be company for Saturday supper—Simon Greenwood, the short-order cook who'd found Laurel and me wandering in the desert. He used to come every week before they took us in, they said. And after that, they thought it best to wait till I was up to it. Apparently they thought that time had come.

I knew this just meant another plate at the table. I should be able to manage that for an hour or so—if Jim had taught me anything, it was how to shut down and fake it on many levels.

But when Saturday came, I could barely function. Back home, for those rare evenings with Jim's friends, everything was decided for me—what to wear, what to say, how to behave. I was groomed to be insignificant. To ask no questions, but to answer them like a Good Wife. To lie if need be.

That evening, I couldn't so much as decide what to wear. I simply couldn't *make a choice*. Any choice. I felt like I couldn't bear to make the wrong one.

I gathered the clothes Jessie and I had sewn together and laid them out. Laurel came in, stroking each piece. She had no trouble dressing herself—a green skirt with white daisies, a blue-and-black blouse, red socks.

"Let me pick for you, Mommy," she said.

At least I knew better than that. I chose something close at hand and buttoned myself into it—a subdued sleeveless column dress of soft cotton. But as I turned to head downstairs, I caught myself in the standing mirror in the corner of the bedroom. I don't have much to do with mirrors anymore, but this time I straightened and drew close for a better look.

What my reflection told me was that Jessie was a fine seamstress and knew how to cut and sew fabric to fit. I was still too pale, my eyes too guarded. But I wasn't as bony as I remembered. And the dress, though simple, skimmed my figure in an elegant line. Its bronze hue tempered my complexion from sallow to cream and brought out the color of my eyes, which are the same quartz green as Laurel's.

I ran a finger along the scar bisecting my left eyebrow. I looked at myself so rarely anymore, it startled me to see it.

My hair was still a lank, neutral brown, without the body or auburn hues it once had. There was a time when women would stop me on the street to ask what brand of color I used. They wouldn't believe me when I told them it didn't come from a bottle.

Those days were gone.

I pulled it back from my face, twisting it behind in a swift, practiced movement, fastened it with clips and headed downstairs.

Laurel sat in a wicker chair on the porch, keeping an eye out for the dinner guest. It was the same chair I used every evening to keep a lookout for her father.

The table was laid with bone china, old polished silver and fresh linen. There were tall beeswax candles in silver candlesticks. Olin made a last sweep of the kitchen, dipping his finger in the pear glaze for the chicken before Jessie smacked his hand away. I filled the water pitcher and set it on the table.

Finally Laurel called out from the porch: "Here he comes!"

I peered through the screen door at a man heading toward the arching footbridge, a big tan dog at his heels.

He was taller than most, slim, his hair springing up in short, woolly waves—light brown, with streaks of sun-bleached blond. He was wearing a butcher-style apron, carrying a bottle of wine in one hand and a fistful of flowers in the other. I could hear him talking to the dog as they neared.

He noticed Laurel, now chafing at the porch railing, and smiled and waved to her.

"Laurel," I murmured. "Come inside."

"But, Mommy, I want to say hi."

"*Now.*"

She grumbled, but obeyed. I pulled her close.

Olin stepped outside to greet Simon like an old friend. "Go on in," Olin told him. "The ol' woman's waitin'."

I retreated with Laurel to the far side of the room.

The man stepped through the door, where Jessie was waiting to plant a kiss on his cheek.

"'Bout time," she said, and there was rare affection in her voice. "That your apple wine?"

He handed her the bottle. "Yours now."

With a word he sent his big dog to lie on a hook rug by the fireplace. Then he looked up. Something flickered in his eyes when he saw me—recognition? I certainly didn't recognize him.

But he did surprise me. He was younger than I'd expected—mid-thirties, maybe. I imagined he'd be closer in age to Olin and Jessie.

His face was tanned, his eyes a gray-blue, heavily hooded in a sleepy sort of way, with creases that deepened when he smiled.

Laurel twisted her hand from mine and rushed to him.

"I'm Laurel," she said.

He crouched to one knee. "Simon. Pleased to make your acquaintance."

"Those flowers are pretty," she said. "Are they for Miz Jessie?"

"Matter of fact, they're for you. Picked them in a meadow behind my cabin this morning. You look like a field of wildflowers yourself, so I figure they'll feel right at home."

"Come on, honey," Jessie said as Laurel took the bouquet. "Let's go put those in a vase. Won't they look nice on the table?"

Simon straightened and turned to me.

"This here's Joanna," said Olin. "But I reckon you two already met, after a fashion."

"How're you feeling?" Simon asked.

He sounded too earnest to be making small talk, and it unsettled me. "Good," I said. "I'm good. And you?"

He smiled. "Just fine, thanks." He looked quizzically at Olin. "Mind?"

"Go on up," Olin said.

Simon nodded as he passed, heading for the stairway. I turned in confusion to Olin.

"He needs to wash up before supper, workin' a grill all day," Olin explained. "This way, he don't have to drive out to his place, turn around and drive all the way back."

I could hear the shower start upstairs.

Laurel and Jessie returned with the flower vase and set it between the candlesticks. Then Laurel ran to the dog, still lying on the rug. As she stroked his neck, his tale thumped the floor. "What's his name?"

"Pal," said Olin, settling into a chair beside her. "Golden retriever mostly, but collie and shepherd in there, too."

"We had a dog once," Laurel said thoughtfully, running her fingers through the fur. "She ran away."

"Now, that's a pity," Olin said. "Pal here—he must've strayed from his people, too. Simon gives him a good home, though. No dog could have a better."

Jessie returned with the wine bottle, uncorked now, and two glasses. She handed me one and poured. "Just taste," she said.

"Simon makes this?" I asked.

"With apples from his own orchard," Jessie said. "Doesn't lay in many bottles every year, but that just makes them worth the wait."

"How long have you known him?"

"Why, I met that boy when he first entered this world, bare beamed and buck nekkid."

Laurel whooped.

"Helped deliver him," Jessie said with a smile. "Women did, in those days. Doctors were scarce."

Upstairs, the shower shut off.

"Has he worked for you long?" I asked.

Jessie pursed her lips in thought.

"After the war, he drifted a bit," she said. "Had to find his way again. Happens sometimes to men who see too much. When he came back, he built that little cabin of his and took a job at the café. Been there ever since."

I wasn't sure which war she meant—the Gulf War? Iraq? Afghanistan?

Before I could sort it out, Simon came bounding down the stairs, dressed now in jeans and a blue plaid shirt open at the collar. His hair was damp, the waves combed back from his face. He was freshly shaven, trailing a light scent of something warm and spicy.

"You smell nice," Laurel told him.

"Not me," he said with a smile. "That's bay rum."

Olin stood and stretched, his joints cracking. "Let's dig in!"

Laurel claimed the seat beside Simon, stealing sidelong glances. He took the chair across from me. Soon he, Olin and Jessie began rattling on about who was traveling where, building what, spending time with so-and-so.

If I'd been uneasy before, it was all the worse now. Family dinners back home were strained, even on good days. Small talk only irritated Jim, and for me it carried risk. I never knew from one day to the next which word or comment, however innocent, might set him off. Silence became my sanctuary.

Suddenly I was picturing that table again—wondering if Jim was sitting there, a single plate in front of him, a single glass, a knife, a fork, a spoon. Did he even bother with such things anymore? Or did he just root through the fridge, then stand at the counter eating over the sink like a bachelor? Was he thinking of us, wondering where we might be, biding his time, stoking his rage?

I glanced furtively around Jessie and Olin's table, only vaguely aware that Olin was regaling them with a story about a horse he'd had as a young boy—a big, feisty Appaloosa that first taught him to swear. The others were laughing—even Laurel, her eyes bright. I took the cue and forced a smile.

A faint ringing started in my ears, growing louder.

More words then, more banter, but coming as if from a distance—disconnected, like static buzzing on that old radio in the front room, the needle casting back and forth for a clear signal to lock onto.

I wiped cold sweat from my upper lip and sipped at my water, willing my hand not to shake, fighting the rising panic.

I'd dreaded—even resented—the thought of company tonight, as if it were an intrusion on me. But now it was clear that I was the intruder. I was the outsider, a stranger in every sense, not this man sitting so easy, so appreciated, at their table.

I took up my knife and fork and began to saw pieces of chicken—sweet with the pear glaze but tasteless on my tongue. I cut the bits smaller and smaller and smaller . . .

Finally I stopped and stared at my plate, now sliding out of focus. My chest was tightening, squeezing the air from my lungs. I could feel myself surrendering to the growing static, drifting with it, the voices fusing together, receding to a rushing noise not unlike that creek outside . . .

"How about you, Joanna?"

The sound of my own name cut through the panic—through the rattle and noise filling my head to bursting. It seemed to come from a far place, but it was coming only from across the table, where Simon was watching me, holding the wine bottle, waiting. I blinked at him stupidly.

"Sorry?"

"More wine?" he asked.

I drew a steadying breath. "Yes, please. A little."

He poured a small glass. "I understand you like to write. You must like books, then."

"Yes."

He waited, apparently expecting I had more to say on the subject. I struggled to oblige him.

"I don't read much anymore," I said. "Not since . . . not for a long time."

"What did you like to read, when you did?"

His expression was open, friendly. He was only trying to engage me.

"Poetry," I said at last.

"Anyone in particular?"

At least that question was easy. "I always liked Yeats."

Simon paused, then began to recite: "'Where the wandering water gushes from the hills above Glen-Car . . .'"

I gave him a thin smile. This poem I knew—as familiar as Laurel's favorite bedtime books, read and reread a thousand times.

I finished the line for him: "'In pools among the rushes that scarce could bathe a star.' That's from 'The Stolen Child.'"

Laurel looked startled. "Somebody stole a child?"

"It's a poem, sweetie," I said. "About a fairy that tries to tempt a mortal child away from the troubles of the world."

"Did she go?"

"Well, yes. The last stanza goes like this:

'He'll hear no more the lowing
Of the calves on the warm hillside
Or the kettle on the hob
Sing peace into his breast,
Or see the brown mice bob
Round and round the oatmeal chest.' "

I surprised myself, recalling those lines. I hadn't thought of that poem in years. And the book was long gone.

"That's sad," said Laurel. "Not seeing the mice anymore. Or the calves."

"That would be sad," I said. "But think of the wonderful life with the fairies. And no reason to be unhappy again, ever. That's a good thing, don't you think?"

"Maybe. But if you didn't come, too, I wouldn't go."

"That's right, honey," Jessie said, patting her hand. "You stick with your mama. And if those fairies come round, you tell 'em to scat."

Later, as Jessie passed around the dessert plates, I felt Simon's eyes on me. I forced myself to glance up. His gaze was steady, speculative.

Olin cleared his throat, then spoke: "Simon, how you holdin' up down at the café? We sure did leave you shorthanded of late."

"I understand—you've been busy."

Jessie was shaking her head. "Still, a shame you don't have some help. Even for a day or so a week."

I took their meaning then. It wasn't that I was unwilling to help out in their café, but I'd never done restaurant work before. Or held any real job. After we were married, Jim wouldn't allow it.

But it wasn't only lack of experience that unnerved me. It was imagining Jim pulling up at that café one day—stepping out of his unit with his spit-shined shoes, his Sam Browne and .40-caliber pistol, unsnapping his holster. Working there, I'd be sticking my head out of my hiding place.

On the other hand, I realized he could just as easily pull up at Olin and Jessie's door.

So what I really had to decide was when I would stop letting Jim make my decisions for me—control me, even in absentia. Again I was staring at my plate, this time wrestling down my own survival instinct. I took a deep breath.

"If you like," I said at last, "I could help. But I've never waitressed before—I might be lousy at it."

"Oh, honey," said Jessie, "the way you do around here, you can handle yourself. I'll teach you all you need. Then I'll leave you in Simon's hands."

I glanced at Simon, who was still watching me steadily. And for some unearthly reason, I blushed.

The Café

$\mathscr{It}$ took a few days to muster the nerve to cross the footbridge, but one morning I woke before dawn feeling something like resolve, pulled on a skirt and blouse and left a note for Jessie.

I paused on the front porch. The yellow pickup was already parked next to the building and the neon sign and windows were lit up.

To the left of me, the Mountain was a massive silhouette under its snowcapped peak. I stepped off the porch, averting my gaze even as I sensed *it* still watching *me*.

I started toward the café, my eyes fastened on the path. There was little ambient light, but enough to navigate. My movement must have startled something in the brush—I could hear a rustle and scurry of some small animal, receding fast. Something was throwing shadows of piñon and juniper all around me, and I glanced up ahead to see a full moon on the wane, low and fat in the sky and visible just above the flat roof of the café.

And there it was again—that inescapable force of gravity, latching on to me. It wanted me to turn. Wanted me to look. The prospect was terrifying—and yet thrilling at the same time.

I'm not sure it was my decision to stop.

Or to turn.

The sun hadn't breached yet, but light was spreading out from the east. There was an anemic layer of stratus clouds hanging low in the sky, and as the dawn grew their underbellies bled out from scarlet to salmon to pink.

The face of the Mountain was changing, too—from flat silhouette to deep shadows, cut with shards of light. It seemed to be shifting, rearranging, from the rising sun or some other catalyst.

And there at the summit I saw it, shining from the crags.

A fixed, flawless white light.

I'd never noticed this before—in fact, I'd never seen the top of the Mountain except in daylight. The light seemed set at such an altitude, and so inaccessible, I couldn't imagine what it might be. Or how someone had managed to put it there. Or why.

It didn't move or blink or strobe. A beacon of some kind? A warning?

A cool breeze swept in from the east and I pulled my sweater close.

The sun was cresting now, inching higher with each passing second. As it rose, the light on the Mountain faded in kind, shrinking to a pinpoint, then to extinction, even as the Mountain itself seemed to rouse to life.

It took an effort to disengage and turn back to the path. The air held a new snap and static, as if a thunderstorm had just passed through.

Across the footbridge, I rounded the café to the front. Through the windows I could see the place was compact and retro, with little red tables and a curving Formica counter. In a corner was a large, silent jukebox with art deco chrome and blinking colored lights.

I opened the door and a bell jangled overhead; I could hear soft music coming from the back. There was movement near the jukebox, where Pal was rising stiffly from a rag rug. He pushed his nose into my hand till I scratched his ears.

"It's me!" I called out. "Joanna!"

Simon's head appeared above the half wall that separated the dining area from the kitchen. He broke into a smile.

"You've come to rescue me."

"I'm hardly the cavalry," I said.

"Can you tell time?"

"I . . . Of course."

"Then in ten minutes, open this oven and pull out the biscuits." He handed me a pair of oven mitts. "I got a feeling we'll be busy today. Relatively. Jessie on the way?"

"I left a note," I said. "But this morning I wanted to . . ."

"Fly solo?"

"I guess. Can I help with anything while I wait on the biscuits?"

The next half hour flew. I wiped down tables and counters, wrapped sets of silverware in paper napkins, refilled napkin holders, straw dispensers and condiment bottles.

When Jessie arrived, she walked me through the menu,

showed me how to take orders and leave the slips for Simon. To serve and clear and work the cash register. She was direct and encouraging.

Soon customers began filing through the door. My heart skipped with every jangle of the bell, but every face was that of a stranger. The first time I screwed up an order, I froze and braced for the fallout. But the customer waved off my apologies, insisting the blueberry pancakes I brought him were better than the buttermilk he'd ordered.

A dozen people must have come through that morning—farmers, ranchers, store owners, laborers. None of them asked prying questions. At lunchtime came a second round.

"To get a look at the new waitress," said Jessie.

"They didn't know there'd be a new waitress," I said. "Even I didn't know till I woke up this morning."

Jessie smiled but didn't answer. By two o'clock, she untied her apron and left for the day. Only four customers remained. I refilled their coffee mugs as Simon beckoned me to the counter.

"How about lunch?" he asked.

I'd been so busy, I hadn't thought to break for a meal.

"How does it work?" I asked.

He shrugged. "Just tell me what you'd like."

I hesitated. It had been a long time since I'd ordered in a restaurant.

"Well," I said, "I haven't had a cheeseburger and shake in ages."

I took a seat by a window on the western end of the valley. The sun through the glass was warm on my face and arms. Only two trucks remained in the parking lot, belonging to the last customers.

Simon set two plates on the table—one in front of me with a cheeseburger and fries, and an identical plate on the other side. He left and returned with a chocolate shake for me, a vanilla one for himself. He sat down and thumped a ketchup bottle over his fries.

"So tell me," he said. "How was your day?"

I shook my head. "I'm surprised I survived."

"You did great."

"How would you know? You were back at the grill."

"I see and hear plenty back there," he said. "And careful—you have a limited quota of discouraging words before you violate the menu."

I blinked at him. "What?"

He flipped over a menu and ran his finger along a line at the bottom: *Seldom is heard a discouraging word.*

"Olin's idea," he said. "To keep folks civil. And if they aren't . . ."

"You kick them out?"

He paused, considering me carefully. "For you, a new rule," he said. "You'll have to drop a coin in the jukebox over there and play any song I choose."

"I don't know," I said. "You might have rotten taste in music."

"I happen to have swell taste in music. And every record is crackerjack."

"Are those real vinyls? Forty-fives?"

"Not just forty-fives," he said. "Some are seventy-eights—all of them requests from customers. Jessie orders them special. Sometimes people would just like to hear a song that means something."

"What's your favorite?"

He smiled at me over his burger. "One of these days, I might tell you."

I pegged him for country-western. A ballad, though, not a rowdy bar song. Nothing about cheating—Simon didn't seem the type. And not a patriotic anthem, either. Not after what Jessie had told me about his war experience.

Jim had a particular taste for country-western. I'd listened to song after song about whiskey and beer and pickup trucks, true lovers and cheaters. After a while, it all ran together like manic-depressive white noise.

A few years ago, though, Jim took a break from music. All of it. That was after a country band came out with a song about a wife who'd had enough of her abusive husband and decided to get rid of the problem—rat poison in the grits and rolling out the tarp . . .

One day Jim came home from work and caught me listening to it. I hadn't planned to—it just came over the radio as I was cooking. But as it began, as I listened, it stopped me in my tracks. Jim caught me standing there, so focused, so fascinated. Maybe he thought I was taking notes. Maybe I was.

He yanked the power cord from the wall, then slammed the radio against my head.

It was cheap plastic and splintered easily, so it didn't do as much damage as you'd think. Jim must have thought so, too, because for good measure he took the pot of stew cooling on the stove, stood over me where I lay stunned on the linoleum and poured it on my back. I was five months' pregnant with Laurel then.

"Is something wrong?" Simon asked.

I couldn't look at him.

"If I ask you something," I said, "will you answer it?"

"I don't see why not."

I swallowed hard.

"That day . . . that day you found us. I don't remember it. Any of it. And I need to know what happened."

"It's no mystery, Joanna. I was driving down the road here, heading toward the highway. Once you're over that hill, it's all steep curves toward the interstate, and soon enough you hit desert again. I saw buzzards circling half a mile or so from the road. And on the ground right under them, I thought I saw something move."

His tone was mild. Matter-of-fact. Almost indifferent. When he said the word "buzzards," I looked up to lock eyes with him.

I didn't see indifference there, but sympathy. It stung me.

"I was able to off-road the pickup halfway in," he continued. "By then, I could tell it was someone staggering along, barely able to keep to their feet. I got out and sprinted the rest of the way. You were stumbling, but still standing. You were holding Laurel, and she was passed out—it was all I could do to pry your arms off her. You didn't want to let her go—in fact, you fought me quite a bit.

"You must have been out there awhile. You were dehydrated, sick from the heat. Your clothes were ripped up, legs swelled from cactus spines. I slung Laurel over my shoulder, propped you up as best I could and half carried you back to my truck. Olin and Jessie were the closest. I knew they'd take good care of you."

I couldn't bear to look at him anymore, and turned to stare out the window. But this time I wasn't seeing the green valley, but the awful scene Simon had just described.

"Did you find our car?" I asked finally. "A little Toyota. Silver."

"No car. I even drove back along the road once you were safe at the house, and back and forth along the interstate looking for one. In case there was an accident and someone else might be hurt."

"Did I . . . Was there blood . . . on my clothes?"

Simon might have been picturing an accident, but I wasn't. I was picturing rat poison and just deserts with a sick fascination.

"Some," he said. "From scrapes and cuts. Not much, though. You heal up fast."

"I have lots of practice with that," I said bitterly.

We both went quiet.

It was nearly three o'clock—closing time—and the last customers were leaving, calling their good-byes to Simon, dropping cash on their tables. The bell on the door jangled as they left. Their trucks pulled out and headed south toward the foothills.

Then all was silent again.

"Guess you'll have to kick me out after all," I said.

Simon didn't answer. He pushed his chair back and headed to the jukebox. He studied the selections, then slid a coin in the slot and punched some buttons. The machine whirred and clacked; a record slid into place.

It was soft rock from the sixties, a hit from before I was born. But it was timeless, and I knew it well. This was the more recent remake, the same version Terri and I would play in our dorm room at Hokona Hall whenever we pulled an all-nighter or just wanted to cut loose.

Don't worry, baby—everything will turn out all right. Don't worry, baby . . .

I smiled, and Simon looked pleased. We listened to it together without speaking, and when it was over he sent me back out the door.

Good Night Air

$\mathcal{I}$ tugged Laurel's nightgown over her head. Her hair was damp from her evening bath, the ends rolling like tiny sausages. She could use a trim.

Before she slipped under the covers, she pulled a thin book from the nightstand and handed it to me. Jessie had borrowed it from the library in town. Laurel was too old for it, really, but she loved it. So did I. It was comfort reading, the book equivalent of tomato soup and grilled cheese sandwiches.

After the book ended, after all the familiar "good nights" were said, Laurel was still wide-awake, watching me solemnly from her pillow.

"Mommy, are we living here now?"

I set the book on my lap.

"For a while, sweetie. Do you like it here?"

She nodded, rubbing one eye with her knuckles.

"But are we staying? Is this forever?"

"Well, forever's a long time," I said.

Laurel's hand dropped to the covers and she leveled a look at me even more solemn than before. It was a piercing, knowing look, and I'd never seen it come from such a young face before. Especially hers. It gave me the distinct impression she knew something I didn't. And *knew* she knew, and was only waiting for me to catch up.

I set the book back on the nightstand.

"Laurel, honey," I said. "Do you remember the day we got here?"

She squinted at me, puzzled.

"I woke up," she said. "And I was here."

"Here?"

She jiggled her feet under the covers and smiled.

"Here. In bed. Miz Jessie brought me strawberries."

I brushed stray hair from her temple.

"And what about before that?" I tried to keep my voice light. "Do you remember Mr. Simon bringing us here?"

She thought for a moment, then shook her head.

"And before that?" I asked even more lightly than before. "Do you remember Daddy? Out on the road?"

This time her eyes were fixed on me intently.

"Do *you*?" she asked finally.

I couldn't tell if she was being curious or trying to prod my memory. Either way, it was disconcerting.

"No," I said. "Maybe you can help me remember."

She shook her head once more.

"I can't."

Can't? I thought. *Or won't?*

How old does your child have to be before she starts keeping big secrets? I felt a pang of guilt. Maybe that was something she'd learned from me.

Laurel yawned and stretched, settling deeper under the covers. "Mommy?" she asked.

"Yes, sweetie?"

"I heard Tinkerbell today."

My breath caught in my throat. "Wh-what?"

"She was barking. Up on the Mountain. I think she's trying to find us."

In a flash I was back in our yard in Wheeler, Tinkerbell scratching at the shed door, Jim heading inside with the shovel . . .

"That . . . that's just not possible, Laurel. If you heard a dog, it could have been any dog. They sound alike from far off."

"No, Mommy. It was Tinkerbell. And we gotta go get her."

I stood up from the bed, rattled to the core. I wasn't going up on that mountain. And certainly not to hunt for a dog I knew full well I'd never find.

"Time to go to sleep now," I said.

"But, Mommy . . ."

I stooped for a quick kiss to her cheek, then switched off the table lamp.

"Good night."

Bee in a Thunderstorm

Not long after Laurel told me about Tinkerbell, Jessie said a few ladies from town would arrive the next morning—they were holding a bee to finish up a wedding quilt for the local schoolteacher. She invited me to join them, and pressed till I felt no choice but to accept. She looked pleased when I did.

"It'll be fine weather for it," she said. "These old bones know."

Olin was behind her at the dining room table playing dominoes with Laurel. He looked up at me and winked.

Early the next morning came a menacing rumble. I glanced out my bedroom window to see heavy clouds crowding in from the east. A gust of wind lashed the bedroom curtains. You could smell the storm brewing.

Wooden deck chairs already sat under the oak tree, arranged in a tight circle that Olin had set up the night before at Jessie's instruction. But it seemed the ladies were about to get rained out.

Then I noticed Jessie in the vegetable garden below, standing between rows of tomato plants. Her hands were on her hips and she was glaring. She raised the skirt of her apron and waved it, the way she does to chase off a stray hen.

"Shoo, now! Shoo!"

But there was no hen in sight, and Jessie wasn't looking down, but up—up at the storm clouds.

Another rumble, a louder volley than before. She shook her head and retreated back inside.

We didn't eat breakfast at the outside trestle table, but at the little oak one in the kitchen—all but Olin, who said he had business in the fields.

He'd been outside all morning, but had been vague about where or why. Earlier, I'd spotted him off in the distance—as still and straight as a soldier at inspection, far outside his fieldstone fence. He had faced east, too, just like Jessie.

I almost called out to him then, but something stopped me. Somehow it felt like an intrusion. Now here he was again, running off.

Another battery of thunder; the storm was drawing nigh.

"A pity about your bee," I told Jessie. "You could always bring it inside."

She looked at me thoughtfully. "We always have it outside. Never you mind."

The ladies arrived soon after breakfast. Liz LaGow was dark and sturdy—not tall, but vigorous. She was carrying a thick bundle wrapped in cloth and trussed with twine. Her dark, probing eyes took me in from ponytail to sandals. I knew she and her husband owned the general store. She arrived with her sister, Molly Knox, who was taller than Liz, and slimmer, with finer features. She had a coil of brunette braid at the crown of her head and eyes that were less penetrating than her sister's. Molly owned the hotel in town.

Like Jessie, the sisters wore simple belted dresses hemmed a prim distance below the knee. I couldn't get a handle on how old they might be—they seemed ageless, but had the same bold energy as Jessie. For some reason, I could clearly picture the three of them marching hundreds of miles alongside Conestoga wagons, raising children on hardscrabble farms on the frontier.

The teacher, though, was altogether different. Bree Wythe was younger than I—petite and lively in jeans and a sleeveless blouse of coral silk. She wore a string of small turquoise nuggets around her neck. Her hair was ash blond, styled to her shoulders. Her smile was warm as she took my hand.

"I'm so happy to meet you," she said in a voice with slight Southern notes. She linked her arm through mine as we followed the others through the house toward the back door. "Thanks for helping on the quilt—I don't know about you, but I've never finished a stitch in my life."

We stopped just inside the kitchen, where Jessie and the sisters stood at the open doorway to the backyard, staring at a bank of black clouds that now nearly eclipsed the sky. Wind whipped the branches of the old oak. Lightning crackled; thunder growled.

The three women exchanged grim looks, then without a word forged ahead into the yard. The wind smacked their long skirts about their legs and tore at their hair, pulling it loose from buns and braids.

I paused in the doorway with Bree and stared after them. I expected Bree to be as rattled as I was, but she only smiled and tugged on me until we were heading for the oak, too.

Liz was loosening the twine around her bundle, drawing out a large quilt. The others opened small sewing bags to withdraw scissors, needles, thimbles and spools of thread. Deftly they stretched the quilt into a four-legged frame, then settled back in their chairs. Bree and I took our seats, and the five of us tucked into the quilt as if the wind weren't howling or the clouds about to split open.

The scene was so outrageous, so surreal, I couldn't speak.

Molly handed me a needle, spool and thimble, and Jessie did the same for Bree. Numbly I snipped off a length and bent to thread the needle, but of course it was impossible with the wind whipping the thread, and though it was only midmorning, it had grown as dark as dusk. I was about to give up when Molly passed me the needle she'd just threaded, apparently with little trouble.

Conversation would only have been drowned out, so the women bent to their own work, needles darting.

Thunder exploded directly over our heads in a long, furious roar that rattled the windows of the house. I could taste the electrical charge.

"We should go inside!" I shouted.

The women paused long enough to stare at me, then shook their heads. Molly leaned in close. "This is nothing, Joanna. Just wait."

Thunder again, followed hard by lightning. I stared about, my heart in my throat.

Then, just as I was about to bolt for the house, everything abruptly changed.

The banshee noise broke off as suddenly as flipping a switch. The thrashing branches of the oak eased till they were rocking like cradles. A rift began to open in the clouds directly overhead, wider by the second, splitting apart to expose a strip of cobalt blue sky. Shafts of yellow sunlight cut through the rift and hit the oak tree.

"There, now," Jessie muttered with a sigh. "Much better."

She and the sisters laid down their needles and calmly began to tuck their hair back in place. I watched them, stunned. I could only guess we were in the eye of the storm, although I'd never heard of thunderstorms having eyes. But they must, for this storm was clearly far from over.

On every side of us it still raged, hammering down the grass all along the bowl of the valley, whipsawing the trees. Fields of corn and wheat rolled like great waves. Clouds boiled, black and green and sickly yellow. In the distance, rain fell in flat unbroken sheets. Lightning flashed—not in single jagged bolts but in branching spectacles that lit up the sky. Thunder bellowed, but it wasn't rattling the windows anymore.

There was chaos all around while we sat undisturbed in an acre of oasis.

Liz began to rub her shoulder as if she'd strained it. "About time," she muttered. "Couldn't hear myself think with that racket."

"I . . . I don't understand," I said. "What's happening?"

Liz frowned at me dismissively, then turned to Bree. "Honey," she said, "tell us about the wedding. At the hotel, is it?"

Bree looked relieved to lay down her needle. "Middle of

December. Reuben says it's a slow time at the ranch. Joanna, you're more than welcome."

I stared at her, still confused. December was a long way off—I couldn't imagine still being in Morro by then. Bree was just being polite.

"Thank you," I managed finally. "If I'm still here."

Jessie dropped her hands to her lap and stared toward the barn just as Olin emerged with a deck chair under each arm, Laurel trailing behind. "Speak of the devil," she muttered. "What's that old fool up to now?"

He stopped in a patch of grass well within our sight and set the chairs side by side facing the western end of the valley, which was now bearing the brunt of the storm. Then the two of them took their seats to watch as calmly as if they were in a movie theater.

Liz was bristling, clearly feeling provoked. Molly was stifling a smile.

"Pay him no mind," Jessie said airily. "Don't give him the satisfaction."

Olin pulled the caps off two pop bottles and handed one to Laurel. It was then I noticed Bree studying me curiously.

"Joanna, summer's about over," she said. "School's starting soon. Will you be enrolling your daughter?"

The question caught me off guard. The last time Laurel had left school, she'd brought home her first-grade certificate, launching our escape.

I shrugged, feigning indifference. "I haven't made any plans."

I was sure Jim had alerted Laurel's school by now, and they'd let him know about any request to transfer her records. Enrolling her anywhere else would be firing off a flare.

"If it's a matter of documents, I wouldn't worry," said Bree. "I'd never turn a child away because of paperwork."

"And don't forget," said Jessie. "We're not county. We do things our own way out here."

"But there must be a school board," I protested. "Officials to account to."

"Honey"—Jessie gestured around the circle—"most of the school board is sitting right here." She looked meaningfully at Liz and Molly, who nodded in return. "All right, then. It's settled."

Apparently the discussion was over. And Laurel was enrolled in school.

"You been to town yet?" Liz asked. "No sense putting it off," she said when I shook my head. "We don't bite. Come on up and visit the store. We got everything you need, and most everything you'd want."

"Check out the hotel, too," Bree urged. "A lovely old Victorian. High tea on weekends. Very authentic."

"Yes, indeed." Liz smirked. *"Authentic."*

Molly's cheeks reddened. "And why not?" she said. "George has been very helpful."

Liz and Jessie said nothing.

"Who's George?" I asked finally.

"Oh," said Jessie. "He's Molly's gentleman caller."

"George is from Bristol," Molly said stiffly. "England."

I didn't ask how they'd managed to meet, but couldn't imagine it was through any online dating site. In fact, I couldn't picture Molly—or her sister or Jessie—on a computer at all. Jessie didn't keep so much as a microwave in her house.

What I could picture—quite suddenly and with utter

clarity—was one or the other placing a lonely-hearts newspaper ad. I could see photos exchanged—formal poses in sepia tones—then letters back and forth over many months, many years. The progression of their courtship washed over me with surprising surety.

Jessie laid down her needle and gazed about. "Storm broke."

It had broken long ago over our heads, of course, but now it was breaking in earnest over the rest of the valley. Lightning streaked soundlessly far off to the west, where thunderheads were in galloping retreat.

I paused, too, taking in the aftermath. The valley appeared to be standing still, catching its breath, set loose from time and space. It felt as if every clock in the world had wound down and suddenly stopped.

Even the air was motionless, leaving the valley as composed and vivid as a diorama. As wild and reckless as the storm had been, so profound now was the calm that followed it. The lull was contagious—it washed over me and through me in a wave of warmth. I'd never felt so at peace. I didn't want it to end.

None of us spoke. None of us moved. We sat together in stillness and silence under the oak tree, caught up in a consecrated moment.

A second passed. Then another. And with the next, the clocks began to tick again. Rain began to drip from the leaves and the rooflines. Birds stirred in the branches, and in the distance Willow Creek rushed noisily from the downpour.

The valley felt purged. Revived.

"Well, ladies." Jessie sighed. "Gather up."

Sewing bags opened up again, and back went needles, thread and thimbles. Liz and Molly unframed the quilt, folded it and slid it back into its fabric bag.

Olin still sat with Laurel at the far corner of the barn. He turned toward me and raised his pop bottle in salute.

And I knew what he was telling me: *You're welcome.*

A Still, Small Space

After the storm, after the sisters had left with Bree, I packed the last of the deck chairs back in the barn and stood alone in the open doorway. Dusk was falling, and lights were switching on in the farmhouse. Scraps of voices drifted outside, rising and falling in conversation. The radio broke into a twangy two-step, something about "Too Old to Cut the Mustard."

I stared about me at every homely and familiar object, every bit of landscape, as if they had suddenly become alien to me. As if at any moment they could transform into something else altogether, or vanish outright. Plow, tiller, scythe. Fence, tree, house. Even as I turned from one to the next, they seemed to pulsate, their lines blurring. I blinked, and they were back.

It was then I realized that the question I'd been asking— *How did we get here?*—was painfully inadequate. Suddenly it was almost irrelevant that I couldn't remember what happened that last day in Wheeler, between the frantic sprint toward Albuquerque, the flashing lights in the rearview and waking up in that bed upstairs.

This wasn't just a matter of recall.

It was a matter of *here itself.*

My stomach heaved and my knees buckled. I slid down the doorjamb, pushing off to land on a ladder that was lying along the barn wall. I closed my eyes and sucked in deep breaths, willing every particle to be very, very still.

"Gettin' a handle on the moment?"

I blinked up at Olin, standing over me in the doorway, his head quirked. His fingers worked a leaf of rolling paper packed with a line of loose tobacco, deftly snugging it into a cigarette. He licked the seal closed, stuck one end in his mouth and pulled a matchbook from his shirt pocket. When the cigarette was lit, he puffed twice as he slid the matches back into place. Then he offered me his hand.

"Join me outside," he said.

He eased me up and led me from the barn to the trestle table. As we sat, I barely noticed or cared that its benches were still soaked from the rain. Olin watched me for a long moment over his cigarette. He seemed expectant.

"Stew for supper," he said finally. "If you can eat."

I shook my head. I started to say something, then stopped. Words had become meaningless.

"Or," Olin continued, "we could just sit here and talk about the weather."

I stared at him and he gazed back, placid as ever. His lines never wavered, never shifted out of focus. It gave me encouragement.

"I thought it was me," I said. "With the Mountain. The way it pulls at me. Almost . . . talks to me. But it isn't me, is it?"

Olin took a drag on his cigarette, the tip flaring cherry red in the gathering dusk, mirroring pinpoints of light in his eyes. The smoke when he exhaled smelled sweet. He waited for me to continue.

"And you and Jessie—you're not just old-fashioned, are you? I can't explain it, but you're . . . somehow you're out of time and place."

If I expected Olin to be offended, he wasn't. Nor did he protest. Instead, he smiled indulgently.

I glanced at the western sky as the first stars sparked into place, much like the lights in the farmhouse. There was no trace of storm clouds left.

"And that thunderstorm. Deny it if you want, but . . ." I hesitated. The evening air wasn't cool, but I was starting to shiver.

"Go on," Olin urged.

"I think . . . I think you made it. Called it down. Whatever. And Jessie and the sisters—" I shook my head again as if to clear it. "Somehow they busted it up right over us, didn't they? Stopped it smack in its tracks. So they could have their bee. Jessie said they always have their bee outside."

"They surely do."

"Rain or shine, right? Only it never rains. At least not where they are. Olin, what is this place? You have to tell me. And tell me like I'm four years old, because that's about all I can handle right now."

He bent his head and flicked ash off the tip of his cigarette. He scraped his thumbnail thoughtfully along his chin, as if considering how best to approach the subject. I watched him in fascination and fear, hardly daring to breathe.

"A while ago," Olin began slowly, "we had a fella come through, said he was a rabbi. From Brooklyn, he said. And him and me, we got to talkin'. He told me about this place by the name of *Olam HaEmet*. A 'Place of Truth,' he called it. He said there comes a time when you go to this Place of Truth, and you stay put till you figure things out. Reflect on all the things you did in your life. Or maybe on all the things you should've done but didn't. He said that's where he was headed."

I started to laugh, but it snagged in my throat. A rabbi? Olin in a tête-à-tête with a rabbi—a tallit slung over his shoulders and tefillin boxes strapped to his head? But overriding the sense of the surreal was the gist of Olin's words. And even more, the meaning between them. I wanted him to fill in those gaps for me unbidden. At the same time, I wanted to scream at the top of my lungs for him to stop. I tried to lick my lips, but my tongue was as dry as dust.

"And this place, where do you find it?" I asked.

"Not so much *where*," Olin said gently, "as *how*."

I was shivering so hard now my teeth began to clatter. I tried to rub the gooseflesh from my bare arms, but my fingers were icicles. The fact was, I remembered reading something about Olam HaEmet, a long time ago. Except the writer had called it the "World of Truth." It's a place observant Jews believe waits on the Other Side. A place for reflection.

A place for departed souls.

"No," I whispered.

"You never know about expectations," Olin said mildly. "Everybody's got his own, I guess. When they first cross over."

Cross over? What the hell . . . ?

A faint ringing started in my ears and my body felt as weightless as balsa wood.

"You're crazy," I said. "Or I am. This isn't happening."

"Give me your hands, Joanna."

I glared back at him as if this—all this—were somehow his fault. Some cruel prank.

He said it again, this time more firmly: "Give me your hands."

His tone was still soothing, but there was a note of command in it, too. I found myself reaching for him, my hands now shaking so violently they looked palsied. I shuddered as he took them. The infusion of warmth I felt the first time he ever touched me—that first morning at breakfast, at this very same table—was nothing compared to the jolt of heat that coursed through me now, driving out the bone-chill. The shivering began to ease.

"This can't be." Tears were sliding down my cheeks. "*I* can't be."

"Go ahead; cry it out if you want. Won't make it any less so."

"But how? I don't know how . . ." An accident on the road? Had I hit another car or careened off the highway to escape that speeding cruiser? Another realization struck, and I pulled my hands from Olin's to stare in horror at the house. "Oh, dear God . . . Laurel . . ."

"Now, now. It's all right. Don't she look all right to you?"

All right? Since we'd come here, Laurel had never looked healthier. Or seemed happier. Suddenly I thought about that night in her room when she'd asked if we were here forever. If *this* were our forever . . .

"Does she know?" I asked.

Olin considered for a moment. "Not exactly. She's workin' it out—children, they catch on when they're ready. But she ain't quite there yet."

Five minutes ago, I would've said I wasn't quite there yet, either. Not ready to catch on. Not ready at all. But I had been suspicious, asking questions and grasping for answers, and Olin had only been obliging me.

Now he was regarding me with sympathy, as if another shoe were about to drop.

"Joanna, when we first met, you recall what I said? That you had the look of a gal who wouldn't be stayin' long."

"A short-timer. I remember."

He nodded. "Now, that's the thing. Near all the folks who come through, they go on eventually. But there's some, a few— they up and turn back."

"I don't understand."

"It ain't their time. They ain't fixed in one place yet, nor the other. So they got a choice to make. To stay or go back."

"Are you— Olin, what are you saying?"

"Near as I can tell," he continued, "you're here for a reason. You were in a bad way, and for a long time. Back in Wheeler."

I ducked my head, unsure how much Olin knew, even without my telling.

"This here—" Olin glanced up and down the valley, nearly eclipsed now by the gathering dusk. "Think of this as a place to rest. To get strong and straight inside. Think of it like your own Place of Truth. To consider where you come from, and what you might do different if you go back."

Jim's face flashed in front of me, and I shuddered involuntarily.

"That man of yours," Olin said knowingly. "Seems to me he was bleedin' the life out of you for a long time before you ever made it here."

"And he sure as hell won't stop if he gets the chance to do it again."

"No, he won't. It ain't in him to stop."

"So why would I *ever* want to go back?"

"That ain't for me to say."

I leaned on the table, burying my face in my hands, anxious for the moment to be over. More than anything I wanted to look up again and find no trace of Olin or the farm or that Mountain. I wasn't ruling out insanity, either—his or mine. I'd sidled up to it often enough over these last few years. But when you've finally lost it—lost it good and proper—do you even realize it? Do you know if you've given up, crawled inside your own head and pulled the ladder up after you? *Die Gedanken sind frei,* my Oma used to sing. *Thoughts are free . . . The darkest dungeon is futile, for my thoughts tear all gates and walls asunder . . .* For all I knew, I was still out there staggering in the desert, just as Simon had said, my broken brain cooking up this mirage . . .

And yet . . .

And yet I did know—knew marrow-deep—this was no delusion. No mirage. I knew because, with all my heart and soul, I wanted it to be. But no such luck. Not for me.

Finally I raised my head. "I don't— Olin, I have so many questions . . ."

"You hold on to them," he said. "Now ain't the time for questions, and I sure ain't the one for answers. What's important—well, it's best we all figure out the important things on our own. In our own way."

Suddenly I felt wrung out, weak as an infant. "What should I do?" I asked. "I don't know what to do."

"First off, you go on inside and get yourself some supper. You get yourself a good night's sleep. You wake up tomorrow and praise the day. You be mindful. And the next day, and the day after that, you get up and do it all over again. *You live.*"

Was that all? Eat, sleep, wake, work—in the afterlife, the same rules applied? I had no idea of the proprieties here. The physics. Were there other short-timers? Was everyone who crossed paths here a departed spirit? If not, would I know the difference? Would *they*? Olin and Jessie spoke of Wheeler as if they'd been there many times. As if they went there still . . .

"Olin," I whispered, as if Jim could be within earshot. "Can my husband find us here?"

Olin looked past me for so long I thought he didn't intend to answer. Then he did.

"That ain't for me to say, neither."

Little Yellow Boots

$\mathscr{T}$ woke on the porch, curled up like a fetus on the wicker settee. It was early morning and a dank chill hung in the air. I pushed myself up and a blanket slid off—someone must have laid it over me while I slept. I felt sluggish, as if my brain had been working overtime through the night. I rubbed at eyes that were dry and sore, trying to recall how I ended up sleeping outside.

And in a flash it came back . . . The sisters and the bee. The thunderstorm. Olin. The Place of Truth.

I swung my legs to the floor and nearly toppled an empty wine bottle sitting at my feet. It was one of Simon's—the apple wine he supplied at Saturday suppers. I'd sneaked it from Jessie's cupboard after they'd all gone off to bed. Then I'd slipped outside to get as snockered as circumstances would allow. I considered it a necessity. A palliative. Even an experiment. And what I discovered was that circumstances allowed snockered, sure enough. But apparently not sloppy. Or maybe for sloppy you needed two bottles.

The noises of a waking household were coming from inside. Jessie would be back in the kitchen, setting her cast-iron skillet on the stove, grinding coffee beans, sending Olin to the henhouse for eggs. I pulled the blanket back over my shoulders and stood. The planks of the porch felt cool and sure against my bare feet. I padded to the front railing, keen for any signs of the supernatural. I wasn't sure what that might be—a melting landscape like something out of Dalí, maybe. A second sun flaring overhead. A herd of bush elephants trumpeting across the valley floor, white tusks flashing . . .

How had Olin called it? *Getting a handle on the moment.* But how do you get a handle on a moment like this? Take it one day at a time, like a recovery program?

Then again, maybe this was meant to be an easy, familiar passage. Like leaving one room to enter another. Otherwise, how could you bear it?

The rattle of an engine came from the hills to the north where the road reared up and disappeared. An old Ford pickup appeared, its black paint faded to dull, piebald grays, coughing blue smoke from its tailpipe. It puttered past the diner on its way south, a ladder poking from its bed, a red rag knotted around the last rung, whipping in the wind like the wings of a scarlet bird.

For some reason, the sheer banality of it heartened me. This, I could handle.

I picked up the empty wine bottle and slipped it under the blanket, out of sight. When no one was looking, I'd drop it in a waste can. Apart from sparing myself some embarrassment,

I intended to use it as another experiment—to see if I was entitled to secrets here.

Breakfast proceeded the same as every other morning. Olin gave no hint that anything was amiss. As if he hadn't lobbed a virtual grenade in my lap hours before.

Hours. Were there still hours? I wasn't sure anymore.

But there was continuity. Familiarity. You sugar your coffee. Spoon the jam. Sop gravy off your plate with hunks of biscuit. You talk about the day ahead, ticking off what needs doing. By the end of breakfast, I was reacquainted with the rhythm, nearly myself again. If I wasn't ready to praise the day, at least I was ready to participate.

Dishes washed and dried, I stepped back outside to find the chill had gone, the sun blazing overhead. It was what Laurel calls a shiny day—so bright and clear your eyes ache with it. She'd gone with Olin to the coop earlier, and her sneakers were caked with mud from the storm the day before. I took a bucket to the yard and was scrubbing her sneakers when Jessie suggested we walk to town to get Laurel a pair of rain boots. I wiped a stray bit of hair from my face and stared at Jessie, searching for a sign on hers—anything to indicate she was aware of what Olin had told me last evening. A hint of complicity. Of *knowing*. Maybe even of sympathy.

But it was Jessie as Jessie had always been—her gray hair coiled to a tight bun, her sturdy frame as straight as a fence post, brooking no argument.

She tied on a straw sunbonnet and handed me another. It was wide brimmed, and from long habit I slung it low to hide my face. I brushed Laurel's hair into a ponytail and the three of us set out.

This was the first time I'd ventured off the farm, and even

now—even now—I couldn't imagine heading along this road without running into a deputy's cruiser, slanted off to the side, engine idling, windows dark. And Jim hunched like a vulture behind the wheel. But I knew that if I hid out on this farm much longer, I'd only be making myself a prisoner on purpose.

We struck out for town—toward the Mountain—an easy walk not only for its length, a mere two miles or so, but also because it felt as if the road sloped down a tick, although to my eyes it seemed level enough. The effect was of some force drawing me on, compelling me to *come*.

As we walked, Jessie pointed out wildflowers on either side of the road. So many, and such variety. She began to name them: fiddlehead and soap tree yucca, thistle and red pussytoes, lupine and Indian paintbrush, chicory and biscuit-root, sagebrush and mountain dandelion, heartleaf and pearly everlasting.

The only sound aside from Jessie's voice was the faint basal hum of cicadas. Their drowsy noise always reminded me of high-voltage transmission wires, and a thought struck. I looked about, and there were no transmission towers in sight. No power lines anywhere, in fact. No telephone lines or utility cables. No poles to string them on. No cell towers, no radio towers. Behind us, no poles or lines running electricity to the farmhouse. Yet the house *had* electricity. Something was powering the lamps, the radio, the sewing machine, the oven, the clocks . . .

I glanced at Jessie, at my daughter walking so easily with her, the two of them holding hands like great friends.

Jessie glanced back at me, her expression obscure, still reciting the names of flowers in a singsong voice as soothing as a lullaby.

. . .

By the time we rounded that first foothill, I had few expectations of Morro. Olin had said it was long forgotten, and I'd seen bypassed towns before: the bitter decay of empty storefronts and boarded-up windows, littered streets and broken sidewalks.

But Morro was nothing like that.

It wasn't big, consisting of but a single street. But that street was more like a broad boulevard that ran for blocks, and smoothly paved. At the town line a sign read:

WELCOME TO MORRO

Beyond the sign, sidewalks with rows of shade trees that branched thirty feet and higher lined each side of the boulevard. On the outskirts of town stood handsome family homes with deep lawns, while at the center well-kept commercial buildings bustled with people. And right in the middle of the boulevard stood a large domed gazebo.

Jessie stepped briskly to the sidewalk, making for the business center of town. Laurel and I followed. There were few cars, and no traffic signals. We passed a sidewalk café and an Italian bakery selling gelato from a walk-up window. An antiques store, an art gallery, a butcher shop, a green grocer's. Across the street was a lending library and a redbrick building with a sign that read, *Town Hall*. Beyond that were more shops, then more homes lining the far end of town.

But the anchors of this place were clearly the general store—a three-story building that took up the better part of a block—and across from it a grand Victorian hotel called the Wild Rose, painted in flamboyant shades of red.

I walked slowly, the better to take it all in.

There wasn't a single crack in the sidewalk, no hole in the asphalt. No chipping paint. Not a stray bit of litter skittering down the street.

Morro was idyllic—a town Norman Rockwell might have dreamed up.

Or me.

Jessie led us past the hotel, where a couple emerged—very elegant, in their thirties, with dark hair and skin. The man wore a tan sport coat and open-collared shirt; the woman, a beautiful sari of apricot silk. I tried not to stare—they seemed so cosmopolitan, and in their way as anachronistic as Olin and Jessie.

At the general store, its massive front windows were papered with flyers for club meetings, recitals, the weekly farmers' market, a school play. And inside, the building seemed cavernous, with row after row of well-stocked aisles.

Jessie led us to the shoe section, where we searched the shelves for rain boots in Laurel's size. But we found few children's boots at all, and none small enough for her.

Jessie called out for assistance, and a big man sorting boxes nearby left his pallet and joined us. I recognized him from the café—Faro LaGow was the customer I'd brought blueberry pancakes by mistake but who graciously took them anyway.

He was muscular and ruddy, with a short graying beard and close-cropped ginger hair. He put me in mind of an old ring fighter.

He grinned at Jessie. "What can I do you for today?"

"We'll take a pair of rubber boots. For this child here. Something sturdy."

Faro considered Laurel for a moment. "You're seven if you're a day."

Laurel nodded.

"Not sure we got anything on the floor to fit," Faro said. "But a shipment's just come in. First, young lady, why don't you tell me what sort of boots you had in mind."

Laurel's eyes widened. I could tell she was delighted to be consulted, but with an imagination like hers the possibilities were endless. So I answered for her: "Just rain boots. Anything her size."

Laurel yanked her hand from mine and tossed her head at me. *"No!"* she said.

Faro leaned low till he was level with her. "I take it you got your own ideas."

I didn't like where this was going. Of course Laurel would have ideas, but they would likely be wildly unrealistic. Faro seemed to be needlessly stoking her hopes, inviting disappointment. Just the sort of game Jim liked to play.

Laurel took a moment to consider the options, biting her lip thoughtfully.

"Yellow boots," she said finally. "With polka dots."

"What color polka dots?"

This time she didn't hesitate: "All colors."

Faro straightened, rubbing his chin with a hand the size of a boy's baseball mitt. His knuckles were stitched with faint scars. "Well, now, let me go poke through my stock."

By now I was sure the man was toying with her. Whether he meant it unkindly or not didn't matter.

"No," I insisted. "Don't bother."

"Worth a look," he said, and winked. Then he turned on his

heel and headed toward the back, disappearing behind an un-marked door.

"Laurel, honey, he's gone to check," I said. "That doesn't mean he has them."

"If he doesn't," she said, "I don't want any."

Her young face was pure petulance now, and I only hoped she wouldn't pitch a fit right there in the aisle when Faro La-Gow showed up empty-handed.

While we waited, Jessie wandered off for boxes of salt crackers and roasted coffee beans. She collected a can of boiled linseed oil and a horsehair brush for Olin to refinish his gunstocks.

At last Laurel hissed with excitement. "Here he comes!"

Faro was approaching, his hands hidden behind him. "Well, now, young lady. Will these fit the bill?"

And from behind his back he drew a pair of rain boots: bright yellow, covered in polka dots of every color.

Laurel squealed, snatched the boots up and ran to me. I turned them over, checking for signs of fraud, however well intentioned. But there was no drying paint, no stickers. And they were just the right size: seven.

I stared at Faro in disbelief, and he grinned back.

"These are . . . perfect," I managed. Then to Laurel, "What do you say, honey?"

"Thank you, Mr. Faro. Can I put 'em on now?"

He looked at me and I nodded. Laurel pulled on the boots and paraded back and forth for us to admire them properly.

I struggled with how to feel about this. The man had either dug up Laurel's dream boots back in that stockroom through sheer serendipity or had somehow managed to conjure them out of thin air, made-to-order. I lacked the nerve to ask the obvious question: Where on earth had these come from?

Jessie linked her arm through mine. She was gazing at Laurel indulgently, the ghost of a smile on her lips.

We checked out and left with our parcels, returning the same way we'd come, Laurel bounding ahead.

Let There Be Light

That evening, Laurel kept her boots on all through supper. She kept them on as she and Olin played checkers at the table, Jessie reading nearby, half-moon glasses tipped low on her nose. The radio was playing a set by the Artie Shaw orchestra.

I sat for a good hour alone on the dark porch, watching the road, recapping the day, struggling yet again to ground myself. Now and then my attention strayed to the foothills, and to Morro beyond—the pitch-perfect town where whims can come true.

When I came back inside, I paused at the table lamp by Olin's empty chair near the fireplace. The base was a ceramic Remington cowboy astride a cattle pony.

I turned the switch and the lamp sprang to life—the round bulb glowing under the linen shade. I studied the base again, checking all around the pony's four hooves where they attached to the heavy metal stand. I could find no power cord to run to an electrical outlet. On the nearest wall, there was no outlet.

I turned the lamp off again.

Then on.

Anatomy Lesson

$\mathcal{I}$ slept fitfully. Every time I woke, I'd lie very still and listen to the silence. An old wind-up alarm clock had sat on the nightstand, but I went and buried it in a laundry basket inside the closet where I couldn't hear its *tick-tick-tick*—like a heartbeat, but mechanical and mocking. In the dark, too, I listened to my own heart. I could feel the steady pulse at my neck, my wrist. And when I pressed my palm against my chest, there it was.

Tick-tick-tick.

The upshot was to make me doubt Olin, or want to. But I couldn't tell if my resistance sprang from strength or weakness. I kept shifting back and forth. One minute, Olin was an old soul doing me a kindness. The next, an old coot feeding me a line. In the dark, anything and everything seemed possible.

My brain wouldn't shut off.

I rubbed my temples, feeling the soft skin stretch across

the hard cradle of skull. Anatomy itself was a mystery now. In the Place of Truth, in Morro, in whatever or wherever this was, how much was illusion and how much was real?

And what was the purpose? Or even the power source? What keeps a lamp going here? Or a heart?

One night when I was a little girl my mother drove us down some desert highway in our old Rambler wagon. I lay in the backseat staring at a black sky bristling with stars. My brain wouldn't shut off then, either. For the first time, I was struck by the vastness of the universe, pure and perfect, and my own place in it. As I stared, the stars began to shift, inching across the sky like a pinwheel. And I knew it was revealing itself to me, and only me. And a voice that was no voice at all began to fill my head with thoughts so big, so frightening, they set it to spinning, too . . . and soon enough my whole body seemed to spiral like those stars, toppling headfirst toward the sky.

The shock, the enormity, had made me pull back. I closed my eyes and shut my brain down—like pulling a pot off a stove before it boils over. As if whatever I was about to discover threatened to burn me alive. It was all too vast. Too terrible.

After that, the stars were never the same. In time, like anyone else, I learned the names of the major constellations, the North Star, the Evening Star. But I never again trusted myself to get lost in them.

That had been a lesson learned, and I decided to apply it again. There are things too big to take in all at once. And thoughts so deep they might send you pinwheeling off to disappear in the dark.

I couldn't handle Awe when I was four, and still couldn't as a woman of thirty.

I wanted surety and safety and continuity. I wanted to wake in this bed in the morning, wash my face, comb my hair, wake Laurel and get her ready for an unremarkable day. I wanted a long march of unremarkable days just like it.

I wanted it for as long as I was able. Or allowed.

The Lady from Mississippi

Since sleep wouldn't come, I decided to get up early to make my second trip to the café. This time the dog, Pal, wasn't dozing in his corner but sitting just inside the door as if expecting me. Simon came from the kitchen to hand me a mug of hot coffee, already flavored with cream and sweetener.

"How'd you know?" I asked, unable to hide a note of suspicion.

He shrugged. "I've seen how you take your coffee."

"No, I meant how'd you know I'd be here this morning?" It had been well over a week since I'd first helped out.

He nodded toward the back. "There's a window. I could see you heading down the path. Didn't think I was psychic, did you?"

His explanation came as a relief, and I smiled. "Not psychic. Just . . . nosy."

"I prefer 'observant.'"

"Most nosy people would."

He laughed and turned back to his work. He was dressed in a red plaid shirt, the sleeves rolled up past his elbows; his forearms were tanned.

He gestured toward a radio on a stool. "Mind if I turn this on?"

Soon a piano was playing in the background—classical, which surprised me. Chopin, I think. Apparently Simon wasn't such a country-western fan after all.

I took a deep breath and dove in, setting to work as I had the first day, wiping down surfaces, refilling canisters. I slid trays of loaves and biscuits in and out of the oven, setting them on racks to cool. Now and then I glanced at Simon, moving so easily, so confidently, about his work. I would take my cue from him.

There weren't as many customers this morning. One was a plump and pensive woman who said she was the town librarian, although she hardly fit the type.

Jean Toliver wore a skirt to her ankles, a long-sleeved velour blouse cinched at the waist with a silver concho belt. Hanging low on her chest was a magnificent squash blossom necklace of silver and turquoise.

I learned she was from a small town in upstate New York near the Adirondack mountains, but had a lifelong interest in Southwestern Indians, so I imagined she meant it as an homage to dress like many traditional Navajo women. I'd also seen very traditional ones wear their hair twisted at the nape into a sort of stiff, vertical double twist, but Jean wore hers in a simple braid down the back.

Her skin was so milky I suspected she rarely made it beyond the library stacks. Her eyes were the color of nougat behind round-rimmed glasses.

"You're the new one," she said.

I wasn't sure how to answer her.

"You like books—I can tell. Not everyone does," she continued, glancing around the café with disapproval. "A few of us started a monthly book club. You should come."

She opened a canvas tote, drew out a flyer and handed it to me. "Our next meeting." Then she smiled, and two deep dimples gave her a girlish look.

I slid the flyer into my apron pocket. As I turned to leave, Jean tapped my arm.

"We have monthly poetry workshops, too," she murmured. "At the library. You should bring some of your work."

I hadn't told Jean I wrote poetry. Or rather, that I used to, eons ago. In fact, I hadn't told anyone.

"I wouldn't be good enough," I said. "But I might sit in one day, if that's all right."

Jean nodded. "Anytime."

By late morning the breakfast shift had eased up, and it was my first chance for a break. I poured a glass of lemonade and took a seat on a stool. Simon turned off the grill and leaned on the counter, a dish towel slung over his shoulder.

"This is the speed most days," he said, nodding at the tables, most of them empty. "Second gear. Occasional shifts into fourth."

He struck me as a curiosity. A short-order cook who liked Yeats and classical music. Served in the military. Traveled. Had even, as Jessie said, fought in a war.

"Don't you ever get bored here?" I asked.

He paused. "There's a saying: 'May you live in interesting times.' That happens to be a Chinese curse. There's a lot to be said for the simple life."

"That's funny—I said the same thing once to a college friend about a hundred years ago. But interesting times have a way of ambushing you, don't they?"

"They do."

Simon had a frankness about him. An easiness that invited conversation. Even, to an extent, confidences. But just how far did that extend?

I bent over my lemonade, unable to look him in the eye.

"You're from Morro originally, aren't you?" I asked.

"Third generation. My people are from Maryland and Virginia, but my grandparents settled here before the Civil War."

"Then you left."

"Not strictly by choice. Sometimes there's a job to do, and you're called to do it. A lot of men were."

"Jessie said you were in the war. Iraq was it?"

He drew a deep breath and turned away. His strained expression made me regret probing the subject. Roadside bombs, snipers, multiple deployments, post-traumatic stress—not every veteran could reassimilate easily or quickly after trauma like that.

"I'm sorry," I said. "I shouldn't have asked."

"Don't look so distressed, Joanna. I made it home just fine."

"I see."

"Besides, *simple* isn't the same as simplistic. Don't get me wrong—some days all I want to do is drop everything and head out for some far corner of the earth."

"Why don't you, then?"

He grinned. "Who says I don't?"

I looked at him then, full on. There was humor in his eyes, but there was earnestness there, too. Did he really get a wild hair some days and strike out for far-flung places? And if he did, did he book a plane ticket or just click his heels together like Dorothy and let out something like, *There's no place like Nepal?*

All at once Simon broke into a laugh that made me blush. Then he turned to head back to the grill.

I was ringing up a customer when the man muttered, "Oh, my Lord." He was gaping over my shoulder through the front windows, and I turned to look, too.

The *prettiest* car I'd ever seen had just pulled up—a two-tone convertible, powder blue and white, stretching from a chrome hood ornament to what looked like chrome missiles mounted on the rear fender. It had whitewall tires with polished rims. The soft top was down, and the noon sun set the white leather seats to shimmer.

Simon came out front to look, too, and gave a long whistle. *"That,"* he said, "is a 1956 Cadillac Eldorado."

The car door swung open and the driver stepped out—a tiny black woman in a lavender suit and red kid gloves. A red silk scarf was wrapped around her head, its ends dangling down her back like two giant rose petals. She removed oversized white sunglasses to glance at the café sign, then headed inside. She took a seat, stripped off her gloves and untied her scarf to reveal a cap of smooth, marcelled hair.

"Honey, you got sweet tea?" she asked, picking up a menu. Her voice was high-pitched and Deep South.

I brought the tea, and the woman ordered pork chops and fried apples. When I gave Simon the order, I asked if she'd been in before.

"Nope," he said. "I'd remember the car."

Simon brought her plate without waiting for me to retrieve it. Then he stood beside me for a better view of the convertible.

From what I could see, it had no dents, no scratches, no markings of any kind. As pristine as if it were still sitting on a showroom floor.

"Not a speck of dirt," I murmured.

The woman gave me a puzzled look.

"Take a load off, honey," she said, nodding at an empty chair at her table. "I know how it is, on your feet all day. My name's Lula. You had lunch yet?"

Soon Simon was back at the grill, frying up more pork chops and apples while Lula told me about her home in Mississippi.

"Natchez—on a bluff over the river, up from New Orleans," she said. "I was a hotel maid there from fifteen on—and they *worked* you. Big white house, portico two stories high, big ol' columns, acres of lawn."

"Like a plantation," I said.

"Used to be, long time since," said Lula. "Family fell on hard times and sold it for a hotel. One night a car pulled up like what I got now, and out they stepped—him in black tails and her in yellow satin—lookin' like *somebody*. Swore to God one day I'd get me a car like that. See what there was to see in this world. Stay in fine places, too."

Simon arrived with two more plates and joined us.

"What if you break down out there on the road?" I asked.

Lula leveled her eyes at me over her tea glass. "What if I don't?"

And in a flash of certainty I knew that the Eldorado outside would never break down on her. It would take Lula wherever she wanted to go, with never a blown tire or a boiling radiator. It would never run out of gas. And should she ever want to drive to China one day, or whatever destination she might fancy, somehow it would get her there.

"You still have people back in Natchez?" I asked.

"Not for ages," said Lula. "My grandmother, she raised me. We lived in a shotgun shack outside Dunleith till she passed. I took on my two brothers and went to work. Otis, he up and died—wasn't but seven at the time. Been seizin' up all his life, and one day he just grabbed ahold of his head and dropped. My brother Lester, he took to the bottle. Gone a long time. Heart give out."

She shook her head. "I'd say wasn't nothin' of family left in Dunleith but what they planted in the old Baptist cemetery, but even that ain't there no more. A few years ago, they up and moved it."

"Excuse me?" I said. "They moved the cemetery?"

"The church house, anyway—loaded it on flatbeds and drove down the gravel road to Long Switch. Wasn't no congregation no more—folks died off or left. So a big company come and turned the land to crops."

"What'd they do with the people buried there?" I asked.

"Not a blessed thing."

I wasn't sure she understood me. "I mean, before they started plowing—what did they do with the bodies in the cemetery?"

Lula braced her forearms on the table and leaned toward me, her smile indulgent.

"Honey, they left 'em. Said they wasn't no bodies. I know for a fact that cemetery started out back in the slave days. Wasn't much used after that but by a few old families. When I was young, they was a boy sweet on me—he's there. His great-grandmother, too—she had the *sugar*. By the time the company come, grave markers was mostly gone. Onliest thing left was that ol' beat-down church, and land turnin' wild like it was back when the Indians had it."

"You mean . . . they're *farming* the graveyard?"

Lula nodded. "Soybeans mostly. Some cotton."

It was a horrifying image—furrows dug, seeds planted, then roots growing down, down toward bones lying six feet under, smooth as those stones Olin pulls from his fields every spring.

Lula leaned toward me again. "Don't you fret none—they's more to eternal rest than where your bones are planted. It don't make the situation less despisable to me, but ain't a thing to be done but get on with life."

She sat back with a smile and asked if we had chocolate cake for dessert. She had a thick slice and a cup of coffee before wrapping her scarf back around her head and picking up her gloves. She paid her bill and turned to leave, but before she got to the door she stopped to throw her arms around my neck.

"You take care of yourself," she said. "Your little daughter, too."

Her earnestness startled me. But it wasn't until the café had closed for the day, the farmhouse chores were finished, Laurel was tucked in and I was back in my room readying for bed that it struck me:

I hadn't told Lula I had a daughter.

Rain, Rain, Come

I'd been working in the vegetable garden for a good hour when I stood to give my back a stretch. The air was listless and hot. We'd gone nearly two weeks without a good soaking, and the plants weren't the only things feeling it. I fingered the wilting butterhead lettuce in my basket, then looked up, eager for signs of weather. But the clouds were as thick and dry as cotton batting, and stalled out.

I licked at my parched lips as sweat slid down my back. I was about to head inside for a drink of water when a notion struck that stopped me short.

I turned toward the same field where Olin had stood the morning of the quilting bee—so motionless and unyielding he might have been carved from his own fieldstone, looking for all the world like a man with a purpose. And when he was done, a thunderstorm had swept through this valley.

Olin was a man of many skills; was rainmaking one of them?

Tentatively I looked around, but no one was in sight. I closed my eyes.

So . . . what does a rainmaker say? What does a rainmaker *think*?

Does she think *rain* and the clouds come? Can thoughts get caught in an updraft, pulling in water vapor, seeding the atmosphere until they're plumped up and ready to fall as raindrops?

Suddenly the absurdity of the moment—standing in a garden, trying to catalyze a downpour—cut me to the quick. I felt like a grown woman caught playing hopscotch. I opened my eyes.

But there was more to it than mere discomfiture. While a part of me knew, all evidence to the contrary, that conjuring up a storm was a load of hocus-pocus, still another was sure that even if it *were* possible, it wasn't child's play. It couldn't be.

And yet . . .

I turned toward the Mountain. A prickle ran up my spine as I sensed it looking back, as if taking my measure. Curious to see what I could do.

Skepticism? Or a challenge?

I set my basket at my feet and shut my eyes again.

This time I didn't think—not in words, anyway. Instead, I pictured the sky overhead just as it was—a palette of white and blue, the sun a brilliant ball radiating ferocious heat and light. The images clicked into place almost willfully, like pieces of a jigsaw puzzle.

Then I added a rain cloud. Just one.

I concentrated with all I had to shape it, sculpt it. To make it realer than real. I made it darker than the others—gray as granite, and swelling with moisture. I placed it just at the sharp arête of the Mountain. Heavier and heavier it grew—until it was so swollen, so heavy, it couldn't keep its altitude anymore. It began to sink . . . skimming lower and lower . . . whipping down the Mountain slope . . . out of control now and picking up speed . . . making for the garden . . . for me . . .

My eyes flew open and I was startled to find I was panting, struggling to catch my breath. Sweat was running down my face, the salt of it stinging my eyes. I used my shirttail to wipe it away.

I glanced up again, and the sky was just as it had been. The Mountain . . . still vigilant.

But what was that hugging the ridge?

It was a cloud like the others—only this one was not quite so white, not quite so high. Its underbelly was a pigeon gray, as if a charcoal pencil had only begun to shade it in.

Even as I watched, the cloud began to shred and dissipate. Fainter and fainter, until finally it dissolved into the same thin air it was made of.

As if it had never been there at all.

Nastas

Olin had built a freestanding fireplace and grill on the patio behind the house, with a pumice stone core and faced with sandstone flags. Jessie said they used it deep into winter, bundling up like Eskimos. There was no need to bundle yet—it was only the end of August, according to Jessie, although I couldn't see how she kept track. The two of them owned no calendar—Olin said there was nothing a calendar could tell him that the elements couldn't.

"Except birthdays," Laurel said.

"That's what the wife's for," said Olin.

Simon suggested a barbecue, and he'd bring the venison steaks. By now Saturday suppers were settling into routine, and no longer a cause for panic. I still left the bulk of the conversation to the others—I'm not garrulous by nature, but can appreciate those who are. Even Laurel has a better talent for it than me.

We were on the patio when Simon arrived. He showered and joined us, his eyes skimming my yellow sundress. I turned my back to finish laying the table, awkwardly smoothing the fabric over my hips.

Simon was a creature of habit, too, and as usual he took a seat facing me while Laurel claimed the chair next to his.

Olin took charge of the grill, forking the steaks onto a platter for Jessie to distribute. She started with Laurel.

"Ever had venison before, honey?" Jessie asked her.

Laurel frowned suspiciously. "What's that?"

"Deer meat," I answered, cutting her steak for her. "Give it a taste."

She chewed cautiously at first, then nodded. "Good!"

"Atta girl," said Olin.

"Mommy?" said Laurel.

"Yeah, sweetie?"

"I heard her again."

"Who's that?"

"Tinkerbell."

My heart stuttered in my chest. I set down my knife and fork.

"Not now," I murmured, handing her the breadbasket with a warning shake of my head. "Here, have a slice."

Olin looked intrigued. "What's this?"

"Nothing at all," I said.

"Tinkerbell," said Laurel. "She's up there."

She twisted in her seat and pointed high on the Mountain. Olin squinted, trying to make something out.

"It's nothing," I repeated.

Laurel pressed her lips in a stubborn line. "She was barking again," she insisted. "I *heard*."

"Is this your pup, hon?" Jessie asked her. "The one that run off?"

Laurel nodded. "I looked and I hollered, but she never came back."

"Now, that's a shame," said Jessie.

"Mommy, we gotta go get her."

"Please stop, Laurel."

"But, Mommy—"

"Laurel! Stop! Now!"

She was shocked to silence. But I could see the fury brewing, every ounce of it plain on her face, until she broke into howls of misery.

I took a deep breath and tried again, this time without the snap in my voice.

"Tinkerbell got lost a long way from here," I said. "She couldn't have walked this far. In fact . . . In fact, I bet some other family took her in by now."

A lie is forgivable, I figured, if it hides a wicked truth. And I had enough to handle as it was, without the worry of that poor, wretched dog.

Olin smiled at Laurel. "Why, that's very likely," he said. "Folks would take in a lost pup, quick as that."

Laurel didn't look convinced, but the howls were trailing off to wet hiccups, and she wasn't fussing anymore. She wiped her eyes with her sleeve.

"Simon," said Olin, "I hear you got yourself a new horse out at your place."

"Four-year-old gelding," said Simon. "Underweight at the moment, but good form. He'll fill out fine."

"Bring him over when he does."

"Or come see him yourself. It's been a while since you and Jessie were up. And, Joanna, you haven't seen my place yet. You and Laurel."

Before I could answer, Olin accepted for all of us. "You'll need a corral, though," he said. "Got any help?"

Simon hesitated. He glanced uncertainly at me before answering. "Davey's been lending a hand."

Olin and Jessie traded a queer look and fell silent. I'd never heard them—or Simon—ever mention anyone by the name of Davey before.

Simon cleared his throat. "Till the corral's finished, the horse boards close by. Grazes behind the cabin."

Laurel was looking curiously at Olin and Jessie. Even she could sense the shift in the air.

"Who's Davey?" she asked.

More silence. Finally Olin spoke.

"Why, a local boy," he said lightly. "Lives on a ranch outside town. Takes on odd jobs to help out his folks. Smart as a whip. Good with his hands."

Jessie was nodding in agreement. From the description, I couldn't see why the mention of the boy's name would scupper the conversation. None of them offered more than that.

I turned to Simon. "Do you have other horses?"

"This is my first," said Simon. "He'll be a handful when he's filled out. Do you ride?"

"I took lessons one summer when I was a kid. English style. I had what they call horse fever—read every book on horses I could get my hands on. But I can't say I'm a rider. Lessons ended before I got the hang of it."

"Why didn't you keep it up?"

Ending the lessons hadn't been my idea. The summer I turned thirteen, I was living—yet again—with my Oma in her little house outside Taos. Every time my mother took on a new man, sooner or later she'd pack me off to my grandmother's, which suited me fine. I guess when I was younger she meant to spare me the sight of strange men at the breakfast table. But as I grew older, she started to see me as competition.

That particular summer, my mother and I were living in a town in west Texas, and the new man was an assistant city planner who laughed too much and drank too much and had sweaty palms that he liked to drape over my shoulder in a friendly sort of way, casual, as if he weren't trying to run his fingers down the curve of my breast. One day my mother caught him at it, and the next I was on a Greyhound to Taos.

There was a small stable near Oma's house, and she signed me up for riding lessons. I took on babysitting jobs to help pay for them. It was a wonderful summer, until my mother's affair flamed out, as they always did, and she packed a cooler with six-packs and drove up to fetch me—at first because she wanted someone to comfort her in her latest hour of need, but eventually because she needed somebody to blame.

After that, we moved to another new town where my mother could put the booze and the past behind her. Start fresh. One more time.

"Riding lessons . . . they're expensive," I said finally.

"They are," said Simon. "But there's horse people round about that could help you take up where you left off. Olin here was a real rider."

"Good enough," said Olin.

"More than good enough," Jessie said affectionately.

Olin squeezed her hand. "A tale for another day. But if you're up to it, Joanna, I could make a real cowgirl out of you."

. . .

One morning not long after, I woke to the sound of whinnying. I belted my robe and headed to my bedroom window. There was a man on horseback below, speaking with Olin at the open gate of the corral.

And the corral was no longer empty, but held four horses. I pulled on jeans and a shirt and hurried outside.

"Mornin', Joanna!" Olin called. "This here's an old friend—Morgan Begay."

The man looked to be in his sixties, with a barrel chest, graying hair to his shoulders and deep brown eyes magnified by bottle-thick glasses. He wore a work shirt with a black vest and dungarees. Around his neck was a fetish necklace strung with polished stones carved into bear shapes.

"Are these your horses?" I asked him.

"From my herd." His voice was deep, with a clipped accent.

"They're beautiful."

"Begay's from the other side of the Mountain," Olin said. "He'll be leavin' these horses awhile. Wanna try one?"

"Now?" I asked.

"Which one you like?"

It had been so long since I'd sat a horse, I wasn't sure I wouldn't just mount up and slide off the other side again. I took a step back.

"Buck up, now," said Olin.

I looked the horses over. The first three were a handsome blood bay, a pinto and a big roan.

But the fourth horse was a sleek liver chestnut—a hand or two smaller than the others, with the swan neck and small, shapely head of an Arabian.

When I was thirteen, this had been my dream horse, like Lula's Eldorado.

"He's a beauty," Olin said, following my gaze. "Name's— what's he called, Begay?"

"Nastas."

"That's right—Nastas. What's it mean in Navajo? 'Leg-Breaker'? Or 'Never Been Rode'?"

I laughed. "Sure it doesn't mean 'Call an Ambulance'?"

"Atta girl," Olin said. "Actually, it means 'Curve Like Foxtail Grass,' for that neck of his. Come on over and I'll make the introductions."

Begay had already dismounted and was leading Nastas to the gate where I stood. The horse seemed much bigger up close. His ears swiveled at the sound of my voice.

"Good boy," I murmured nervously, running my hand down the firm muscles of his neck. Olin handed me a carrot, and I held it to the horse's muzzle until he snorted and grabbed it in his teeth. All the while, Begay was settling a blanket on the horse's back, then a saddle. He cinched it snug.

"His mouth is soft, so easy on the bit," Begay said as he worked. "Ask him—don't tell him. He knows."

"Okay, boy," I murmured. "I'll go easy on you if you go easy on me."

"All set?" Olin asked, gripping the bridle. "Don't worry— he likes you."

"Yeah?" I said shakily. "Let's see him show it."

I stepped to the side and slid my left foot into the stirrup, grabbed a handful of mane and pulled myself into the saddle. While Begay adjusted the stirrups, I ran through those old riding lessons in my head—*back straight*, *toes up*, *heels down*.

"Take the reins in your left hand—this is Western style, not English," Olin said. "Grip 'em in front of you. Not too tight. That's right."

Begay led the horse forward at a slow walk. We moved halfway around the corral like that, till he let go and moved to the side. Then it was just me and the horse making a circuit all by ourselves.

"How's it feel?" Olin called out.

I smiled. "Like riding a bicycle. A really big bicycle."

"Doin' good," Olin said. "Ready for the lesson?"

"I thought this was it," I said.

He and Begay laughed.

"Aw, now, you can do better'n this," said Olin.

Begay approached again. He patted the horse's neck and said something in a language I couldn't understand. Then he looked up at me.

"Listen to Olin," he said. "You can do better."

He stood back to give the horse a light slap across the flank, and Nastas set off at a hard trot that jarred every bone in my body. In desperation I tried to post, which I knew wasn't Western, either. Olin called out for me to sit and relax. Find the rhythm.

Instead, I pulled on the reins to make it stop before I could fall off. Nastas shook his head, his mane flying. He was disappointed; he wanted to run. I had a feeling this wouldn't end well.

"Whoa, boy." Olin was grabbing the bridle again as Nastas ground to a halt. "You're fightin' 'im, Joanna."

"I wouldn't fight anything that outweighed me this much. Maybe this wasn't such a great idea."

"Now, now, I can tell you rode before," Olin said. "You just don't trust your horse—so he don't trust you. And you're too afraid to fall off."

"I don't think that's unreasonable."

Olin chuckled. "Say you do. Then what? You climb back up and try again." He stepped back. "Ready? Kick with your heels. You can do it."

Nastas needed only another grazing swat to break into another trot that had me sliding to the side, grabbing for the saddle horn with my free hand.

"Keep goin'!" Olin called out. "That's it! You ain't bouncin' near as much as you think!"

I grit my teeth. I was still landing hard, fighting the urge to call it quits and yank on the reins again.

This was grim—not at all the joyful experience of my childhood. The horse's ears had flattened out; he was miserable, too.

I willed myself to try to locate some rhythm, but my entire body had clenched like a fist and refused to unknot. I wasn't just bouncing in the saddle, but sliding all over it. I knew I couldn't keep my seat much longer.

Frantic, I bent my knees, pulled up my heels and pressed hard—

And suddenly I wasn't bouncing anymore, but flying—cresting on rolling waves, up and down, up and down. Nastas had exchanged that punishing gait for a springing gallop.

Olin was shouting as if I'd managed to accomplish something, beyond not getting pitched to the ground.

We circled the corral several times before I reined in again.

The horse slowed to that awful trot, but I reined more firmly and he curbed to a walk.

Olin and Begay were outside the corral now, leaning on the top fence rail.

"A good start," said Olin. "Before you know it, you'll be stickin' to him like a burr and won't need those reins near as much. A good horse and rider—they're like one animal. You lean and turn, press with your legs, and he'll read you right enough."

"So when I bent my knees and pressed—"

"You were tellin' him, 'Let's hightail it!' So he did."

"And here I thought I was just hanging on for dear life. Can I give it another go?"

Lesson over, Begay rode off toward Morro, leaving me and Olin to ready four stalls in the barn for the new horses.

The others from Begay's herd were Kilchii, Yas and Tse.

Kilchii, the blood bay, and Yas, the pinto, were no strangers to the farm—Begay apparently would bring them over now and then for trail rides; Olin and Jessie had given up their own horses a long time ago. Kilchii means "Red Boy," for his deep copper coat. He was Olin's mount. Jessie's was Yas, which means "Snow," because he loves to roll in it.

The third horse, Tse, was the big roan mare, intended for Laurel. Tse was unflappable and solid, Olin said, so her name meant "Rock."

"They'll mean a lot more work around here," I said. "I'll take it on, in exchange for the lessons."

"Fine idea," said Olin.

"I know what you're doing," I said.

Olin blinked at me, but said nothing.

"First the café, now this. You're nudging me out of my rabbit hole."

"That right?"

"But you have to understand—there are reasons I jumped in there in the first place. And pulled Laurel in with me."

"I'm a fair listener."

I shook my head. "Don't nudge too hard. Just know . . . there are bad things out there."

Olin gave me a smile. "Don't forget," he said. "There's good things, too."

The Periwinkle House

The grade school in Morro is a one-room wood-frame structure that came from a mail-order catalog, just like Jessie's sewing machine. It arrived by boxcar in the 1920s in pieces by the
thousands—from the lumber, siding, roof shingles and nails
right down to the paint cans and varnish—ready to be assem-
bled on-site. The men of Morro put it together over two days
on an acre of land at the edge of town.

It was painted white, and stayed that way for years. It was
Bree's idea to repaint it lavender, with shutters and trim a shade
darker, and the front door darker still. Someone called it the
Periwinkle House, and the name stuck. It was even printed on
a brass plaque by the door.

The schoolhouse took in younger students, and there was
a second school with its own teacher for older ones. I learned

all this from Bree after Jessie dropped me off one morning to get Laurel formally and finally enrolled.

The big room was bright and colorful—with maps, photographs and posters, children's drawings and paintings, a mobile of the solar system and shelves filled with books. There were a dozen children studying at desks, grouped in a reading circle, working math problems on a whiteboard or gathered around a terrarium feeding whatever was inside. No different from a classroom you might find anywhere.

Laurel twisted her hand from mine and ran off to join the group at the terrarium. Before I could call her back, Bree stopped me.

"Let her make friends."

"I don't know how you handle so many grades under one roof," I said.

"It wasn't that long ago that schools like this were commonplace in rural areas," she said. "Besides, when you mingle the grades, older students encourage the younger ones."

She pulled a folder from a pile on her desk and leafed through it.

"I've already started a file for Laurel," she said. "I'll give her a few placement tests to see where she stands."

"I guess you have forms for me to fill out."

Bree closed the folder and tossed it back on her desk with a smile. "Nope."

Of course not. Why would she?

I watched Laurel at play with the other children; she was oblivious to me.

"It's pretty painless, isn't it?" I said.

"She'll be fine," said Bree. "And so will you. By the way, I told Reuben how you helped with the wedding quilt, and he'd love to meet you. I'm cooking dinner next Friday night—can you make it?"

Before I could come up with an excuse, Bree took my arm just as she had at the bee and walked me to the door.

"I'm not the greatest cook, but I do know wine," she said. "Come around six. My place is on the second floor here. The entrance is on the side."

She opened the door and ushered me through, then closed it firmly behind me.

The Dog That Didn't Bark

"*Mommy!* Come quick!"

Laurel ran into the living room to grab my arm, her small fingers digging in. She was burning with excitement, eyes wide.

I dropped my broom to snatch her by the waist for a quick once-over, top to bottom: no cuts, no bruises, no blood.

"What's wrong?" I demanded. "You okay?"

Before she could answer, before I could even think clearly, an awful thought hit me: *Jim.* He'd tracked us down. He was outside even now, heading for the door.

I rushed to the front window, where the curtains were open and the view was clear. There was no vehicle in sight, aside from Simon's yellow pickup at the café, same as always.

Laurel pulled my arm even harder, this time with both hands, desperate to get me to the door.

"Hurry! Before it stops!"

I stared down at her. Before *what* stops?

I let her tug me onto the porch and down the front steps. In the yard, she dropped my arm and turned toward the Mountain, wiping stray strings of hair from her flushed face.

She pressed a finger to her lips. "Sssssshhhh."

Then she pointed.

I looked where she was directing me—at a point near the crest, just below the tree line. Yet again my stomach lurched.

I knew very well what Laurel was so anxious for me to hear. I closed my eyes with a shiver, and listened.

And heard nothing. Nothing but the birds, the running creek and Laurel's quick, expectant breaths.

Simon's Cabin

After the horses arrived, it became my routine to lead them from the barn every morning and put them to pasture. Their range was the stretch of valley that started at the barn and ran due east. It wasn't fenced, but Olin said Kilchii and Yas knew the area well and never wandered far, and Nastas and Tse would keep close by.

While they grazed, I would get out the wheelbarrow, grab a pitchfork and muck their stalls. I carted the soiled bedding to the compost pile and laid down a fresh layer of straw. Olin taught me to clean their hooves, then groom them with curry-combs and brushes. Sometimes Laurel helped, standing on an upturned bucket to braid Tse's mane.

While Olin gave Laurel lessons in the corral, I rode Nastas in the pasture, practicing leg pressure and shifting movements.

Then, one morning after lessons, Olin saddled Kilchii and suggested he and I take a trail ride. Rather than head along the valley, though, he led us south on the hardpan road into Morro.

We cantered until we reached the town limits, then slowed to a walk, past the welcome sign and onto the smooth asphalt.

From Nastas's back, I could reach the lowest branches of the big elms, their leaves now turning a vivid gold. For all the notice we drew, a trail ride through town was nothing unusual.

We passed the Wild Rose and the general store, the gazebo, the library, the town hall and every door and shingle in between. We passed a cluster of boys huddled in an alley, fascinated by the contents of a small container.

"What's in the cigar box, boys?" Olin called out.

The boys looked up guiltily. "It ain't cigars, Mr. Farnsworth," one said.

"I'm sure it ain't. Best set it loose before long, or I'll know why not."

"Yes, sir," the boys replied.

"How'd you know they had something in that box?" I asked him.

"I didn't," he said. "But I do know boys."

I hadn't seen this side of Morro before—I'd never ventured this far. The asphalt stopped at the town limits and the hardpan picked up again, veering left into the Mountain. But there was a narrow secondary road splintering off to the right.

I reined Nastas to a firm halt. Olin pulled up, then circled back and drew alongside me.

"Somethin' wrong?" he asked.

The pull of the Mountain had grown more intense the closer we came, and now we were right at its feet. Resisting was taking real effort, and my head was throbbing as if the barometric pressure had plummeted.

"Are we going up there?" I asked warily. Nastas took several steps back.

Olin shrugged. "Figured to," he said. "Trail's good, and your mount knows it. You can trust 'im."

Nastas pulled at the reins and snorted, his eyes wide now. "Whoa," Olin murmured, and the horse steadied himself.

I gripped the reins tighter, staring at the fork in the road, struggling to steady myself, too.

"Courage," Olin said softly, "is a kind of salvation."

"What?"

"Somethin' an old Greek said once. Long time ago."

"Right."

He shifted in the saddle to take in the Mountain with me. "It's a far piece to the summit," he said. "Ain't never been myself, but I know some who trekked it. I don't figure to go anywhere near that far today. Just up a ways." He looked at me and smiled. "Then back down again."

Nastas was motionless now, his ears pricked as if awaiting instructions. I stared at Olin, willing him to say something that would buck me up, too, but he only sat in his saddle as if he had all the time in the world for me to make up my mind.

I drew a deep breath and tapped Nastas with my boot heels.

We moved forward.

Olin led the way, taking the narrower road to the right—a wide dirt track with a low incline for a mile or so before it began to climb. As it climbed, it wound through thickening forest. Sunlight sifted through the trees, and I could hear birds, the rustle and snap of twigs, the distant rush of water.

If I'd been afraid that this Mountain would rear up and

swallow me whole, it wasn't happening. There were no bogey-men in these woods, no fires, earthquakes or floods. My nerves began to settle.

We leveled out again and Olin, still riding ahead, turned in the saddle and called back, "Let's pick it up."

"I'm game," I replied shakily.

Then he was off at a canter, Kilchii on his long legs disap-pearing down the road. Nastas chewed his bit and bobbed his head, nearly pulling the reins from my hand.

"Okay, boy. Think you can take him?"

I tucked my legs and pressed, and Nastas lunged after them. Of the two, he was the smaller horse but not the slower, and he was eager to prove it. We drew up on them fast, Olin glancing at us as we overtook and passed them. Now the road ahead of us was wide-open.

Half a mile on I reined in and could hear Olin and Kilchii coming at a fast clip. They pulled up level, and Olin looked pleased.

Both horses had worked up a lather, so we set them at a walk to cool down. Nastas was still straining at the bit, snort-ing hard.

"He has more steam to blow off," I said.

"We'll set 'em loose up the road here," said Olin.

We rode on in easy silence. After another mile the forest began to clear on the left, opening onto a broad meadow. As we neared I could see the meadow wasn't empty, but held a small cabin, painted slate blue, with black shutters and white trim, a table and chairs on the porch.

And there in the narrow drive was a familiar yellow pickup.

Behind the cabin, two figures were sawing and hammering on a corral that was nearly finished. By then, I wasn't surprised to see that one of them was Simon. The other was much slighter, wearing a tan cowboy hat.

Simon straightened as we approached. He spoke to the person with him, who looked briefly in our direction. Then he headed toward us across the meadow, Pal hard at his heels.

Simon's hair shone nearly blond in the bright sun. He was bare chested, his work shirt knotted around his waist. As he walked, he loosened it, swung it around his shoulders and pulled it back on, but left it open in the heat.

"Come on up to the house!" he called. "I'll get us some cool water."

"Corral's comin' along," Olin said as we dismounted.

"Couple more days, I figure." Simon wiped his sunburned neck with a bandanna. "Sorry I'm not too presentable."

"You're a workin' man," said Olin. "Don't apologize for lookin' the part. We was out for a ride and figured to drop in."

"Glad you did."

Olin led his horse to a patch of shade on the far side of the house, then headed for the porch. I started to do the same with mine, when Simon fell in beside me.

"Here," he said. "Let me."

He took the reins from my hand and led Nastas to the same patch of shade. When he returned, he examined me curiously. "Your hair's different, Joanna. Very becoming."

I'd left it hanging loose this morning, held back with a band of ribbon. I could only imagine what a rat's nest the ride had made of it.

"It could use a good combing," I said.

"Looks better this way."

"You're an easy man to please, then. All a woman has to do is throw away her hairbrush."

He laughed. Then he called out to Olin, still waiting for us on the porch: "Go on in, have a seat."

The idea didn't appeal to me. None of this did. I knew Olin meant well—pushing me out of my comfort zone, challenging me to be brave. But this was too far, too fast. This felt like an ambush.

"Olin, we can't stay long," I said.

"At least rest awhile on the porch," said Simon. "I'll get some water. The horses could use some, too. Davey can see to that."

So that was Davey working on the corral—the boy whose very name at the barbecue a few weeks ago had stalled the conversation. From a distance he looked wiry and slim.

Simon called out for the boy to take the horses around back to the trough; then he brought a water pitcher and glasses to the porch table. Olin sank back in his chair. "All I need now's a smoke," he said.

"Can't help you there, my friend," said Simon. "Promised Jessie."

"She's right," I said. "She's worried about your health."

Simon and Olin traded smiles, and I realized my foolishness—in Morro, did Olin really need to worry about the afflictions of tobacco smoke?

"What gets her is the smell," Olin explained. "Says I should stick with a pipe. But she really took against cigarettes the night I burnt down the ol' outhouse."

"You didn't."

"It was years ago—burnt clear to the ground. Folks saw it from miles off and come to watch. Then they took to speculatin' as to what caused it, and I said it all started with Jessie's bean chili. She ain't quite forgive me for that."

I chuckled despite myself. "I can't blame her. You insulted her cooking."

"There's chili cooks would consider it a compliment."

"We use her recipe at the café," Simon said. "Now you know why it's called the 'house' chili."

"No! Poor Jessie."

"Naw, she thinks it's a humdinger," Olin said. "Just too proud to admit it."

Simon drained his water glass. "Would you like to see the new horse? He's out back."

The meadow behind his cabin was covered with thick blue grama grass and wildflowers past our knees. It was an easy slope to the tree line, where the Mountain started to climb again. There was a raised vegetable garden and a small grove of apple trees, stacked rows of honeybee hives and a tall smokehouse on a stone foundation.

Davey stood at an outbuilding with our two horses, a water bucket at his feet.

Simon pointed toward the apple grove, and I could see nothing at first. But when he whistled, a horse emerged from the trees.

He was tall—as tall as Tse. And you could tell he must have been beautiful once.

Now, though, his gray hide stretched across sharp hip bones and jutting ribs. His broad back swayed as if it carried an oppressive weight.

"Mind if I take a look?" said Olin.

"He's gun-shy," Simon cautioned as Olin headed toward the grove. Then he turned to me. "Well," he asked quietly, "what do you think?"

I didn't know how to answer him. Certainly Jim had proven

just how wretchedly an animal could be abused, but I'd never seen neglect like this. Still, I knew Simon wasn't fishing for compliments.

"He looks awful," I said. "What happened?"

"He was a racehorse once. Not a good one, I guess. Or his owner didn't think so. He was sold for dog food to some outfit down in Florida. Since he wasn't worth the cost of feed, they let him starve. He was just skin and bones when I got him."

"Worse than this?"

"He's improved quite a bit. And he'll get better still. Watch."

He whistled again and gave a call. The horse broke into a canter along the tree line, apparently unwilling to get too close. He pulled up and shook his big head, then finished his circuit across the field.

"There, now. See?" said Simon. "They didn't break him."

It pleased me to hear him say it. Most people wouldn't see much worth in salvaging an abused creature like this.

"He'll make a good trail horse one day," I said.

"No—thoroughbreds don't do well out here for trails or cattle. Their legs are too fragile; the country's too rugged."

"So you'll race him?"

"Oh, no."

"Then what on earth will you do with him?"

Simon hesitated, watching the horse turn and bolt back toward the grove.

Then he shrugged. "Let him run."

The horse was moving at a speed that seemed wholly unsupportable for his gaunt frame and gangly legs. But he tore up the distance with little effort, disappearing again in the apple trees.

"Almost like he has wings," said a voice behind us. "Like Pegasus."

We turned to see the boy, Davey, a few yards away in dungarees and a damp T-shirt, his cowboy hat shading most of his face.

"Pegasus, huh?" said Simon. "Could be a fine name. What do you think?" He was asking me.

What I thought was that even if that horse had actual wings sprouting from his withers, he looked barely fit enough to carry a child, much less Zeus's thunderbolts. But I had to admit he had spirit.

"I like it," I said. "Some names you just have to grow into."

Simon made the introductions, and Davey stepped forward to shake my hand. The boy pulled off his hat, and for the first time I could see his face clearly . . .

The slight arc to the bridge of his nose . . . the squared-off chin . . . and the hair—a deep mahogany brown.

The resemblance to Jim was uncanny.

I snatched my hand from his. It was then that I noticed the eyes looking up at me from that eerie, familiar, terrible face were the same quartz green as Laurel's. As mine.

"Joanna . . . ?" Simon sounded concerned.

I was staring at the boy with open revulsion. I couldn't help myself. I stared as he flushed a deep red, then ducked his head in confusion. He took a step back . . . recoiling from me.

The rational part of my brain was struggling to intervene. *This is only a child*, it said. *We don't choose the features we're born with*. And yet . . .

"I—I'm sorry," I managed to say. "I thought . . . we'd met before."

"No, ma'am," said the boy.

"No," I said. "I'd have remembered."

I dragged my eyes away from that face and turned toward the apple grove. I cleared my throat.

"How'd you come up with a name like Pegasus?" I asked finally. "Do you like Greek mythology?"

"Sure, I like stories about the old gods," Davey said. "Olympus and the Underworld."

"I did, too, when I was a kid," I said. "I discovered them when I was eleven. How old are you?"

"I turned nine in June."

I swallowed hard. "Nine in June."

The boy nodded. "I write my own stories, too."

"Best grades in his class," Simon said. "Davey, can you go water Pegasus?"

The boy bolted off, eager to please Simon. And no doubt just as eager to escape the crazy woman with the Medusa stare. When he was gone, I turned to Simon: "Tell me about his family."

He hesitated. "They have a little place on the other side of the Mountain."

"I remember," I snapped. "From the barbecue—ranch folk, respectable people. And he's their only child?"

"They have a couple more. Older boys."

"But he's . . . their *natural* child?"

Simon didn't answer, but watched Davey refill the water bucket, Pegasus at his side. Olin joined them and was running his hand over the horse's bowing back, then down each reedy leg.

When Simon spoke again, I could see what a careful, neutral mask his face had become.

"Davey was a foundling," he said. "They took him in as a baby. His natural parents—they've never been part of his life."

"They *found* him? On their doorstep?"

"I'm not sure what you want to know, Joanna."

I wasn't sure, either. How do you say, without sounding like a lunatic, that a boy you just met looks like a child version of your husband, but with your eyes? Like he could be your natural-born son?

A son that, in point of fact, had never actually been born.

I'd been about ten weeks along when Jim gave me that punch to the stomach. The fetus had barely been an inch long—it hadn't even registered a heartbeat. But I knew from pregnancy books that all its organs were in place. That it had ears and eyelids and a nose . . . a tiny body cabled with muscles and nerves. That it was distinct down to its fingerprints and hair follicles.

I'd never had an ultrasound and could never have asked the doctor, but I knew—in my heart I knew—he'd been a boy.

And for years I'd been imagining him: his features, his temperament. I'd been dreaming him up out of whole cloth, like Laurel with her rain boots. A boy who wouldn't inherit the malice of his father, but a finer, sweeter spirit.

And every year he grew older—a presence that only I felt. Only I missed.

If I'd carried him to term, he would have turned nine this past June.

And the name I'd chosen for him all those years ago—but never told a soul—was David.

Tea and Empathy

Back from Simon's cabin I withdrew again, hunkering down until it was almost like the bad old days under Jim's boot. I couldn't buck the feeling I'd stumbled onto something I shouldn't have—a glimpse of the baby I couldn't save . . . the boy he might have become if I had. I couldn't stop picturing his face—every line, every curve, every inch of it. I was floundering in grief and guilt.

Olin had said Morro could be a Place of Truth for me, but that nugget of wisdom should have come with a warning label. Truth wasn't just something that could set you free—it could kick you in the gut ten times over. In its way, truth could be as brutal a bastard as Jim ever could.

I kept to my room, just like the early days when we'd first arrived. Jessie brought me meals on a tray again and didn't ask what was wrong or where it hurt. At night, Laurel climbed up on my bed and slipped under the covers.

This was new territory. With Jim, it was constant survival mode—every morning armoring up for one more round. I could never have surrendered like this around him, or he would've eaten me alive.

But here . . . here, I could shut down. I could lie in bed— neither asleep nor awake—and just *drift*. Aimless and mindless as a dandelion seed. And know with utter surety that if I only let go, let go for good and all, I could rise and rise . . . a sweet, numbing *nothingness* sluicing over me, through me, warm and solacing . . . until I dissipated at last, like the cloud that day in the vegetable garden.

Courage is a kind of salvation.

It was Olin's voice.

Olin's words in my ear, so close he might have been drifting on the wind beside me. I could smell the tang of cured tobacco . . .

My eyes flew open, and instead of a blank, open sky above me there was only the bedroom ceiling. I concentrated until the light fixture slid into focus.

Courage? Forget it—wouldn't know it if I tripped over it.

And what's courage, anyway, but delusion? You pick yourself up only to get beat down all over again. That doesn't make you brave—that makes you a punching bag. I stayed ten years with a sadist because I was too witless to see him for what he was. And when I did, I was too big a coward to get the hell out.

And yet . . .

I focused again on the ceiling. On its vast, vacant depths.

And yet . . . I did get out, didn't I?

. . . a kind of salvation.

I *did* get out. And brought Laurel with me. We broke free of him. Whatever else, we were in a good place now, with good people. And after all this time, he still hadn't found us. Hadn't managed to make his own way here, for all his threats to never let us go. *Ever.* That was something, wasn't it?

Whatever else Morro might be, at least it was getting that job done. Even a rabbit hole can keep a wolf at bay.

I pulled myself up and leaned back against the headboard. My body felt leaden and sluggish, as if it had been weightless for a while and needed to acclimate.

There was a food tray on the nightstand. The tea was still hot.

Night-light

Later, I grew restless in the wee hours and got up. Laurel had slipped into my room again and lay fast asleep on the far side of the bed. I slid into my robe and headed down the hallway to the stairs, then down to the living room. Jessie hadn't drawn the front curtains—they were still wide-open to the darkened café and the empty road. The room felt exposed. I hadn't sat vigil on the porch in a while.

I unlatched the front door and stepped out. The narrow valley was hushed except for the pulsing chirp of crickets. I headed to the railing on the far side of the porch where I could see the Mountain clearly. And, no surprise, that tenacious light. Anywhere else, that light might be nothing more than a cell tower. Here, it was more likely a burning bush.

It was a riddle, but there were others—the stars here were strange, too. *Strangers*. For weeks now I'd been trying to trace the Big Dipper, the Little Dipper. The Lion, the Hunter, the Big Dog, the Hare . . . any of them. But they just *weren't there*. My constellations were gone. The stars here kept to their own patterns, their own boundaries, and I didn't know their names. Old ship captains used to orient themselves by the stars. Celestial navigation, they called it. If they tried that here, where would these stars lead them?

A cold wind gusted through, and I pulled my robe close and headed back inside, latching the door and drawing the front curtains. Then I turned.

Across the living room, a light emanated from the kitchen.

And there in the open doorway was the dark shape of a man.

Years of reflex kicked in and I yelped and stumbled back, hitting the wall with a painful thud.

"Whoa, Joanna, it's me."

Olin's voice.

I gasped, clutching my throat. "You scared the life out of me!"

Then he was beside me, taking my arm, steering me toward the kitchen. "I just made some cocoa," he said. "Come sit."

On the table, a teapot was steaming on a serving tray. He fetched a mug from the cupboard and filled it, then settled across the table. Jessie's half-moon reading glasses were perched on his nose and there was a magazine in front of him—a *Farmer's Almanac*. He gave me a rueful smile. "Better?"

"Yeah," I said. "It's just . . . I guess I still startle easily."

"What're you doin' up this time of night?"

"Couldn't sleep. Guess I had my fill lately. I'm sorry."

"Sorry?" he said. "What for?"

"Leaving Laurel to you and Jessie. And the horses—all the work."

"Don't you worry—some days I'm not fit company, neither."

He took off the glasses and laid them on the *Almanac*. I examined the cover more closely—even upside down it was easy to make out the year.

"Olin," I said. "That magazine is from 1938."

"A good year," he said, wiping cocoa from his mustache. "Got more of 'em in my den. We visit now and again."

If he sounded absurd, who was I to judge? I hid scraps of paper in a tea tin under a floorboard.

"Penny for your thoughts," said Olin.

"They aren't worth that."

"Seems to me you saw somethin' from the porch just now. Ain't a coyote, was it?"

"No," I said. "Not an animal."

I might have left it at that, but I was picking up the faint scent of tobacco again, just as in my room earlier when I was ready to give up and scatter to the four winds, until it latched onto me like gravity . . . like a rescue . . .

Olin's hair was lifting in white tufts all around his scalp, as if he'd just come from bed without bothering to comb it into place, and for one wild second, backlit by the lamp behind him, it seemed to glow.

"Olin," I ventured. "That light on the Mountain—what is it?"

"Well, now, that's been there so long, I don't think about it no more. It just is."

"But who put it there?"

He shrugged. "Always been there, far as I know."

"Nobody ever checked it out?"

"Sure did."

"And what was it?"

"I never asked. They never said."

I shook my head in frustration and looked down at my mug. I could feel Olin's eyes on me for a long moment before he braced his arms on the table and leaned in.

"Laurel's got a night-light," he said finally.

"Yes . . ."

"Makes her feel safe."

"I guess."

"So if she wakes in the dark, scared maybe, she knows it's just a light, but she feels better. Watched over."

"Olin," I said slowly, "you're telling me the Mountain has a night-light?"

"It pleases me to think of it on the same principle."

I frowned down at the *Almanac* again—at the cracked and curling corners, the yellow cover filled with gourds, twining vines and sheaves of wheat, sketches of spring, summer, autumn and winter frozen in time. It read, *146th year. Price: 15 cents.*

I picked up Jessie's reading glasses and turned them over in my hands. "You two have the same prescription? I guess you really are a perfect match."

"Me and her was meant for each other."

The phrase was cliché, but he made it sound like truth.

"Soul mates?" I asked. "What an awful thought."

"How you figure?"

"I don't mean you and Jessie—you're happy. But when you're not—when you're with someone who makes your life hell—the idea of being bound for eternity . . . God, I'd go insane."

"And I wouldn't blame you—but that ain't it. The one you're meant to be with ain't always the one you end up with."

"What . . . ?"

"I figure if soul mates find each other right off," he continued, "that's best. But if they don't, they can still make a good life—with somebody else or on their own. But sooner or later, if you're meant to be, you find each other."

"Olin, you're a romantic. And how do they manage that?"

He snapped his fingers. "I forgot. The ol' woman'll skin me."

He stood and headed for the butcher-block table by the stove. When he returned, he handed me a small parcel in brown wrapping.

"Simon heard you was under the weather," he said. "Left this for you."

I pulled off the wrapping, and inside was a book of poetry—selected works of Yeats. It was the same volume I'd had in college, only mine had fallen apart over the years. This one was pristine, the spine still stiff.

I opened to the cover pages, and there Simon had written in surprisingly fine penmanship: *Joanna, for inspiration.*

Inspiration? To do what?

As if in answer, Olin turned to pull open a drawer and fish something out. When he returned, he set a blank notepad and a pen in front of me.

Dinner at Bree's

The next afternoon I stood at my bedroom mirror and for the first time in ages was pleased with what I saw. I wore a light cotton cardigan of buttercream yellow with short sleeves and shell buttons, and a tan pencil skirt. I pulled on flat pumps for the short hike into town for Bree's dinner.

I ran my hands down my arms, feeling the firm cords of muscle under the skin. Even after lying in bed for days, they felt strong. I leaned toward the mirror and stared hard. The old scar along my eyebrow—the one Jim sliced open with his pinkie ring with a sharp backhand—was fading. In fact, I could barely make it out now.

I ran a brush through my hair and noticed my little finger—the one Jim had broken when I dropped a dish—was limbering up, starting to bend. That bone had never been set, and the finger had healed crooked and stiff. Now here it was, straight as a pencil. I flexed my fingers. Even the twinge in the knuckle was gone.

What was it Olin had said? *Get straight and strong inside.* And apparently outside, too.

Jessie called up the stairs. "Joanna! Best set out now!"

I smoothed the skirt over my hips and gave myself a last once-over. Jim would never have approved of these clothes— not the cardigan that flattered me, not the skirt sized to fit, not the sleek pumps with their pointed toes.

But Jim wasn't here.

I undid the top button of my sweater and headed down-stairs.

The Periwinkle House had a tiny landing at the top of the side stairwell, with a lavender door under a striped awning.

I'd never met Bree's fiancé and knew nothing about him other than his name and that he worked on a ranch. So I ex-pected a polite and reserved young man sunburnt to beef jerky. But when the door opened, it was a young Navajo standing there, flashing white teeth in a handsome, round, inquisitive face. He wore cowboy boots, black jeans and a silver-tipped bolo with his dress shirt.

"Joanna, right?" he said. "Reuben. Let me help you with that."

He reached for the cheesecake I'd brought as Bree called from inside. "Sweetheart, don't leave her standing there."

Reuben stepped aside, and I could see Bree at a little gas stove in a pink sundress and thick oven mitts.

"Look at you!" she said. "You should wear yellow more of-ten. Reuben, honey, put that in the fridge."

"Sure there's room?" I asked.

The refrigerator was sized to fit the tiny apartment, which was a half story with sloped ceilings. The main room was an open kitchen and living room with a white couch and chair spaced around a Navajo rug. Off the kitchen was a small round table that was laid, I noticed warily, with four place settings.

Bree hadn't mentioned another guest.

"Can I help with anything?" I asked.

"Just grab a wineglass," said Bree. "Sweetheart, can you pour? Tell me what you think of the Riesling, Jo. It's from Virginia. And the fish"—she lifted the lid off a narrow steamer pot—"the fish is domestic, too. The boys caught them."

"The boys?" I asked.

She pulled off the oven mitts. "Reuben and Simon. He should be here any minute."

And that explained the fourth place setting.

"How about some music?" Bree said.

There was a small stereo on a console behind the couch. Reuben switched it on and turned the knob, catching station after station. When he hit soft jazz, Bree smiled.

There was a knock at the door and Reuben answered it. It was Simon, and he didn't look the least surprised to see me. He stepped in, kissed Bree on the cheek and handed her a small paper bag. She opened it and began to set cucumbers and tomatoes on the counter. Simon wasn't wearing jeans this time, but a dark sports coat and slacks.

"Evening, Joanna," he said as Reuben handed him a glass of wine.

"Why don't you two have a seat?" said Bree. "Dinner won't be a minute."

Simon pulled out a chair for me and waited.

I found myself unsure how to act with him. This wasn't a

Saturday supper at the farmhouse, so what was it? A double date? A setup? I felt blindsided.

This was also the first time I'd seen him since the trail ride to his cabin. Since Davey.

Altogether, it left me feeling vaguely bruised and resentful.

"How's Laurel?" he asked as I took the chair he offered. "Does she like her new school?"

I nodded.

"She making friends?" he asked.

"She's my little helper," Bree called from the kitchen.

"I want to thank you for the book," I told him a little stiffly.

"Not at all," he said. "Maybe it can help you find your voice again."

Before I could answer, Bree was standing over us with a platter.

"All set?" she asked. "I hope y'all have an appetite."

She and Reuben brought more food dishes, nearly overwhelming the little table. Reuben uncorked a second bottle of wine.

"My father says you're getting to be quite the rider, Jo," he said. "He's not an easy man to impress."

"Your father?" I asked blankly. As far as I knew, I'd never met the man.

"Morgan Begay—he brought the horses."

"Oh, yes," I said. "But I haven't seen him since."

"He must get updates from Olin. They're tight."

"Reuben's been teaching me, too," said Bree. "I have more room for improvement than you, Jo."

"You didn't ride back home?" I asked. "Virginia, right?"

"Hampton Roads. Very old family. My parents are both at NASA Langley. I, on the other hand, always wanted to teach."

"But not in Virginia . . ."

"Oh, I did, for a while. After I graduated William and Mary, I taught for a bit in Norfolk. Third grade. But one night . . ." She frowned as if trying to pull up a faded memory. "One night, that all changed."

She sounded oddly wistful.

"What happened?" I asked.

Bree concentrated harder. "I was out with friends at a concert at the Coliseum. Little Phish. I was heading home right after, and there was a trucker talking on the cell with his boy, saying good night. The phone slipped. He went to catch it and jerked the wheel just enough to cross the center line. Hit me head-on."

"Oh, God," I said. "I'm so sorry. Were you hurt bad?"

"About as banged up as you can be. I'm fine now, of course. The poor trucker, though—I doubt he's gotten over it."

"I don't know if I could be so forgiving," I said.

"I bet you would," she said. "Anyway, I needed a change. That's how I ended up in Morro—just felt drawn to the place. And after I met Reuben, I knew why."

Drawn to the place? I wondered if she had the same reaction to the Mountain as I did.

Bree took Reuben's hand and squeezed it, and Reuben gazed back at her with every ounce of heart and soul right there in his eyes. I felt a pang of envy—no man had ever looked at me that way.

"How'd you two meet?" I asked.

"She stabbed me," said Reuben.

Bree groaned. "I *didn't*. It was a little dart and never touched a lick of skin. It hit your *boot!*"

Simon noticed my confusion. "The pub down the road has

dartboards," he explained. "And, well, some people have better aim than others."

Reuben pointed to the toe of one worn cowboy boot. "I still have the hole."

"I'll buy you another pair," said Bree.

"I like these just fine," he said, pulling her hand to his lips to kiss her fingertips. "Even if they do leak when it rains."

That was when my old habit kicked in, and I began to watch them over my wineglass for telltale cracks in those happy, shiny surfaces. For a note too sour, a look too sharp . . .

But I could detect nothing wrong. Nothing rang false or out of place between them—not a single, solitary fraudulent thing.

And I felt thoroughly ashamed of myself.

"Joanna," said Simon, "you and Reuben have something in common. You both studied in Albuquerque, right?"

"Another Lobo, eh?" Reuben asked.

"It was years ago," I said. "Only three semesters."

"Double features at Don Pancho's . . ." he said with a smile. "Ice cream at the Purple Hippo . . ."

I smiled back. I knew those places well. "Cinnamon buns at the Frontier—that's where I packed on my freshman ten," I said. "The Living Batch Bookstore . . ."

Memories that had been long dormant came rushing back in an instant—familiar, yet foreign, too. As if they were from somebody else's life. It didn't seem possible it had once been mine.

"I had no idea those places were still around," I said. "But they must be—you couldn't have graduated that long ago."

"I didn't graduate, either. A couple years, I was back home. I missed my family. I missed—" He shrugged. "I missed my father. And by then I was drinking. My uncle in Shiprock took me to help with the ranch. Herding ponies on motorcycles, whipping in and out of arroyos . . ." His eyes began to shine. "That was a good year. But even that wasn't enough. We'd go to Wheeler to drink our paychecks—no alcohol sales on the rez. I started to hate the idea of going back to the ranch. And one day, I didn't."

I understood. Wheeler used to be notorious for weekend bar traffic—thousands pouring in from reservations or rural towns. A core group of alcoholics never left. At night, cops would round them up and haul them to the drunk tank at the edge of town to sleep it off. Come morning, they'd be sober enough to straggle to the nearby soup kitchen run by Catholic nuns. After that, they hit the streets again—panhandling, petty theft, pawning their blood—to score more alcohol.

When the weather was good, the system worked—even when officers couldn't find everyone who'd passed out in the bed of a pickup or collapsed in a dark doorway.

But in winter the temperatures could drop to freezing at night, and it wasn't that unusual to find someone dead of hypothermia by sunup. The city kept a running tally. Jim called them popsicles.

Reuben leaned close. "You know Mother Teresa?"

"Of course," I said.

"She came to the mission once. One morning we were sitting there with our cheese sandwiches and heard a ruckus. I looked up and there was this shrunken little woman in white robes, face like a walnut and the saddest eyes. My first sober thought that day was, 'Holy shit, it's Mother Teresa.' She was walking through, nuns at her heels. Photographers, TV cameras. An hour out of the drunk tank, this is the last person you expect to see, right?"

I knew about that day—Mother Teresa had come to town several years before Jim brought me to Wheeler. It was her Sisters of Charity that ran the soup kitchen. People still talked about that visit.

But that happened—what, fifteen years ago? Twenty? If Reuben had seen her in town, he would've had to be around Laurel's age at the time . . .

"So she's passing my bench," Reuben continued, "and I stagger to my feet. Then I drop to my knees, holding my arms up like I'm a referee and somebody just nailed a field goal. And I'm not even Catholic. She totters over and for a second or two lays her hand on mine. Then she goes on her way."

He shook his head slowly. "It was one of those moments, you know?"

I nodded. "Life-changing."

"Hell, no! I went out, pawned some stolen hubcaps, bought myself a bottle—business as usual. Things didn't change till that winter. I was in an alley one cold night, massively stoned, thinking how strange it was that I couldn't feel my arms or legs anymore. And that if I wasn't careful, I could lose everything. *That* was my wake-up call."

Bree was giving him a small, consoling smile.

After dessert, Bree suggested a walk to Schiavone's bakery down the block to cap off the evening with genuine Italian coffee. It was mid-September by my best guess and the air had chilled considerably. It felt like the first bite of autumn, and I chafed my arms against the cold.

Simon peeled off his sport coat and, before I could object, draped it over my shoulders. It was warm and smelled of cedar wood.

"But now you're in shirtsleeves," I protested.

"I'm fine. We mountain men defy the cold."

"I thought mountain men defied the cold by wearing animal pelts, not by shucking their clothes."

He chuckled and fell in beside me on the sidewalk.

Bree and Reuben were a few paces ahead, arms linked. Bree was leaning into Reuben, whispering in his ear. Now and then she glanced back at us, her expression conspiratorial.

Lampposts were lit all along the main street and strings of lights were wound around tree trunks and branches. Most stores had already closed for the day, but others remained open: a fifties-style malt shop, its counter packed with young people; a steakhouse and saloon, the kind with swinging doors and frisky piano music inside. The Wild Rose had a candle burning in each window, and the pub looked like it had been transported stone by stone from an Irish village. I imagined it was there that Bree had punctured Reuben's boot with the dart.

Schiavone's had a half dozen café tables on a patio, and most were taken. Bree and I found an empty one while Reuben and Simon went inside for the coffees.

The lights were still on at the town hall across the street, and Bree explained it doubled as a community center for plays and concerts; some evenings they hung a screen for a movie projector.

At the next table sat three older men with intense, angular features, wearing worn cloth coats and drinking from espresso cups. They were deep in conversation in a language I couldn't begin to place.

"This is like nothing I've ever seen in Wheeler," I murmured.

"I've been to Wheeler, so I know what you mean," said

Bree. "Me, I prefer farther afield. Reuben and I just trekked through Scotland. Next summer, we're hitting the Amalfi Coast." She laughed. "My Reuben may come from a desert people, but he loves the sea."

Reuben was approaching with a tray, Simon close behind. He placed four foaming glasses on the table, along with four forks. I thought he'd made a mistake in the cutlery till Simon set down a small plate: on it was a huge cinnamon bun— exactly like the ones from my late-night binges in college.

Simon handed me a fork. "They even warmed it," he said. "Shall we?"

They waited for me to take the first bite. It tasted just as I remembered, down to the sweet, dripping butter.

"They make these here?" I asked.

"Not ordinarily," Simon said vaguely. "You have to know who to talk to."

Later that night, Simon insisted on driving me home. He opened the passenger door of his truck and offered his hand to help me inside. I ignored the hand and climbed in on my own. The bench seat was upholstered in soft cowhide that warmed my legs, despite the deepening chill.

Simon started the engine, then turned a knob on the dashboard. "Doesn't take long for the heat to kick in."

"I'm fine."

I slid his coat from my shoulders and folded it neatly. I laid it on the seat between us.

"Are you?" he asked. I knew he wasn't talking about the chill.

The evening had been surprisingly pleasant, but now that Simon and I were alone, the resentment was back and doubling down. Just how was he expecting this lift back to the farmhouse to end? With the two of us parked in the driveway steaming up the truck windows? Sloppy kisses on the porch?

Besides, I couldn't look at him without seeing Davey pulling off his cowboy hat, exposing that face . . .

I turned toward the side window and watched as Morro swept past. The truck left the asphalt and hit the dirt road with a faint bump. As we drove on toward the farm, I shifted in the seat to look behind us.

Tonight the snowcap on the Mountain shone with a kind of phosphorescence. And there near the top was Olin's night-light.

If I climbed up and found that light, if I touched it, would it burn like fire? Or like ice?

Simon was reaching for the knob on the dash again.

"Corral's almost finished," he said as warm air fanned my legs. "Pegasus has even jumped the rails a few times, but he always comes back. I wouldn't have thought he could hurdle that high—not in his shape. Maybe he's got wings after all."

I dragged my eyes from the Mountain and straightened in my seat. "You're keeping the name?"

"Wouldn't want to disappoint Davey," he said.

"He seems like a nice boy."

"He is."

"Yes," I said tonelessly. "And he looks *exactly* like a nine-year-old version of my husband." The words tasted bitter as rue on my tongue. "Except he has my eyes. Didn't you notice?"

I turned to stare at the window glass. I could feel Simon studying me, but he was silent for a long while. Then, "I knew there was something."

We were almost at the house now; the drive from town

wasn't long. Despite the warm air in the cab, I was shivering all over again.

"Yes," I said. "There was something."

Simon didn't answer. He kept his hands level on the wheel, his eyes on the road. And just . . . *waited*.

I felt no demands from him. No expectations. No judgments.

I knew we could ride the rest of the way without another word being said—we could drive clear up to Canada as silent as two monks—and it would be perfectly fine with him.

But this time the truth sat painfully in my throat, straining to burst free. This time there was no one compelling me to speak.

And that meant no one to resist.

"I was pregnant once before," I began quietly. "Before Laurel, I mean. I lost the baby early. If he'd been born—" I shook my head. "His name was David. At least, that was my name for him. His due date was in June. Nine years ago. Sound familiar?"

I was startled to realize my cheeks were wet. I wiped at the tears, then stared at my fingers.

We were drawing up on the farmhouse, pulling into the drive. The porch light was on; a single lamp shone through the front window. The rest of the house was dark. It wasn't late, but Olin and Jessie kept farm hours.

Simon switched off the engine and made no move to exit or to help me out. Instead, he rested his left arm on the steering wheel and eased himself in his seat, angling in my direction. Still he said nothing.

If he'd questioned me then, I couldn't have gone on. I would have shut down, just as I'd done with the doctor in the clinic and with Alicia from the prosecutor's office. It wasn't from obstinacy or defiance. It was just that some wounds run so deep, they can cut you all over again in the telling.

But almost before I knew it—there I was, telling Simon. It helped that it was too dark to see his face well, or for him to see mine.

I told him about Jim's jealous rage that day, and the punch to the stomach. About the emergency trip to the clinic two days later. I even told him something I'd forgotten till that very moment—about rushing to the bathroom in the clinic before the exam because I was bleeding through my clothes. And somehow there was my blood all over the bathroom floor, the walls, and I panicked, pulling paper towels from the dispenser, frantic to clean everything up before anybody found out I'd made such a mess.

Then, after the exam, the curettage, with Jim hovering and the doctor advising us to go try again, we stood in line to pay the bill, just one more couple like any other in the room. An office assistant was soothing a fussy toddler, holding him over a machine to copy his tiny hands till he laughed.

As I stood there watching them, it was the first time—the only time—I shed tears over the baby. A nurse pulled us out of line and hustled us to a desk in a quiet corner to handle the payment in private. Jim went through the motions of a man comforting his wife, his hand a vise on my shoulder.

Once home, he warned me never to mention the baby again. And so I hadn't.

"Joanna, I'm so sorry." Simon reached for me, but I shrank from him.

"I appreciate it—I do," I said apologetically. "But I don't think I could handle a single bit of kindness right now. Does that make sense?"

"It does."

"I always thought I'd break into a thousand pieces if I ever dared tell anyone about Jim. Like there'd be some punishment— from Jim or, I don't know, from God, for all I knew. As if the two of them were one and the same. Crazy, right? I mean, if one of them existed, the other couldn't possibly."

"It's hard to make sense of the world when people do terrible things."

"And get away with it—don't forget that. *And get away with it*. If God protects fools and drunks, he sure as hell protects bastards, too. Where's all that righteous anger of his, anyway? I've seen plenty of anger out there, but never his. If he hears the smallest prayer, he sure as hell can hear a scream."

Simon was looking off in the distance. He had an earnest grip on the steering wheel.

"It can seem that way sometimes," he said, his voice low. "In our darkest hours, it can seem like there's nothing out there. When you're fighting for your life, weeks into a battle— outgunned, outmaneuvered and so exhausted you don't know if you're awake or just trapped inside your own nightmare. Watching your buddies disappear one by one in a blast of shells—just *gone*—or ground up like raw meat under tank treads."

His voiced trailed off. I was watching him then, mesmerized by his profile, by the strain in his voice—so unlike him. I waited for him to go on.

"Artillery, mortar fire, tanks raking you from all sides . . . explosions so close your ears bleed. You wipe at the mud and the blood, knowing there's nowhere to run. *Nowhere.* So scared all you want to do is crawl up inside your own helmet. And you hear the screams. You hear the prayers, too. Impossible to miss." He turned and gave me a thin smile. "Trust me. Impossible."

"Simon . . . I'm sorry. I had no idea."

"No reason you should."

"You make me ashamed."

He cocked his head. "Why on earth?"

"I forget other people have scars, too. Where were you? Afghanistan?"

He didn't answer.

"No," I continued slowly, "that couldn't be right. We haven't had battles like that over there. Weeks and weeks, against tanks . . ." I waited for an explanation, but he wasn't offering one.

"You know," he said finally, "maybe some prayers aren't answered right away. Maybe we have to wait for it. Or *work* for it."

"A bootstrap theology."

"Not quite," he said. "We don't always have to go it alone, you know."

Suddenly I was remembering Bernadette.

"There was someone who helped me once," I said. "And for no good reason I know of. She said it was because I asked her, but even so, I don't know many people who would've done that. Jessie and Olin would have. *You* would have."

"Joanna, listen. When you first came, you could've knocked on any door and been taken in. That's just the way it is. I believe that's how most people are, given a chance."

"I wish I could believe that," I said.

"Give it some time."

I drew a deep breath; the choking knot in my throat was gone.

"Better?" he asked.

"I feel empty," I said. "But in a good way—lighter, cleaner. You're a good listener."

"Happy to lend an ear. Anytime."

"You must be kidding. Why in the world would you want to hear about the hot mess that is my life?"

He pulled on his door handle. "It's late. I'll see you to the house."

Olin's Kachinas

$\mathcal{I}$ was raking oak leaves in the yard when Laurel bolted outside with a shout. She ran up and latched onto my leg. "Mommy! Mr. Olin plays with *dolls!*" She chortled.

Olin had followed her onto the porch, looking tickled.

"Honey," I told her, "I'm sure Mr. Olin doesn't play with baby dolls . . ."

"No!" she said. "With little wooden Indians."

I understood then what she meant: kachinas. They were in every souvenir shop in Wheeler—cheap, clunky carvings decked out with gaudy paint and feathers, glued to wooden stands.

"Those aren't dolls, sweetie. They're—" I fumbled for something inoffensive. "They're special figures in Indian culture."

"That's near the point, punkin'," Olin told her. "But there's more to it than that. Come on—I'll show you."

"You, too, Mommy."

"In a minute. You go on—I want to get this done before Simon comes."

I was finishing up when Simon and his dog rounded the café, heading for the house. I waved, and he raised his arm in turn. Pal must have thought I was giving him a signal because he put on speed and bulleted right at me. I dropped the rake just as he reared up, his front paws ramming my shoulders. I staggered from the impact.

Simon whistled and Pal jumped down and swung around, waiting for his master to catch up.

"Sorry. Did he get dirt on you?"

I brushed at my sweater. "No harm done."

Simon gestured. "Missed a spot."

"Where—here?"

"No." He hesitated, then picked a crushed leaf from my shoulder. "There—now you're perfect."

"And you're full of it."

He laughed. We climbed the porch steps together, and I leaned the rake against the house. He glanced around curiously. "Where's my little lookout?"

"Inside. Playing with Olin's kachinas."

"Ah. That could take a while. Have you seen them?"

"Not yet. Thought I'd look in when I was more presentable."

His eyes swept over me again, this time down to my capris and bare feet. I'd kicked off my sneakers while I raked.

"You look just fine," he said. "I should . . . go on upstairs."

I nodded.

He took one final glance before disappearing inside. I followed soon after, checking in with Jessie in the kitchen to see if she needed help with supper.

"Not a thing," she said. "What on earth are you smiling about?"

"What?"

"Child, you look right pleased with yourself. What's going on?"

"I don't know what you mean. I'll get Laurel washed up. Olin's showing her his kachinas."

"Those?" Jessie muttered. "I hope he doesn't frighten the poor thing."

She pulled off her apron and dropped it on the butcher block, then headed for the living room.

I hadn't seen Olin's den yet—I knew it was his personal retreat, but could only imagine what it looked like: deer heads mounted on the wall, a gun safe in the corner, a cracked leather sofa by a fireplace . . .

The door to the room was open and I followed Jessie inside. Olin was bending over Laurel, his palm outstretched.

"And this here they call the 'Priest Killer,'" he was saying.

"Land's sake! Don't show her that!" Jessie snapped.

Olin was holding a figurine so tiny I couldn't make it out from the doorway. Laurel was staring at it, her eyes wide.

"Can I touch it?" she asked.

"Olin!" Jessie growled.

Before Olin could reconsider, Laurel snatched up the figurine. It was impossibly small—two inches, if that. And she looked mesmerized.

"Is that a knife with *blood* on it?" she asked. "Is he holding somebody's *head*?"

I drew closer. It was a stocky figure in a leather cape, loincloth and red moccasins. There were two red squares where his ears should be and an orange ruff around his neck. He had a black wolflike snout. In one hand he was clutching a decapitated head; in the other, a knife tipped with red.

"Why did he kill the priest?" Laurel asked.

"Well," said Olin, "Indians didn't much appreciate other folks sayin' their ways was no good, tryin' to make 'em follow theirs. So one day they up and went to war. Attacked a mission."

"They didn't want to believe in God?"

"They did believe—in the Great Spirit. Believed other things, too. In the Earth Mother, in balance and cycles to life. And spirits everywhere—not just in people, but in trees and animals and every God-made thing."

Laurel looked thoughtful. "I like that."

"Me, too," said Olin.

"I think the oak tree outside has a spirit."

"I often thought that myself."

"Why do people fight over things like that?" she asked.

"It'd take a wiser man than me to figure it out. Till a man goes to his reward, he don't know nothin' for sure. Till then, arguin' over it is like blind men arguin' over the color blue."

Gingerly, Laurel handed the figure back to Olin.

"Mommy," she said, "look at these."

She pressed her face against a display case filled with carved figures of every size—from miniatures like the Priest Killer to others topping two feet. All were made of cottonwood root. Some were very rough, very old. Others were large and resplendent, finely sanded and painted, dressed in real feathers, soft fur and leather. None looked anything like the knockoffs in those tourist shops in Wheeler.

Olin explained that the older, plainer carvings were Hopi—

the pueblo tribe that originated the kachinas. The Zuni and Navajo had adopted them later.

By tradition, he said, there are hundreds of kachinas, each representing a supernatural being that protects, teaches, amuses or disciplines. They're also messengers to the spirit world.

Just before spring, the kachinas leave their ancient home in the sacred mountains to live among the Hopi, to help with the hunt and the harvest. Then in midsummer they hold the Home-Going Dance before they return to their mountains.

Some appear in animal form, while others are mudheads, or clowns, with fantastical headpieces. Ogres teach children right from wrong. And still others, said Olin, aren't strictly kachinas, but dancers. Many are revered for their virtues— their wisdom or healing, their skill as hunters or warriors. Some help the rains come.

Laurel found a tiny Warrior Mouse that Olin said saved a village from a hawk that was gobbling up all its precious chickens. The mouse taunted the hawk till it dived and impaled itself on a sharpened greasewood stick.

"What's 'impaled'?" Laurel asked.

"A fine thing to have to explain," Jessie muttered, heading for the door. "Supper in fifteen minutes."

She left just as Simon entered. "Impaled?" he murmured, so close that his breath brushed my ear and I could smell the Lifebuoy soap on his skin.

"Some story about a Warrior Mouse and a hawk," I said.

He nodded.

"Well," Olin began slowly, rubbing his chin, "when the hawk dove to the ground, that greasewood stick was stickin' up just like a little spear, see? And the hawk, he flew smack into it before he even knew what happened."

Laurel looked intrigued.

I pointed to a nearby figure. "What about this?"

Olin smiled. "Now, that's right special—and not just to Hopis. He's the Hummingbird."

He picked it up—a figure less than a foot high, with a straight body painted aqua and yellow, arms crooked at the elbows. It was dressed in a white leather skirt, a green mask and green moccasins, and crowned with a ruff of Douglas fir. It didn't look any more remarkable than the others; in many respects, it looked much less so.

"The Hopis, they send the Hummingbird up to ask the gods for rain so the crops can grow," Olin explained. "One time, when the whole world caught fire, it was the Hummingbird who gathered all the rain clouds to put it out."

A colorful legend, I thought, but I wasn't sure why a Hummingbird that could summon rain was any more special than, say, the Antelope or the Long-Haired kachinas, which could do the same.

"And the Apaches, they got a story about a warrior named Wind Dancer who saved Bright Rain from a wolf," Olin said. "He died and Bright Rain took to grievin', and the whole world settled into a long winter. Bright Rain, she set out on long walks, and a hummingbird took to flyin' with her, whispering words of comfort in her ear, restorin' the balance. Turns out, that hummingbird was Wind Dancer. And after a while, Bright Rain stopped her grievin', and winter broke and spring come again."

Laurel was tracing the crown of the Hummingbird kachina. "Too bad Bright Rain didn't turn into a hummingbird, too, so they could be together."

Olin smiled down at her. "When her time come, maybe she did," he said gently. "Maybe heaven ain't all harps and halos."

But he wasn't finished with the lesson. "Go back far enough," he said, "the Mayans thought the hummingbird was the sun in disguise. And the Aztecs—to them, hummingbirds was warriors that died in battle."

He was eyeing the figure thoughtfully. "And out of all of the kachinas, only the Hummingbird ever flew high enough to see what was on the other side of the sky."

That intrigued me. "What did he find?"

Olin shook his head. "As the story goes—nothin'."

Jessie's voice rang out from the kitchen: "Supper!"

The lesson was over. We put the figures away and headed for the dining room.

"Mr. Olin," Laurel asked, "do all old people know as much stuff as you?"

He chuckled. "Li'l gal, I been thinkin'. I figure 'Mr. Olin' is a mite formal for good friends like us."

"But what should I call you, then?" she asked.

"What'd you like to call me?"

"Can I call you Opa?"

I shushed her. "Laurel, no."

Olin looked puzzled.

"*Opa* is German," I explained. "It means 'Grandpa.'"

He considered for a moment. "Sounds easy enough to pronounce, for bein' German. You call me Opa anytime you want. What should I call you?"

"My name's Laurel."

"True enough. But how 'bout I call you Honey Bunny?"

Laurel giggled.

"Only sometimes I might call you Honey for short, and other times just Bunny. But Honey Bunny for more formal occasions."

Laurel took his hand. "What do you think heaven is, Opa?"

He looked around the room—from his wife to the hearth to the table set for supper.

"Well, Bunny, I think heaven is whatever, wherever and whoever makes you happiest."

After supper, Olin and Jessie began clearing the table and Laurel headed upstairs to get ready for bed, leaving me to see Simon off. From the porch, I could hear bluegrass music on the radio inside. I pulled one of Jessie's woolen shawls around me as Simon turned to leave.

He hesitated on the porch steps.

"It occurs to me you haven't been to the pub yet," he said. "I wonder if you'd care to rectify that."

"What?"

"I mean, with your interest in Irish poetry, and the proprietor of the pub being Irish—it just makes sense."

"You're trying to set me up with the pub owner?"

He laughed. "I'm not trying to set you up with anyone. I'm asking, in my clumsy way, if you'd care to go to the pub some evening. With me. The pub owner's married."

"Simon, there are so many reasons to say no, I couldn't begin to list them all."

"Then don't say no. Say you'll think about it. Then think about it."

I hugged the shawl tighter. "Laurel's waiting. I told her I'd read to her before bed."

"Night, then."

He turned and headed to his pickup truck. I waved as it pulled away, certain he was watching.

As I entered the house again, I noticed the door to Olin's den still ajar. I could hear him and Jessie puttering in the kitchen, so I slipped inside for another look, pausing just inside the doorway.

I looked around at the sage green walls and white molding. His rifles and shotgun were mounted on a far wall, along with an old-style cavalry carbine. No deer heads, though, and no leather sofa. Instead, there were two overstuffed club chairs slipcovered in yellow flowers; both looked comfortable and well used. There were shelves lined with books flanking a deep stone fireplace, and on the mantel a display of Indian pottery, pewter mugs and candlesticks, and an enameled tobacco box.

As I turned to leave, I spotted a photograph in a silver frame on a small table. It was an old black-and-white of cowboys in slouch hats, kerchiefs knotted at their necks. They were surrounding a standing figure that looked remarkably like Teddy Roosevelt. As I read the caption, I realized it *was* Teddy Roosevelt: *Rough Riders, 1898.*

Several of the men were on their feet while others knelt on one knee or sat cross-legged on the bare ground. The landscape looked like Southwestern desert.

I scanned the faces—the young and cocky, the stern and worldly-wise. Kneeling in the foreground was a youthful cowboy with dark hair and a bristly mustache, grinning into the camera, cradling a carbine very like the one now mounted on the wall.

I leaned closer. The cowboy looked like a young Olin Farnsworth.

"See the resemblance?"

Olin was behind me, gazing over my shoulder at the picture.

"I didn't hear you come in," I said. "What a time you must have had . . . storming San Juan Hill."

Olin paused. "Well, that ain't exactly the case. Not all Teddy's boys made it to Cuba. When orders come, they wasn't enough room on the transport ship." He nodded at the picture. "Some had to stay behind in Florida. Most of the horses and mules did, too, which wasn't an ideal situation for a crack cavalry outfit. And that's why the Rough Riders took San Juan on foot."

I looked over the kachinas one last time. All those intermediaries between people and their gods. All that blind faith in the unknowable. Faith that something better was waiting, just out of sight. And spirits ready to step in, if asked. To guide and protect. To fend off mortal enemies.

And what of those enemies? Do they have their own spirit champions? And when they die, do they ever get to see what's on the other side of the sky?

"What about someone who does bad things?" I asked finally. "Does he deserve to be happy? Does he deserve heaven?"

"I figure a man can't be all that happy if he does bad things. And it ain't up to me to say what he might deserve. But I figure when he passes on, he's where he oughta be."

"Some people . . . some people don't believe in Judgment, a reckoning. Any of that."

Olin shrugged. "I figure it ain't up to them."

Red Bird

This is a dream

I wade through wet cement ... straining to *run* ...

A scarlet bird flies in my face, wings flapping like a Fury. My head explodes like shattered glass and I fall and fall until I can't fall anymore

I smell heat rising from red rock ... I taste grit ...

This is a dream

My mouth opens to scream, but no sound comes. I scream again and again until my throat is scoured raw. But no sound comes

I know this is a dream

I fight like a demon to *wake up wake up wake up* but can't move ... only my mouth moves, gaping like a canyon, mute as rock

.   .   .

I bolted upright in the dark, gasping for breath like a drowning woman breaching the surface.

Like a cornered animal, I threw wild eyes around me at every shadow.

There was no cement, no scarlet bird.

I was in my own bed at the farmhouse. My nightgown was drenched with sweat and I couldn't suck in air fast enough.

No cement. No scarlet bird. No explosion inside my head. I groaned and buried my face in my hands.

The nightmare still gripped me like a claw. Every smell, every taste. Every fresh stab of fear. I could even hear it—the screams that wouldn't come. But they were coming now, high-pitched and howling . . .

. . . and down the hall.

I threw off the quilt and ran toward Laurel's room. I burst in to find her kicking and thrashing on her bed, eyes clamped tight, moaning and shrieking. I ran to gather her up, hugging her against me to quiet her, to stop the thrashing.

"It's all right, sweetie," I crooned over and over. "It's all right."

It was a long while before she could hear me, before she opened her eyes and looked at me, staring as if she hadn't seen me in forever. She reached out and fingered my hair as if I were some foreign thing.

Then she burst into sobs and flung her arms around my neck. I let her cry it out, holding her close, walking the room with her as if she were a baby again. Olin and Jessie were watching from the doorway.

"I'll heat up some milk," Jessie murmured, and headed for the stairs.

Laurel's face was buried in my neck and she was mumbling

something over and over that I couldn't make out. I stroked her hair. "What is it, honey? What are you saying?"

She shifted her head until she could speak more clearly.

"He's coming," she whispered.

"Who's coming, sweetie?"

She buried her face in my neck again, but this time when she spoke I could hear her plain enough:

"Daddy."

The Ravenmaster

Jim didn't come that night. Not the next night, either, nor the one after that. It was painfully obvious that my daughter dreaded her own father the way other children fear monsters under the bed. But in her case, she had every right to.

Laurel insisted she didn't remember much about her bad dream, but it was a while before she settled down to sleep. For the rest of that night, though, and for several nights after, she slept with me.

I didn't mention to anyone my own nightmare that had coincided with hers—the last thing I wanted was to compare notes. But I wanted very much to understand what it augured. Was it her own fears manifesting? A premonition?

Or had Olin's kachinas and his stories of life and death and spirits sparked something in her? In me?

Her dream didn't repeat itself, and in no time she seemed to have forgotten it.

I didn't.

Soon enough, for the first time since we came to Morro, there was frost on the ground when I set the horses to pasture. The days were growing short, and Laurel grumbled about waking in the dark. She dressed for school as I packed her lunch, then bundled her in a jacket for the walk to town with Olin.

I was working the café that morning, and when I arrived there was already a stranger sitting quietly at a window table—a tall man with a bottlebrush mustache wearing a green tweed coat; a slouchy tweed cap sat on the table in front of him. There was a canvas knapsack at his feet and a walking stick propped against the wall.

When I greeted him, the man turned and blinked as if he'd just noticed where he was and that someone else was with him. He nodded.

In the kitchen, Simon was tying on his butcher's apron.

"Who's the early bird?" I murmured.

"Showed up just after I did," he said. "Told him I wasn't quite open, but he said he'd wait."

"I'll start the coffee."

"Better make it tea—he's English."

Earl Grey steeping at his elbow, the man examined the menu. "Let's try something exotic," he said. "Spanish omelet. When in Rome, eh?"

He handed back the menu, and when I returned with the order Simon came with me.

"I'm just getting my sea legs, as it were," the man said as

he ate. "This . . . traveling takes getting used to. You know, we'd always talked of moving to the American Southwest one day, the wife and I. Running a bed-and-breakfast."

"Oh, is she with you?" I asked.

"No—back in Surrey. Keyes, by the way."

"Pardon?"

"My name. Albert Keyes."

"Joanna. And this is Simon."

"Delighted."

Simon took a seat at the counter. "You're far afield, aren't you?"

Keyes nodded. "I'll be returning before long, once I've seen a thing or two. Like your town here—Morro, is it? And your desert." He gazed wistfully out the window. "And, perhaps, the Northwest."

Pal rose from his quilt and headed for the window, his ears pricked, his eyes trained like gun barrels on something outside. In the growing light I could just make out a huge black bird perched on a signpost across the road. It seemed to be staring back.

"Look at the size of that crow," I said.

"Raven," Keyes replied. "A very old friend, and now my traveling companion. His name is Gruffydd." He spelled it out. "It's Welsh. After a prince who fell from the White Tower in a failed escape, a very long time ago."

Simon smiled at my confusion. "I believe he's talking about the Tower of London," he said.

"That's right," said Keyes. "I was a yeoman warder there a number of years, after service as a regimental sergeant major. Began as deputy to the ravenmaster. He retired some years ago, and I took over."

He nodded toward the black bird.

"That's how we met. Raised him from a fledgling. Named him as well. At one time, all the birds were named for the Queen's regiments. Now they're often named for old gods, or for those who find them. Or rescue them. I named Gruffydd there for the prince that couldn't fly."

Simon leaned back against the counter, crossing his arms. "I remember the ravens," he said thoughtfully. "I was in London a few weeks before shipping out. Took a tour of the Tower. The ravens were *something*. Six of them. Bigger than you'd think. Must be a huge responsibility, taking care of them. What is it they say? If the ravens ever leave the Tower, the empire will fall?"

"That's the legend, anyway," said Keyes. "But there have been episodes when the ravens have been absent—toward the end of the war, for instance—with no detriment to the monarchy."

"How do you keep them from flying off?" I asked. "You don't keep them caged, do you?"

"They are, indeed, caged at dusk. I whistled them in for bed, but at dawn they were out again, roaming the grounds. I fed them from my own hand—raw meat from Smithfield Market. Boiled egg every other day. Bird biscuits soaked in blood— a delicacy. The odd roadkill. And they don't fly off because their wings are clipped—or one wing, at least—every few weeks. They can still fly a bit, but no appreciable distance."

There was affection in his voice, but it still seemed a cruel fate for such wild creatures.

"They are wild," Keyes said thoughtfully. "But they're natural mimics, and very intelligent. And they do have their fun. Gruffydd was always my favorite. Every day he tells me, 'Good morning.' When I fill his water bowl, he says, 'Cheers.' He used to stake out a particular doorway at the Tower, lying in ambush for tourists. If you wore a hat, he'd try to grab it. And if he made off with it, he'd be off to a restricted area and battle that hat like billy-o."

Pal plopped his rump down heavily on the tile floor, still training on the bird. He licked his chops and whined. Simon tapped his leg. "Here, boy." Ever obedient, Pal rose and moved to sit next to him.

"Don't worry about Gruffydd," Keyes said. "He can manage, should the dog get out."

I wondered what sort of bond this man and that raven could possibly share. If Keyes whistled, would Gruffydd come? Perch on his shoulder, clutching the nubby tweed? Say "Good morning" and "Cheers" on cue for a boiled egg or beef?

Keyes sighed. "Twenty-five years—he was getting on, you know. After his de-enlistment I brought him back to Surrey. My wife is still there—did I say?—puttering about the garden."

When he was ready to head out, I rang the man up as he pulled on his cap and gathered his things. I cleared his breakfast dishes and delivered them to the back. By the time I returned, Keyes and Gruffydd were gone.

For the rest of the day, I couldn't get that raven out of my head—picturing him perched on weathered stones in high places, buffeted by winds that would never bear him away.

The Parting Glass

The librarian, Jean Toliver, arrived at the farmhouse one morning dressed in the long skirt, velvet blouse and squash blossom necklace I now took to be her uniform. I imagined she'd come to press me to attend her club meetings, but soon found it was to invite me to a poetry reading set for the following week. Amateur poets, most of them local.

Then she asked where I'd like to appear on the program, and somehow by the time she left she'd inked me in for a slot.

I'd never enjoyed reading in public, and had only ever done so twice: at a student event in college, and a small community reading by a pair of unknowns—myself and a coffeehouse barista.

Both times, I'd nearly backed out. But for the first reading, Terri had been there to make sure I made it to the podium. I managed the second only after a shot of vodka from a hip flask the barista had stashed.

This time, I not only lacked the nerve, but the material as well.

That night I sat in the rocking chair in my room and opened the notebook Olin had given me—I'd been using it as a journal, after many failed attempts at poetry. Apparently Yeats no longer had the power of inspiration over me. Or I was no longer a likely vessel.

I came to the notebook that night with fresh purpose and not a little desperation, but with the same result: after a good hour, the page was still empty. There was nothing for it. Words weren't failing me—I was failing them.

I slapped the notebook closed, capped my pen and returned it to the nightstand, the blank page just another white flag of surrender. Tomorrow I would withdraw from the reading. The decision came as a relief.

And a vague sting of disappointment.

Over the years I'd grown keenly aware of risk, and adept at avoiding it. The risk here, it occurred to me, wasn't in standing before a roomful of strangers to read my own work. It wasn't even the struggle to find my own voice.

It was finding out if I had anything worth listening to in the first place.

And the only one who could determine that was me.

I looked down at the notebook in my lap. I opened the cover and leafed through the pages—the journaling I'd been doing nearly every day since I'd received it. The pages already filled with words.

My words.

By the night of the reading, I had two poems in hand. If I wasn't ready, I was at least resolved.

Jessie enlisted a girl from town to sit with Laurel; then Olin washed and waxed the old Ford pickup he stored in the barn and drove Jessie and me to town. He opened the pub's heavy oak door and I hesitated in the doorway until Jessie did just as Terri would have, and urged me inside.

The Parting Glass was a series of small cozy rooms strung together, and it was just as I imagined an old pub should be—coal fires and pipe smoke, beamed ceilings, odd recesses and crooked corners.

"There you are!"

It was Jean near the entrance, checking names off a clipboard. "Your table's in the second room, through the archway," she said. "Name's on the placard. Simon's already there."

Then she broke into a broad, dimpled smile. She had tiny round teeth, barely bigger than seed pearls.

"Who else is reading?" I asked.

"Only seven tonight. Don't look so worried—people at these things are ready to like everything they hear. You're"— she consulted the clipboard—"sixth up."

Through the archway, the second room was much larger than the first. One side was lined with booths, and on the side opposite was a small stage and podium. In between were tables, nearly all of them occupied. Bree and Reuben called out from one of them.

"How wonderful," said Bree. "You're a poet."

"That remains to be seen," I said.

"Jean says you're good."

How would Jean know any such thing? I hadn't written these poems until a few days ago, and she'd never read them.

Jessie tapped my arm. "Honey, we're off to say hello to Liz and Molly. Meet you at the table."

The sisters Liz and Molly were there, with Liz's husband, Faro, from the general store and a second man I'd never seen before. He was lively and middle-aged, dressed in a brown suit with a windowpane pattern and wide lapels. He had an infectious laugh—head thrown back, Adam's apple bobbing. From the way Molly was smiling at him, eyes glistening, she was clearly smitten.

So this was George, from Bristol.

Simon was sitting at a corner booth. In front of him was a tall beer, and at his side was a young woman, unreasonably pretty, her blond hair pinned back on either side to fall in a soft wave to her shoulders. She was leaning toward him, her pink lips moving. Then they were both smiling, as if at some shared joke.

"That's your table," said Bree, watching me.

I hadn't thought much about Simon attending the reading tonight. Still, when Jean had mentioned him, it hadn't been a surprise. Part of me had expected him to be here, as a gesture of support.

I just hadn't expected him to bring a date.

I'd never thought of Simon with a woman. Certainly Jessie and Olin had never mentioned him seeing anyone. Not even casually. Maybe this was someone new in Morro. Newer than me. Or maybe she'd had her eye on him for a while now and was finally making progress.

Had she been up to his cabin yet? Gone for rides in his pickup? Cooked him dinner? Shared pastry under the stars? Had he invited her to the pub because I'd turned him down?

As I approached, I pulled a smile that felt forced, and too big for my face.

"Hey!" I said.

"You're here!" Simon looked pleased, and not a whit embarrassed. He stood. "There's someone I'd like you to meet. Joanna, this is Meg."

To my dismay, Meg was even prettier up close. "I've heard so much about you," she said. Her voice was warm, her smile sincere. "I'm glad we could meet."

I took a seat across from them. "I'm glad, too. But I have to say I never heard—"

"Simon never mentioned me? No surprise. He's off in his own world sometimes." She shook her head at him affectionately. "You're settling in, are you? At the farm?"

Before I could answer, a big man appeared, shirtsleeves hitched above his elbows.

"This the new one, is it?" His Irish accent was thick, and he was gesturing at me with a toothpick. "You can call me Mahenny. You like Italian food, do you?"

"I . . . adore Italian food," I said.

"Lovely, then. I'm an old mick, but my wife's from Firenze. She's the cook. I recommend the lasagna."

He glared, as if daring me to refuse.

"I'll have that, then," I said.

"Brilliant. I usually only take orders at the bar, but on this particular occasion, I'll make an exception. Understand?"

No, I didn't understand. But I wasn't about to tell him that.

"I appreciate it," I said.

"Now, for wine you got two choices: red or white."

I was sure any pub owner—married to an Italian, no less—knew what to serve with lasagna. Mahenny was playing with me.

"Surprise me," I said.

The glare softened. "That I will, darlin'. Lasagna all 'round, then?"

"Not for me," said Meg. "I'm off to rejoin my husband."

Husband? I smiled with relief.

Meg smiled back with what looked like—understanding? Apology?

"His name's Will," she said. "You can meet him later."

Then Meg and Mahenny were gone, leaving me sitting across from Simon in an awkward silence. Simon broke it first, but not on the topic I'd hoped.

"He seems gruff, but he's a sweetheart," he said. "Not that he can't toss a guy out on his ear if he has to. His wife—she's the sister of Schiavone, the baker."

"And Mahenny's not from these parts, either."

"County Armagh."

I nodded. "Meg seems like a sweetheart, too," I said lightly, trying to strike the right note of disinterest.

"We've known each other for years. She's the kid sister of an old friend. Back then, she was just a tomboy, trailing me like a puppy. Then one day I turned around and the tomboy was all grown up."

Mahenny swooped past, setting a wineglass in front of me. Then he was off again. I took a sip and smiled—Chianti. I focused on its rich red color, the better to avoid Simon's eyes.

"A long time ago," he continued, "Meg and I were sweet on each other, but . . . things didn't work out. She and Will are very happy. Five kids."

"Five?" I stared at him in disbelief. "With that figure? That has to be . . . physically impossible."

He laughed. "You can meet them someday. Meg and Will are heading back to Colorado tomorrow."

He reached for my poems, and I slapped the pages back on the table.

"Sorry," I said. "I'd rather you didn't. I can't explain it—"

He didn't seem offended, but amused. "Artistic temperament," he said. "I can wait."

Jessie and Olin joined us—Jessie already pink cheeked from the sherry in her hand, Olin nursing a bottle of Rio Grande beer. Lasagna arrived for the four of us; Mahenny was right—his wife was an excellent cook.

Soon, Jean stepped to the podium with her clipboard, tapping the microphone to test the sound, then introduced the first of the poets. One by one, they took the stage, reading from note cards, from paper or from memory.

A tense older executive type in horn-rimmed glasses went first, followed by an academic with white hair and precise diction. I was surprised to see Faro take the stage next. He closed his eyes and clasped his hands behind him, just as he'd done before he produced Laurel's yellow boots, and let loose with a love poem that had Liz looking cross, then pleased. After him, Jean read three works—compact and clipped works that reminded me of Emily Dickinson. Then a young woman with multiple piercings on her pretty face read fierce free verse about an ill-fated love affair.

Then it was my turn.

Olin was beside me on the bench seat, and stood to let me out. He squeezed my shoulder encouragingly.

As I made my way to the podium, I was suddenly very grateful for the Chianti—I was sure it was giving me the courage to go through with this and not bolt for the exit. It nearly steadied my hand as I adjusted the microphone. I was grateful for the darkness of the room that blurred the faces all around me, and for the many brands of beer Mahenny stocked to loosen up the audience.

I stared down at my papers and cleared my throat.

"This is for a woman I met in the café," I said. "Lula told me about a cemetery back home in Mississippi—a black cemetery, mostly forgotten now, being farmed over. It's called 'Brother Stones.'"

I couldn't stop my hands from shaking. I drew a deep breath and began:

Brother stones rise to the plow,
crack the topsoil
in a catch of breath
audible only to the blue boneset
and the Quaker ladies.
A barren harvest of white stones,
then seed is thrown back:
soybean and cotton.

This gravel road between Dunleith
and Long Switch runs past
an empty space
where the Baptist church
once stood, dug up by its roots
twelve years ago to become
another wide load rumbling
across the Mississippi Delta,
a far piece from empty sockets
in the fractured earth where
uprooted metal markers lay,
one by one.

"There was no cemetery there."
There was a child, seven,
cradled his head and rolled
to the kitchen floor
of the shotgun shack.
There was the child's brother.

There was a young man, drowned
in the River, his great-grandmother,
dead of the "sugar."
A hundred others or more
planted in this earth,

a quiet population
under a blowing field of cotton,
a disjunction of bones and teeth
rising like smooth stones
through the earth,
a terminable progress

from this place where they are not,
up toward the cotton in fruit,
toward the topsoil, sunbaked to fissures,
toward the vigorous light,
to break the fresh furrows finally
with a gasp.

I could hear murmuring as I switched papers, smoothing them under the bright podium light, still struggling for control.

"And this is for Keyes, an Englishman who passed through

Morro with a raven named Gruffydd. I call this 'Six Ravens at
the Tower of London' ":

>They are the darlings of the Yeoman Warders
>who named them after regiments
>of the Queen, who feed them
>eggs and bread and meat,
>who clip their wings, jealously pinch back
>their bold growth
>toward the sky.
>
>They perch regal and wild and wary
>on the wrought-iron gate, dwarfed
>by the thousand-year stones
>of the White Tower.
>Here, a captive Welsh prince once leapt,
>spread his arms and
>did not fly.
>
>If these creatures fly off,
>England will fall.
>By royal decree, then,
>they will never leave.
>For four hundred years these stones
>have been their keep.
>
>Their black, bottomless eyes
>stare at a silence worn smooth
>by a river of centuries,
>restless as the London mist,
>tameless as Cuchulain's
>horses of the sea.

A thousand voices speak to them
each day in every tongue
but their own.

I gathered my papers. Without daring to look at the audience, I left the podium.

As I stepped from the stage, the applause began. The other readers had had their share of applause, of course, but this applause—this applause was for me.

This was mine.

And it felt . . . *wondrous.*

At the booth, Jessie and Olin hugged me in turn. Then Simon was standing in front of me, looking unsure. I laughed breathlessly. "I'd better sit before my knees buckle," I said.

Back in the booth, Simon leaned across the table. "You were marvelous," he said.

"I was okay. But I appreciate it."

My head was spinning so fast I still can't recall the last reader of the night—for all I knew, it could have been Yeats himself.

The readings didn't close out the evening. Mahenny removed the podium, and three Irish musicians took the stage. The lead singer had ferocious red hair and a bird's nest of a beard, and the three didn't just sing their songs—they attacked them. Tables and chairs were pushed aside to clear a dance floor.

George threw off his jacket and swung Molly around in a bucking polka, and the young poet with the piercings paired off with a cowboy in a starched shirt and handlebar mustache.

Bree stopped by with Reuben. "Jo, you were terrific." She had to shout to be heard above the reel blasting from the stage.

Reuben leaned close. "The family's throwing a shindig in a few weeks for my brother's birthday. You're all invited."

"How old's he now?" asked Simon.

"Turning sixteen," Reuben answered as Bree pulled him back to the dance floor.

Olin stood and offered his hand to his wife. "Honor me?"

Jessie's smile as she took it dropped decades off her.

"You know," I told Simon as I watched them on the floor, "they dance like this more nights than not. Turn on their old radio and off they go. I don't know where they get the energy. I'm starting to wonder what he packs in that rolling paper of his."

Then it was Simon who stood and stepped to my side. "May I?"

I stared at his open hand.

"Simon," I said, "I haven't danced in years. And I've never tried a reel in my life."

He glanced toward the stage, then back at me. "This song's about over. If the next is a slow one, will you dance?"

The Irishmen had been playing only jigs and reels. They could read the crowd, and the crowd wanted to *move*. I felt safe in agreeing.

"Sure," I said.

Almost as soon as I said it, the reel was over. There was a pause, and the three musicians exchanged a look. Without a word, one of them took up a penny whistle, the second an electric guitar and the third an electric bass. The bass beat a deep, rhythmic thrum while the flute broke into a slow, melancholy tune.

"What are the odds?" I murmured.

Simon was gazing at me steadily now, arm outstretched.

I laid my hand in his and he pulled me gently to my feet.

Even after a decade, I still managed to remember whose arms went where. What I'd completely forgotten was the initial thrill of stepping into a man's embrace—the feel of skin against skin, of warm breath against my temple.

I moved stiffly at first—for so long, physical contact with a man was something I'd tried very hard to avoid. And I was painfully aware that I was just as skittish as I'd been at my first junior high dance. But if Simon was aware of it, he didn't show it.

He didn't pull me tight or let his hand roam, nor could I ever imagine he would. Not like that. He pressed his palm lightly against the small of my back, and the warmth of it seemed to percolate through my clothes, through my skin, down to my core.

The music was almost primal—a minor bass chord, over and over, like the beat of a drum, the flute raveling against it like a keening voice, prickling every hair on my arms.

I closed my eyes and there were images of landscapes I'd never seen before—immense, ragged mountain ridges carved by receding glaciers. Deep valleys exploding with yellow gorse and purple thyme. Lush lowlands sweeping down to the North Sea, waves pounding against the rocky coast, so close you could breathe in the cold salt spray . . .

The scenes were so intense, so vivid, that when I opened my eyes again it was disorienting not to see the surf crashing on the rocks right in front of me . . . to feel the salt water on my face, or taste it on my tongue . . .

And there was Simon, watching me with the slightest smile, and those knowing, careful, hooded eyes.

Climbing a Mountain

It took a while to identify what I was feeling lately. I ran through the usual roster, but nothing fit.

At last, I put my finger on it: I was *happy*.

It had been so long. Jim had taken so much—lopping away bits and pieces until there was nothing of the essentials left. Till Joanna was gone, boiled down to baser elements.

Now here she was again in the mirror, gazing back at me. Not quite what she had been, not yet. But no longer the lump of potter's clay on Jim's wheel, either.

The feeling persisted until I filled up the notebook, then started another. I had so much to say, and every word on every page felt like a victory. A battle won. I reveled in it.

But there was a part of me that didn't trust it. A part that knew better.

And she wasn't wrong.

Late one afternoon I stepped out back to call Laurel in for supper. I heard nothing in return but the cluck of hens and sheets snapping on the line.

It was a peculiar, yawning silence, and I could feel the skin on my arms prickling to gooseflesh.

I called again.

Olin appeared in the open barn door, wiping his hands on a red bandanna. He was alone. He latched the door behind him and headed toward the house.

The sun was close to setting, shadows slanting low.

My heart skipped a beat. An alarm was clanging in my brain.

"Where's Laurel?" I demanded. "Not with you?"

Olin shook his head. "Not for a good while. Said she was headin' inside to help with supper."

I swallowed hard. "When was that?"

"Oh, nigh on a couple hours."

I swiveled and started to round the house at a fast clip, scouting the landscape for signs of her. Not by the creek. Not in the fields. She wouldn't have gone so far as the foothills, would she?

I turned one corner, then another, till I'd nearly circled the house, calling her name over and over.

Jessie swept through the front door onto the porch. "Somethin' wrong?" she asked.

I turned and stared, incapable of speech.

Wrong?

There were lots of reasons a curious seven-year-old might slip off and disappear for a while. None of them meant a thing to me in that cold-blooded moment.

By then, Jim had finally shrunk down from monster-sized

to something more manageable—a toothless jackal prowling the perimeter. I could go entire days without his name, his face invading my thoughts. Weeks without sitting sentinel on the porch, watching the road.

Stupid, stupid, stupid.

I ran up the porch steps, pushing past Jessie into the house. I took the stairs by twos up to the second floor and Laurel's room at the end of the hall. Empty. I ran to mine. Empty, too. The bathroom, Jessie and Olin's room, back downstairs to the den, the kitchen, calling Laurel's name in a ragged voice.

I pulled up in the middle of the living room, my heart thumping so hard it made my chest ache. Jessie was back inside by then, watching me gravely as I began to tick off Laurel's movements like a trail of bread crumbs that would end with her smiling up at me as I reached the last one.

"She came home from school . . . then with Olin in the fields . . . then heading inside . . ."

Then what? Then Jim intercepted her? Bundled her up, threw her in his Expedition? Drove back to Wheeler? Daring me to come get her?

Is that even possible?

Laurel's nightmare came back to me: *He's coming . . . He's coming . . . Daddy . . .*

Olin was inside now, too.

"I need your truck keys," I said, brushing past him to the cabinet where he kept his ammunition. I slid open a drawer and grabbed two boxes of shotgun shells.

"What on earth?" Jessie murmured.

"I'll need your 12-gauge, too."

I didn't wait for permission. The shotgun was still mounted on the far wall of his den, next to the pair of Winchesters and the antique carbine. I took it down, broke open the breech, mastered my trembling hands long enough to slide a cartridge into each barrel, then snapped it to.

Olin was watching from the doorway. "Keep the safety on."

"Not for long," I said, pocketing the boxes of shells.

He followed me as I made for the barn and his truck sitting inside. It might be old, but it sure as hell would get me three miles over the break of hills and thirty miles due west.

In the barn, I opened the driver's door and slid the shotgun behind the seat. Finally I turned to Olin, my hand out for the keys.

But Olin was looking toward the far wall of the barn, at the row of horse stalls. They were empty—the horses were still pastured outside.

"Hold on . . ." he said, moving away.

"Olin, there's no time to waste," I said.

"Hold on now," he repeated, more firmly this time.

Then he was standing by the tack, eyeing bridles, halters, reins, martingales hanging from wall hooks, leather saddles slung side by side over a broad beam.

"*Olin,*" I barked.

"Her saddle's gone," he said. "Looks like she tacked up."

He turned and left the barn, making for the pasture. I followed, and we both stared at the three horses grazing there.

Three horses. Not four.

Tse—the big roan, Rock, Laurel's horse—was gone.

"She couldn't have," I said.

"She knows well enough how to do it," said Olin. "It'd take some effort for a mite like her, but she could do it."

Relief pulsed through me till I thought my head would burst. I tried to laugh but I huffed instead, catching my breath.

So Laurel hadn't been kidnapped after all. Jim hadn't snuck in while my guard was down and snatched her up.

"But why?" I said. "And where?"

Once more I scanned both ends of the valley, east and west. Then north at the foothills darkening under the setting sun, this time looking for a rider.

But Olin was peering up.

Up at the Mountain.

"I figure," he said, "she went a-lookin' for that little dog of hers."

Simon arrived by the time we'd saddled the three remaining horses, but supper would have to wait. It was decided Jessie would stay behind in case Laurel came home on her own. Simon would take Yas.

The three of us made for town at a canter, pulling up once we hit the asphalt. There we could see another rider waiting in front of the general store, watching us approach. It was Faro LaGow on a big Appaloosa.

"Heard your little gal went up the Mountain," he told me as we pulled up. "Figured to help out."

I didn't ask how he'd heard—he was one more pair of eyes on a good horse, and a cold night was falling fast.

"Thank you," I said.

At the far end of town where the main road and the secondary splintered off, we stopped to carve out a plan. While the men briskly sorted it out, I glared up at the Mountain, impatient to be off.

This time there was none of the old, fearful reluctance. Its magnetic pull was just as sharp, but this time I wasn't resisting it. This landmass was a barrier between me and my daughter, and as far as I was concerned it had lured her there under false pretenses. Played on her affection for a dog that was long gone. This time I couldn't assail it soon enough.

It was decided that Olin and Faro would take the steeper main road that switchbacked up the side, while Simon and I took the narrower one that rounded it at a lower pitch and led to his cabin and beyond. I knew both routes also had any number of trails leading off into the forest.

I half expected someone to raise an objection about the futility of searching in the dark, especially with no clear sense of where to start and so much ground to cover. I thought someone might even suggest waiting to fetch some hunting dogs to try to sniff out a proper trail. If I'd been in my right mind, I might have suggested such a thing myself.

Olin wheeled Kilchii around to fall in beside me. His slight smile was meant to be comforting.

"Young'uns have lit out on their own before, up the Mountain or down the valley," he said. "And we always find 'em safe and sound. We'll find your girl, too."

There was a choking lump snagged in my throat. I nodded.

Then Olin and Faro trotted off to the left without a backward glance, disappearing into the gloom and the first bend in the road.

I turned to Simon, who was watching me with sympathy.

"Ready?" he asked.

Again, all I could do was nod, flick the reins and kick off.

Simon rode ahead where I could barely make him out in the darkness. But I could hear him plainly enough, calling Laurel's name. I called, too, our voices carrying into the dim woods on either side of us. Now and then I'd hear a dry rustle in the distance or the call of some creature or other, but never Laurel's voice calling back.

After an hour or so, Simon pulled up and handed me a canteen. It was coffee, still hot. He offered a sandwich Jessie had packed, but I had no appetite. Laurel was out there somewhere. Likely hungry and scared. Had she taken her jacket with her? Her mittens? Had she even thought that far ahead? Or had she just figured to point Tse in the general direction of that barking dog and be back with Tinkerbell in time for supper?

"How cold is it expected to get tonight?" I asked.

Simon was tucking his canteen back in his saddlebag. "Try not to worry."

"Freezing?" I continued, ignoring him. "Even if it doesn't drop that far, hypothermia can set in well above freezing."

I ran a guilty gloved hand down the arm of my warm sheepskin coat. The moon was slipping out from behind a bank of clouds; it was still a few days from full but bright enough now that I could make out my breaths hitting the chilly air in puffs.

I heard a voice then, calling from farther up the road. But deep—the voice of a man, not a child. "Hello up ahead!"

Simon and I turned as one toward the sound. "Hello!" Simon shouted in return.

Out of the darkness appeared two riders at a hard trot. They were nearly upon us before I recognized them—Reuben and his father, Morgan Begay.

They reined in as they reached us. They didn't offer pleasantries or explanations about how they, too, had joined the search.

"Nothing on the road this side," Begay said in his clipped voice. "We'll double back. Hit some trails."

Simon nodded. "We'll take some trails, too. She's headed up—we know that."

"She kept hearing a barking dog," I said to Begay. "Any idea where it might be coming from?"

Begay shrugged. "Hard to tell. Lots of dogs here."

"You find her, fire off three shots," Simon advised him. "And we'll come fetch her."

He said it as casually as if they were talking about a child who'd wandered off in a supermarket: *You find her in aisle three, give a holler.*

"She won't be lost long," Reuben said gently, watching me. "Tse has a mother spirit."

A mother spirit? What on earth did that mean? That made as much sense as Simon telling me to "try not to worry."

I wanted to light into both of them, kicking and punching. When your daughter runs off God knows where into the freezing cold, lost and alone, *you* try not to worry.

We divided again, each pair returning the way we'd come. Except this time we didn't go far before Simon pulled up beside the barrel-sized trunk of a nearly leafless oak tree. It stood next to a narrow path I hadn't noticed the first time we passed.

"Started out as a deer track," Simon explained. "Hunters use it mostly."

My heart dropped.

"We must have passed dozens of these," I said. "We don't have time to check them all."

"Farther up the Mountain, a lot of them join together, like a big tangle," he said reassuringly. "But the layout makes sense, once you know what you're dealing with. And I've been here awhile. I know what we're dealing with."

The track cut up the Mountain at a steep, snaking incline— so steep in places that Nastas and Yas had to strain to climb as we stood in the stirrups, leaning forward for balance.

On either side, trees towered over us, many of them bare and black as woodcuts, others shaggy pines; together with the clouds snuffing out the moon, they made it impossible to see far in any direction. Now and then we'd stop and call, then keep still for a response, ears pricked, the horses under us panting from their effort in the thin air. Morro already sat at high altitude—more than a mile high. This mountain was taking us higher still.

Finally we stopped to call out again, and this time I heard something in the distance.

Not a voice. Not a human voice, anyway.

But a whinny.

I held my breath and waved for silence.

There it was again.

"Over there!" I said excitedly.

"I heard it," said Simon. "Wait here. I'll check it out."

"Like hell," I said, wheeling Nastas toward the sound and kicking off.

The forest was thick, and Nastas had to maneuver carefully, picking his way on slim legs through a natural obstacle course of dead tree trunks toppled at weird angles, over brush and limbs and large rocks. I could hear Simon and Yas close behind. But Yas had surer footing in rough terrain and soon lunged around us, Simon urging him on. I tried not to think Simon was worried about what I might find if I got to the source of the whinnying first.

But soon there it was, in a clearing some fifty yards off.

It was Tse.

Riderless.

Her saddle was empty and slightly askew, as if it hadn't been cinched tight enough; the reins hung loose from the bridle. She stamped and whinnied again as we neared.

Simon was well in front then, and I could hear him murmuring, "Whoa, girl," as he got to her and reached from Yas's back to gather up the reins.

It was then that Tse—gentle Tse—reared up, lashing out with her hooves. It startled Yas, who reared up, too, then landed and bucked.

It wasn't a hard buck, but it caught Simon just as he was leaning to the side, off-balance, and pitched him to the ground. He landed with a cry of pain.

I dismounted and ran toward him. He waved me off.

"Get the horse," he said with a gasp.

I saw that Yas had turned to launch himself back through the brush, leaping and hurdling toward the track we'd just come from. Fleeing faster than I could possibly manage, even on Nastas.

"No!" Simon cried. "Get Tse!"

I turned in confusion toward Tse, who wasn't hurdling headlong anywhere, but standing almost motionless at the edge of the clearing. She appeared to be watching me.

I approached carefully, murmuring, unsure if she would rear up again. But this time she was her familiar gentle self. I took the reins and led her back toward Simon, who had propped himself up to a sitting position but seemed unable or unwilling to get up. I tied Tse's reins around a low branch and went to him.

"It's my leg," he said as I knelt down. "Twisted a bit. Not broken, though."

"Can you stand?"

"We can try," he said.

"Here—put your arm around me."

He slung one arm around my shoulders and pushed off with the other, and together we managed to get him back on his feet.

"Son of a—" he muttered with a grimace.

"Can you put any weight on it?"

"Not without doing some serious damage to your eardrums," he said.

"Hang on."

I left him balancing on his one good leg to search the ground for a branch straight and strong enough to bear his weight. When I found one, I helped him limp to a seat on a nearby boulder.

"Wait here," I told him.

"I'm not going anywhere."

I hitched a deep breath and walked deliberately to the edge of the clearing, nearest the spot we'd first seen Tse. I scanned the dark undergrowth for a flash of color, of pale skin glowing in the shank of tepid moonlight. Then I began to call Laurel's name.

I circled the clearing as I scanned and called. I heard nothing in return. When I ventured deeper into the woods, Simon called me back.

"You won't see your hand in front of your face in there," he said. "You'll only get lost. Then we'll need two search parties."

"You can't ride," I said. "And I can't just stay here."

He patted a spot beside him on the boulder. "Sit down," he said. "Let's think this through."

Even thinking seemed like a luxury of time I couldn't afford.

"I can't sit," I said, gazing almost longingly at the dark woods. "I have to do something."

"Then get me some coffee. Jessie packed some in your kit."

I stared at him, mutinous.

"Please," he said firmly.

Nastas was still under a tree branch I'd hitched him to, chewing on his bit. I dug around in the saddlebag and pulled out a thermos. I returned and tossed it to Simon.

"You can't understand," I told him as he caught it. "You've never had a child."

"True enough," he said.

"You can't—" I stopped short.

He couldn't possibly know—the guilt, the loaded gun with a hair trigger that always seemed trained on your daughter. And all you could do was try to keep her, if not absolutely safe, at least blissfully ignorant.

"I failed her enough," I said. "I won't fail her this time."

"I believe you."

"This . . . *Mountain* can't have her."

Simon gave a slight smile. "You talk about it like it's alive."

"I know—it's crazy."

He didn't answer.

"How rich," I said, suddenly deflated. "If all that time with Jim she never got a scratch, but a few months alone with her mother she ends up—"

"Here's an idea," Simon said abruptly. "Take Tse and give

her her head. Let her go wherever she wants. There's a chance she'll go back to where she left Laurel."

"Simon, there's an even better chance she'll head right back to the warm barn. Why would she take me to Laurel?"

"You might ask her to."

I shot him an angry look, expecting he was making light of an unspeakable situation. But even in the thin moonlight I could see he was dead serious.

Tse stood quietly while I readjusted the loose saddle and tightened the cinch. I lowered the stirrups to fit me. I leaned in close to where Tse could hear, but Simon, still seated on the boulder, could not.

"Come on, girl," I whispered. "Take me to Laurel."

I mounted up.

"I'll be back," I called to Simon.

"I'll be here," he said.

The climb began in earnest as Tse—the reins slack, no guidance from me—picked her own path up the Mountain. There were moments when, just as Simon had said, I could barely see my hand in front of my face. But Tse seemed to move as if she were on a mission.

As the way grew steeper, the trees began to thin out. They were mostly pine by then, and aspens with their slim white trunks and quavering yellow leaves. A half hour or more we climbed, till I was standing almost steadily in the stirrups and Tse was grunting from the effort. Soon her hooves began to slide out from under her.

I dismounted and led her to a young aspen, knotting the reins about its banded, chalky trunk. I patted her neck.

"I'll take it from here, old girl," I said.

Before I left, I took the signal pistol from the saddlebag and slipped it into my pocket. I had no idea where I was headed, only that Tse had tried to get me to some fixed point on the Mountain. She hadn't tacked back and forth to make the way easier. She hadn't turned and headed for the warm barn. She'd plowed on with what looked like purpose. And so would I.

The snowpack didn't start till much higher on the peak, but the air already felt glacial. I was panting from the climb, and my lungs felt chilled, too. The effect wasn't debilitating, but oddly bracing. On the ground, thin patches of snow glistened almost preternaturally bright in the moonlight.

What had felt before, from far below in the valley, like the magnetic tug of the Mountain had become at this altitude not just a *pull*, but also a *push*. As if now there were also a wind at my back, like an unseen hand.

But this time, I wasn't resisting. Not a whit. Not if it might get me closer to Laurel.

Suddenly I caught a flash of movement out of the corner of my eye. Something small and nimble darting through the trees. I turned toward the movement, and it was gone.

I held my breath and listened, and heard nothing but the rasp of aspen leaves.

Still, I'd seen something. I was sure of it.

I changed direction, heading toward the movement. It hadn't looked big enough to be a seven-year-old child, but then again, I hadn't caught a good, full-on look. And if it was a wild nocturnal creature, I expected to either flush it out or make it scurry off.

"Laurel?" I called tentatively, scanning the woods as I moved.

No response.

"Laurel!" I shouted, then paused, listening harder.

Snap.

I swiveled at the sound, and there it was again to my right, vanishing behind a giant ponderosa pine—a flash of what looked like fur. Four legs. A tail. It might have been a large raccoon, but for what looked like patches of white on its body. White fur, maybe. Or snow crusted to the animal's hide.

Either way, I could feel the hair bristle on the back of my neck.

As I stepped toward the pine, I stripped off my gloves and felt for the signal pistol in my pocket. I drew it out and switched off the safety.

The pine trunk was so big it would have taken two of me to wrap my arms around it. Its scaly bark was the color of oxblood in the dark and had that familiar faint scent of vanilla.

I rounded it carefully, eyes pitched toward the ground.

But there was nothing on the other side of the tree trunk. Nothing but a thin, crusty patch of snow. I knelt and looked closer. The snow was unbroken. No paw prints.

I glanced around. I had the uncanny sensation I was being led somewhere. Lured.

A copse of aspen trees, white and reedy as ghosts in the moonlight, lay up ahead, snow gleaming at their deep roots.

And there it was again among the trunks. A flash. White and dark together, in a quick, sylphlike movement.

Then it was gone.

My heart began to race, and it had nothing to do with the altitude or the thin air or the cold. Even under my wool sweater and my warm coat, the skin on my forearms was contracting painfully. My palms were so slippery with sweat, I had to rub my gun hand against my jeans to get a dry grip.

I knew—*somehow I knew*—there was something in those trees that I didn't want to see.

Just as I knew I had no choice but to see it.

This time the Mountain was no help. It neither pulled nor propelled me. It waited for me to choose to walk the thirty feet, then twenty, then ten to the stand of aspens, which clumped together almost protectively in a rough circle.

And inside that circle was a small dark shape curled on the ground, motionless.

The back was to me, so I couldn't make out the face. But I could see the hair—honey blond and splayed loose upon the snow.

My breath caught and held. Hot tears spilled down my cheeks. My mouth opened, but no sound would come.

I dropped to my knees beside Laurel and the gun fell from my hand. I reached out to stroke her soft, cold hair. Then her cheek.

And her cheek was warm.

Her skin was flushed with warmth. It felt hot against my trembling fingers.

I leaned close and saw the warm breaths puffing from her parted lips.

I moaned and gasped with relief, convulsing into dry sobs.

Between the sobs, I managed to gasp out her name again. *Laurel.*

She stirred then, and yawned.

And then I saw it. What her little body had been curled

around. What her arms had been embracing as she lay fast asleep at the base of the trees.

A furred head popped up and blinked at me with brown eyes lined like Cleopatra's. It had foxlike ears, a white ruff and a lush caramel coat.

It was Tinkerbell.

Back Again

Laurel sat on the kitchen floor stroking Tinkerbell so tenderly it made me wince. Jessie had given the dog a little hook rug to lie on next to the warm stove. It was resting, eyes closed, its pretty, perfect head buried in its paws. A food dish and water bowl had been licked clean.

I sat heavily in a kitchen chair and watched them. All it had taken was three signal shots of the pistol to bring Olin and Faro, Reuben and his father right to the aspen trees. In no time at all. We'd gathered up Simon and Nastas on the ride down, and found Yas on the road, waiting right at the trailhead.

Laurel was none the worse for wear, despite a tumble from the loose saddle and a few hours in the cold. She was as unblemished, as unmarked, as the dog.

Wordlessly, Jessie brought me a cup of hot tea and squeezed my shoulder.

Dark Night

Olin worked the root vegetable beds. Jessie hung laundry in the thin autumn air. The dog would trail behind one, then the other. They both spoke to it, patted it, filled a water bowl for it from an outside spigot. It licked their hands gratefully. It stretched languidly, stealing quick naps in shafts of sunlight.

For whatever reason, it never came to me. Small favors. I couldn't look at the creature without reliving that wretched afternoon behind the shed all over again—the object lesson that broke the last of me.

For everyone else, something wonderful had happened. A little dog was lost, but now was found. Laurel said it even remembered the rollover trick she'd taught it last year.

The first night, and the next, I refused Laurel's pleas to let it sleep in her room. So when she begged the third night, I could tell by the surprise in her face that she wasn't expecting me to answer as I did: *yes.*

That night, Laurel bathed and dressed for bed. From the kitchen, I could hear the dog scramble up the stairs as Laurel took it to her room.

Hours later, when the house was dark and hushed, I dressed in jeans and a jacket and took my boots in hand. I tiptoed in stocking feet down the stairs.

In the kitchen, I eased open the catchall drawer and drew out a flashlight. Out the back door, I sat on the stoop and pulled on my boots. The moon was full now, and so bright I made my way easily to the barn, unlatched the door, slipped inside and waited for my eyes to adjust to the darkness.

Nastas nickered softly. I switched on the flashlight to make my way to his stall. He nuzzled my shoulder as I saddled him, then led him outside. I latched the barn door and mounted up.

The bedroom windows of the house were still dark, the curtains drawn. I nudged Nastas to a walk to the dirt road, then reined him south at a canter toward Morro.

We cast a long, loping shadow all along the road, the air so biting it made my teeth ache. The snow on the Mountain stretched halfway down its hulking side now, so deep that the serrated ridge at the crest could barely punch through. And still that burning beacon shone. Fixed and watchful.

As we hit town, we slowed once more to a walk, Nastas's hooves falling with a dull rhythmic *clomp.* I'd never seen Morro when it wasn't bustling with life. Now all its windows were dark or shuttered, but for a few random panes still softly glowing. Many were strung with orange Halloween lights and cutouts of witches and ghosts.

At the fork at the end of town, I took the smaller secondary road on the right and nudged Nastas back into a canter.

After a mile or so, just as before, the road began to climb through thick forest before leveling out again.

It was only then that it occurred to me Simon might not be awake by the time we reached his cabin. That he was surely in bed by now and sound asleep. Why wouldn't he be? He started work early. It was already past midnight.

I reined Nastas to a halt.

I pictured myself on Simon's porch, pounding on his door in the dark, Pal raising a ruckus. Then Simon blinking at me from the doorway, groggy and confused.

And then what? Asking him if this was a nice time for a chat?

Just ahead and still out of sight was the clearing where I knew his cabin sat, with the new corral and the orchard behind, the smokehouse and the little stable. An hour ago, this had seemed like a good idea. No—a *necessity*. Now it felt more like lunacy.

Nastas stamped hard, shifting to the side. He yanked his head, trying to turn us both around. He wanted to be back in the barn, in his warm stall. At that moment, there seemed no sensible reason why he shouldn't.

I patted his neck. "Sorry, boy."

I started to rein around, glancing one last time at the road ahead.

Wait . . . Had that glow been there before?

It was faint and seemed to be coming from the clearing on the left. I nudged Nastas forward.

As we neared, the glow grew more distinct. Brighter.

Then, as the trees began to clear, brighter still.

We broke the tree line into the clearing, and there was Simon's cabin. And there I could see where the light was coming from.

The oil lantern on the porch was lit, casting flickering shadows over the table and chairs there.

Something stirred in one of those chairs. A slim figure rose, moved to the porch steps and paused at the top.

My heart leapt. Had Simon been expecting me?

I didn't have to guide Nastas to the porch—he moved in all on his own. I jumped down, looped the reins around the saddle horn and let him loose. I knew he wouldn't wander far.

Nearer the steps, I could make out Pal sitting at the bottom, gazing calmly in my direction as if seeing me ride up in the middle of the night was nothing out of the ordinary. I moved past him and up the stairs. Simon was still waiting at the top, now with his hand outstretched. When I was close enough, I took it.

Then I burst into tears.

I couldn't tell how long I stood there, gathered in his arms, leaning into him, my face buried in his shoulder, shaking with sobs that I was both embarrassed and relieved for him to see. He didn't ask why I was there, or why I was crying. He just kept murmuring that everything was going to be all right, his lips now warm against my temple, now brushing my cheek.

It felt so safe, so lulling, I didn't want to pull away, even after the tears had subsided. If I could have pulled some lever then, releasing us both from time and space, I would have.

When I finally did pull back, wiping at my eyes and nose, the only thing I could say was, "You're not wearing a coat."

He shrugged. "I've got a fire going inside."

He paused as if considering what he'd just said. Then we both laughed.

"Come on in," he said.

This time there was no hesitation. The cabin had a great room with fireplaces on either side, one of them already lit and crackling before a deep sofa. On the opposite side was a dining table and chairs. In between was a stairway to the second floor.

Simon led me to the sofa, only the slightest hitch in his step from his fall a few days ago on the Mountain. An end table was set with a bottle of whiskey and two empty glasses.

"I was about to have a drink," he said. "Like one?"

I don't usually drink hard liquor and was about to tell him so. Then I realized that whiskey sounded exactly like what I needed. I pulled off my jacket and threw it over the back of the sofa before taking a seat.

"A small one."

He poured them both out, handed me the smaller, then settled in beside me.

"How's your leg?" I asked.

"Nearly good as new. How's Laurel?"

I sipped the whiskey carefully; it was bracing, not burning. "I've never seen her happier."

"You don't look happy about that."

It was an invitation to open up. All I had to do was take it: *No, not happy. Not happy at all. Here's why . . .*

"Why are you up so late?" I asked.

He gestured in the general direction of the meadow out back. "Checking up on Pegasus. He was restless tonight." His voice was low and familiar, perfectly pitched for firelight. "He isn't the only one."

Another invitation. I focused on the glass gripped in my lap. "I couldn't stay at the house tonight."

"Talk to me, Joanna. That's why you're here, isn't it?"

I drained the glass and handed it to him. "Can I have another?"

He smiled. "Irish courage, eh?"

"I'll take any kind I can get."

The refill he returned with wasn't as small as before. I had to down half of it before I was ready to begin. Even then it wasn't soon, and in little more than a whisper.

"That dog back in Laurel's bed right now?" I said. "It didn't just run away—that's only what I told her. That dog is . . . Jim killed it with a shovel. Made me bury it in the yard. I can't . . . I can't even bear to look at it. It's ghoulish."

I paused and glanced at him, but he said nothing.

"There's so much I don't understand," I continued slowly. "Olin has told me a few things. The rest he said I need to figure out for myself. But I don't know the rules." My voice began to rise. "I don't know what's real or not. *Who's* real or—"

Simon raised his hand, cutting me off. "Do you feel safe here?"

The question caught me off guard. "What?"

"Do you feel like you belong?"

I shook my head at him, still confused.

"Belonging can mean a lot of things," he continued. "As for me, I was born not far from here, on a little ranch my father built. This is where I grew up, so I know this country. This is where I *fit*. Where I want to be. This is new terrain for you, and I don't just mean the landscape. You're bound to have questions."

"New terrain . . ." I repeated. "Yes."

"You don't know how you ended up here, beyond me finding you wandering around lost, holding on to Laurel for dear life. You see things you can't explain. You sense things, but don't know how."

"Not everything," I said. "Laurel used to tell me she could hear the dog barking on the Mountain. Even when I couldn't."

"The dog," he said. "What else?"

He was coaxing me, guiding me. And at once in my mind's eye I could see the Mountain—the way it loomed over me that first day at the breakfast table, and every day since, urging me to come . . .

"That was no mistake," said Simon, and I knew he was seeing the Mountain with me, feeling its gravitation. "You were heading for it when I found you. Do you remember?"

I shook my head.

"It's got a will of its own, hasn't it?" he asked. "More intense at first. I've seen people traveling through and they're single-minded. They want to hike right to the top, and no mistake."

"Simon, I don't want to hike to the top."

He smiled. "You've got a will of your own, too."

"Free will . . ." I murmured. "Really? Even here?"

"Even here. Nobody brings anything here they didn't already have. The good, the not so good. The idea, as far as I can tell, is to keep *trying*."

"Trying what?"

"Not exactly clear on that one myself," he said with a small chuckle. "Maybe to follow our better natures till we get it right. Or maybe it's different for each of us. But the thing to bear in mind when Morro confuses or frightens you is that it's a community like any other. And the people here, they're just *people*. And you . . . you've got time to figure things out."

"How much time?"

He hesitated. "As long as you need to make a choice."

"You know about that, too."

"Yes."

"Olin told me—'Stay and get strong,' he said. 'Then decide.' Simon, did you have a choice? When you first came?"

His expression shifted. There was a fixedness to it—the mask was back.

"No, Joanna," he said finally. "Few people do."

"This is a good place," I said. "I feel like it fits me, too. Olin seems to think I should go back. And face my husband."

"Did he say that?"

"Yes. Well, no—not exactly. He said I should consider this like a Place of Truth for me. To think of the things I'd done. Or failed to. And what I'd do with a second chance."

"A second chance . . . sounds tempting."

"You don't understand. Neither does Olin. It would mean going back to . . . a monster. Jim wasn't just a rotten husband and it wasn't just a rotten marriage. *Even here* I've had nightmares about him. Laurel, too. She dreamed he was coming for her. She was terrified."

Simon was watching me steadily.

"Do you recall the day I found you?" he asked.

"I don't. Not everything."

"Try. What do you remember?"

I tried to oblige him. To dig deep. Like Bree when she was remembering the trucker who had hit her head-on as she drove back from a rock concert.

"We were on the way to Albuquerque," I said. "Running for our lives, really. Jim had threatened to kill me so many times. Even showed me how he'd do it. How he'd get away with it." I downed more whiskey, my hand shaking now. "I remember looking in the rearview at his police unit. The flashing lights. The siren."

Simon shifted on the sofa. His face was averted, but I could still make out the furious cast of it.

"Why'd you stay with him?" he asked.

"God, that's a cruel question."

"I'm sorry," he said. "Don't answer it."

But it was the obvious question, too. And now it was the bell he couldn't unring.

"Because it wasn't so bad in the beginning," I managed finally. "Because I did love him . . . once. Because I was weak. All of the above."

"Joanna—"

"Really, the first six months, the first year, it was great—or that's what I thought. And I wanted so much to make it work, even if I didn't have a clear idea how. I'd seen my mother fail at so many relationships, and I didn't want to live like that. Jim was like the ideal husband at first—charming, attentive, handsome. So when things started to go bad, I thought it was *me*. That I was doing something wrong. Failing somehow. I thought all I had to do was change *me* and everything would be all right again.

"By the time I realized what was really going on, it was too late. I was alone, cut off. He had me trapped and wasn't about to let go. Till death do us part . . ."

I tipped my glass in toast, but didn't drink. Simon took my free hand and held it.

"It's all right," I assured him. "That's all over. He'll never do anything like that again. I'd kill him first."

The words were out of my mouth before I realized they were ever in my head.

And I meant every one.

"Oh, God," I said. "Does that shock you?"

He smiled. "Honestly, Joanna, it would take more than that to shock me."

"That's good. Because if Jim is unfinished business . . ."

I hesitated, and Simon waited for me to continue.

"This thing with Jim, a part of me knows it's not over," I said. "I get the feeling, even as I'm sitting here, that I'm still running. Sometimes when I try, I can almost feel the hard rocks under my feet, the dry wind on my face—I'm literally *running*. And I . . . I don't know how to stop."

Simon squeezed my hand gently.

"And to think I came here to talk about Tinkerbell," I said.

"Aren't we?" he asked.

"Simon . . ."

"All right—Tinkerbell. Is she the same dog you remember?"

"To the smallest detail."

"And this dog was up there on the Mountain, sticking to your daughter when she was alone and scared."

"But not in danger . . ."

"There are real dangers here, Joanna. Not always the kind you expect. So Tinkerbell stuck right with her. Till you came to the rescue."

I shook my head. "No . . ."

"That's right. Till you rescued them both."

Rescued them both. Hot, grateful tears sprang from nowhere. "Yeah," I said wryly. "I was the cavalry riding over the hill."

"Hey, now. That's just the booze talking."

I laughed, and he smiled back. The whiskey was bolstering me, true enough. Its warmth was soothing. But it wasn't only the drink.

Suddenly, as if for the first time, I was aware of Simon's nearness on the couch, and it seemed to unstitch me. He was so close I could feel his breath on my face as he spoke. So close that, if I leaned toward him, I could kiss him without any trouble.

The image was so clear in my mind that I could feel the heat rise in my face. I also found myself wondering if he was entertaining any such thoughts about me.

As if in answer, Simon slowly, purposefully turned my hand over in his grasp. I couldn't help but stare in fascination, as if his hands were disembodied things, acting independently of the man they were attached to.

His fingers traced their way lightly, slowly, along my palm. A thrill surged through me far stronger than the whiskey. Then he brought my palm to his warm lips, kissing the places where his fingers had just been.

I wasn't sure I could speak even if I wanted to. His lips felt branded on my skin.

He took my glass and set it on the table, then drew me to my feet. Then he drew me into his arms.

He didn't try to press or persuade. I could feel his lips move like a caress over my cheeks, my closed eyes. Then they were on my mouth, kissing me over and over . . . And once more I was leaning into him, and his arms were around me, pulling me to him, to his beating heart.

His lips slid to my neck, the stubble on his cheek scraping my skin. When they moved back again to my mouth, I wrapped my arms around his neck and pulled him tighter till he sighed deep in his throat, still kissing me, and drew himself up till my feet left the floor.

I'd never felt so giddy, so breathless. His body against mine was a foreign country, but at the same time as familiar as the bay rum I could taste on his skin. As if holding him were the true muscle memory, and every moment that had ever come before only a waste of body and soul.

Forgiven

I raced the dawn back to the farmhouse that morning. The house was still asleep as I slipped Nastas back into the barn. I stripped off his saddle and set it back on the railing. He returned of his own accord to his stall, and I swung the door closed; it latched with a click.

I stood in the yard and watched the sun crest, wishing Simon were there to see it with me. Leaving him had been hard, even knowing I'd see him again soon at the café.

But before I got ready for work, there was something I had to do.

Inside the house, I returned the flashlight to its drawer and climbed the stairs again in stocking feet. From the top landing, I didn't head for my bedroom, but for Laurel's. Her door was ajar, a night-light glowing in an outlet near her headboard. I stepped inside and heard a rustle on the bedding. A small, furry head popped up near her pillow, peering in my direction, followed by the rhythmic thump of a tail against the quilt.

I could hear Laurel's deep, regular breaths before I was close enough to brush stray streaks of hair back from her face and tuck the quilt close. Her forehead was cool when I kissed it.

As I straightened, the tail thumped more energetically. I skirted the bottom of the bed to where the dog still lay—she was stretching a bit now, dark eyes blinking, tongue darting nervously in and out. As I approached, her head sank to her paws and she burrowed into the covers as if she wanted to disappear.

As gingerly as I could so as not to wake Laurel, I sat on the bed, then drummed my fingers against my leg. Tinkerbell leapt to her feet at the signal and climbed into my lap, her tongue licking at my face. I stroked her soft coat and scratched at the base of her ears. Felt the firm muscle and bone beneath my fingers, the pulse at her throat. She curled up in my lap, her fox tail wrapped around her body, and sighed.

I leaned down and kissed the top of her head, then buried my face in her fur.

"I'm sorry."

Kindred

"I learned about the Big Dipper when I was a little girl," I said. "The Little Dipper, too. The Seven Sisters."

"Mmm," Simon murmured sleepily.

We were stretched out together in a sleeping bag in the field next to his cabin. I adjusted my head on his shoulder, the better to examine a million brilliant stars in a perfect black sky.

"The Seven Sisters are a star cluster," I explained. "Pleiades. Look at them straight on and they're just a blur. But look off just to the side and you can make them out. Peripheral vision. I figured that out when I was a kid."

"Show-off," he mumbled, stroking my hair.

"It ain't braggin' if it's true." I could feel the rumble of his chest as he laughed. "But no matter how hard I look," I continued, "I can't find the Big Dipper anymore. Or the Little Dipper. Or the Sisters. I haven't seen them since I came here."

Simon's laughter faded. "Does it bother you?" he asked quietly.

"Would it make a difference if it did?"

When he didn't answer, I raised my hand, gesturing overhead. "So tell me about *these* stars."

"That's easy," he said. "Those over there? That's the Spatula. And those? Ten-Gallon Hat. And those five grouped together over that way? Bluebeard and His Wives. But you have to squint and cross your eyes at the same time or you can't see them right."

"Ass." I tucked my arm back inside the sleeping bag, nestling against him with a shiver.

"Sure you don't want to go inside?" he asked.

"No. This is nice. You cold?"

"I'm fine. I've been colder."

"Tell me."

He paused. "A long time ago. Winter. A forest in Germany."

"Ah. One of those trips to far-flung places? Was it beautiful?"

"Used to be."

His tone was light, but there was a finality to it. Like a door closing.

"So, tell me more about when you were a little girl," he said. "Did you have pigtails?"

"Pigtails?" I laughed.

"Sure. The kind boys dip in inkwells."

I raised my head from his shoulder to gape at him. "Inkwells? Just how backward was the school system when you were a kid?"

"We were lucky to have slate boards and chalk. We rode dinosaurs to school."

I kissed him. "Poor boy."

"If I tell you about the outdoor privy, do I get another kiss?"

"Don't you dare." I kissed him again, this time lingering. When I raised my head again, I stroked the hair springing from his temples.

"How'd you manage to stay a bachelor so long?" I asked.

"It takes commitment."

"Seriously. Meg's been married for a while. You must have had . . . other opportunities."

He ran a finger lightly down the bridge of my nose to my lips.

"I didn't want opportunities. I was waiting for you."

"Stop it. I'll believe every word you tell me right now."

"You should." His hand was cupping my cheek, his face solemn.

I nestled back on his shoulder. "Tell me something you've never told anyone before. From when you were a boy."

"Let's see. There was the time my dad and I were driving back from Santa Fe. On Rural 14, through Madrid. A coal town."

"Used to be. They're turning it into an arts colony now."

"Hey, who's telling this story?"

"Sorry."

"Anyway, it got dark and I fell asleep in the front seat. Next thing I knew, my dad was shaking me awake. He wanted me to see the moon."

"The moon? I think I like your dad."

"It was a full harvest moon, on the night of the autumn equinox. Hanging so low over the piñon pines you could almost reach out and touch it. So we sat there on the ground, backs against the truck, drinking Nehi Wild Reds till the moon went down."

"That's a nice memory."

"I remember something else, too."

"What's that?"

"I remember the Big Dipper."

Night Chill

A dull *thunk*, like an ax splitting cordwood.

Spasms of exquisite pain . . .

I woke in my bed with a moan, my hand flying to my skull. To ward off, to stanch—I wasn't sure which. It took a while for the throbbing to go away.

Nightmares had been coming on more often lately, although when dawn came I could remember them only in snatches. Sometimes vague impressions lingered, like a bad taste in the mouth or a heaviness of spirit. But by breakfast, I was usually myself again.

I was learning to see them as clarifying. Like visions that focus the mind. Giving it direction.

But that night, as the pain ebbed, something else took its place. Like a voice, but not quite. It was giving me direction, too.

Get up, it urged. *Get up.*

I did as it told me. I opened my bedroom door and headed down the hall.

Laurel's door was cracked, her night-light glowing. I stepped inside and there she was, asleep in bed. She was curled on her side, peaceful, both hands tucked under her chin.

Tinkerbell was there, too, but awake and crouched protectively against Laurel's back. The dog was growling low, a relentless rumble deep in her throat, her white teeth bared. It shocked me, until I realized Tinkerbell wasn't looking at me.

She was looking at Jim.

Jim was standing over Laurel's bed. Or, at least, some version of him was. There was no real substance to him, nothing to equate flesh and blood. The form was there, with all the right lines in place, but it was colorless, translucent.

I stepped into the room, and Jim turned toward me. His movements were slow and impassive. His face a blank, an abyss. A beam of light slanted steeply through the bedroom window. Not the moon—there was no moon that night. The light had to be coming from the top of the Mountain. And it glinted off an object in Jim's hand. Long, flat, tempered steel. Machete.

A cold, contained fury erupted inside me.

Jim turned again, back toward Laurel, and Tinkerbell snarled and half rose to her feet, primed for attack. I moved then, too. It was only a few steps to where he stood, and I was on him in an instant.

I overtook him in midstep . . .

. . . and he dispersed like fog gusting from dry ice, until there was nothing to grapple with but a clammy chill.

Just like that . . . he was gone.

Into a Fogbound Moon

The night before the birthday party for Reuben's brother came the first snow of the season. We had a dusting just after Thanksgiving, but it didn't last long. This time the snowfall was four inches at least, and it stuck. It was even deeper on the Mountain, where the Begays lived, so we had to get there on horseback.

That morning, Olin and I saddled the horses while Jessie buttoned and zipped Laurel into warm boots and a parka. Tinkerbell had built up a thick coat for the winter, but I wasn't sure if her paws could handle the trail higher up, so I slung an army blanket across my saddle in case she needed to hitch a ride.

We packed up the birthday gifts. I wasn't sure what a sixteen-year-old boy might like, but Liz LaGow had assured me a fleece-lined hackamore was just the thing, because the main present from the boy's family was to be a saddle horse.

As I mounted up, I tried not to stare at Jessie, who was wearing belted woolen trousers—so different from her usual matronly attire that she seemed almost a different woman. Olin winked at me before he gave Jessie a leg up. Jessie reined the pinto into a fast clip toward the road.

"She's a firecracker on horseback," Olin said admiringly. "Even did some barrel racin' as a girl."

"What's barrel racin', Opa?" Laurel asked as Olin swung her onto Tse's broad back.

"That's expert ridin', Bunny." He tucked her boot into the stirrup. "I'll show you come spring."

He swatted Tse's flank as Laurel dug in with her heels, and the big horse took off after Yas, who had slowed to an easier pace toward town. I waited for Olin to mount up; then we cantered after the others, Tinkerbell loping behind.

The broad avenue through Morro was strung with pretty plastic snowflakes—huge ones that lit up every night now. Garlands of ivy and red holly berries were wrapped around each lamppost. Doors and lintels were hung with evergreen wreaths and swags decorated with pinecones and fruit, ribbons and bows. Inside the gazebo was a Christmas tree with handmade ornaments.

We headed past homes where kids were scraping together snow to build snowmen. Others were sliding down the foothills on wooden sleds. Past the Wild Rose, the general store, Schiavone's, the library, the pub. The town hall, according to the sign out front, would be showing *It's a Wonderful Life* this weekend. It didn't strike me as ironic.

Just outside Morro, we bore to the right to climb into the forest on the access road. The snow was still a dry powder, so the horses kept their footing with ease.

I glanced at the spreading snowcap overhead. Ever since that night when I'd found Laurel and Tinkerbell, the Mountain and I seemed to have reached an understanding. Maybe it had lost interest in me and loosened its grip. Or maybe the prospect of getting caught up in its orbit had lost its menace. I'd made my peace with it—like going from a bone-jarring beginning to finding the right rhythm at last.

At Simon's cabin, Pegasus was corralled out back pacing the fence. He'd filled out into a powerfully built animal—nothing like the emaciated creature I'd seen that first day.

But in front of the cabin was a handsome bay I'd never seen before. Simon was snugging the saddle cinch as we approached.

Tinkerbell raced ahead and onto the porch, stretching out beside Pal. Laurel called out, waving her arm like a flag, and Simon returned it. He was wearing a brown cowboy hat and sheepskin coat.

"I'll see if he needs any help," I said, leaping from Nastas's back.

"Fine, fine," Jessie said. Then to Laurel: "Why don't we ride 'round back and visit Pegasus?"

As I headed toward Simon, I watched the three of them disappear behind the cabin.

"Mornin', cowboy. Need some help?"

"Always."

He leaned over as I moved in for a kiss; then another. "You're beautiful," he murmured.

"Your nose is cold."

"You know what they say: 'Cold nose, warm heart.'"

"That's 'Cold *hands*, warm heart,'" I said.

"In that case, I'd better get these off." He was pulling at his gloves.

"Stop that!" I grabbed his hands with both of mine. "You'll freeze."

He tugged me to him. "With you here? Not a chance."

Olin's voice rang out: "Don't forget the saddle, Simon! The boy'll be disappointed if you do."

He and Jessie and Laurel were returning. Simon patted a large lump wrapped in a thick blanket strapped tight behind his saddle. "Right here!"

"Best get started, then," said Olin. "It's a ride."

The Begay ranch lay on the other side of the Mountain. The access road would take us to it, cutting around the Mountain rather than over. Laurel rode ahead with Simon. She had always taken to him, from that first night he came to dinner; perhaps that's why she seemed to accept our being together now without hesitation or fuss. He was pointing out the places he'd gone hunting or fishing as a boy, or where he and his uncle hunted mushrooms or dug up sassafras roots to make tea.

"What's sassafras?" she asked.

"A tree," said Simon. "Deer eat the leaves and twigs, and rabbits eat the bark in wintertime."

"What's it taste like?"

"You like root beer? It tastes like that."

She gave him a look that said she didn't just fall off a turnip truck. *"A root beer tree?"*

He reached for his canteen. "Here," he said, unscrewing the cap and passing it to her.

She took a sip. "It's a little like root beer," she said. "But no bubbles. It's warm, too."

"Like it? Then drink up."

In time, the road hit a steep incline, which the horses took at a slow, methodic pace in snow that was well past their fetlocks. When the road leveled off again, we were high up on the Mountain's south side, breaking free of the forest and overlooking a deep, sweeping valley so spectacular it took my breath away.

I reined in. The others did the same.

The late morning sun hit the slope at an angle that made the snow shine as if every inch were dusted with crystals.

And moving along the deep slope were bison—hundreds and hundreds of them, massive and shaggy, pawing at the ground, blowing out steaming breaths like bellows. Tinkerbell and Pal began to bark, but the bison ignored them—all but one great bull that raised his huge horned head, his muzzle white with rime ice, and heaved a huge snort. The dogs quieted.

Along the valley floor, a river was whipsawing through. Scattered along its banks were buildings of various sizes and shapes. You could smell wood smoke from chimneys and fire pits.

"And over there," said Olin, pointing to the opposite slope, "those are Begay's sheep. Some of 'em, anyway."

A faint jingling noise erupted farther down the mountain road, growing louder by the minute. Finally I could make out a red sleigh on runners, drawn by a horse with silver bells on its harness.

We sidled closer to the Mountain to make way for the sleigh to pass. Seated inside was a woman in a silver fox coat and hat and a man in a wool overcoat and Russian-style fur cap. They were rosy cheeked and giddy, and the woman waved and called as they passed: *"Gruss Gott! Wie geht's?"*

I sputtered after them: *"Gruss Gott—gut, danke!"*

Then I burst into laughter. "Who on earth were they?"

"That looked like Santa's sleigh," said Laurel. "But that wasn't Santa."

"No, sweetie, that wasn't Santa," said Jessie. "Santa's busy at the North Pole this time of year."

I wouldn't have contradicted her.

By the time we made it to the ranch on the valley floor, it was past noon. Morgan Begay met us as we rode up and directed some of the many children on the premises to tend to our horses as Simon unhitched the bundle.

"I'll show you where to put that," Begay said, gesturing for us to follow. A few curious children trailed after us.

He led us to a long stable that was nearly empty; his main herd was out to pasture. Begay nodded toward one of the stalls. "What do you think?"

As we neared, a head popped up and slung over the stall gate. It was the prettiest pinto I'd ever seen: a quarter horse with dark brown and pure white markings, brushed and curried till he glowed like polished wood.

Laurel stretched up to touch the horse's muzzle; he dipped his head so she could reach. "He's beautiful," she said. The children who'd followed us inside giggled.

"Think my son will like him?" Begay asked her.

"I think so. What's his name?"

"The horse? His name is Shilah. It means 'Brother.' My son's name is Trang."

The name of his son didn't surprise me. Simon had already explained that Trang wasn't Navajo, but Vietnamese—an adopted son. But he hadn't said how he'd come into the family.

"Tell me," Begay asked Laurel. "Have you ever seen a sheep up close before?"

When Laurel shook her head, Begay said something in Navajo to the children nearby.

"They will show you around, if you like," he told her. "Show you the cook shed, too, where the food is."

"Go have fun, honey," I told her. "I'll find you later."

Then Laurel and the children were gone, the dogs hard at their heels.

"I could do with some mutton stew myself," Olin said.

"Up to the house, then," said Begay.

The main house was large and rambling and stood out from the smaller structures on both sides of the river. Some of those structures were more modest homes and trailers; the rest were work buildings, barns or sheds.

There was also a hogan on the far slope, distinct for its rough, round shape. I'd seen them before on the reservation, but had never been inside one. I knew they were traditional Navajo dwellings of wood and mud, usually with six or eight sides. By tradition, the doorway faces east. Some Navajo still lived in them, but in more modern times they were usually used only for ceremonies.

Begay led us on, past empty sheep pens and corrals, past a volleyball net strung between two bare trees where teenagers lobbed a ball back and forth.

At the main house, we were hit with a wave of warmth and noise as Begay led us into rooms packed with people. The aroma of roasting meat made my stomach growl. Olin followed Begay to the food table, while Simon disappeared with our coats.

"Jo!"

Bree was moving toward us; she gave me a quick hug, then did the same to Jessie. "You made it! Met the family yet?"

"We just got here," I said. "I wouldn't know who's family and who isn't."

"Darlin', they're *all* family."

"*All?*"

"That's the clan system—everyone's your brother or your sister, your auntie or uncle, grandmother or grandfather. That's why you're not allowed to marry someone from your own clan—too close for comfort. Lucky for Reuben, I came along, huh?"

"Wedding all set, honey?" Jessie asked.

"Every bit of it. Just show up and have fun. Less than two weeks from now—can you believe it?"

Actually, I couldn't. Back at the quilting bee, I wouldn't have believed we'd still be here by now. That Laurel would be thriving like this. Or me.

"Come on," said Bree. "I want you to meet the newest member of the family."

She led us through the crowd to a small bedroom where a handful of young people had gathered. In the center of the room was a lean, angular man whose age I couldn't begin to guess. His wire-rim glasses made him look collegiate, but there was silver in the long black hair flowing down his back, bound loosely at the nape with a leather cord. He was cradling a newborn in the crook of one arm, rocking from side to side. Reuben was standing with him.

The baby began to fuss, and the father broke into a song that seemed half lullaby, half chant as he bounced the baby lightly in time to the music. By the end of the song, the baby was calmer, staring at his father with a frown of concentration.

Bree approached them with a smile, then motioned Jessie and me closer.

"This is Samuel, and he's brand-new. Yes, he is. Yes, he is!" The baby gripped her forefinger in a tight fist.

Jessie patted the man's shoulder. "Fine job, Jasper," she said.

"Want to hold him?" he asked.

Jessie held out her arms and Jasper eased Samuel into them. She handled the baby with a midwife's efficiency. There was warmth in her face, but I could detect an ache there, too.

This was, after all, a moment she and Olin had never been able to share. It reminded me of what she'd said when they'd first taken us in: *A ready-made family.*

Bree moved next to Reuben, who pulled her close. She hugged his waist, her thumb looped through the belt of his jeans.

"Jasper," she said, "tell them about the ceremony."

"Which one?"

"You know—the baby's-first-smile ceremony."

"Well," he began, "the Diné believe that when a baby's born he's still of two worlds: the spirit people and the earth people. So we wait to hear the baby's first laugh. That's when we know he's made the choice to leave one world and join the other."

The choice to leave one world and join the other . . .

For a second, Jasper's words rattled me.

"Then there's a party, with gifts," Bree was saying. "And people bring plates of food so the baby can salt it—why is that again?"

It was Reuben who answered: "To show a generous spirit."

"And how does a tiny little baby manage to put salt on food?" I asked.

Jasper held up his thumb and forefinger, barely an inch apart. "With a tiny little saltshaker."

We laughed, and Jasper took Samuel's walnut-sized fist

and waggled it gently in a pantomime. "Actually, with a little help from his father or mother."

Simon appeared at my elbow with two bowls of mutton stew. "He could start right now, if he likes."

"Don't rush him, Simon," Jasper said with a smile.

Simon handed me one bowl and offered the other to Jessie. She waved it away as she handed the baby off to his father.

"I'm off to find that man of mine," she said. "You two youngsters enjoy yourselves."

Simon led me to the back of the house, where there was a screened porch warmed by a wood-burning chiminea next to a sofa. We sat to eat, spreading a wool blanket across our laps. Through the screen we could see the river snaking past, and the earthen dome of the hogan. We could hear the faint sound of drums and chants.

"They're doing a Blessing Way," Simon explained, nodding toward the hogan.

I'd heard of the ceremony. "They do that for expectant mothers," I said.

"For others, too. Someone who's sick, for instance. Or a warrior going off to battle. Sometimes they hold one because it's been a while and it seems like a good idea."

"Who's this one for?"

He hesitated. "This . . . is to restore balance," he said vaguely. "Health. Strength."

"Did they have one for you, when you went off to war?"

He paused again.

"Not before I left, but when I came back," he said. "It's a different ceremony, though, when you come back. Called the

Enemy Way, and it's more . . . intense. Lasts about a week. It restores balance, too, but first you have to drive away the ugliness, the violence, of battle. Chase off the ghosts of men you've killed."

As he went quiet, I reached for his hand. "Whenever you're ready," I said, "you can tell me anything."

"I know, sweetheart. But not yet."

There was a movement in the doorway, and Reuben and Bree entered.

"How's the fire?" Reuben asked. He hiked up the sleeves of his sweater and laid a small mesquite log inside the wide mouth of the chiminea. Then he and Bree sank into nearby chairs.

"We were just listening to the chanting," I said. "Is it for your brother?"

"The Hozhooji ritual," said Reuben. "It should last a while yet. It's for him and . . . whoever might need it."

He was gazing at me frankly, his dark eyes suddenly unreadable, and it flustered me.

"For little Samuel, then," I said. "Who's his mother?"

"That would be Emmi, my sister."

"Actually," said Bree, "Emmi would be his cousin. But in the clan system, they're brother and sister. Or might as well be."

"Add it all up," I said, "and it makes for one huge family."

Bree laughed. "A real tribe."

"So," said Simon, "is Trang happy about the pinto?"

"Picked him out himself," Reuben said. "From Great-Grandmother's herd."

"He's got a good eye," Simon said.

"He's a long way from Vietnam," I said. "How did he come to be in your family?"

"Quite a story, actually," said Reuben. "When he was little, he lived in a village with his parents. Straw huts, the whole deal. One day his older brother took him fishing, and while they were gone soldiers came through, shot up the place, torched it. Killed his parents. Trang was six or so."

"God. The poor kid," I said.

"That's only the half of it," Reuben said. "After a few years, they made it to the States. His brother got a job on a shrimp boat off Louisiana and they lived there awhile. Then one day his brother was out in the Gulf when a big storm blew through. Swept him overboard."

"Did they find him?"

Reuben shook his head. "Lost at sea. Trang waited a week till the coast guard gave up the search. When the food and money ran out, he packed up one night and hit the road."

"Where did he think he was going?" I asked.

"West. He heard once that he had an uncle in San Francisco—it was all he had to go on. He walked, slept under overpasses and bridges. Hitched rides with truckers when he could. Some of them bought him meals. Then one morning my sister Angela—"

"*Cousin* Angela," Bree murmured.

"*Angela*," Reuben continued, smiling, "was tanking up at the truck stop—you know, the big one outside Grants—when she saw this skinny, scrappy kid thumbing a ride. She picked him up and brought him back here. It was supposed to be for a meal and a bed, then send him on his way in the morning. But the family took to him and he took to us. So he just . . . stayed."

"He must be resilient as anything," I said.

"He's having the time of his life now," said Reuben.

. . .

It was near dusk by the time the birthday gifts were presented. As the big family crowded outside the stable, I tried to pick out Trang from among them, but couldn't.

Teenage boys came running from the direction of the river, jostling and laughing; they were among the group we'd passed playing volleyball when we'd arrived.

They pushed one boy forward—smaller than most, skinny and dark, his glossy black hair shaped in a bowl cut, black brows arching over almond eyes. He grinned up at Morgan Begay, standing at the stable door.

So this was Trang.

Begay gestured for the boy to come closer, then spoke to him. I couldn't understand the words. Then Begay turned and entered the stable. He returned leading Shilah, by then decked out in a handsome silver-tipped leather saddle and full tack, including my hackamore.

I was surprised, though, to see the pinto's white mane and tail covered with dozens of streaming bows of colored yarn. He looked like a rainbow on the hoof. Laurel was standing nearby with Olin and Jessie, beaming.

With others calling out encouragement, Trang stepped to the pinto's side, slipped his foot in the stirrup and pulled himself into the saddle. He kicked off and the horse vaulted forward. Off they rode—down toward the river, then along its banks—hooves throwing up hunks of snow and mud.

Laurel ran to my side. "Did you see my ribbons, Mommy?"

"Honey, I don't think you missed a single color."

"You know," Simon told her, "that's the way they deck out their horses for special ceremonies. Then they all mount up and ride across the valley. It's a sight."

"When's the next one?" Laurel asked him.

"Don't worry—you'll see it."

A waning moon was rising, fogbound and hugging the Mountain. The stinging smell of wood smoke intensified as fires lit up along the riverbank. Laurel took my hand, then Simon's. We headed across the compound, taking our time, toward a white trailer where Begay had said a birthday cake was waiting for the kids.

The trailer door was wide-open, spilling yellow light and the voices of children. Trang sat at a kitchen table facing a big white cake with candles. A gold party hat was strapped to his head. Someone placed a toddler in his lap, and he slid a steadying arm around her.

"You two go on," I said. "I couldn't eat another bite."

Simon looked back quizzically as Laurel pulled him toward the trailer.

"Really, I'm fine," I insisted. "I just want to enjoy the quiet."

I found a seat on a tree stump near a stand of junipers. There was a fire crackling a few yards off, with three men hovering over it watching a skillet of meat and fry bread on a grill. Now and then the burning wood spat out a spark in a soaring arc that was hypnotic to watch.

I turned to the trailer again and the children playing inside, loud and giddy. Each of them had a story like Trang's; I was sure of it. Only—God willing—not so tragic. Stories that were cut short. They looked happy enough, all of them. But how many would choose to stay here, and how many would take up their stories again, if only they could? And Laurel . . . on her next birthday, would she be just as happy here in Morro? Would she turn eight years old, or would she be seven forever, here in the forever place?

That first day at breakfast, Olin had told me I still had something to accomplish. Laurel, too. He'd seemed so certain . . .

"It's the violet hour, isn't it?"

I started at the voice—female, coming from behind me. I turned, and there was a dark shape next to a juniper tree—a shadow within a shadow—not ten feet off. It shifted, apparently to reposition itself in a better light so I could make it out.

It was Jean Toliver, cocooned in a woolen blanket from neck to ankles.

"I didn't startle you, did I?" she asked.

"Well, no."

"Good. I always do like the dusk—don't you? I like to greet it alone when I can."

"Ah," I said, finally getting the drift of her remark. "Eliot's violet hour—'The evening hour that strives homeward, and brings the sailor home from the sea.'"

Jean rose from her seat and moved closer, settling on a fallen log. She drew her blanket over her head.

"Not quite," she said. "I was thinking more along the lines of DeVoto."

I wasn't sure if she was referring to a person or a car—the name meant nothing to me.

"Sorry?"

She turned toward me, and I could see the flames from the grill fire dancing in the round lenses of her glasses. She reminded me of an owl.

"Bernard DeVoto. Historian and author. 'This is the violet hour,' he wrote. 'The hour of hush and wonder, when the affections glow again and valor is reborn, when the shadows deepen magically along the edge of the forest and we believe that, if we watch carefully, at any moment we may see the unicorn.'"

Her voice was tremulous.

"That's lovely," I said. "A poem?"

"A cocktail manifesto. Would you like some?"

The blanket rustled and I looked down. She was holding a small silver flask, half buried in the folds. She put a warning finger to her lips. *"Shhh."*

I choked back a laugh. If the Navajo reservation was dry, apparently Jean would make do.

The flask was etched with Celtic knots. I uncapped it and took a sip. It went down with a scouring that made me shiver.

I handed the flask back to her. "What is it?"

"Rye whiskey," she said, stealing a quick sip before recapping it and tucking it back in the folds. "Chilled."

She murmured the last word primly. Then together we burst into snorting giggles that drew the attention of the men around the fire.

"Too much of that and you *will* be seeing unicorns," I whispered.

"Wouldn't that be charming?"

"And yet a unicorn wouldn't be the strangest thing I've seen since I came here."

"New place, new rules," she said.

"Excuse me?"

"I think the most important thing when you're a stranger in a strange land is to try to enjoy it while you're there. Besides, the farther back you go, there are no strangers, are there?"

I began to wonder how long she'd been tippling from that flask.

"Come, Joanna. You've noticed it—I know you have." Jean was nodding meaningfully at Trang, still framed in the open doorway. She waited.

She was trying to herd me toward something. But what?

I looked at Trang. At the toddler in his lap. At the faces of the other children gathered around the table. What was I seeing? Except for Laurel, nothing but dark eyes, dark hair on dark heads. Nothing unusual. I looked from one face to the next, sifting through . . .

Till I realized: this was precisely what Jean was talking about.

Nothing unusual.

Aside from Laurel, the faces were nearly indistinguishable from one another. Southeast Asian . . . Diné . . . hair, features, skin . . . so similar . . . so familial.

Cousin, kin, clan.

Jean sighed with pleasure and shifted on the log.

"Athabascan," she murmured.

I reached back to my U.S. history lessons and dredged up what I could about Athabascans. Crossed from the Asian continent thousands of years ago. Their descendants became the Inuits in Canada. Then much later some turned south and migrated again—latecomers, compared to other tribes. And their descendants became the Apache, Hopi, Zuni—and the Navajo.

"They crossed the Beringia on foot," said Jean, still watching Trang. "Followed the migrating bison south along the Rockies. They retain so much of the look of their Asian forebears, don't you think?"

In my mind's eye I could see with utter clarity what she was describing. The slow southward progression of clans at the end of the last ice age. If you stretched back far enough, Trang and the Begays could easily share common ancestors.

Unlike those first immigrants, of course, Trang didn't cross the land bridge into Alaska. He rounded the globe from a different direction entirely—to connect through sheer happenstance with cousins a thousand generations removed.

Millennia of separation until—a homecoming.

"It wasn't an adoption," I murmured. "It was a reunion."

"At any moment"—Jean nodded, uncapping her flask—"we may see a unicorn."

We were back in the great room saying our good-byes before heading out when Jessie led me toward the kitchen.

"Let's pay our respects to Begay's grandmother. She's old as they come, and all this"—her hand circled in the air—"all this is hers."

I knew the old Navajo tradition was matrilineal, and it was daughters who inherited livestock and land. But I didn't know it was a custom still followed.

The kitchen was crowded with women talking animatedly in English and Navajo. Seated in a chair against the far wall was a petite, wizened woman, her white wisps of hair twisted into a traditional bun. She wore a red velvet blouse cinched at the waist with a sash, a black skirt to her ankles and soft deerskin boots. Slung over her shoulders was a simple gray blanket with stripes of white and black. The lines of her face were so deep-set, they didn't seem so much the wrinkles of age as the fissures of natural erosion.

She turned in our direction as we paused in the doorway. Then she said something in Navajo and beckoned us closer, her face breaking into a delighted grin, her thin lips parting over teeth almost too white, too perfect. She watched as I approached, her brown eyes probing mine . . . just like Olin at breakfast under the oak tree.

"Yuhzhee," said Jessie as the room quieted. "This is Joanna."

Slowly, deliberately, Yuhzhee raised a wrinkled hand, stretching to touch my face. I had to bend for her to reach. Her fingers were thick, the tips as worn as weathered wood.

I'd never been around someone of such great age before. Jessie and Olin were old, certainly, and my Oma had been in her seventies when she passed, but this woman felt . . . ancient. She didn't seem weighed down by the years, but buoyed by them. Weightless as a cornhusk doll. Or a carving out of cottonwood root.

She said something in Navajo, and I shook my head. "I'm sorry—I don't understand."

I peered about the room for someone to translate, but no one seemed inclined to do so. Finally, a young woman stirring a pot on the stove spoke up:

"She said you shouldn't be here."

I pulled away from Yuhzhee and straightened. Shouldn't be here? I might be a newcomer, but I wasn't a stray cat scratching at their door.

"I was invited," I said stiffly.

Jessie laid her hand on my arm, shaking her head as if I hadn't understood.

"No," the young woman continued, not unkindly. "You're a welcome guest. She means there's somewhere you need to be. Something you need to do." She shrugged. "This is not a bad thing."

The old woman was urging me closer again. And again I leaned down, if more reluctantly.

This time, Yuhzhee fingered a lock of my hair, examining it curiously. She said something and the women in the room burst into laughter. I glanced around in confusion.

The young woman at the stove spoke up again. "She says you have pretty hair. The color."

My hair? Pretty? I never imagined I'd ever hear that compliment again. Especially from a Navajo grandmother in deerskin boots.

And then, of all things, Jim's snarling face flashed in front of me, hurling insults, threatening worse. The man might be invading my sleep or appearing like an apparition in night visions, but this felt different. This felt like an ambush.

Habit alone should've had me bracing for impact. For the familiar surge of panic to freeze me in my tracks.

Instead, I felt prepared. Strong.

My hands of their own volition curled into fists.

Slowly I straightened, Yuhzhee's eyes locked steadily with mine, and behind them I sensed a message she was trying to convey. A question, awaiting an answer.

I felt ready.

"Can you tell her I said thank you?" I said.

The old woman needed no translation. She nodded and gave me another pearly, perfect smile.

Have You Ever Heard of
Little Orphan Annie?

Simon and Laurel were at the edge of the woods, cutting ever-green boughs for the mantels. I could see the two of them through the side window—Laurel pointing out the branches she preferred and Simon tackling them with a pair of loppers, then stacking them in the snow in a growing pile. It had snowed for real last evening, and Simon was wading knee-deep in powder that came up to Laurel's hips. Now and then, if she seemed to struggle in a drift as they moved from tree to tree, Simon hoisted her over his shoulder like a sack of grain, her long toboggan cap of red and green swinging down his back as he cleared a path. I could hear her peals of laughter from here.

By morning, the snow clouds had blown off to the east,

leaving behind a radiant blue sky and snow so blisteringly white it stung your eyes. Another shiny day.

Simon's cabin was already filled with the scent of pine from the blue spruce—an eight-footer we'd cut that morning and set into a cast-iron stand in the living room—and the wild turkey that was roasting in the oven.

I was sitting in the middle of storage boxes, rummaging through lights and ornaments to decorate the tree before dinner. I pulled out tangles of green cables strung with round bulbs. I peeled tissue paper from glass ornaments—balls of every size and color, stars with long spires and tails. There were delicate bird nests, toy soldiers, carousel horses, a tiny cuckoo clock.

At the bottom of one box was a cardboard container the size of a board game, orange and yellow, stamped with a green Christmas tree. It looked well used, but still in good shape. The printing on it read, *Cartoon Character Christmas Tree Lights* and *Made in Japan*. The design was outdated, antique. On the lid were drawings of each character and its name. Some I recognized—Dick Tracy, Betty Boop, Little Orphan Annie, her dog Sandy. As for the rest, I had no idea who they were. A bald man in a black vest and red tie named Andy Gump. Another man with a feckless expression named Moon Mullins. A surly boy in a blue-brimmed hat, his arms crossed, named Kayo.

I lifted the lid. Each figurine was in its place, like eggs in a carton. The paint was bright, but so roughly done it had to have been done by hand. And not very artfully, either. These figures looked like something a child would treasure, not a grown man.

I got up and peered through the window again. Laurel was

loading the cut boughs into Simon's waiting arms, higher and higher, laughing as he pretended to buckle and stagger under the weight. She saw me watching from the window and waved, still laughing. When had I ever seen her laugh like that?

Simon spotted me then. He stopped staggering and stood up straight, dropping the branches in a heap as he waved, too. Laurel cried out in dismay and began to scold him.

I went back to the box with the cartoon character lights. I picked it up again, brushed off the lid, then placed it at the foot of the tree. They could be a family heirloom, passed down from father to son. Simon could have found them in the general store, or special-ordered them. Maybe they were a gift from a friend who appreciated vintage things, and discovered them tucked away in some old shop.

But I knew none of that was the case. I knew those cartoon lights were Simon's. That, when he was a boy, he'd helped string Little Orphan Annie and Smitty and Kayo around his family's tree. That it was an experience close to his heart, a warm memory he'd carried with him since.

The way today would be for me.

The stamping noise on the front porch meant they were back with the evergreens. They burst through the door, and Olin, who'd been napping on the couch, sprang up to take the boughs and carry them to the fireplace, exclaiming how fine they were, while Laurel and Simon pulled off their boots and hung their coats on pegs by the door.

Simon padded over to me in thick wool socks, blowing on his bare hands to warm them. He was windblown, his cheeks ruddy. His tan was faded enough that a sprinkle of freckles showed through.

"Brrr. The frost is really biting today." He embraced me

from behind as I looked the tree over, and laid his cold cheek against my ear.

I rubbed his arms. "It got your nose pretty good."

"I think we even spotted Jack Frost in the woods out there. Isn't that right, Laurel?"

Laurel was at the fireplace with Olin, holding her hands to the fire.

"Jack Frost isn't real," she said. "That was a rabbit."

"Was it a *jack*rabbit?" Olin asked, his mustache twitching.

She pulled a face at him. "Ho, ho, ho."

Jessie called out from the kitchen. "They back yet? There's hot cocoa for those who want it!"

I turned and gave Simon a quick kiss. "You guys go on. I'll stay here and do the bough thing."

As Simon passed by the fireplace, Laurel planted herself in front of him and raised her right arm high. "Let's show her the fireman's carry," she said.

"The what?" I asked.

In answer, Simon leaned down, grasped Laurel's raised arm and swung it behind his neck. When he stood straight again, Laurel was slung around his shoulders like a fur stole, giggling, while Simon held her right leg and arm with one hand, anchoring her in place.

"The fireman's carry," Simon said before turning to head toward the kitchen.

Laurel's head popped up from his shoulder, her hair swinging. "They use it to rescue people," she called as they disappeared through the door.

Their low voices carried from the kitchen as I arranged the evergreens and pinecones on the mantels—the one in the dining area and the other in the living room. I'd found rolls of gold satin ribbon in one storage box, and cut and tied them into bows, placing them here and there among the boughs. I stood thick beeswax candles at either end of the mantels, and lit them. They smelled like honey.

I stepped back and studied the effect. Simple, but not plain.

Laurel padded out from the kitchen, a mug in her hand. "This is yours, Mommy." It was almost too hot to drink, but not quite. Exactly the way I like it. Topped with tiny, melting marshmallows.

Laurel stood in front of me facing the fireplace. She took my free arm and wrapped it around her, holding it with both her hands, which were warm now. I marveled at how much taller she seemed. As if she'd sprouted inches since the summer. I leaned over and kissed the top of her head.

"It looks happy," she said quietly. "I don't think I've ever seen a happier fireplace."

We'd never decorated a mantel for Christmas before, so I didn't doubt it.

"Me, either."

She tipped her head back to peer up at me. "I like it here."

"Really? What do you like about it?"

"I like Oma and Opa. I like Simon and the dogs. The horses." She paused, lowering her head again to look at the fire. "And I like you. You're not like back home, scared all the time."

I drew a deep, steadying breath.

Out of the mouths of babes . . .

So. Despite all my efforts, I hadn't been able to shield her. Not from everything.

Not from me.

"You used to be only two colors. Maybe three, on good

days," Laurel said, as if she were drawing me in crayon. "Now you're all of them."

I couldn't speak for a moment. And I couldn't disagree with a single word.

"I think . . . I think that's the nicest thing anyone's ever said to me. Thank you."

She tipped her head back again. This time she was smiling up at me.

"You're welcome."

I leaned over and kissed her again. "Want to help with the tree?"

We started with the strings of lights. Before long, Jessie, Olin and Simon came from the kitchen to join in, Jessie ordering Olin about to make sure the lights were well distributed around the tree.

The last string to go up was the one with the old cartoon figures. I handed the box to Simon. He stared at it thoughtfully, moving his hand slowly over the characters on the lid as if he weren't standing in that room anymore but in another one, at another time. A smile flickered. When he looked up again, I was still studying him, seeing the boy he'd been and the man he'd grown into. I reached to brush his cheek. He caught my hand as I pulled it away, and kissed it.

Then he turned to Laurel, who was fingering the yarn manes of the tiny carousel horses. "Look, Laurel," he said, holding out the box for her to see. "Have you ever heard of Little Orphan Annie?"

When every ornament was in place—every shiny ball and spired star, every wooden soldier and nesting bird—we stepped back, waiting for Simon to plug the lights into the outlet. Right before he did, he warned us that the strings were old, that if a light had burned out since last year it could break the circuit for an entire string. Maybe we should have tested them first, he said, before we went and put them all up. I wasn't sure if he was trying to lower our expectations or build the suspense. Probably both.

He plugged it in and the tree lit up at once. No light had burned out; no circuit was broken.

"Whoa," said Laurel.

"Wait till the sun goes down," Jessie said, making a small adjustment to an ornament. "Then you'll really see something."

It was time to set Simon's little table for dinner. Jessie spread a damask cloth and handed Laurel linen napkins to roll and slide into copper rings. I took the white plates she'd stacked on a kitchen counter and began to space them around the table.

When I was finished, I noticed something was off.

"Jessie," I said, puzzled, as she set a basket of cutlery on the table. "There's an extra plate here."

"Is there?"

"We're five, not six." I took up the extra plate.

"There's six napkins, too," Laurel said, counting them off.

"My, my," Jessie said absently. "What was I thinking? Well, just set 'em aside."

Finally Jessie called everyone to supper. Pal and Tinkerbell trotted out from the kitchen and slipped under the table.

The turkey was a deep golden brown, with cherry and chestnut stuffing, set on a platter of roasted vegetables. Laurel leaned into it before she took her seat, and sniffed.

"Can't wait," she said.

"You have a biscuit, honey, to keep you," said Jessie.

Simon took on the turkey, dismantling it as efficiently as if he did it every day.

"I do appreciate a man who knows his way around a carving knife," Jessie said.

"Then, ma'am," said Simon, "what you need is a short-order cook."

He was serving up the turkey slices when I heard it: a distant rumble that seemed uncannily familiar.

And utterly out of place.

It was so faint I thought I might be imagining it. No one else seemed to notice.

Until it came again—a faint roar now, but growing louder.

"Does anyone else hear that?" I asked.

Simon, Jessie and Olin exchanged glances. Laurel closed her eyes, frowning in concentration. The roar was growing even louder, coming even closer, until it was clear it was a powerful engine heading toward the cabin.

Laurel dropped her fork on her plate with a clatter. "It's the lady!"

She pushed off from the table and raced to the front window, wiping condensation from the glass to stare down the road.

The lady?

It couldn't be, could it? Here? Now? After all this time?

I left my chair to join Laurel at the window, wiping at the glass, too, staring out in disbelief. The road was empty, still packed with snow from last evening, lined with bare deciduous trees and bottom-heavy firs. Anyone trying to make it up this mountain in anything with tires and a motor, let alone a motorcycle, would have to be crazy as a wildcat.

So, yes, I thought: *Bernadette.*

In another moment, we saw her, her Harley breaking through the forest road at the edge of the clearing, moving steadily but not fast, tires skittering and sliding in snow that nearly buried them. It had to take considerable skill to keep the bike upright and plowing through two feet of powder.

"Oh, my God," I murmured as I watched her finesse it.

She still wore her black leather jacket with the zippers and studs. She had on black snow pants that, at the moment, looked more snow than pants, and her red bandanna was replaced by a red scarf. She had on black Oakley sunglasses—the wrap-around kind that mercenaries wear in Hollywood movies.

My mind raced, questions flying. What was she doing here? How had she found us? *What does this mean?*

With a last, snarling burst, the bike slid into the driveway behind Simon's pickup. The rear wheel sprayed snow in the front yard just as it had kicked up grass and dirt when she'd peeled out from the house in Wheeler that day back in June.

She checked out the cabin, adjusting her sunglasses. Then she dismounted and set the kickstand.

There was something else new: a leather saddlebag strapped behind her seat. She opened it and lifted out a small drawstring bag that looked filled to the brim. She slung it over her shoulder like a biker-chick Santa and headed for the porch.

Laurel ran to open the front door. Her eagerness astonished me. She'd seen this woman just once, months ago, and so briefly. She couldn't have known what Bernadette was doing at the house that day.

Or could she?

Bernadette stomped her boots on the porch mat as Laurel held the door wide-open for her. Then she stepped inside. She pulled off her sunglasses and looked me up and down.

"Good God, Jo! Look at you! You clean up fine!"

She was just as tall, just as striking, just as imposing as the first time I'd seen her in the Javelina Saloon, when the crowd had parted for her like the Red Sea for Moses. With the red scarf around her head and earrings of tinkling silver coins cascading to her shoulders, she was like some gypsy Amazon. I embraced her like a long-lost sister.

When I let go, I brushed the tears from my eyes.

"Hello again, *niña*," Bernadette said to Laurel. She pulled the drawstring bag from her shoulder and handed it to her. "Here—why don't you take this? Go ahead and take a peek—there's something funny inside."

Laurel set the bag down and pulled excitedly at the drawstring. She drew out a present wrapped in glossy yellow paper topped with a bow. She stared at the gift tag, then up at Bernadette.

"It's got my name on it," she said.

"See, that's the funny thing—I got these from a guy in a red suit on the way up here. I thought they were for me, but then I peeked inside and saw your name, so I thought I'd bring it by."

Laurel turned to me. "Can I open it?" she asked.

"Honey," I said, "Christmas is still a couple weeks away."

She screwed up her face, girding for battle. A spoiled evening was only a tantrum away.

"All right," I relented. "But just this one."

She tore at the wrapping as I made the introductions. Then Bernadette pulled off her jacket and boots and set them by the door. She unzipped her snow pants and stepped out of them to reveal slim black jeans.

"You'll stay for dinner," Jessie said.

I retrieved the extra plate and napkin Jessie had set out

earlier; now I understood why she had. I filled the plate to overflowing and set it before Bernadette.

Laurel's gift was a book: *Charlotte's Web*.

"I liked it when I was a kid," Bernadette told her. "Of course, all I could tell you about it now is it's about a pig and a spider."

"It's perfect," I said. "Laurel will love it."

"Hey, *niña*," said Bernadette. "Why don't you go see what else Santa put in there?"

Laurel ran back to the bag, pulling out more gifts. "Mommy! There's a present for Simon, too. And Oma and Opa. And one for you."

I looked at Bernadette questioningly. She arched her eyebrows at me, then mimed locking her lips and throwing away the key.

I scanned her smiling face, searching for answers—how had she come here? did she know what Morro was?—but afraid of what I might find. Comprehension was trying to settle in, but I was beating it back.

Laurel ran to the table to pass out the rest of the presents, and Bernadette insisted they be opened at once. Simon's was a Leatherman knife. Olin's, a pipe of polished sandalwood. And Jessie's, a pair of fine kid gloves, dyed a deep scarlet.

I wasn't sure Jessie would approve of such a brassy color, but her eyes sparkled as she tugged one on, stroking the soft leather.

Bernadette shot me a look that seemed to say, *Every lady needs a little red in her life.*

Finally, I turned to mine—a box wrapped in silver with a silver bow. But as I began to unwrap it, Bernadette placed her hand over the box to stop me.

I looked at her in surprise. Her face was solemn. When she spoke, her voice was pitched low, for me alone.

"Not now. Open it before you go to sleep tonight."

How odd. I couldn't fathom why. But without a word I set the box on the floor by my chair.

Olin held up his pipe, admiring the slim black stem and the wooden bowl shaped like an old-fashioned corncob. "I'll break this in after supper," he said. "I thank you, Bernadette."

"Use it well," she told him. "And you can call me Bern—suits me better." She licked the tip of her finger with a hiss: "*Tsssss.*"

Olin laughed.

"Where you from, honey?" Jessie asked, still wearing her scarlet glove. "Your people from around here?"

"Nope. Cuba. Not the island—the town north of here." She took a bite of cherry stuffing and moaned. "*This* is delicious. Did you make this, Jessie? Good God. For this, you deserve a little red hat to match those gloves. Think I'm kidding? Just wait—next time I come through."

Color sprang to Jessie's cheeks. "Have some more—there's plenty."

"My family has a sheep ranch outside Cuba," Bernadette continued, her nose wrinkling in distaste. "I grew up on boiled mutton, mutton stew, lamb stew. I lived with sheep, played with sheep, wore sheepskin and slept under it. Hell, till I was five, I thought I had a fleecy tail."

Laurel giggled.

"I got outta there when I was fourteen," Bernadette said. "A wild child—not that you can tell." She winked at Olin. "As for my people, they go back to the conquistadors, the Towering House Clan and the Irish Potato Famine. A real pedigree, huh?"

"Towering House?" Simon asked. "Our friends the Begays are part of that clan. One of them is getting married day after tomorrow."

"Mazel tov," said Bernadette.

"I mean, I'm sure they'd like to have you. Unless you have somewhere to be."

Bernadette set her fork down, frowning in thought. "Well, I was planning on a bike trip . . . *Whoa* there!" She leaned back in her chair, lifting the tablecloth and peering underneath. *"Hello,"* she said.

I'd forgotten Tinkerbell and Pal were still under the table, eager for scraps.

Bernadette looked at Olin. "You have dogs?"

"A couple."

"Good. No cause for alarm, then." She took two pieces of turkey from her plate and tossed them under the table. "Here ya go."

Simon rose from his chair and gave a low whistle. Pal darted out, Tinkerbell close behind. He gestured to a blanket by the fireplace, and the two dogs settled onto it, licking their lips.

"Sorry about that," Simon said as he took his seat again.

"No harm done," Bernadette said.

"Well, if your trip can wait a bit," I said, "why not come to the wedding? It's only two days. At the hotel in town."

"The big red one? I'm staying there tonight."

"Stay a couple more nights, then."

"Well," she said slowly, tapping her lips with a black-lacquered nail. "I guess there could be diversions." She glanced at Olin. "How's that saloon I saw on my way through? And the pub? Either of them disreputable?"

"No, no," he said reassuringly.

"Well," Bernadette drawled, shaking her hair back till her earrings tinkled like bells. "They will be when I get done with 'em."

Bernadette didn't stay long after supper—night fell early, and she wanted to make it back to the Wild Rose before then. We made plans to meet at the pub the next evening—there was so much I had to ask her, to tell her.

In the living room by the fire, Laurel settled on the couch between Jessie and Olin to read *Charlotte's Web* to them. Simon and I were in the kitchen washing the dinner dishes, the radio on the counter playing Christmas music. Sometimes we sang along, making up the lyrics we couldn't remember.

Before long, we'd saddle the horses and ride back to the farmhouse. Tomorrow, I'd help Bree finish up the hotel ballroom for the wedding. Simon would open the café early, and Jessie would help out for a few hours. The schoolhouse was on winter break, so Laurel would tag along with Olin at the farm.

In my mind's eye, I could see the day play out. And the day after that, and the weeks, the years after that—stretching like an unbroken winding road toward a chosen horizon.

I swished my hands in the warm water, staring down at the suds. Simon was at my shoulder, drying plates with a dish towel. I could feel his eyes on me.

"What do you see?" he asked.

I turned to him, blinking to clear my head. "Hmm?"

"You're staring so hard, like at a crystal ball."

"I don't believe in fortune-telling."

"No?" he said. "What do you believe in?"

TAMARA DIETRICH

I almost smiled, but the magnitude of what I believed at just that moment was too sobering. As were the consequences.

"Choices," was all I said. I pulled the rubber stopper in the sink and the water began to drain with a sucking sound.

His towel froze for the merest second. "You decided, then."

The window above the sink looked out on the meadow behind the cabin. In the dark, the trees had disappeared except for the snow coating their limbs, etching them in white.

"I can't tell you how much I love this place," I said. "But you know that." I turned to him. "Laurel, too, because here she has people who love her. Protect her. That's something I didn't do."

He moved toward me. "Sweetheart—"

"No, please. Let me finish." I took a step back, away from him. "I've been offered a rare thing, right? You said it yourself—not everyone gets a second chance, so there must be a reason. These things can't be random, can they? At the Begays', the birthday party, Trang turning sixteen . . . I think about Laurel, and what I want for her is *real* birthdays. Growing up, growing older. Learning about the world, making her way in it."

"That can happen here," said Simon.

"I'm sure. In its way. But it would always be . . . an imitation, wouldn't it? No—an *echo*." I shook my head. "No, that's not right, either—at least an echo begins with the real thing. She hasn't had that. She never will. And *she* had no choice in this. Any of it. This was . . . forced on her. Because *I* failed to make the right choices back in Wheeler."

I paused, struggling to untangle a knot of feuding emotions. Simon waited for me to continue.

"And Jim. He won't let us alone—not even here. He's invading this place, our dreams. It's like we're *fused* somehow. Or

306

maybe we're bringing him with us because we can't let *him* go. I even saw him one night in Laurel's room—or a vision of him—standing over her while she slept. You said there are risks here—even here—remember? I'm her mother. I'm supposed to protect her. Maybe I do that by going back and getting it right. Doing what I should have done, or just doing things differently. Maybe that's what Olin meant. Maybe that's my truth."

Simon was watching me as if he was dealing with his own feuding emotions. I willed him to move, to speak, but he didn't. Or wouldn't. Above all, I didn't want to leave him. Didn't want to disappoint him. And I didn't want the three feet of empty space between us to turn into a chasm that couldn't be bridged, ever.

I moved to him and wrapped my arms around his waist, burying my face in his shoulder, holding on for dear life. The tears started, dampening his shirt.

After a moment, Simon coaxed my head up and brushed the hair from my face. He kissed the tears on my cheeks.

The truth was, I might not understand Morro—its physics or how we ended up here—but I did understand it was a sanctuary for us. But sanctuaries aren't forever—that's their nature.

"I told you I fit here, and I do," I told him. "I fit with *you*— I've never been more sure of anything. But not like this. Not . . . yet."

He kissed my lips, then leaned toward the radio and turned the dial.

"You asked me once about my favorite song," he said.

"And you said one day you'd tell me."

He stopped on a ballad, low and slow. A woman's voice. An old song from when crooning was popular.

His arms were around me again, and we began to sway to the music. The song was from the 1940s, but I knew it. Redone . . . how many times? It made me think of Manhattan nightclubs, swing bands and cigarette smoke, tear-filled good-byes at train stations, soldiers shipping off to war half a world away.

I pulled back just enough to look into Simon's face. And at last I saw none of the guardedness he could slip on like armor. No careful neutrality. His eyes shone the deepest grays and blues, and his whole heart and soul were in them.

"This isn't good-bye," I said. "I'm coming back."

"I know," he said. "I'll be here."

At the farmhouse, Laurel was tucked into bed, Tinkerbell curled beside her. Olin had ducked outside to the kitchen stoop, stealing his last cigarette of the day.

I stood outside on the porch, hugging my coat around me.

There was a slim fingernail of a moon. Not enough to cast shadows or illuminate much. I stared up at the Mountain, lying as quiet and still as a great hibernating beast. It was completely blanketed in fallen snow that filled and tempered its deep ravines and blunted the long, rocky ridge along its crest. It wasn't watchful anymore, or even restless in its sleep. The point of light near the crest was faint now and for the first time it was flickering, like a flame about to go out.

Behind me, Jessie opened the front door and stepped onto the porch. She was already in her thick bathrobe, her bun undone for bed, her gray hair plaited down her back. She stood beside me, silent, her gaze following mine to the mountaintop.

"This was a good day," I said softly.

She slung her arm around my shoulders and squeezed.

"There'll be more, sweetie."

. . .

In my room, I dressed for bed and turned out all the lights, save for the one on the nightstand. I sat in the rocking chair and held Bernadette's present, with its shiny silver wrapping, in my lap. It had a familiar shape and heft. For a long moment I stared at it, then began pulling at the paper.

Long before the paper was torn away, I recognized it.

It was my old tea tin. The secret one from the house outside Wheeler where I kept my Life Before. The one I hid from Jim under a loose floorboard in the storage space under the stairwell.

And it should still be there—on Insurrection Day, I'd done exactly as Bernadette had told me, and taken nothing from the house. Not even this.

I opened the tin and, one by one, pulled them out: The first-place certificate from the high school poetry contest. The clinic receipt from the baby I'd miscarried. The letter from my mother. The warning note from Terri.

They were gathered on my lap, as familiar to me as my own face. Except this wasn't my face anymore. The features might be the same, with the same curve to the cheek and jaw, the same coloring. But there was a different woman behind them now, looking back.

I stared down into the tea tin and saw something else. Something that wasn't there before. Had, in fact, never been there.

It was a small piece of white paper, folded and lying at the bottom. I picked it up and smoothed it out.

The handwriting was familiar, too. It was my Oma's, and it contained a single word: *Mut.*

Courage.

Part III

*What Is Past,
or Passing,
or to Come*

What if you slept? And what if, in
your sleep, you dreamed?
And what if, in your dream, you went
to heaven
and there plucked a strange and
beautiful flower?
And what if, when you awoke, you
had the flower in your hand?
Ah, what then?

—Samuel Taylor Coleridge

Rattlesnake

black bitter tang of copper gravity wrenching me down down down slammed against hard rock screams shards of glass twisting inside my skull screams

Laurel

eyes don't open don't open but then they open on red on red on red everywhere red my hand inches from my face red fingers twitch on red rock twitch like dying animal inches from my face
    blink and blink eyes blur sting with red and salt and wet and warm running in the sockets

Laurel

pulsing roar in my ears push and push can't move rock won't let me go let me go rock *move move move* let me move twitching fingers hand jerks hard pushes out pushes away dead air rock won't let me go

let me go rock

Eyes close tight no screams now no screams. *Laurel.*

Lungs spasm, hurt, buck for air. Shuddering breath rolls into me, throws me onto my side. Temple, shoulder, hip scrape warm sandstone. Eyes open, red rocks everywhere—above and below and beside and forever.

Blink hard against the blur. Against the sun. Against skull full of nails shredding my brain.

And there's Laurel.

Dangling weightless, little cornhusk doll, from Jim's up-raised fist, over the mesa's edge.

Laurel, back in her summer clothes of many colors. No parka, no snow, no trees, no valley, no farmhouse. Only mesa, sun, heat.

And Jim, his back to me. In his summer uniform, shiny oxfords, Sam Browne, just like that day in June when we last saw him.

In his other hand, the machete, slick with blood.

Something more than human strength surges in me, my limp arm twists, limp hand flops to my side, palm flat, to push off.

At last the rock lets me go.

Struggle to my feet, teeter like an old woman, head dangling, wet hair sticky on my face. Shake my head and the ends of my hair rain down splatters of blood everywhere. One step forward, then another and another toward Jim, who stands there beguiled by the power he has over life and death.

Another step, another. My foot stubs against a rock. Pale gray, not red like the others, but gray like Olin's fieldstones. I stoop, fight for balance, pick it up, feel its heft, its potential, another step, another.

I'm behind Jim now, so close I smell sour sweat, see it stain the back of his shirt along the spine, the armpits. My stomach heaves. My hand curls, clamps around the rock. The other reaches out, loops fingers through the rear strap of his Sam Browne. I yank with all my weight, pulling him with me, back from the brink. Laurel is still in his grasp, and he stumbles backward, struggling to keep his feet, legs pedaling like crazy.

As he hangs there, off-balance, he sees my face, my fist, the rock coming at him, and for a second I see it register in his eyes—the disbelief, the betrayal, the gall—before I bring the rock down hard against his head.

It sounds like an ax hitting cordwood. *Thunk.*

He hits the ground with a groan, face contorting. He loses his grip on Laurel and she falls on the ground in a heap. I lose my footing and crash down next to him. Something snaps in my wrist; pain shoots up my arm.

Jim rolls away from me, his hand flying to his forehead. "Mother*fuck*!" he mutters, sits up, dazed, swaying, blinking at the blood on his fingers as he pulls them away. He looks from his fingers to me, and his expression shifts. His dark eyes now as cold and empty as twin coffins. They move from me to the machete, dropped near the edge of the mesa, a few feet away.

Still fixed on it, he leans forward to stand back up, slow, methodical, like there's a job to do and no particular hurry to do it.

But as he leans in, bracing to stand, I swing the gray rock

again, wide and for effect, and it's as if he's moving right into the blow, in profile. I wonder that he didn't expect I'd put up more of a fight. It hits his handsome Roman nose and I can hear, can feel the cartilage crunch underneath. Blood spurts from his face, down the front of his police shirt, sprays on my forearm.

I pull back and hit him again. His face is averted now and the rock hits his cheekbone, just below his right eye. *Crack*. He falls back, his eyes roll, and in an instant, with a strength and speed from no earthly source, I straddle him, pound his face, his head, over and over and over. He catches and grips my injured wrist till I think he'll wrench it off, and white-hot pain convulses my body. My teeth sink into his fingers till I feel bones break. He screams.

"Bitch!"

And still I hit him, hit him, hit him, till his own face is blood, pulp, not Jim. Till I don't have the strength to strike even one more blow. Till he stops moving.

I roll off and kneel panting on the ground, light-headed, fighting nausea, fighting for breath. Then I straighten and let the bloodied rock go.

I crawl to Laurel and feel for a pulse at her throat. It's faint and rabbity. But it's there. Her face and arms are full of scratches, from the tumble or from Jim, but otherwise she looks whole. I close my eyes, roll on my back beside her, lungs heaving, push sticky hair from my face. The wet is still running down my scalp, seeping into sandstone. My body, too heavy to move now, wants to sleep.

A whisper, an echo, low and urgent, coming from nowhere, from everywhere, coming from the rock, calling me.

Joanna.

It doesn't want me to sleep, wants me to move move move again. I blink up at the sky, blue as a cornflower, but with a bank of gray clouds moving in fast.

I roll onto my good arm. It pushes me up till I'm sitting beside Laurel. We need to move. With my wrist, my head, I know I can't carry her, so I call to her, a croak, from tongue dry as dust, "Laurel, please wake up. Please."

She moans; her eyelids flutter but don't open.

I look around me, not sure for what. I don't know where we are, how we got here. Only that we're somewhere in the red rock mesas east of Wheeler. That somehow we went from winter to summer in a heartbeat. That Laurel and I are both dressed in the same clothes we fled Wheeler in, back in June. Miles of empty in every direction.

I push to my feet, totter to the edge of the mesa. I see the four-lane interstate below in the desert, in the distance. Now and then a car, a truck, speeds along. Getting there is our best hope.

I stagger to Laurel, kneel down to pat her cheek, my blood dripping onto her chalky skin, try to wake her, but can't. There's nothing for it. We have to get out of here. I have to stop the blood. My good hand shakes as it works the buttons of her blouse, undoing them one by one, then strips it off her, down to her yellow camisole. The sleeves are long, and I use them to tie the blouse around my head like a gypsy scarf, knotting it with my good hand and my teeth.

I pull Laurel up, nearly toppling under the deadweight of her limp body. I crouch and grasp her right arm, loop it around my neck. Then slowly I straighten, holding her slung around my shoulders in a fireman's carry.

I stand for a long time, head throbbing, to judge if I have

the physical strength for this. To climb down off the mesa carrying Laurel on my shoulders. One slip and we could fall. I could kill us both.

I turn and look at Jim, lying there motionless, arms flung out at his sides in some sort of surrender, face pulped, blood pooling beneath his head.

Then I turn away and start to walk.

I skirt the edge of the mesa till I find what looks like a steep, narrow trail going down. Maybe this is how we climbed up to begin with. It hardly resembles a real hiking trail. More of a goat track cutting between boulders.

I stare down at it and my vision blurs, fades to a sick gray. A buzzing grows in my ears; bile rises again in my throat. I close my eyes and will my vision to return, my stomach to settle.

Desperate, I appeal to the powers that be: *If I have a concussion, let it do its worst. So be it. But not yet. Not yet. Not till I make it to the highway and flag down help.*

Gradually, my head begins to clear. I shift Laurel on my shoulders and start down the track.

One small step, then another. Feet slide on loose gravel. Focus, focus, pick out a path. I miss a turn, hit a crevasse, turn, a boulder blocks the way, miss another turn, dead-end into a wall of sandstone, turn back, turn again. Focus, focus. I don't know how, but I keep to my feet. I pause for breath, steady myself against a boulder, rest, close my eyes.

A small stone pings against the boulder, inches from me, bounces off and hits the ground, tumbles ten feet down the path. I open my eyes and stare at it.

"I see you."

The voice is Jim's. It's Jim's, but it sounds off. Like he has a head cold and can't breathe right through his nose. It's coming from above, to the left.

I drag my eyes from the stone and turn to look. He's standing on an outcropping not forty feet away. A perfect vantage point to see the trail, right down to the bottom of the mesa. To see us. To see me.

He stands there, looking down, head cocked. Wipes at his face with his shirttail, then drops it.

"I'm coming."

He turns and disappears.

Adrenaline hits me, launches me from the boulder and back on the trail. No more small step, small step, but lunges down and down. Still I know I can't outrun him. Not even if I were whole and healthy. As I lunge, I glance around, frantic for a place to hide out, to foil what's coming down the trail after us. To regroup.

Finally I see it. A tangle of small boulders and rocks, seven, eight feet high. A small opening at the bottom. Panting, I move to it, kneel down too fast and Laurel slips from my shoulders. I catch her with both arms, wince from the stabbing pain that shoots from my bad wrist. As I catch her, her mouth gapes; her eyes flicker open. She looks at me, fazed, tries to register what's happening. I lay my finger against her lips. Her expression freezes. Her mouth clamps shut. No explanation needed.

I lean over and peer through the opening in the rocks. It's dark, but I can make out a space inside. Just big enough for us to crawl through.

I push Laurel through first. She digs in with her elbows and pulls herself inside. Before I do the same, I glance around again. Nothing in sight. Then I crawl in.

It's cool and dim, the hole just big enough for both of us to sit up. I hug Laurel against me with my good arm. Ready to clamp my hand over her mouth, if I have to. She's trembling, heart rabbiting faster than ever. I know she can feel mine doing the same.

For what seems like far too long, there's silence. No footsteps, no gravel shifting underfoot. I begin to wonder if Jim took a wrong turn, ended up on some other track, lost his way.

But no.

"I see you."

The voice is close. Nasal, and singsong. Like he's playing a child's game.

I squeeze Laurel against me. Whisper in her ear: *"Shhhh."*

If he can see us, he can see us. If not, the bastard's just trying to flush us out.

I won't play.

"You stupid bitch. If I can get Bernadette, you think I can't get you? She was ten *times* the woman you are. And it was easy. *Easy.* Knock-knock. Who's there? Payback, baby. Vengeance is *mine.*"

Payback? Vengeance? What's he talking about?

"You think I wouldn't find out? Put it together? I'm a cop, you idiot. It's what I *do.* I know it was her. At the house today. Must've been right after I left for work. Munoz calls me, tells me you're gassing up the car. Or *trying* to." He's chuckling. "Only there's a little problem, huh?"

The voice is moving, to the left of us, to the right, then back again. Hunting us down.

Laurel shifts, her hand groping for something in her pocket.

"Like I wouldn't find out. Like I wouldn't see the bike tracks in the yard."

I gasp. I remember that. Bernadette peeling out from the house, bike wheels hitting the grass, throwing up sod, just as they threw up snow when she came up the mountain road to Simon's cabin . . .

"Knock-knock. The maid's gonna have a helluva time cleaning up *that* mess."

I shake my head. He's lying. He has to be. I just saw Bernadette. We're meeting at the pub. She's invited to the wedding.

But I know he's not lying. Somehow I know.

My head starts to spin again. It throbs till I want to vomit. I close my eyes tight, lean back against the rock wall. But I still feel like I'm falling.

He's talking like the last six months never happened. Like it's just today that I saw him off at the front door, today that I sat in the chair under the sunburst clock, waiting with my heart in my throat for Bernadette to show up. He's talking like he went after Bernadette just like he's going after me now. Like she's not checked into the Wild Rose back in Morro at all. Like she's still at the Palomino. *A helluva mess for the maid to clean up.*

I can't draw a decent breath. Can't think.

From winter to summer in a heartbeat.

Laurel begins to whisper. So quiet I can hardly hear her. Holding something to her lips like a Catholic with a crucifix.

"Fly away, fly away," she's saying. So faint, like a release of breath. "Fly away."

She whispers it over and over, like a chant.

Fly away, fly away, fly away.

I look close and see then what she's holding to her mouth.

A tiny wooden doll carved of cottonwood root, barely three inches tall. Painted aqua and yellow, wearing a white leather skirt, green mask, moccasins. Crowned with a ruff of Douglas fir.

It's the Hummingbird. The messenger you send to ask the gods for rain. The creature that warriors who die in battle are transformed into. The only bird that ever flew high enough to see what was on the other side of the sky.

I lean close and whisper in her ear: "Where did you get that?"

She turns her head to whisper back.

"Simon."

There's shuffling nearby, and we freeze, the kachina pressed against Laurel's lips again. No whispering now.

I wait for a shadow to fall across the opening of our little cave, but none comes. Soon the shuffling moves off.

I don't trust it. Could be a trap. More games. Or Jim could've moved on, and the shuffling was only a fox, a rabbit come back to find its home invaded.

But we can't stay here and I know it. Sooner or later, moving up and down the trail, Jim's bound to see the opening. Bound to check.

I shush Laurel one more time and maneuver around her toward the opening. I wait, bated breath, then slowly peer out, glancing all around as I go. Ready to pull back at the slightest movement.

Nothing.

Jim's gone for now.

I crawl through the opening, turn to Laurel, who looks ready to follow me through. I push her toward the rear of the little cave.

"No. You can't come with me. You stay here. Quiet as a mouse."

"Like Warrior Mouse?"

I nod. "Quiet as Warrior Mouse. Just as clever, just as brave. No matter what you hear. No matter what happens. Promise me."

Her face settles into something stubborn, and for a second I think she won't promise.

Then she does.

"If I'm not back, stay here till morning," I say. "Then make your way down the trail, careful as can be. At the bottom, you'll see the highway. Go stand near it and wave your arms till somebody stops. Tell them to call the state police. Understand?"

Suddenly she pushes through the opening toward me and I think all bets are off. That she's changed her mind and she's coming with me, like it or not. Instead, she wraps her arms around my neck and for a long minute squeezes tight, like she won't let go.

Then she does. Without looking at me, she turns to dart back through the opening and out of my sight.

I stand on shaky legs, leaning against the big nest of rocks for support. A strange, cool wind buffets me. I glance up at the sky and the cornflower blue is nearly gone now, replaced by storm clouds practically stampeding in from the east. The air temperature has dropped and I shiver in my thin blouse, my slacks; my skin prickles from a snap in the air. I can smell rain moving in on the wind.

I move away from the rock nest, not sure yet which way I'm going. Just that, if and when Jim spots me, I don't want to be anywhere near it. I need to get him away from Laurel's hiding place. My best guess is he's searching farther down the trail by now, but I want a better vantage point. The outcropping he used to spot us would do.

There's a thick branch, like a staff, lying off the trail. I pick it up to use as a walking stick. I lean on it heavily, climbing up and up toward the ledge.

By the time I reach it, my head is pulsing, the pain so bad my eyes are running with tears. A light rain is falling, deepening the red sandstone to a dark brick. My foot slides on the slick surface. The temperature has dropped even more; the wind's picked up, slapping the sleeves of Laurel's blouse around my face. I move carefully to the edge of the outcropping, wary of being seen from below, in case Jim is down there, looking up toward the top of the mesa. The goal is to spot him first.

I peer over the edge. My eyes sweep the desert landscape. A flash of lightning arcs across the sky, stabs at massive black clouds tumbling over one another at a rapid boil.

"I see you."

It's coming from right behind me.

My blood freezes, but there's no panic. No hurry to turn to face him. Nowhere to go.

I straighten, leaning on the staff. Then I shuffle around, till there he is, standing just a few yards away. His face is streaked with blood, misshapen. His eye's swelling shut, nose bashed in.

I look at the damage and feel a swell of pride.

"What are you smiling at?" He's frowning. I notice he's slurring a little.

"Missing some teeth, are you?" I ask calmly.

His good eye narrows to a slit. He takes a step toward me and I see he's unsteady on his feet. A stiff gust of wind hits him and he staggers back. Thunder rolls in the distance like a growl.

And suddenly I remember. I remember the missing bits of that ride out from Wheeler, the mad dash to Albuquerque. The first place for gas was the big truck stop halfway to Grants. The same one where Trang, heading for San Francisco, hitched a ride one day. I was pumping in regular, not sure how many gallons the punctured tank would hold, but sure it would let me know. A redheaded boy with a cowlick and an earplug, who didn't look old enough to drive, wearing a Rolling Rock T-shirt, was at the pump next to me when the gasoline started running out from under my car. "Whoa, lady!" he cried. "You're leaking!"

I bought three gallon containers, filled them with gas and threw them in the trunk. Back in the car, back on the road—I never got the chance to use them. Twenty miles out, I glanced in the rearview and saw a sheriff's unit in the distance, lights flashing, sirens screaming, coming up fast. I knew I couldn't outrun him, so I careened off the road and headed straight for the red rocks, praying for a miracle.

That was where Jim caught up with us. Six months ago. Two hours ago.

I remember it. Like a bad dream somebody told me once. But not my dream. Not anymore.

Now I'm untouchable.

I tip my face to the wrathful sky, eyes shut. Cold rain streams down my cheeks as the storm overtakes us.

"Like it?" I ask. "It's for you."

He doesn't say anything, and I open my eyes. He's staring at me. Staring like he's not sure if I'm contagious.

But he's not moving toward me.

I feel a rush of adrenaline. Not sure what I'm doing. What I'm saying. Why I feel with all my might that I want to poke the rattlesnake.

I stare back, certain I look as bad to him as he does to me.

"You're fucking nuts," he says.

"I'd say you'd know, but that's giving you too much credit. To know what *nuts* is, you need a point of reference. You'd have to know what *sane* is. Do you know what sane is, Jim?" I shake my head sadly. "That would be no. A thousand times no."

The rain is coming down harder now and starts to sting. Tiny ice pellets. Sleet. Jim looks at the sky, at the boiling clouds. He looks at his bare arms, like he's seeing something unusual.

"What the fuck——?"

"Dear God, get a vocabulary," I snap. "Buy a vowel, Alex! Get some consonants! Mix them together. They're called *words*. I'd get better conversation out of a monkey."

His arms drop to his sides. He moves forward. But only a step.

He snarls deep in his throat. "Finally grow some backbone, eh? Didn't know you had it in you."

The adrenaline is pumping so hard now it feels like my head's splitting open. Like I'm levitating off the ledge. Like I'm bristling with clarity. My face is hot. I lean on the staff, eyes locked on his, drilling him down. I can feel a shift in the air between us. Can feel him waver. The dynamic is changing.

"You have no idea what I'm capable of," I say.

Thunder explodes above our heads. Rolls along the mesa like a diesel train. The air shudders with it.

The sleet is gone. Now it's hail the size of peas, the size of golf balls, rattling, thudding against the sandstone rocks, bouncing off, pelting us both.

Jim looks more uncertain than ever. Like he's not expecting this. Like he doesn't recognize me, or what's happening. He holds up his arms to protect himself, shoots a last glance at the cold-blooded sky.

Then he makes a choice. The only choice a man like him can make.

He heads toward me, an odd hitch in his step, fists clenched. "How did you think this was gonna end?" he shouts above the clatter.

He sounds desperate. Petulant. A grown man pitching a fit.

"And, Jim," I tell him. "Bernadette? Don't worry about her. She had a soft landing. You won't."

He's coming at me like a bull. Like old times. When he reaches me, I know the staff is nothing against him. The adrenaline took me this far, but it can't alter muscle mass. Can't unbreak my wrist or teach me judo in seconds flat. I hold it ready anyway. Ready to fight back, even with no chance of winning.

He's reaching for me, his ruined face like a Halloween mask, when I swivel and pivot on the staff at the last second, a clumsy move that puts me no more than a couple feet to the side, but just enough for him to overextend. He has no time left, no balance, when one spit-shined oxford hits an icy patch of red rock and slides right out from under him.

He brushes against me as he topples over the edge, so close I can see the startled look in his good eye.

Sixty feet below, the rocks break his fall.

After the Storm

The hail won't stop. It falls like a blizzard. A stiff wind keeps shoveling it into drifts. The hike back down the trail is slow. Plant the staff one step ahead, inch my way forward. Plant the staff again. Adrenaline's gone. Body's on fire. I slide on the slick path, but don't fall.

The rock nest where I left Laurel is nearly covered with a thick coat of ice and hail. For the first time I notice its shape—a rough dome, like a little hogan.

I call Laurel's name and her face appears at the opening. She scurries out, takes my hand, helps me inside. She's still dressed only in shorts and camisole and sandals. I'm soaked through, feverish. We curl up together on the floor to wait for the storm to pass.

In less than an hour, it does.

Blistered clouds roll off to the west; the sun splits through for the last hour of daylight. When Laurel peeks through the opening again, the air is already so warm the melting ice drips on her head.

She leaves me in a fitful sleep and makes her way down the hail-covered path, not once losing her way. She passes an indistinct shape a few yards off the trail, buried in a four-foot drift. She'll never know it's the body of her father.

She jogs to the highway and stands well to the side.

Minutes later, a plow driver out of Grants is clearing the interstate of the accumulation from a freak June hailstorm when he sees a little girl dressed in green shorts and a yellow camisole jumping up and down, arms flailing. He pulls over to see what on earth is going on.

Epilogue

As it is

It was Sam who told me about Bernadette. I was still in the university hospital in Albuquerque when he showed up with a bouquet of coneflowers he'd bought in the gift shop in the lobby, looking just as grizzled as the one and only time I'd seen him that night in the Javelina.

It wasn't the maid who'd found Bernadette, but Sam.

Sam had known about the escape plan, of course. In fact, he'd pitched in to help fund it. So when Bernadette was discovered, it wasn't hard to come up with a suspect.

Others came to visit while I recovered. Munoz and his wife. Sandoval and CeCe. The sheriff, who couldn't quite meet my eye.

The investigation was brief. Jim hadn't bothered to cover

his tracks. Maybe he'd figured to just disappear once he was finished with us. Start over in some other incarnation. Or maybe my flight had taken him by surprise and he hadn't thought that far ahead.

The first person I saw when I woke in my hospital bed, though, was Terri. Ten years older, beaming at me as if merely waking up was an achievement.

"Girl," she said, "you're *back!*"

When Laurel and I hadn't arrived at the airport in Boston as planned, she and her husband, Greg, had placed enough calls to Wheeler to find out why. They flew out at once. They took care of Laurel till I was released.

It's been two years since Insurrection Day, and I haven't been back to Wheeler since. I sold the house, leased a small one in Albuquerque near the university, started classes again. I'll get my English degree in June. After that, Terri and Greg have invited us to spend the summer with them in Boston— they have a daughter close to Laurel's age, and the two have become great friends. In the fall, I'll start working on an MFA in creative writing, and have accepted a job as a teaching assistant.

On weekends, we drive up to Taos. I found my Oma's little house outside town, abandoned, in disrepair. I used the money from the sale of the Wheeler house to buy it. To replace the rotting boards, repair the leaking roof. We painted it inside and out, and sowed fields of wildflowers all around.

Then we drove stakes of all sizes into the soil and tied links of pretty chain from branches. We used them to mount and hang a dozen hummingbird feeders—sequined glass, brushed metal, a crystal lantern, a dewdrop, giant strawberries and oranges, a red rose, a cobalt blue bottle, a tiny glass chandelier.

When we talk about Morro, about Jessie and Olin and Simon, it's usually there in Oma's house.

Although I've never been back to Wheeler, I did get close once.

It was a few months after I was released from the hospital, a day in late autumn when Laurel was still in school. I rented a four-wheel drive, hit the interstate and drove west. About thirty miles this side of Wheeler, I began scanning the landscape hard.

In time, I spotted the makings of an old dirt road cutting off south from the highway. Or, rather, the remains of a road—overgrown and pitted from rain and wind and disuse, sloping up toward a toothy break of hills and disappearing over the other side.

I pulled off on the shoulder and cut the engine, torn about whether to drive up this particular path or turn around and go back, even if I had just come a hundred miles to find it.

Finally I switched the engine back on and turned off the highway.

It was slow going over the rough terrain, up and up the sloping hills, then over. A mile or so farther on, I stopped again.

This time I left the Jeep and walked to the edge of the road.

The valley cuts east-west here, just as before. But now it's filled with wild grasses, brush, piñon, juniper trees. Gone are the wheat fields, the cornfields, the orchards, the trees of every kind, the wildflowers of every color. There is no Willow Creek tumbling down the Mountain.

There is no mountain.

At least, not the one I was looking for. What's here now has the bulk, the breadth, of a mountain, but it's barely a third the size of the one I knew. Just a moderate incline to a smooth summit of moderate height. Much like any other in the range. Nothing extraordinary.

And from where I stood, I should have been looking at Olin and Jessie's farmhouse. But there was no farmhouse. There'd never been one. At least, not the big house with the wraparound porch, built of gray stones dug up from the soil every spring.

Instead, next to the road were the remains of a little wood-frame, long collapsed in on itself, its fallen timber now scattered and rotted. The only portion still marginally intact was a brick fireplace rising out of the ruin, its chimney toppled.

This was where Olin and Jessie had lived.

It had taken a while to track them down, searching through the microfilm in the periodicals section of the university library. Two small obituaries in the Wheeler newspaper, both dated 1939. Jessie had passed first, in late April. By July, Olin had joined her.

I noticed far off the road a large mound of gray stones, cracking apart from erosion, sprouting so many weeds you could mistake the pile as part of the landscape—not collected over years of farming. But there weren't quite enough stones, not quite enough years, for Olin to build Jessie that farmhouse.

Finding Reuben, Bree and Jean had been easier. They were so recent, by comparison, that an Internet search was all it took. And Trang was difficult only if you didn't know what to look for. His was a brief newspaper notice: Asian male, mid- to late teens, no identification, discovered under an overpass along the interstate just outside Wheeler, hypothermia.

It was a while before I had the heart to look for Simon.

In the periodicals section, I skipped the computer and turned again to the microfilm. Wheeler newspapers, starting with 1942. Reel after reel, month by month, year by year until, in December 1944, a notice that U.S. Army Sergeant Simon Greenwood, thirty-five, 2nd Ranger Battalion, had gone missing in action in the Hürtgen Forest, on the border between Belgium and Germany.

It mentioned a fiancée, Margaret Dahl, but no other family.

I ran through more reels of microfilm, to the end of the war and beyond, but there was no other mention of him.

Margaret eventually married William Carmody in late 1946. There was a picture with the wedding announcement, the couple smiling at the camera, looking much as they had the night I met them in the pub. A computer search turned up a William Carmody who died in Denver fifteen years ago, a retired businessman, survived by his wife, Margaret, his five children, twelve grandchildren and four great-grandchildren. Margaret "Meg" Carmody passed away only two years ago, at the age of eighty-six.

I turned and headed back to the Jeep. When the engine kicked in, I gripped the steering wheel and, for the barest second, wondered if I was going to continue south toward the foothills. If I'd round the bend to see what was left of Morro, the mining town where the copper had played out half a century ago. And to see if, just on the other side of town, there was a road cutting off to the right, heading up to a cabin in a clearing halfway up the mountain.

Instead, I wheeled the Jeep around in a tight arc, kicking up dust, heading back to the highway.

I would leave Morro as it was.

As it is.

As it will be.

TAMARA DIETRICH

This Conversation Guide is intended to enrich the
individual reading experience, as well as encourage us
to explore these topics together—because books,
and life, are meant for sharing.

QUESTIONS
FOR DISCUSSION

1. Jim uses some classic tactics of an abuser to keep Joanna trapped. What are they? Did Joanna have chances to leave her husband, other than through Bernadette's help?

2. Why are the people in Morro there? Some of them seem to be people who have died. But Joanna's unborn son is there as well, which suggests it's a place for souls or spirits of another kind. Is Morro a type of heaven?

3. The Mountain in Morro has a strong effect on Joanna. What does the Mountain symbolize? What could be the "unwavering light" at its crest?

4. Why might Laurel hear the barking dog, but not Joanna?

5. Even though Jim never physically shows up in Morro, Joanna still strongly feels his presence there—why might that be? Is it Joanna and Laurel's inability to break free of him? Or could he be inserting himself in some way?

6. Do you think Morro is a real place? Or is it all just a hallucination of the heroine? And if it is a hallucination, does it matter?

7. Why is Joanna given the option to return to the "real world," while others in Morro aren't?

8. Joanna ultimately decides to leave Morro. Would you have made the same decision?

9. Joanna's final battle with Jim echoes many of the things she's seen or experienced while in Morro. What are some of them?

10. A freak hailstorm helps Joanna defeat Jim. Was it a natural phenomenon, or could it have been more than that?

11. Why do Joanna and Laurel put hummingbird feeders all around their house in Taos? What does the hummingbird symbolize?

12. Will Joanna ever return to Morro? If she does, what might she find there?

Photo courtesy Joe Fudge

Tamara Dietrich was born in Germany to a U.S. military family and raised in the Appalachian town of Cumberland, Maryland. She has wanted to write ever since she could read.

She earned a degree in English/creative writing from the University of New Mexico in Albuquerque, and launched into journalism. Chasing a newspaper career, she has lived in New Mexico (twice), Maine, upstate New York, Arizona and, now, Virginia. Along the way, she has won dozens of journalism awards for news reporting, feature writing and opinion columns.

She now lives in Smithfield in a colonial cottage that predates the Revolution. She has a grown son, a dog, three cats and an English cottage garden. She gets her best writing ideas while jogging with the dog or cycling around Windsor Castle Park.